image comics presents

CHEW

created by John Layman & Rob Guillory

"Taster's Choice"

written & lettered by
John Layman
drawn & coloured by
Rob Guillory

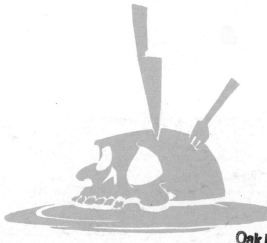

IMAGE COMICS, INC.

Robert Kirkman - chief operating officer
Erik Larsen - chief financial officer
Todd McFarlane - president
Marc Silvestri - chief executive officer
Jim Valentino - vice-president

Eric Stephenson - publisher
Todd Martinez - sales & licensing coordinator
Sarah deLaine - pr & marketing coordinator
Branwyn Bigglestone - accounts manager
Emily Miller - administrative assistant
Tyler Shainline - production manager
Drew Gill - art director
Jonathan Chan - senior production artist
Monica Howard - production artist
Vincent Kukua - production artist
Kevin Yuen - production artist
Jana Cook - production artist
www.imagecomics.com

International Rights Representative: Christine Meyer (christine@gfloystudio.com)   ISBN: 978-1-60706-159-5

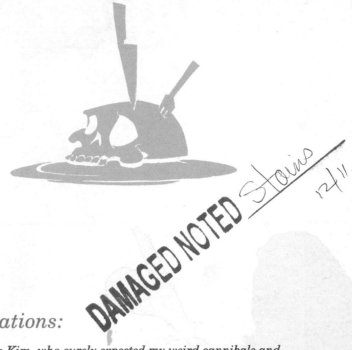

Dedications:

JOHN: To Kim, who surely expected my weird cannibals and bird flu idea to flop, and supported my mad folly nonetheless.

ROB: To April, who makes me think I can lift mountains. And to Mom and Dad, who sheltered my dreams, while not completely understanding them.

Thanks:

Lisa Gonzales, for the coloring assists.
Tom B. Long, for the logo.
Comicbookfonts.com, for the fonts.

And More Thanks:

Robert Kirkman, Eric Stephenson, Brandon Jerwa, Ed Brubaker, CB Cebulski, Kody Chamberlain, Joe Keatinge, Allen Hui, Drew Gill, Matt Fraction, Jonah Weiland, Aris Iliopoulos, Roman Stepanov, foodies Rachelle and Darlene, Dave Crosland, Ben Templesmith, and YOU.

Chapter 1

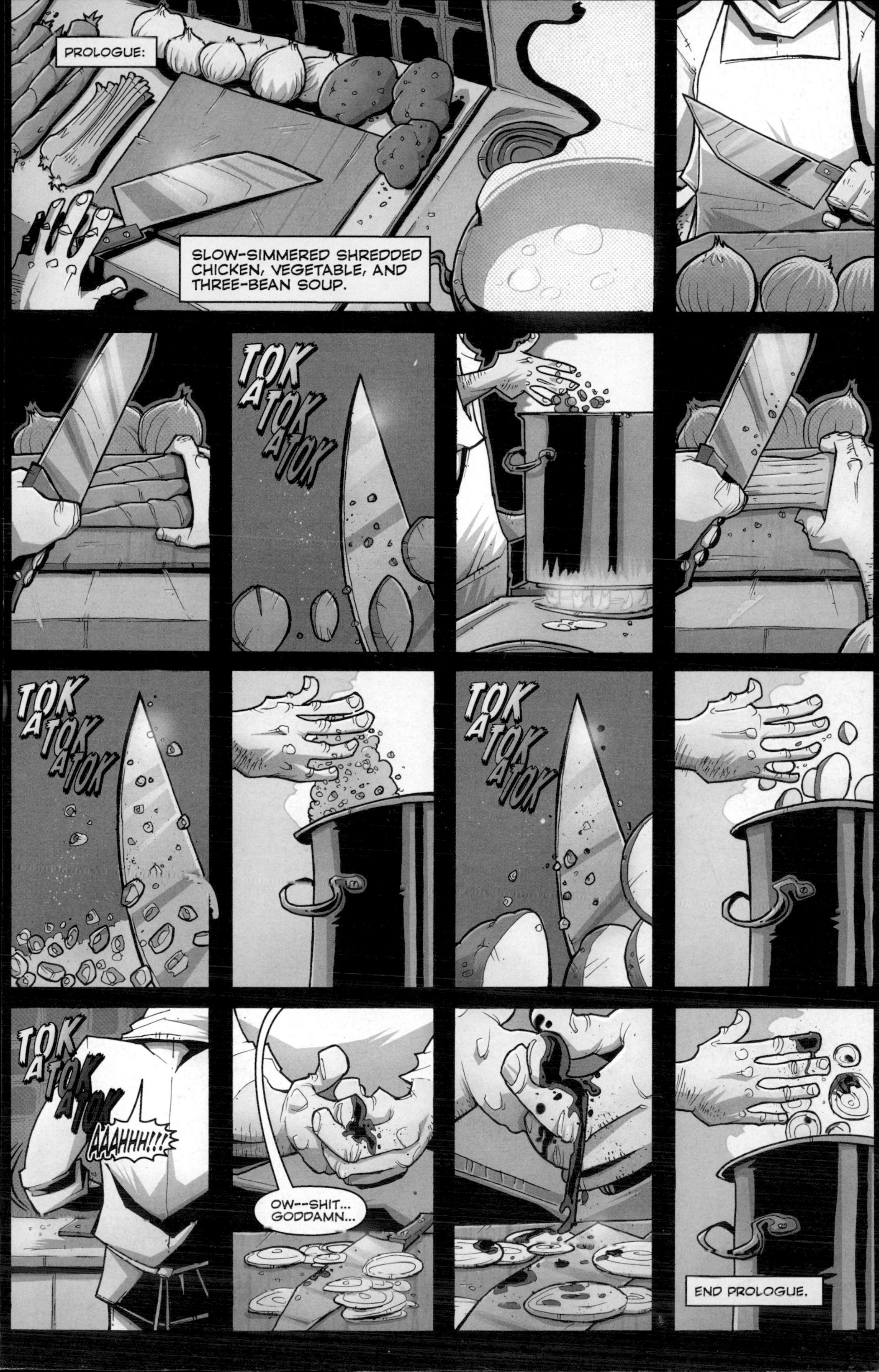
PROLOGUE:
SLOW-SIMMERED SHREDDED CHICKEN, VEGETABLE, AND THREE-BEAN SOUP.
TOK A TOK A TOK
TOK A TOK A TOK
TOK A TOK A TOK
TOK A TOK A TOK
AAAHHH!!!
OW--SHIT... GODDAMN...
END PROLOGUE.

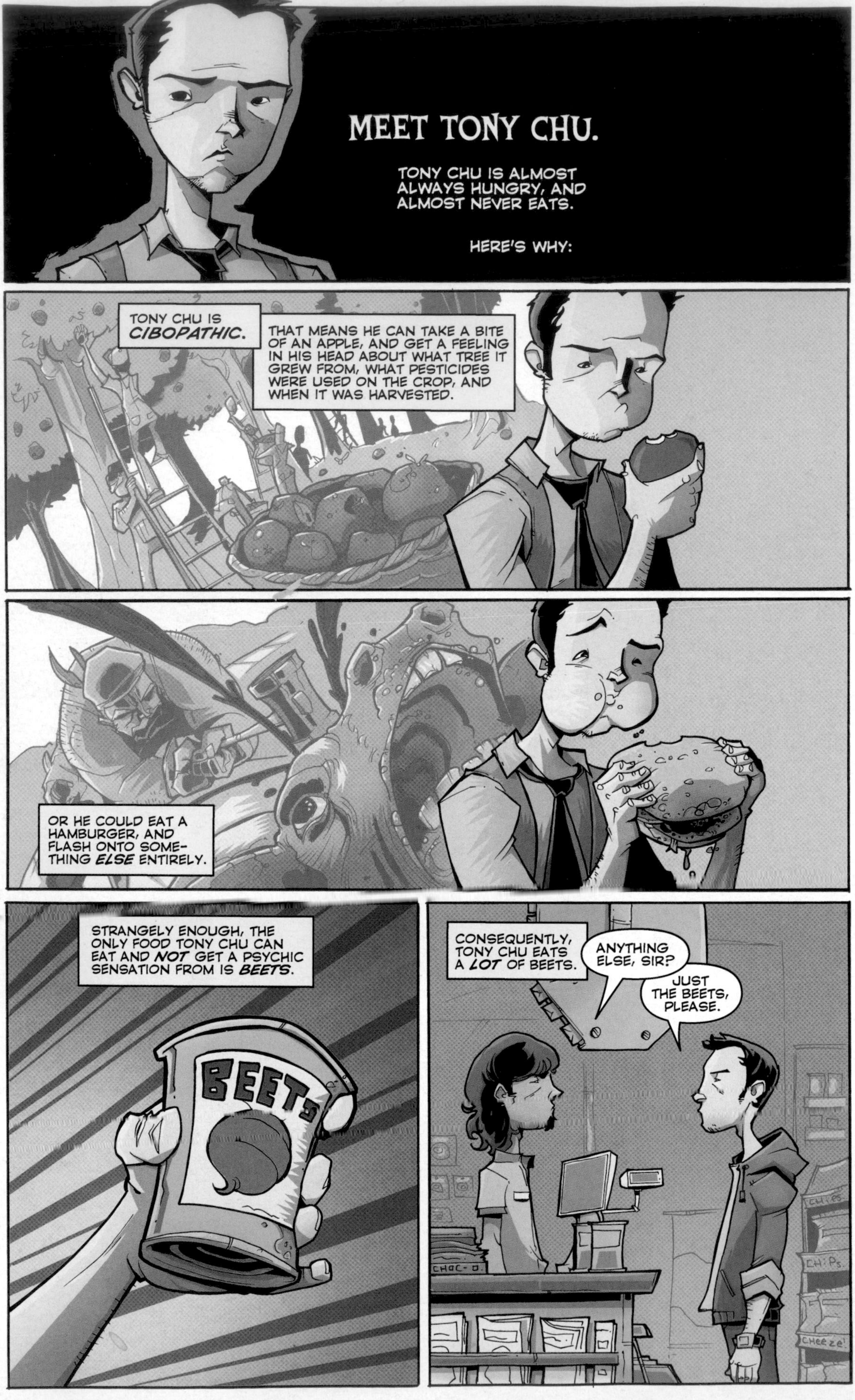
MEET TONY CHU.
TONY CHU IS ALMOST ALWAYS HUNGRY, AND ALMOST NEVER EATS.
HERE'S WHY:
TONY CHU IS *CIBOPATHIC*.
THAT MEANS HE CAN TAKE A BITE OF AN APPLE, AND GET A FEELING IN HIS HEAD ABOUT WHAT TREE IT GREW FROM, WHAT PESTICIDES WERE USED ON THE CROP, AND WHEN IT WAS HARVESTED.
OR HE COULD EAT A HAMBURGER, AND FLASH ONTO SOME-THING *ELSE* ENTIRELY.
STRANGELY ENOUGH, THE ONLY FOOD TONY CHU CAN EAT AND *NOT* GET A PSYCHIC SENSATION FROM IS *BEETS*.
BEETS
CONSEQUENTLY, TONY CHU EATS A *LOT* OF BEETS.
ANYTHING ELSE, SIR?
JUST THE BEETS, PLEASE.
CHOC-
CHIPS
CHIPS
CHEEZE!

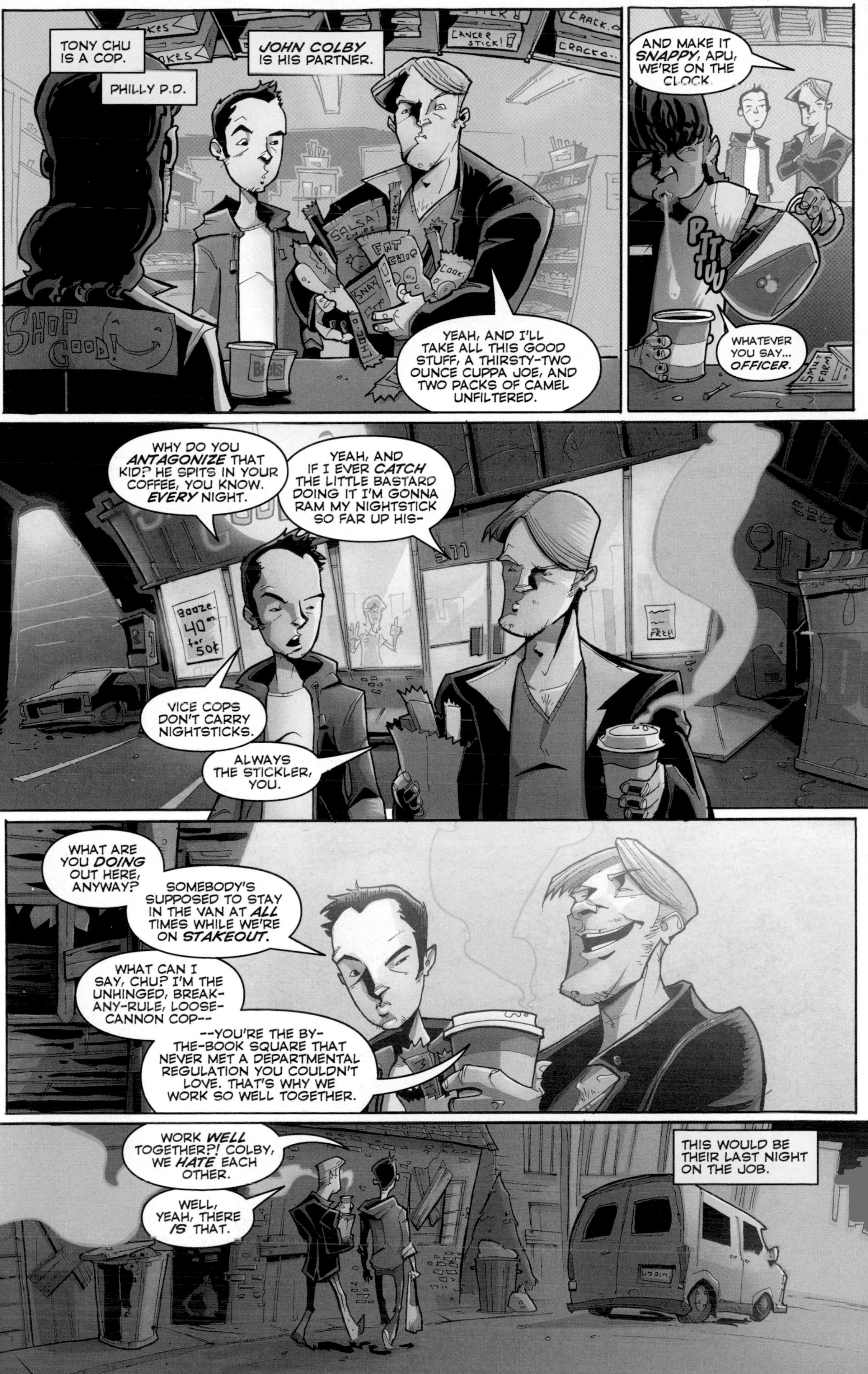
TONY CHU IS A COP.
PHILLY P.D.
JOHN COLBY IS HIS PARTNER.
YEAH, AND I'LL TAKE ALL THIS GOOD STUFF, A THIRSTY-TWO OUNCE CUPPA JOE, AND TWO PACKS OF CAMEL UNFILTERED.
SHOP GOOD!
AND MAKE IT SNAPPY, APU, WE'RE ON THE CLOCK.
PTTTUU
WHATEVER YOU SAY... OFFICER.
WHY DO YOU ANTAGONIZE THAT KID? HE SPITS IN YOUR COFFEE, YOU KNOW. EVERY NIGHT.
YEAH, AND IF I EVER CATCH THE LITTLE BASTARD DOING IT I'M GONNA RAM MY NIGHTSTICK SO FAR UP HIS-
VICE COPS DON'T CARRY NIGHTSTICKS.
ALWAYS THE STICKLER, YOU.
Booze. 40oz for 50¢
WHAT ARE YOU DOING OUT HERE, ANYWAY?
SOMEBODY'S SUPPOSED TO STAY IN THE VAN AT ALL TIMES WHILE WE'RE ON STAKEOUT.
WHAT CAN I SAY, CHU? I'M THE UNHINGED, BREAK-ANY-RULE, LOOSE-CANNON COP--
--YOU'RE THE BY-THE-BOOK SQUARE THAT NEVER MET A DEPARTMENTAL REGULATION YOU COULDN'T LOVE. THAT'S WHY WE WORK SO WELL TOGETHER.
WORK WELL TOGETHER?! COLBY, WE HATE EACH OTHER.
WELL, YEAH, THERE IS THAT.
THIS WOULD BE THEIR LAST NIGHT ON THE JOB.

THE LAST NIGHT OF THE *STAKEOUT*.

Fairmount
Speedy Upholstery

OUT OF BUSI-NESS!!

THANX FOR YOUR PATRONAGE !!!

HEADS UP.

LOOKS LIKE WE GOT SOME *CARRY OUT*.

HMM. WHAT DO YOU THINK?

LET HIM GET A FEW BLOCKS AWAY AND TICKET HIM?

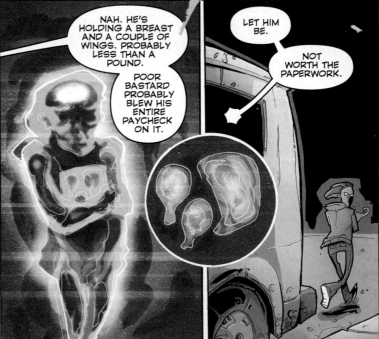

NAH. HE'S HOLDING A BREAST AND A COUPLE OF WINGS. PROBABLY LESS THAN A POUND.

POOR BASTARD PROBABLY BLEW HIS ENTIRE PAYCHECK ON IT.

LET HIM BE.

NOT WORTH THE PAPERWORK.

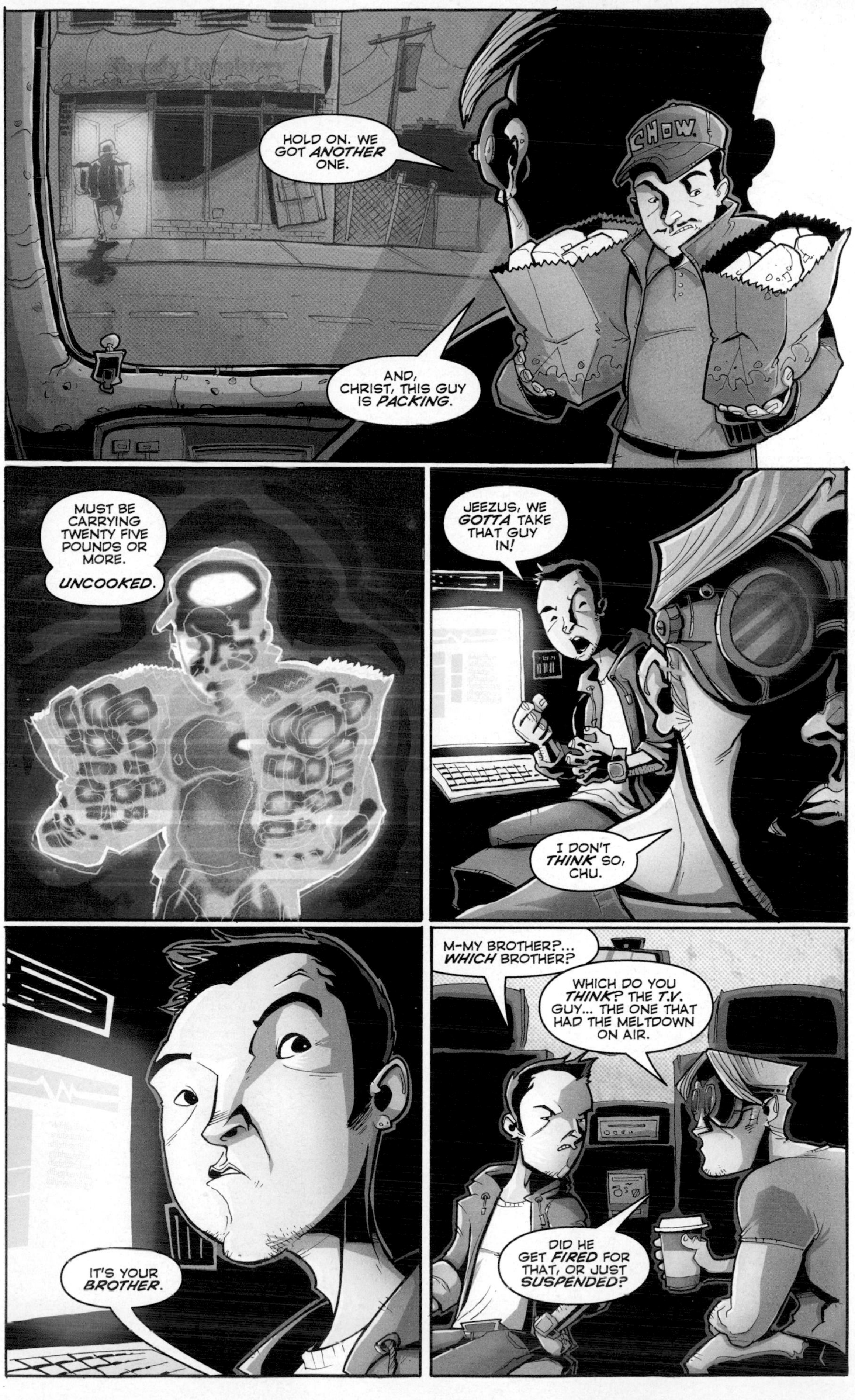
HOLD ON. WE GOT *ANOTHER* ONE.
CHOW.
AND, CHRIST, THIS GUY IS *PACKING*.
MUST BE CARRYING TWENTY FIVE POUNDS OR MORE.
UNCOOKED.
JEEZUS, WE *GOTTA* TAKE THAT GUY IN!
I DON'T *THINK* SO, CHU.
IT'S YOUR *BROTHER*.
M-MY BROTHER?... *WHICH* BROTHER?
WHICH DO YOU *THINK*? THE *T.V.* GUY... THE ONE THAT HAD THE MELTDOWN ON AIR.
DID HE GET *FIRED* FOR THAT, OR JUST *SUSPENDED*?

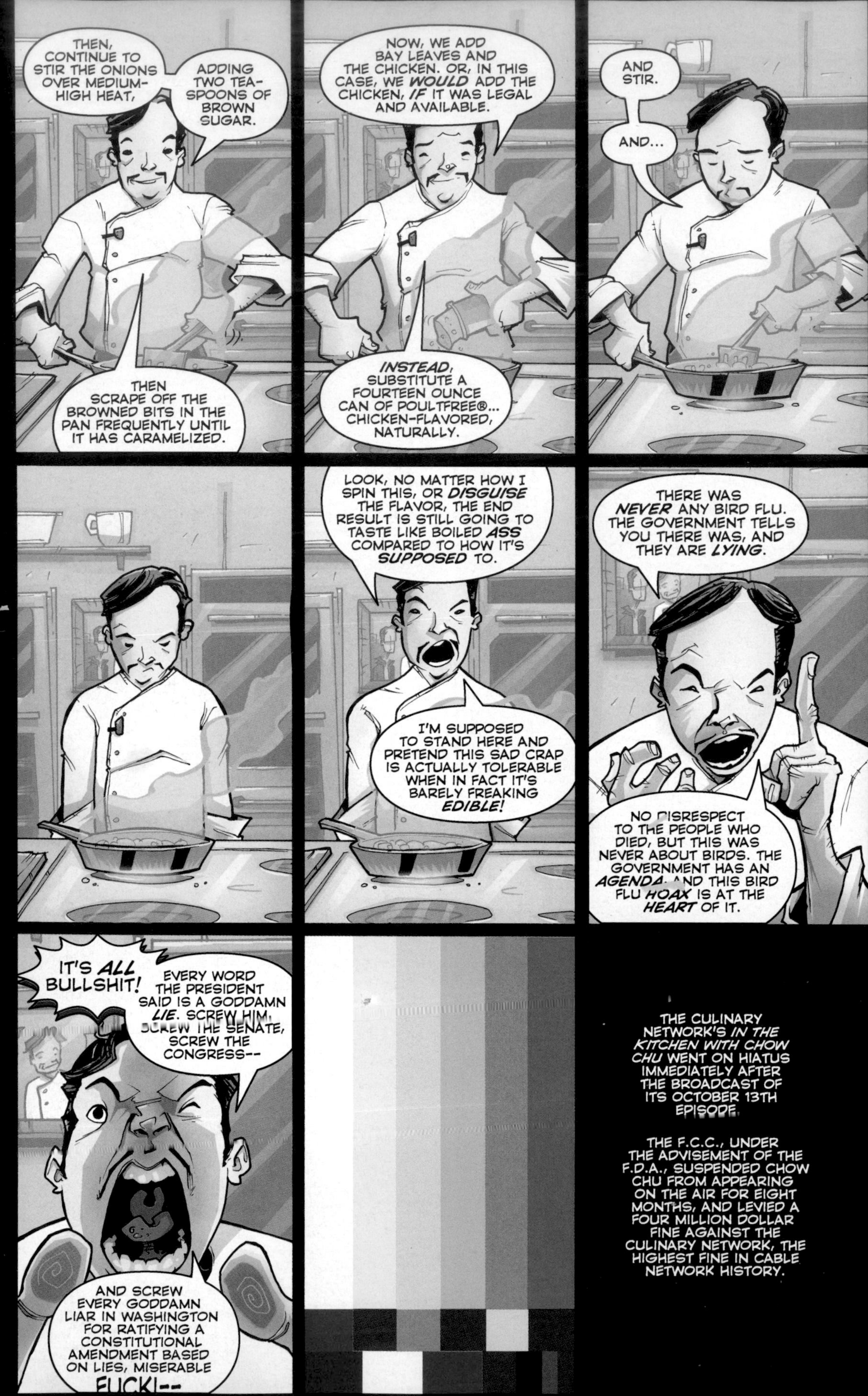
THEN, CONTINUE TO STIR THE ONIONS OVER MEDIUM-HIGH HEAT,
ADDING TWO TEA-SPOONS OF BROWN SUGAR.
THEN SCRAPE OFF THE BROWNED BITS IN THE PAN FREQUENTLY UNTIL IT HAS CARAMELIZED.
NOW, WE ADD BAY LEAVES AND THE CHICKEN. OR, IN THIS CASE, WE *WOULD* ADD THE CHICKEN, *IF* IT WAS LEGAL AND AVAILABLE.
INSTEAD, SUBSTITUTE A FOURTEEN OUNCE CAN OF POULTFREE®... CHICKEN-FLAVORED, NATURALLY.
AND STIR.
AND...
LOOK, NO MATTER HOW I SPIN THIS, OR *DISGUISE* THE FLAVOR, THE END RESULT IS STILL GOING TO TASTE LIKE BOILED *ASS* COMPARED TO HOW IT'S *SUPPOSED* TO.
I'M SUPPOSED TO STAND HERE AND PRETEND THIS SAD CRAP IS ACTUALLY TOLERABLE WHEN IN FACT IT'S BARELY FREAKING *EDIBLE*!
THERE WAS *NEVER* ANY BIRD FLU. THE GOVERNMENT TELLS YOU THERE WAS, AND THEY ARE *LYING*.
NO DISRESPECT TO THE PEOPLE WHO DIED, BUT THIS WAS NEVER ABOUT BIRDS. THE GOVERNMENT HAS AN *AGENDA*, AND THIS BIRD FLU *HOAX* IS AT THE *HEART* OF IT.
IT'S *ALL* BULLSHIT!
EVERY WORD THE PRESIDENT SAID IS A GODDAMN *LIE*. SCREW HIM, SCREW THE SENATE, SCREW THE CONGRESS--
AND SCREW EVERY GODDAMN LIAR IN WASHINGTON FOR RATIFYING A CONSTITUTIONAL AMENDMENT BASED ON LIES, MISERABLE FUCKI--
THE CULINARY NETWORK'S *IN THE KITCHEN WITH CHOW CHU* WENT ON HIATUS IMMEDIATELY AFTER THE BROADCAST OF ITS OCTOBER 13TH EPISODE.
THE F.C.C., UNDER THE ADVISEMENT OF THE F.D.A., SUSPENDED CHOW CHU FROM APPEARING ON THE AIR FOR EIGHT MONTHS, AND LEVIED A FOUR MILLION DOLLAR FINE AGAINST THE CULINARY NETWORK, THE HIGHEST FINE IN CABLE NETWORK HISTORY.

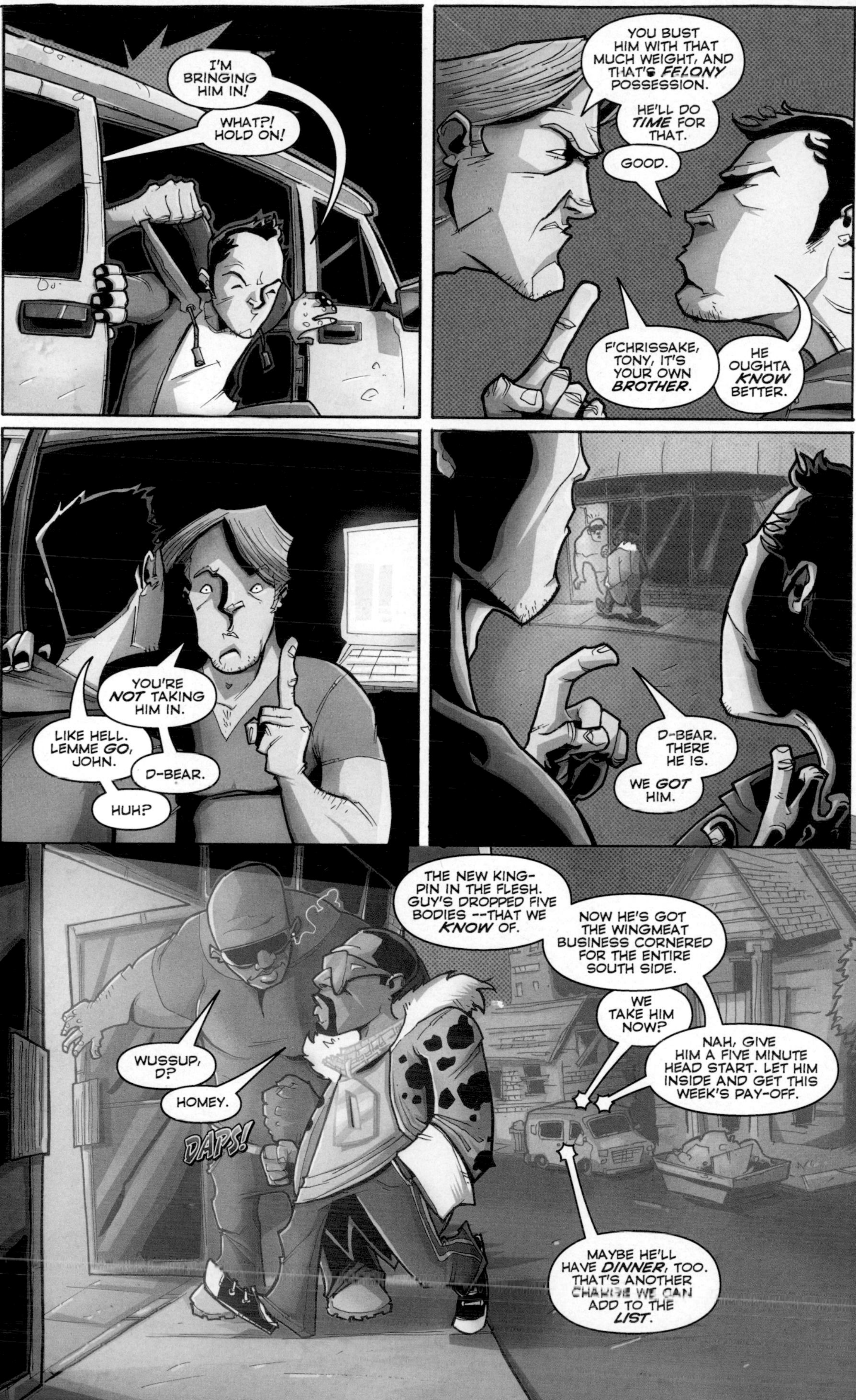

I'M BRINGING HIM IN!
WHAT?! HOLD ON!
YOU BUST HIM WITH THAT MUCH WEIGHT, AND THAT'S FELONY POSSESSION.
HE'LL DO TIME FOR THAT.
GOOD.
F'CHRISSAKE, TONY, IT'S YOUR OWN BROTHER.
HE OUGHTA KNOW BETTER.
YOU'RE NOT TAKING HIM IN.
LIKE HELL. LEMME GO, JOHN.
D-BEAR.
HUH?
D-BEAR. THERE HE IS.
WE GOT HIM.
THE NEW KING-PIN IN THE FLESH. GUY'S DROPPED FIVE BODIES --THAT WE KNOW OF.
NOW HE'S GOT THE WINGMEAT BUSINESS CORNERED FOR THE ENTIRE SOUTH SIDE.
WE TAKE HIM NOW?
NAH, GIVE HIM A FIVE MINUTE HEAD START. LET HIM INSIDE AND GET THIS WEEK'S PAY-OFF.
WUSSUP, D?
HOMEY.
DAPS!
MAYBE HE'LL HAVE DINNER, TOO. THAT'S ANOTHER CHARGE WE CAN ADD TO THE LIST.

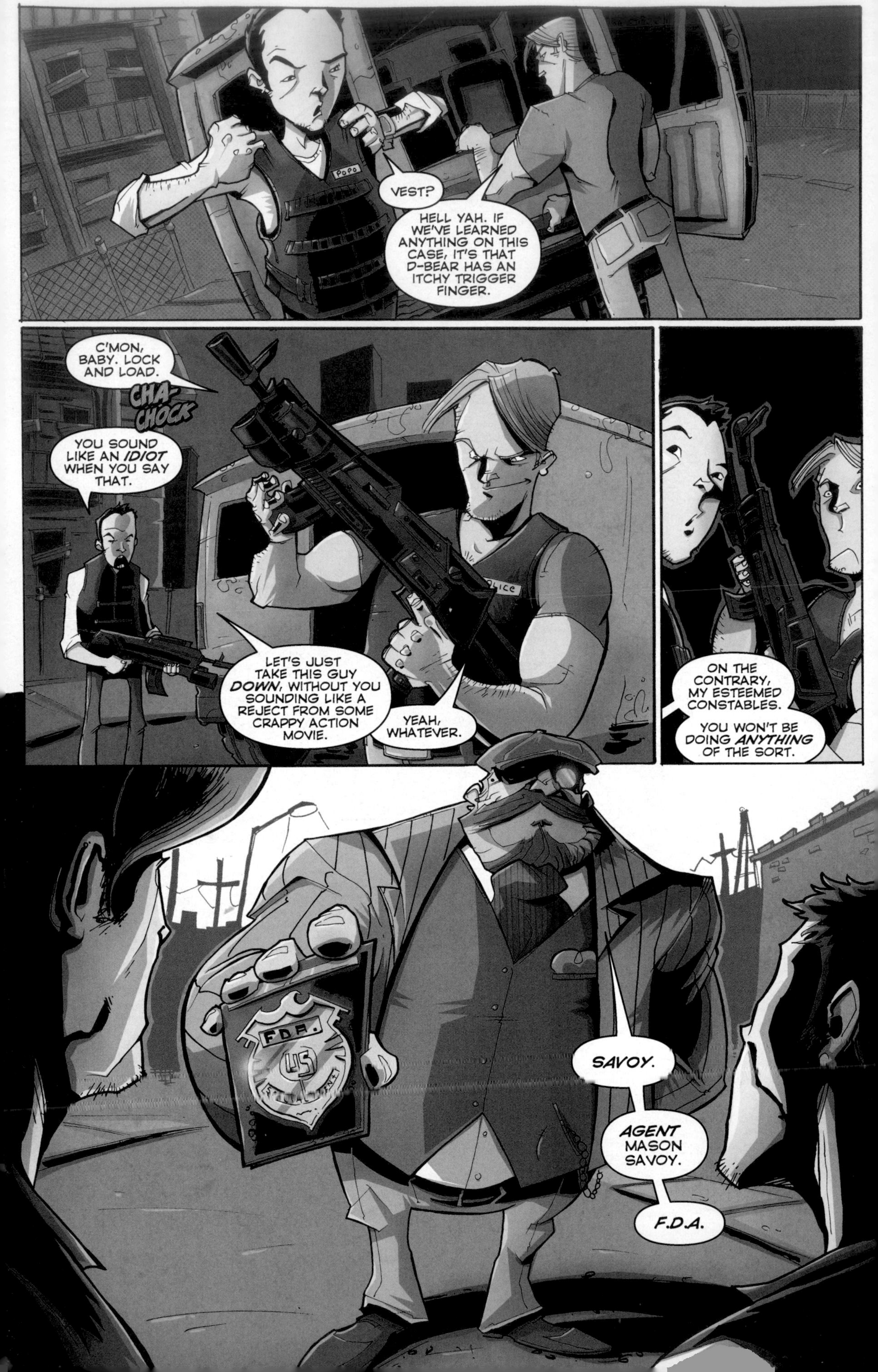
VEST?
HELL YAH. IF WE'VE LEARNED ANYTHING ON THIS CASE, IT'S THAT D-BEAR HAS AN ITCHY TRIGGER FINGER.
C'MON, BABY. LOCK AND LOAD.
CHA-CHOCK
YOU SOUND LIKE AN *IDIOT* WHEN YOU SAY THAT.
LET'S JUST TAKE THIS GUY *DOWN*, WITHOUT YOU SOUNDING LIKE A REJECT FROM SOME CRAPPY ACTION MOVIE.
YEAH, WHATEVER.
ON THE CONTRARY, MY ESTEEMED CONSTABLES.
YOU WON'T BE DOING *ANYTHING* OF THE SORT.
SAVOY.
AGENT MASON SAVOY.
F.D.A.

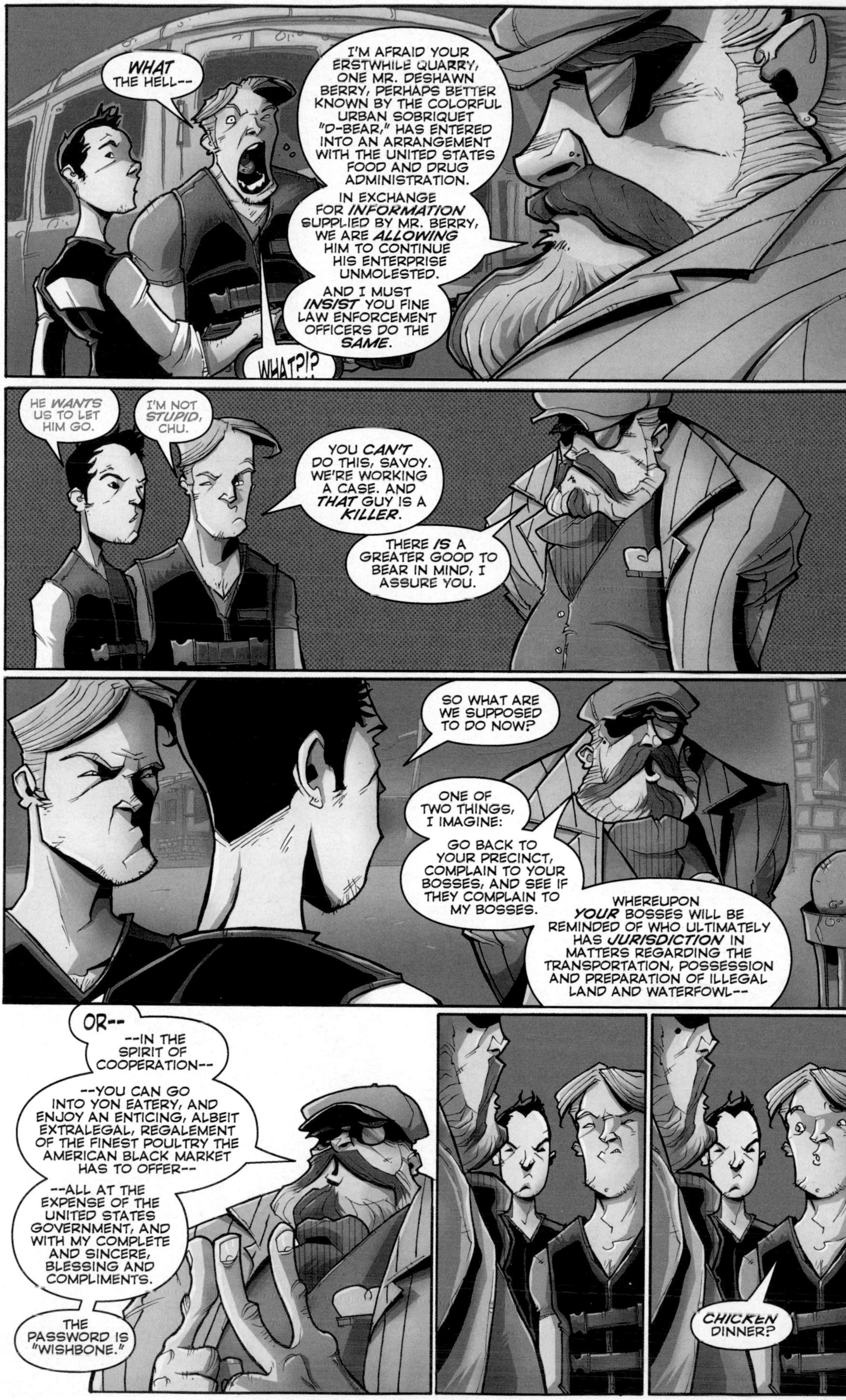
WHAT THE HELL--
I'M AFRAID YOUR ERSTWHILE QUARRY, ONE MR. DESHAWN BERRY, PERHAPS BETTER KNOWN BY THE COLORFUL URBAN SOBRIQUET "D-BEAR," HAS ENTERED INTO AN ARRANGEMENT WITH THE UNITED STATES FOOD AND DRUG ADMINISTRATION.
IN EXCHANGE FOR INFORMATION SUPPLIED BY MR. BERRY, WE ARE ALLOWING HIM TO CONTINUE HIS ENTERPRISE UNMOLESTED.
AND I MUST INSIST YOU FINE LAW ENFORCEMENT OFFICERS DO THE SAME.
WHAT?!?
HE WANTS US TO LET HIM GO.
I'M NOT STUPID, CHU.
YOU CAN'T DO THIS, SAVOY. WE'RE WORKING A CASE. AND THAT GUY IS A KILLER.
THERE IS A GREATER GOOD TO BEAR IN MIND, I ASSURE YOU.
SO WHAT ARE WE SUPPOSED TO DO NOW?
ONE OF TWO THINGS, I IMAGINE:
GO BACK TO YOUR PRECINCT, COMPLAIN TO YOUR BOSSES, AND SEE IF THEY COMPLAIN TO MY BOSSES.
WHEREUPON YOUR BOSSES WILL BE REMINDED OF WHO ULTIMATELY HAS JURISDICTION IN MATTERS REGARDING THE TRANSPORTATION, POSSESSION AND PREPARATION OF ILLEGAL LAND AND WATERFOWL--
OR--
--IN THE SPIRIT OF COOPERATION--
--YOU CAN GO INTO YON EATERY, AND ENJOY AN ENTICING, ALBEIT EXTRALEGAL, REGALEMENT OF THE FINEST POULTRY THE AMERICAN BLACK MARKET HAS TO OFFER--
--ALL AT THE EXPENSE OF THE UNITED STATES GOVERNMENT, AND WITH MY COMPLETE AND SINCERE, BLESSING AND COMPLIMENTS.
THE PASSWORD IS "WISHBONE."
CHICKEN DINNER?

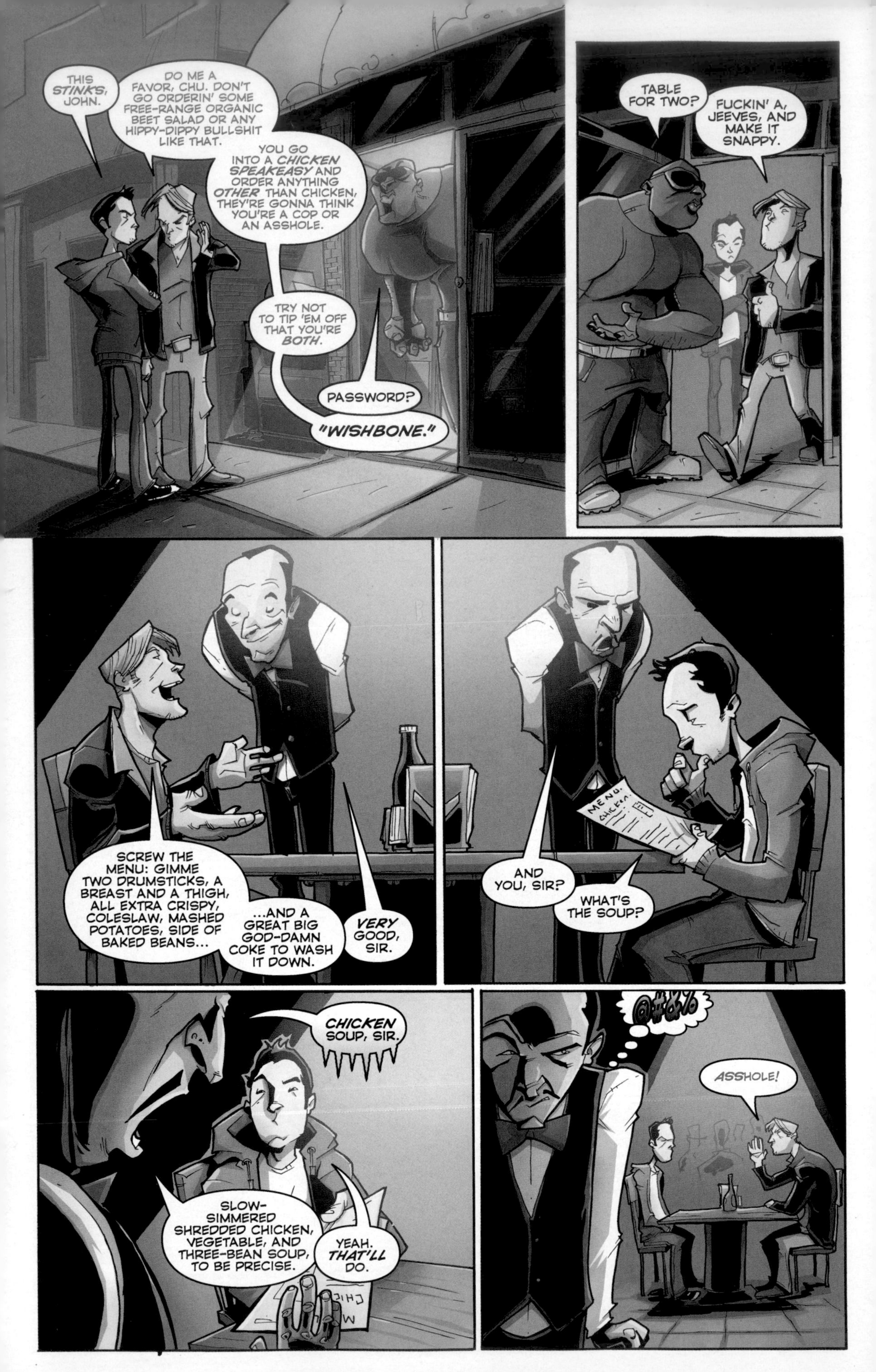

THIS STINKS, JOHN.
DO ME A FAVOR, CHU. DON'T GO ORDERIN' SOME FREE-RANGE ORGANIC BEET SALAD OR ANY HIPPY-DIPPY BULLSHIT LIKE THAT.
YOU GO INTO A CHICKEN SPEAKEASY AND ORDER ANYTHING OTHER THAN CHICKEN, THEY'RE GONNA THINK YOU'RE A COP OR AN ASSHOLE.
TRY NOT TO TIP 'EM OFF THAT YOU'RE BOTH.
PASSWORD?
"WISHBONE."
TABLE FOR TWO?
FUCKIN' A, JEEVES, AND MAKE IT SNAPPY.
SCREW THE MENU: GIMME TWO DRUMSTICKS, A BREAST AND A THIGH, ALL EXTRA CRISPY, COLESLAW, MASHED POTATOES, SIDE OF BAKED BEANS...
...AND A GREAT BIG GOD-DAMN COKE TO WASH IT DOWN.
VERY GOOD, SIR.
AND YOU, SIR?
WHAT'S THE SOUP?
MENU: CHICKEN
CHICKEN SOUP, SIR.
SLOW-SIMMERED SHREDDED CHICKEN, VEGETABLE, AND THREE-BEAN SOUP, TO BE PRECISE.
YEAH. THAT'LL DO.
@#&%
ASSHOLE!

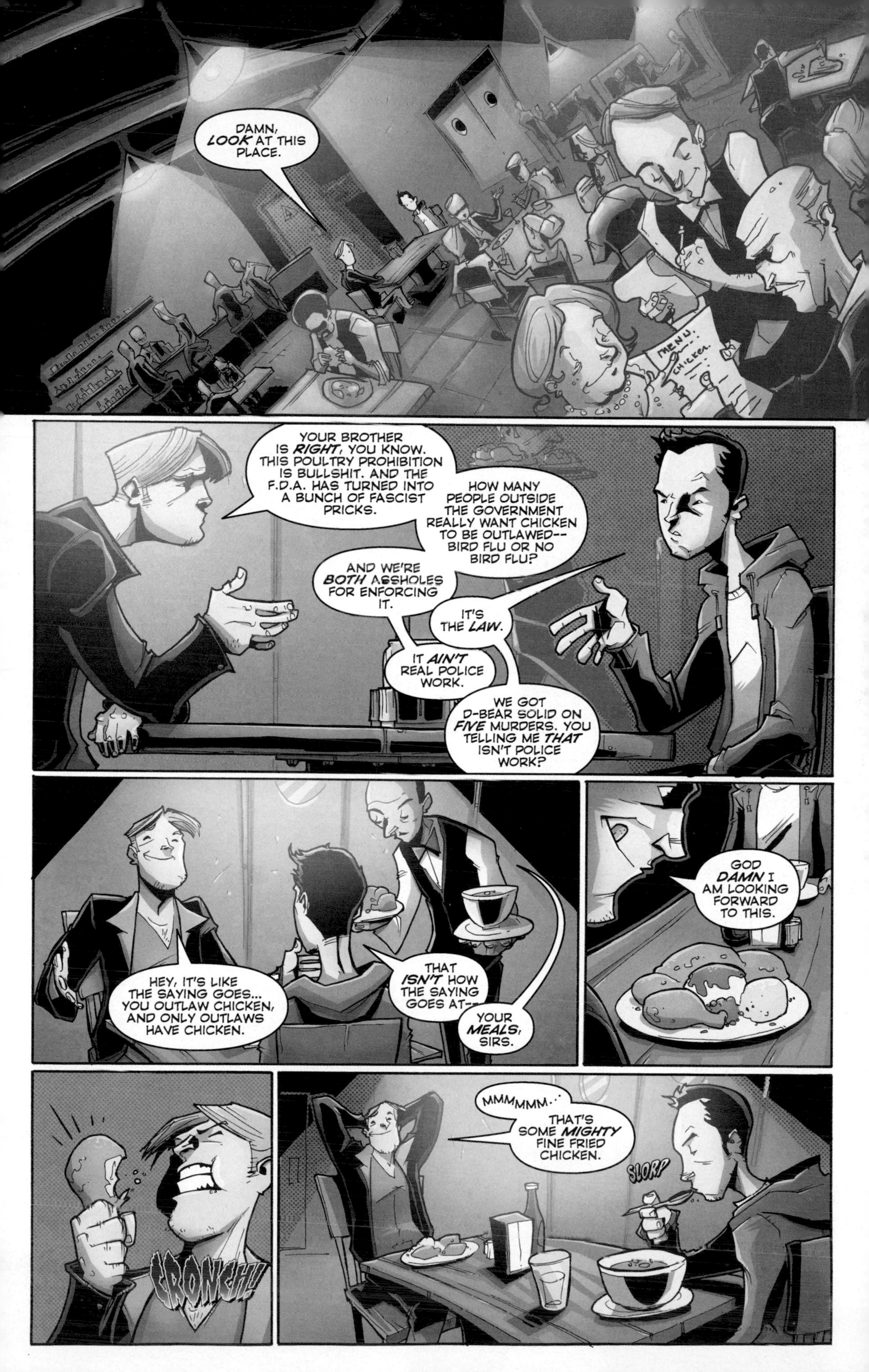
DAMN, LOOK AT THIS PLACE.
MENU. CHICKEN.
YOUR BROTHER IS RIGHT, YOU KNOW. THIS POULTRY PROHIBITION IS BULLSHIT. AND THE F.D.A. HAS TURNED INTO A BUNCH OF FASCIST PRICKS.
HOW MANY PEOPLE OUTSIDE THE GOVERNMENT REALLY WANT CHICKEN TO BE OUTLAWED-- BIRD FLU OR NO BIRD FLU?
AND WE'RE BOTH ASSHOLES FOR ENFORCING IT.
IT'S THE LAW.
IT AIN'T REAL POLICE WORK.
WE GOT D-BEAR SOLID ON FIVE MURDERS. YOU TELLING ME THAT ISN'T POLICE WORK?
HEY, IT'S LIKE THE SAYING GOES... YOU OUTLAW CHICKEN, AND ONLY OUTLAWS HAVE CHICKEN.
THAT ISN'T HOW THE SAYING GOES AT--
YOUR MEALS, SIRS.
GOD DAMN I AM LOOKING FORWARD TO THIS.
CRONCH!!
MMMMMM...
THAT'S SOME MIGHTY FINE FRIED CHICKEN.
SLORP

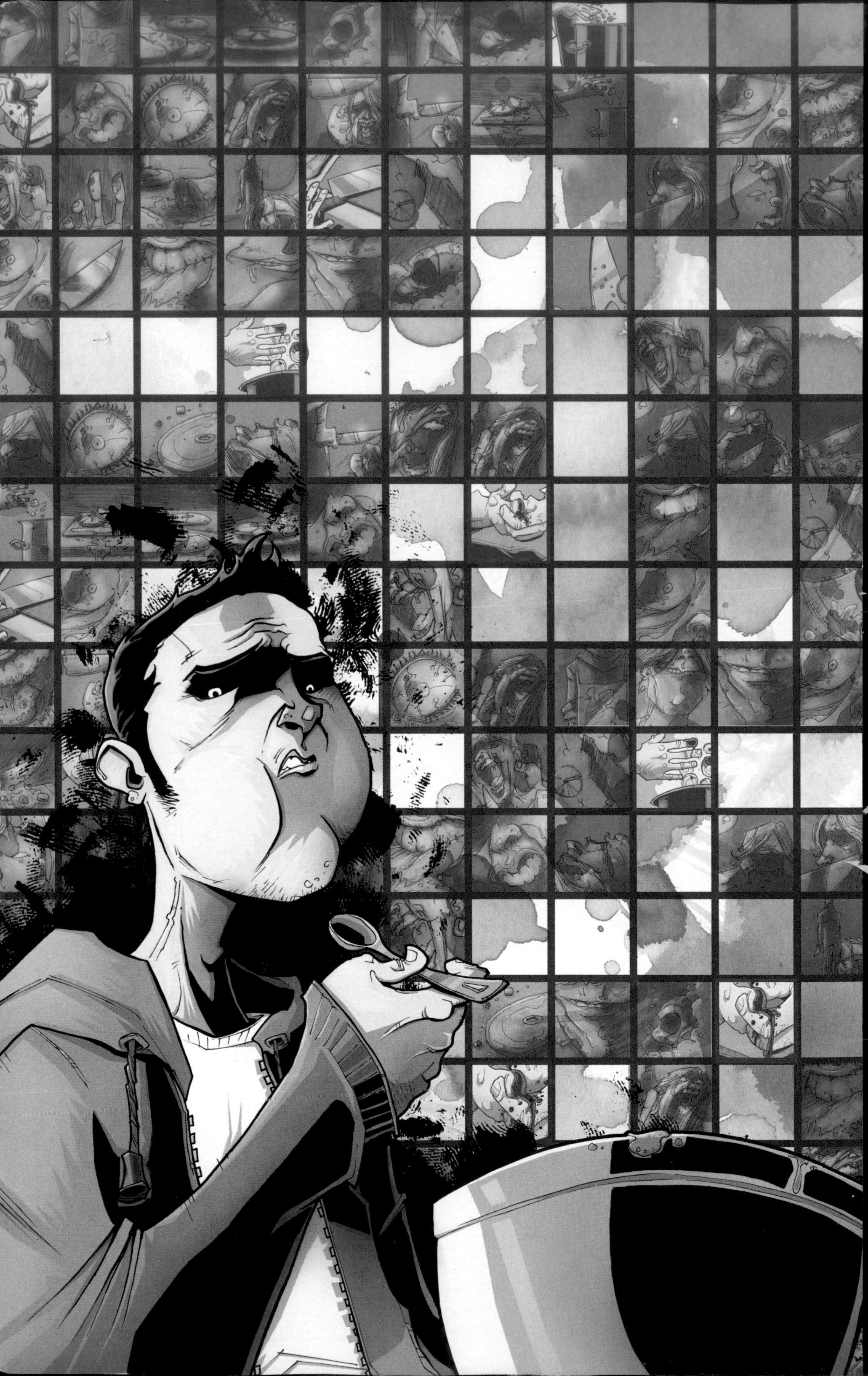

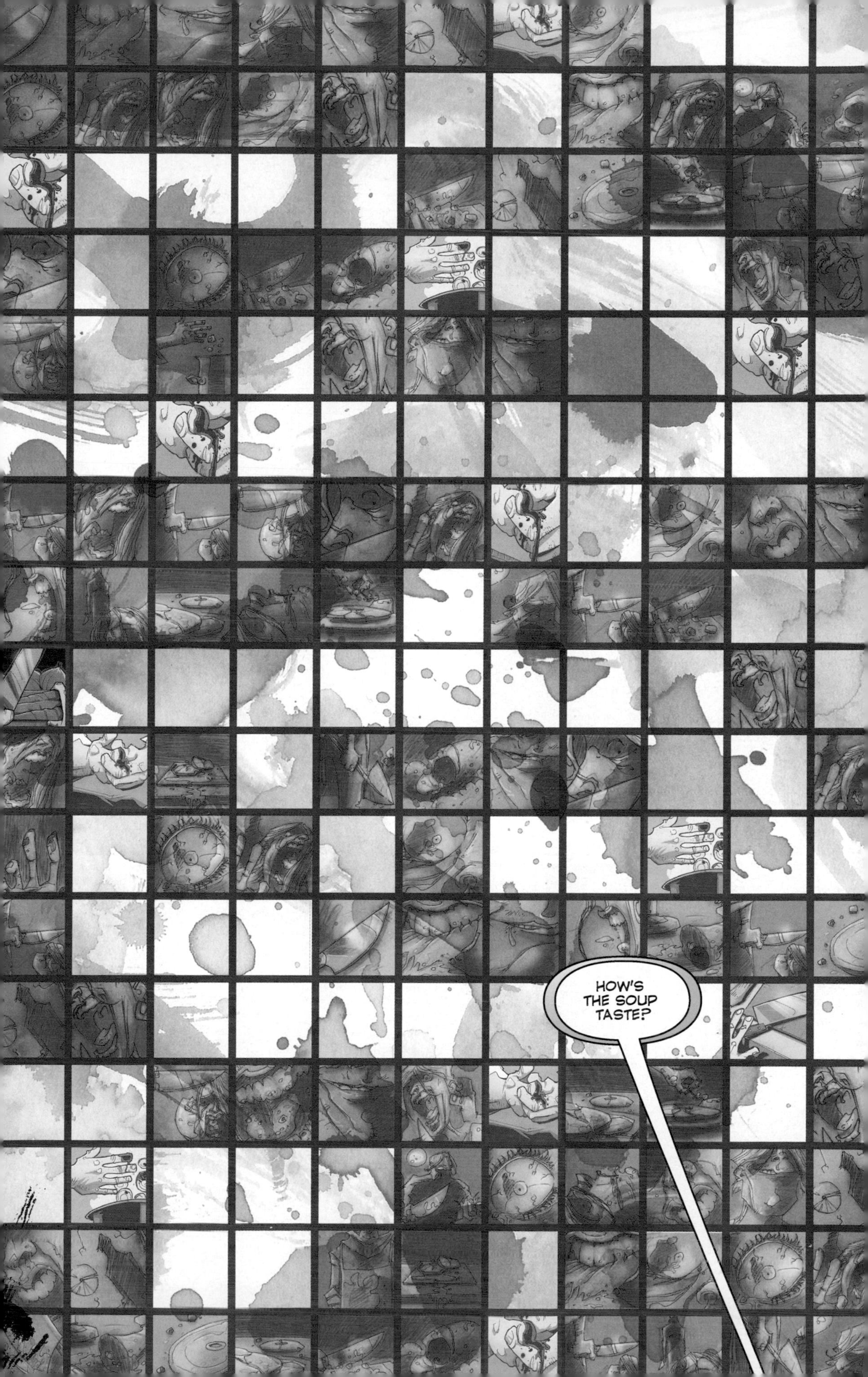
HOW'S THE SOUP TASTE?

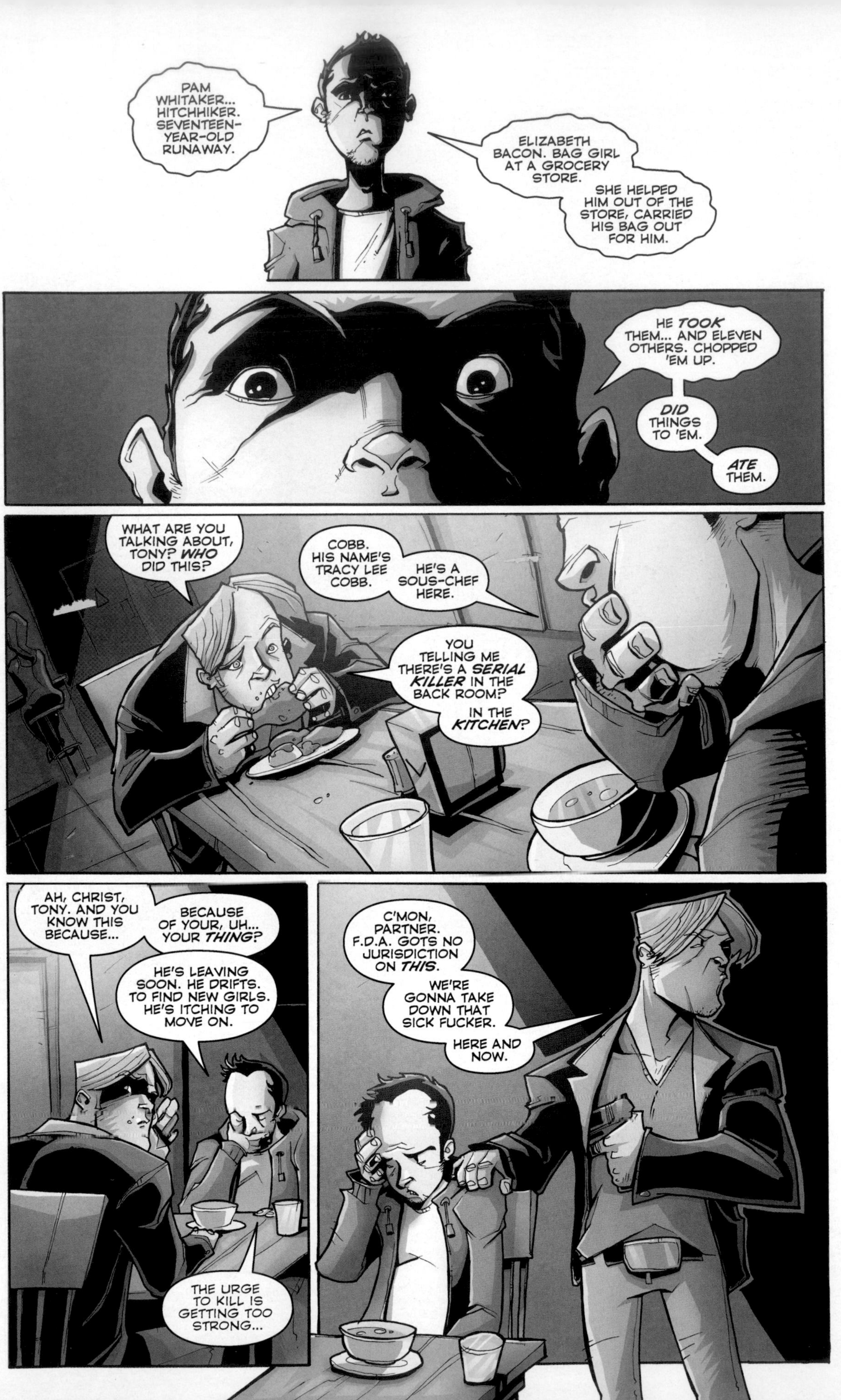
PAM WHITAKER... HITCHHIKER. SEVENTEEN-YEAR-OLD RUNAWAY.
ELIZABETH BACON. BAG GIRL AT A GROCERY STORE.
SHE HELPED HIM OUT OF THE STORE, CARRIED HIS BAG OUT FOR HIM.
HE TOOK THEM... AND ELEVEN OTHERS. CHOPPED 'EM UP.
DID THINGS TO 'EM.
ATE THEM.
WHAT ARE YOU TALKING ABOUT, TONY? WHO DID THIS?
COBB. HIS NAME'S TRACY LEE COBB.
HE'S A SOUS-CHEF HERE.
YOU TELLING ME THERE'S A SERIAL KILLER IN THE BACK ROOM?
IN THE KITCHEN?
AH, CHRIST, TONY. AND YOU KNOW THIS BECAUSE...
BECAUSE OF YOUR, UH... YOUR THING?
HE'S LEAVING SOON. HE DRIFTS. TO FIND NEW GIRLS. HE'S ITCHING TO MOVE ON.
THE URGE TO KILL IS GETTING TOO STRONG...
C'MON, PARTNER. F.D.A. GOTS NO JURISDICTION ON THIS.
WE'RE GONNA TAKE DOWN THAT SICK FUCKER.
HERE AND NOW.

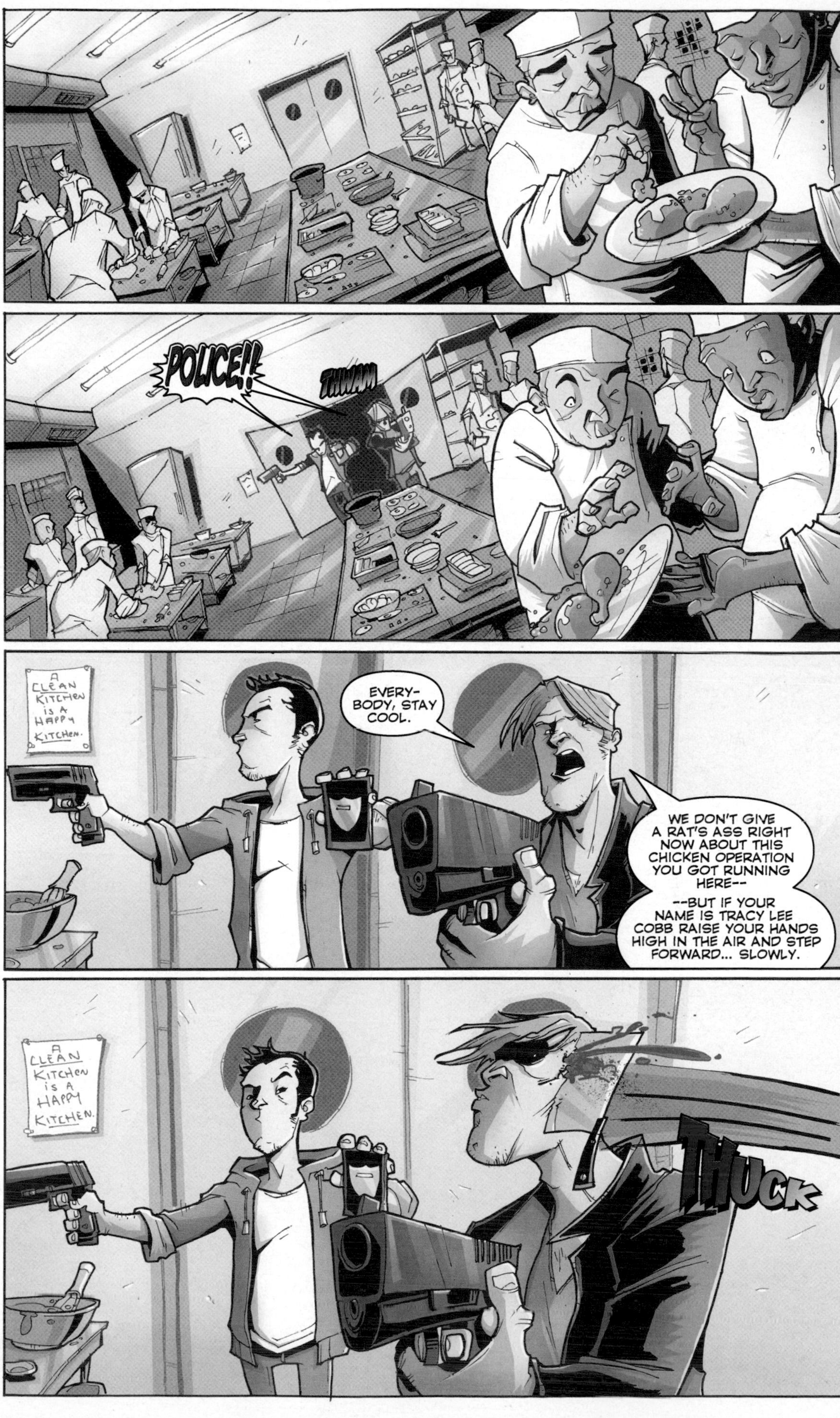
POLICE!!
THWAM
A CLEAN KITCHEN is A HAPPY KITCHEN.
EVERY-BODY, STAY COOL.
WE DON'T GIVE A RAT'S ASS RIGHT NOW ABOUT THIS CHICKEN OPERATION YOU GOT RUNNING HERE--
--BUT IF YOUR NAME IS TRACY LEE COBB RAISE YOUR HANDS HIGH IN THE AIR AND STEP FORWARD... SLOWLY.
A CLEAN KITCHEN is A HAPPY KITCHEN.
THUCK

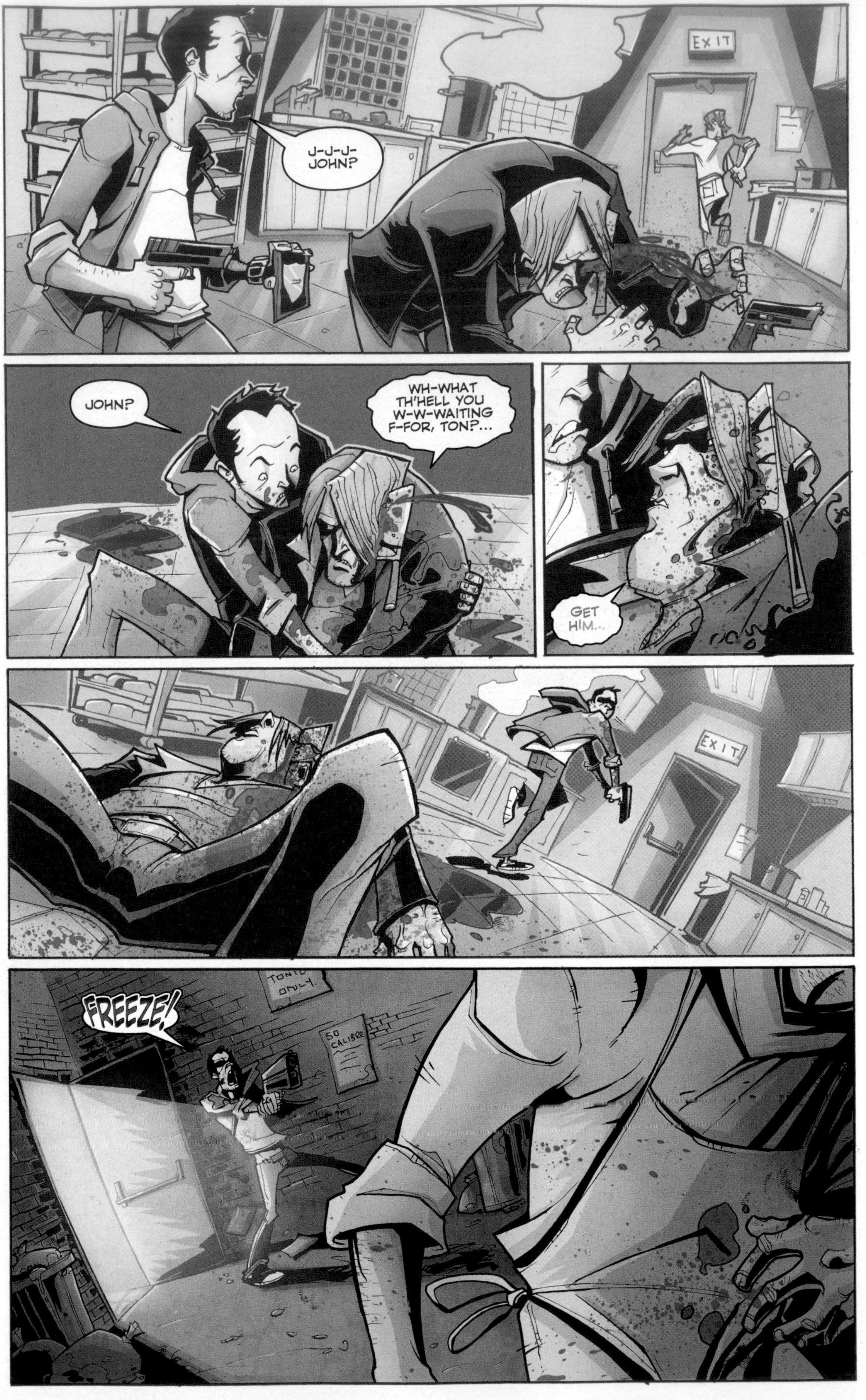
EXIT
J-J-J-
JOHN?
JOHN?
WH-WHAT TH'HELL YOU W-W-WAITING F-FOR, TON?...
GET HIM..
EXIT
FREEZE!

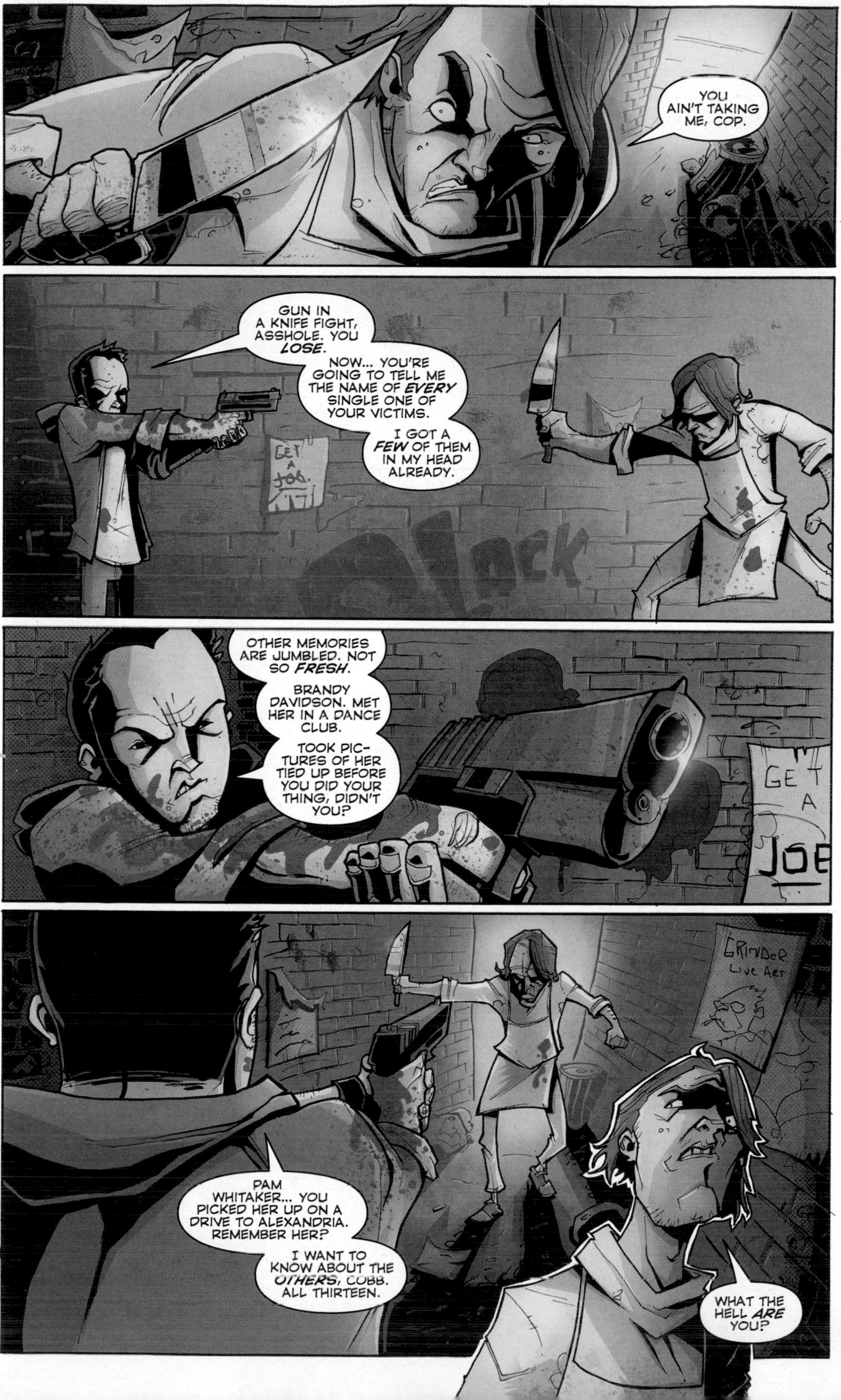
YOU AIN'T TAKING ME, COP.
GUN IN A KNIFE FIGHT, ASSHOLE. YOU LOSE.
NOW... YOU'RE GOING TO TELL ME THE NAME OF EVERY SINGLE ONE OF YOUR VICTIMS.
I GOT A FEW OF THEM IN MY HEAD ALREADY.
GET A JOB.
OTHER MEMORIES ARE JUMBLED. NOT SO FRESH.
BRANDY DAVIDSON. MET HER IN A DANCE CLUB.
TOOK PICTURES OF HER TIED UP BEFORE YOU DID YOUR THING, DIDN'T YOU?
GET A JOB
GRINDER Live Art
PAM WHITAKER... YOU PICKED HER UP ON A DRIVE TO ALEXANDRIA. REMEMBER HER?
I WANT TO KNOW ABOUT THE OTHERS, COBB. ALL THIRTEEN.
WHAT THE HELL ARE YOU?

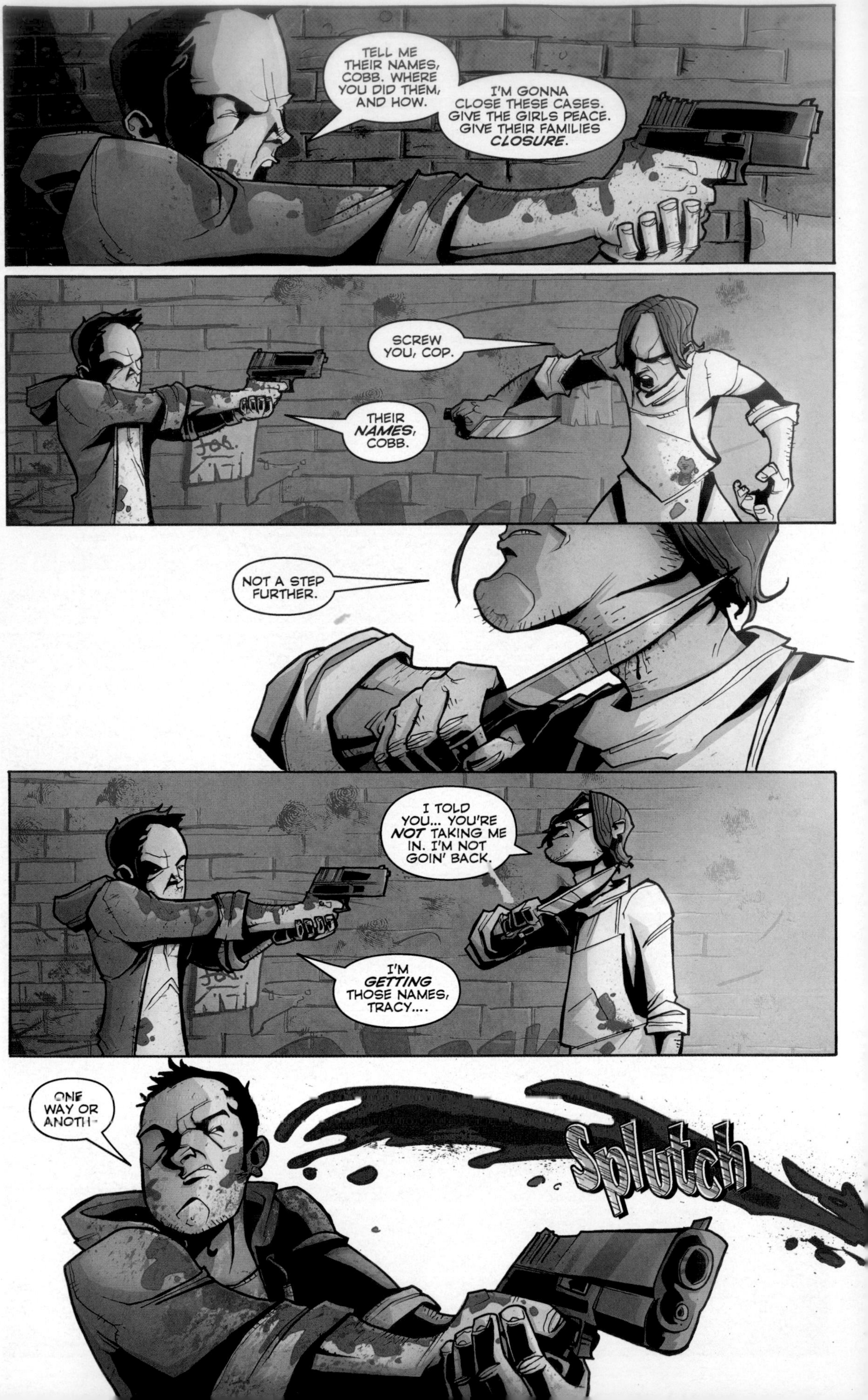
TELL ME THEIR NAMES, COBB. WHERE YOU DID THEM, AND HOW.
I'M GONNA CLOSE THESE CASES. GIVE THE GIRLS PEACE. GIVE THEIR FAMILIES CLOSURE.
SCREW YOU, COP.
THEIR NAMES, COBB.
NOT A STEP FURTHER.
I TOLD YOU... YOU'RE NOT TAKING ME IN. I'M NOT GOIN' BACK.
I'M GETTING THOSE NAMES, TRACY....
ONE WAY OR ANOTH-
Splutch

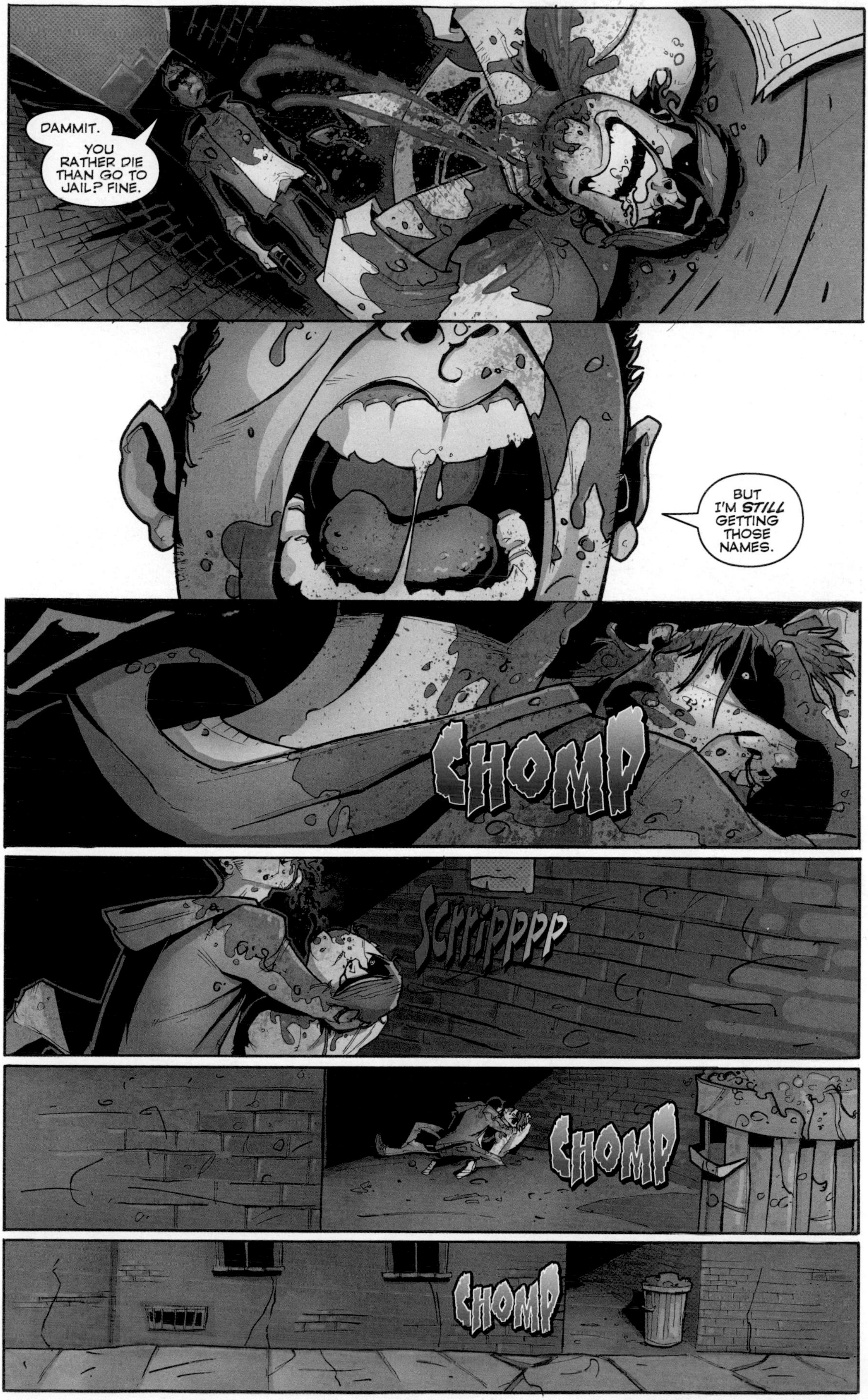
DAMMIT.
YOU RATHER DIE THAN GO TO JAIL? FINE.
BUT I'M STILL GETTING THOSE NAMES.
CHOMP
Scripppp
CHOMP
CHOMP

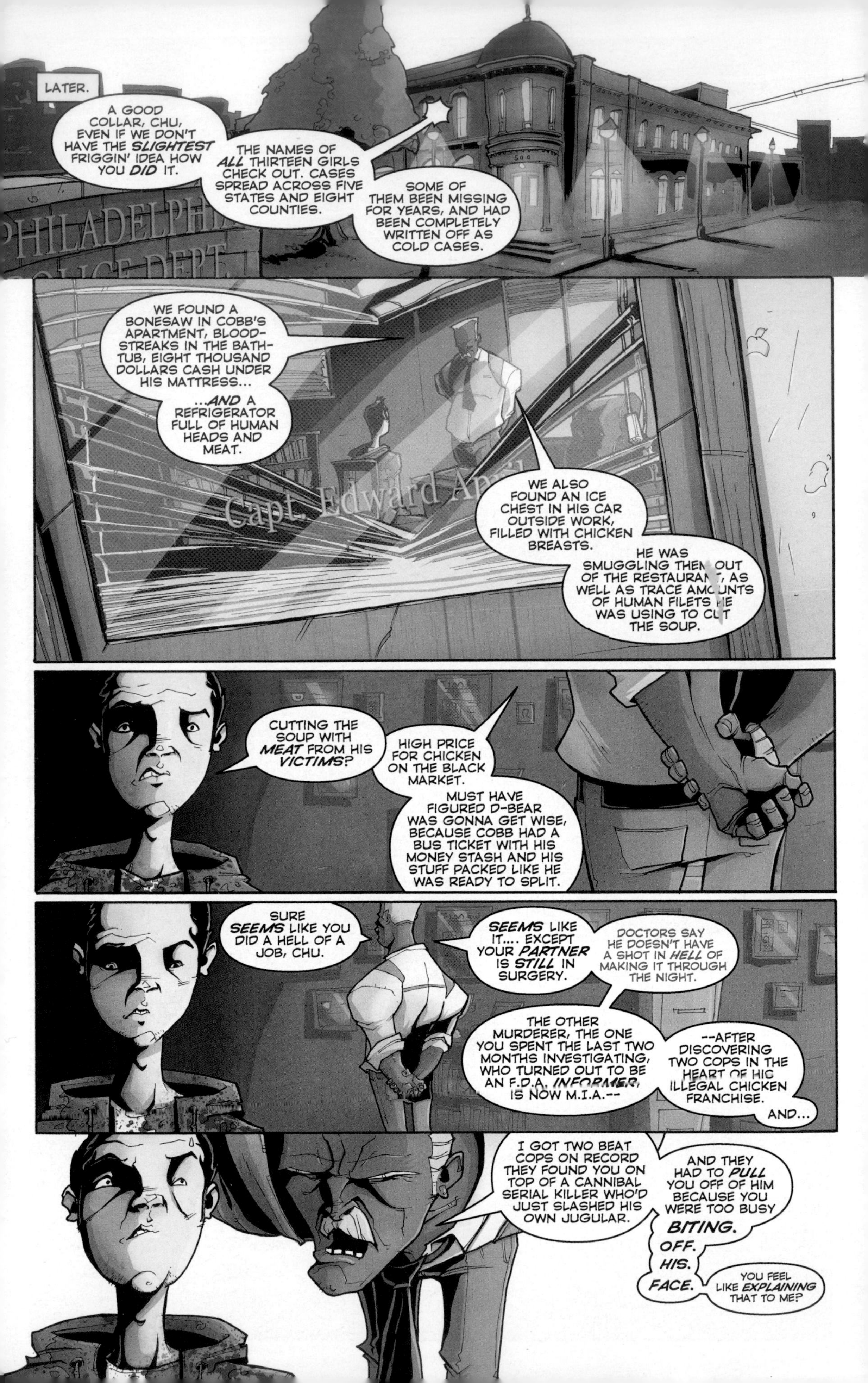
LATER.
A GOOD COLLAR, CHU, EVEN IF WE DON'T HAVE THE SLIGHTEST FRIGGIN' IDEA HOW YOU DID IT.
THE NAMES OF ALL THIRTEEN GIRLS CHECK OUT. CASES SPREAD ACROSS FIVE STATES AND EIGHT COUNTIES.
SOME OF THEM BEEN MISSING FOR YEARS, AND HAD BEEN COMPLETELY WRITTEN OFF AS COLD CASES.
PHILADELPHIA POLICE DEPT.
WE FOUND A BONESAW IN COBB'S APARTMENT, BLOOD-STREAKS IN THE BATH-TUB, EIGHT THOUSAND DOLLARS CASH UNDER HIS MATTRESS...
...AND A REFRIGERATOR FULL OF HUMAN HEADS AND MEAT.
Capt. Edward April
WE ALSO FOUND AN ICE CHEST IN HIS CAR OUTSIDE WORK, FILLED WITH CHICKEN BREASTS.
HE WAS SMUGGLING THEM OUT OF THE RESTAURANT, AS WELL AS TRACE AMOUNTS OF HUMAN FILETS HE WAS USING TO CUT THE SOUP.
CUTTING THE SOUP WITH MEAT FROM HIS VICTIMS?
HIGH PRICE FOR CHICKEN ON THE BLACK MARKET.
MUST HAVE FIGURED D-BEAR WAS GONNA GET WISE, BECAUSE COBB HAD A BUS TICKET WITH HIS MONEY STASH AND HIS STUFF PACKED LIKE HE WAS READY TO SPLIT.
SURE SEEMS LIKE YOU DID A HELL OF A JOB, CHU.
SEEMS LIKE IT.... EXCEPT YOUR PARTNER IS STILL IN SURGERY.
DOCTORS SAY HE DOESN'T HAVE A SHOT IN HELL OF MAKING IT THROUGH THE NIGHT.
THE OTHER MURDERER, THE ONE YOU SPENT THE LAST TWO MONTHS INVESTIGATING, WHO TURNED OUT TO BE AN F.D.A. INFORMER, IS NOW M.I.A.--
--AFTER DISCOVERING TWO COPS IN THE HEART OF HIS ILLEGAL CHICKEN FRANCHISE.
AND...
I GOT TWO BEAT COPS ON RECORD THEY FOUND YOU ON TOP OF A CANNIBAL SERIAL KILLER WHO'D JUST SLASHED HIS OWN JUGULAR.
AND THEY HAD TO PULL YOU OFF OF HIM BECAUSE YOU WERE TOO BUSY
BITING. OFF. HIS. FACE.
YOU FEEL LIKE EXPLAINING THAT TO ME?

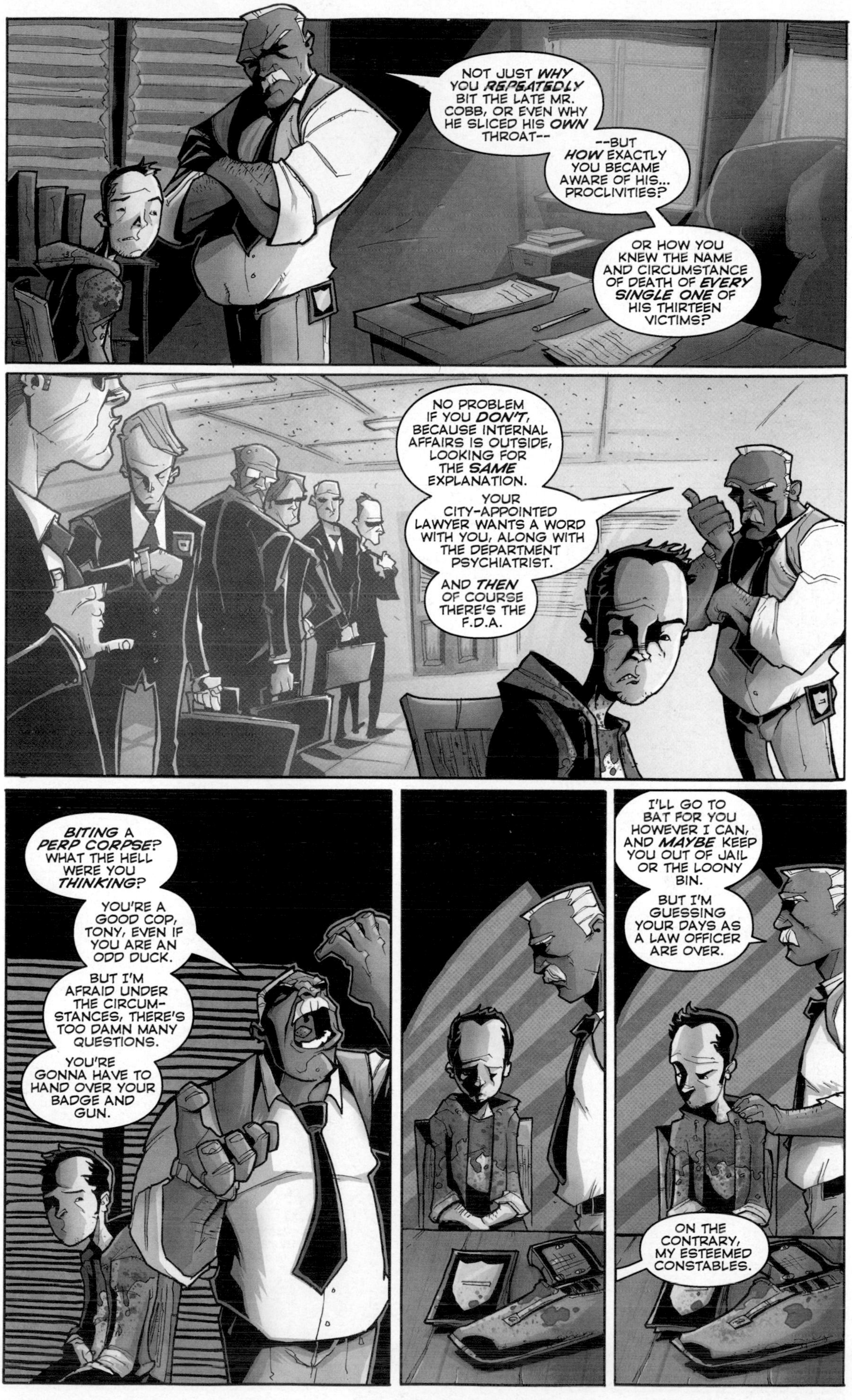
NOT JUST WHY YOU REPEATEDLY BIT THE LATE MR. COBB, OR EVEN WHY HE SLICED HIS OWN THROAT--
--BUT HOW EXACTLY YOU BECAME AWARE OF HIS... PROCLIVITIES?
OR HOW YOU KNEW THE NAME AND CIRCUMSTANCE OF DEATH OF EVERY SINGLE ONE OF HIS THIRTEEN VICTIMS?
NO PROBLEM IF YOU DON'T, BECAUSE INTERNAL AFFAIRS IS OUTSIDE, LOOKING FOR THE SAME EXPLANATION.
YOUR CITY-APPOINTED LAWYER WANTS A WORD WITH YOU, ALONG WITH THE DEPARTMENT PSYCHIATRIST.
AND THEN OF COURSE THERE'S THE F.D.A.
BITING A PERP CORPSE? WHAT THE HELL WERE YOU THINKING?
YOU'RE A GOOD COP, TONY, EVEN IF YOU ARE AN ODD DUCK.
BUT I'M AFRAID UNDER THE CIRCUM-STANCES, THERE'S TOO DAMN MANY QUESTIONS.
YOU'RE GONNA HAVE TO HAND OVER YOUR BADGE AND GUN.
I'LL GO TO BAT FOR YOU HOWEVER I CAN, AND MAYBE KEEP YOU OUT OF JAIL OR THE LOONY BIN.
BUT I'M GUESSING YOUR DAYS AS A LAW OFFICER ARE OVER.
ON THE CONTRARY, MY ESTEEMED CONSTABLES.

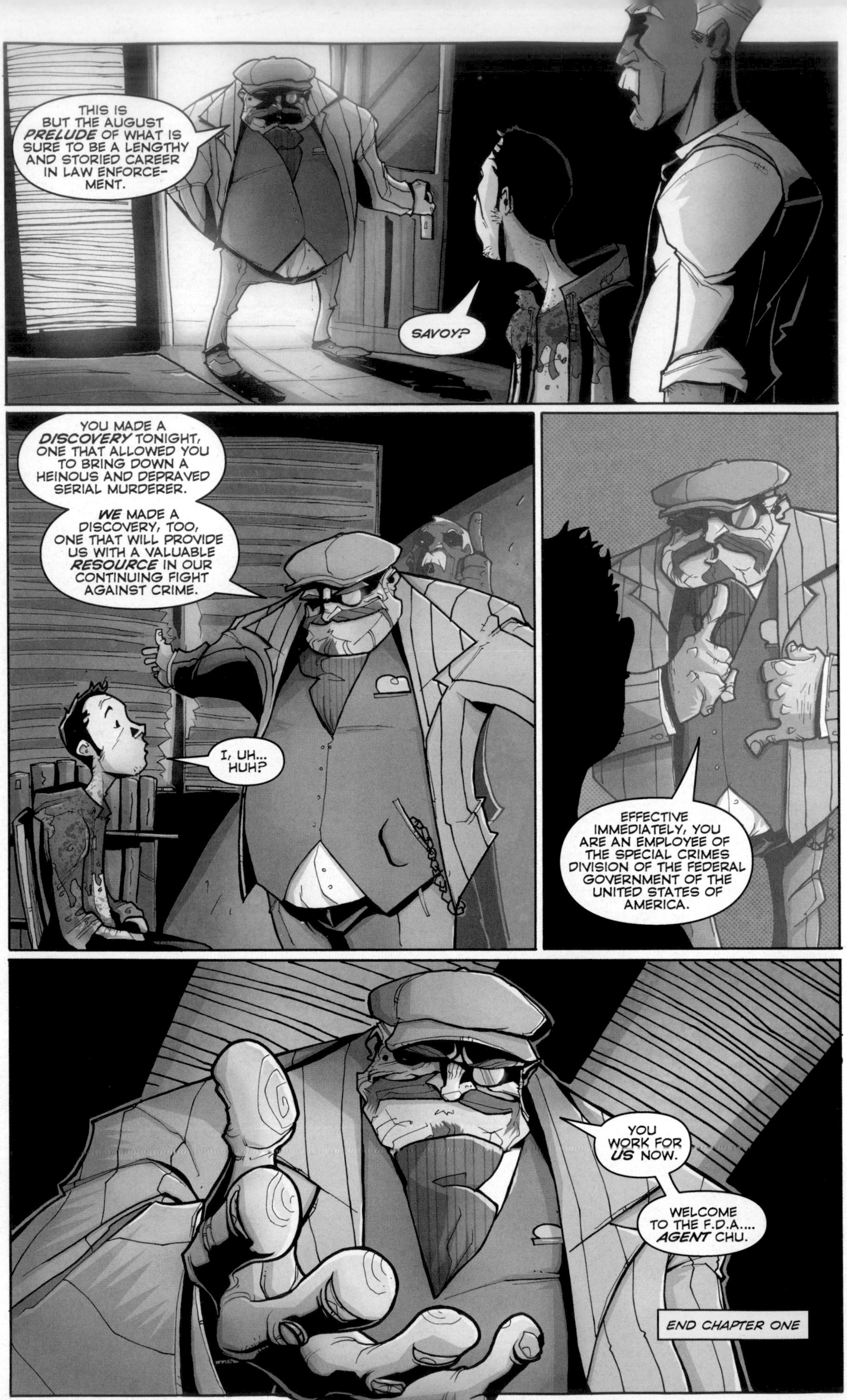
THIS IS BUT THE AUGUST PRELUDE OF WHAT IS SURE TO BE A LENGTHY AND STORIED CAREER IN LAW ENFORCEMENT.
SAVOY?
YOU MADE A DISCOVERY TONIGHT, ONE THAT ALLOWED YOU TO BRING DOWN A HEINOUS AND DEPRAVED SERIAL MURDERER.
WE MADE A DISCOVERY, TOO, ONE THAT WILL PROVIDE US WITH A VALUABLE RESOURCE IN OUR CONTINUING FIGHT AGAINST CRIME.
I, UH... HUH?
EFFECTIVE IMMEDIATELY, YOU ARE AN EMPLOYEE OF THE SPECIAL CRIMES DIVISION OF THE FEDERAL GOVERNMENT OF THE UNITED STATES OF AMERICA.
YOU WORK FOR US NOW.
WELCOME TO THE F.D.A.... AGENT CHU.
END CHAPTER ONE

Chapter 2

戦
GRADE
F

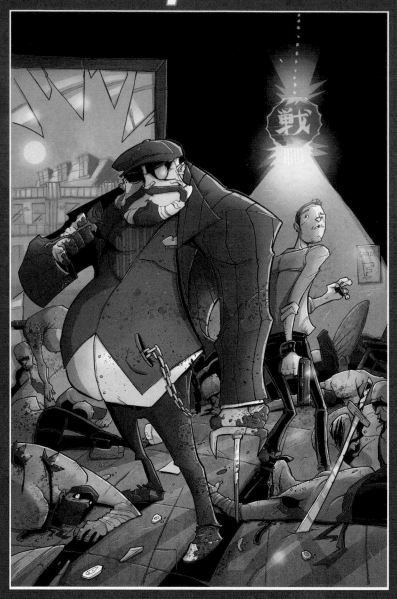

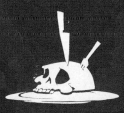

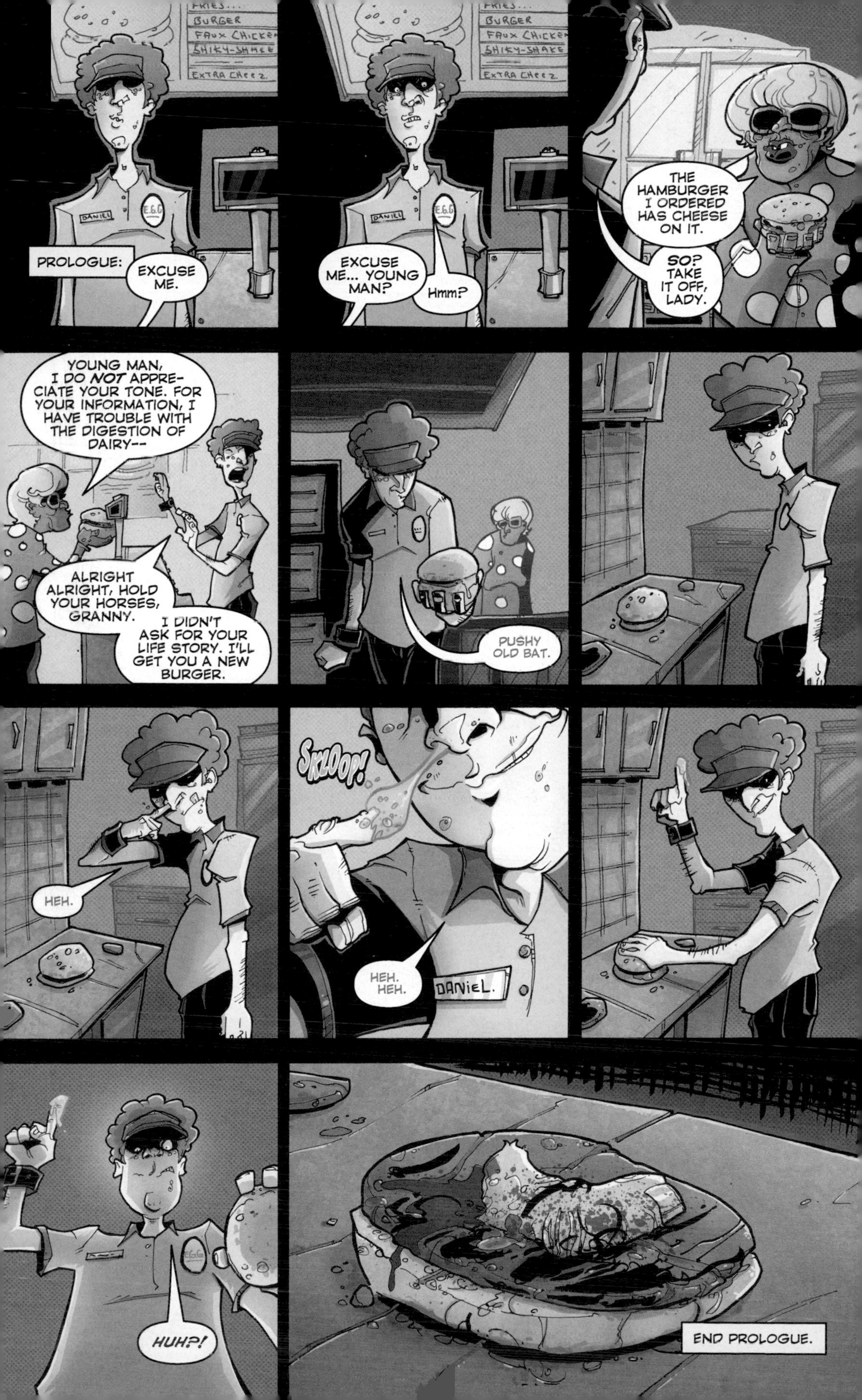
FRIES...
BURGER
FAUX CHICKEN
SHIKY-SHAKE
EXTRA CHEEZ.
DANIEL
E.G.G
PROLOGUE:
EXCUSE ME.
EXCUSE ME... YOUNG MAN?
Hmm?
THE HAMBURGER I ORDERED HAS CHEESE ON IT.
SO? TAKE IT OFF, LADY.
YOUNG MAN, I DO NOT APPRECIATE YOUR TONE. FOR YOUR INFORMATION, I HAVE TROUBLE WITH THE DIGESTION OF DAIRY--
ALRIGHT ALRIGHT, HOLD YOUR HORSES, GRANNY.
I DIDN'T ASK FOR YOUR LIFE STORY. I'LL GET YOU A NEW BURGER.
PUSHY OLD BAT.
HEH.
SKLOOP!
HEH. HEH.
DANIEL.
HUH?!
END PROLOGUE.

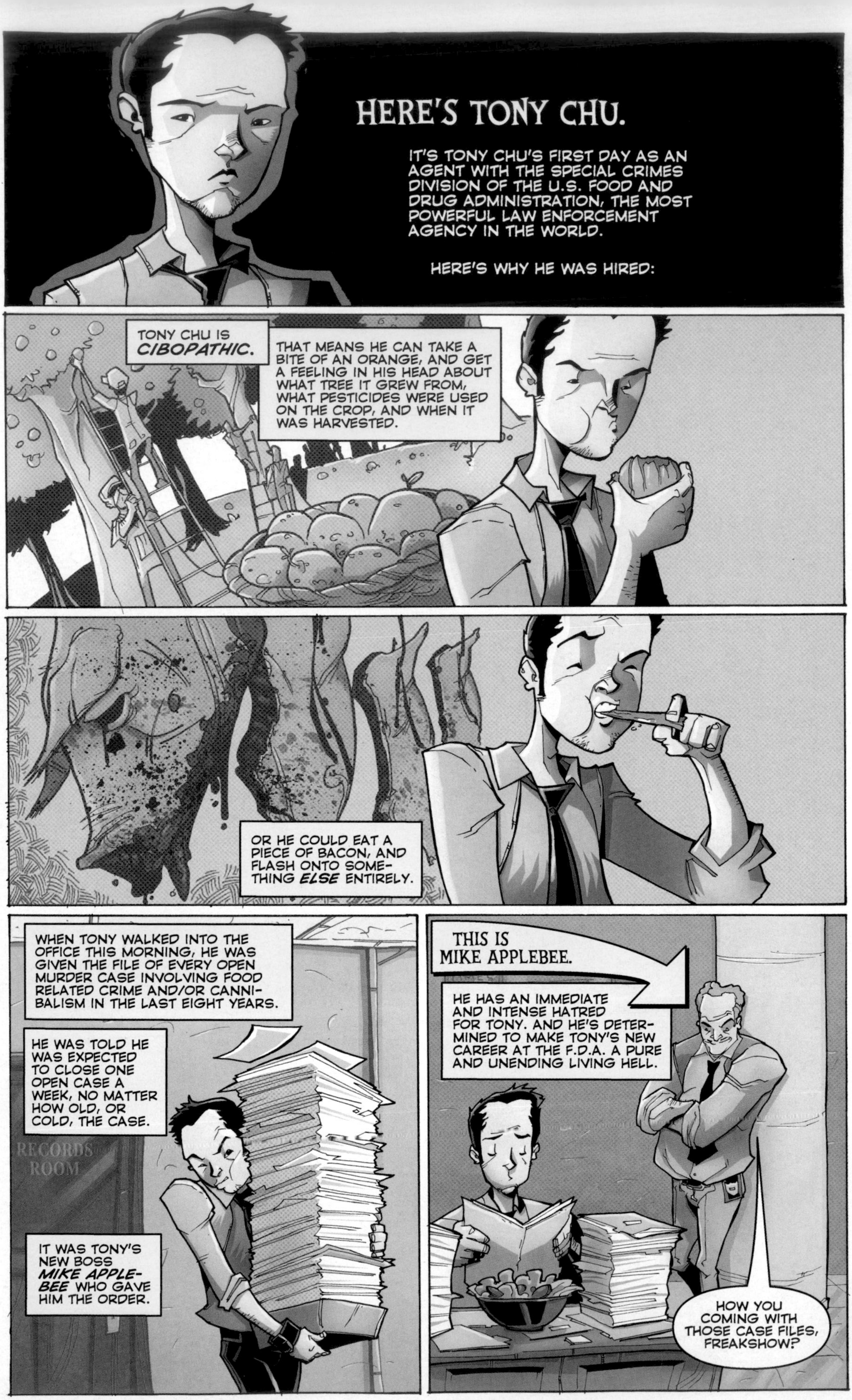
HERE'S TONY CHU.
IT'S TONY CHU'S FIRST DAY AS AN AGENT WITH THE SPECIAL CRIMES DIVISION OF THE U.S. FOOD AND DRUG ADMINISTRATION, THE MOST POWERFUL LAW ENFORCEMENT AGENCY IN THE WORLD.
HERE'S WHY HE WAS HIRED:
TONY CHU IS *CIBOPATHIC.*
THAT MEANS HE CAN TAKE A BITE OF AN ORANGE, AND GET A FEELING IN HIS HEAD ABOUT WHAT TREE IT GREW FROM, WHAT PESTICIDES WERE USED ON THE CROP, AND WHEN IT WAS HARVESTED.
OR HE COULD EAT A PIECE OF BACON, AND FLASH ONTO SOMETHING *ELSE* ENTIRELY.
WHEN TONY WALKED INTO THE OFFICE THIS MORNING, HE WAS GIVEN THE FILE OF EVERY OPEN MURDER CASE INVOLVING FOOD RELATED CRIME AND/OR CANNIBALISM IN THE LAST EIGHT YEARS.
HE WAS TOLD HE WAS EXPECTED TO CLOSE ONE OPEN CASE A WEEK, NO MATTER HOW OLD, OR COLD, THE CASE.
RECORDS ROOM
IT WAS TONY'S NEW BOSS *MIKE APPLEBEE* WHO GAVE HIM THE ORDER.
THIS IS MIKE APPLEBEE.
HE HAS AN IMMEDIATE AND INTENSE HATRED FOR TONY. AND HE'S DETERMINED TO MAKE TONY'S NEW CAREER AT THE F.D.A. A PURE AND UNENDING LIVING HELL.
HOW YOU COMING WITH THOSE CASE FILES, FREAKSHOW?

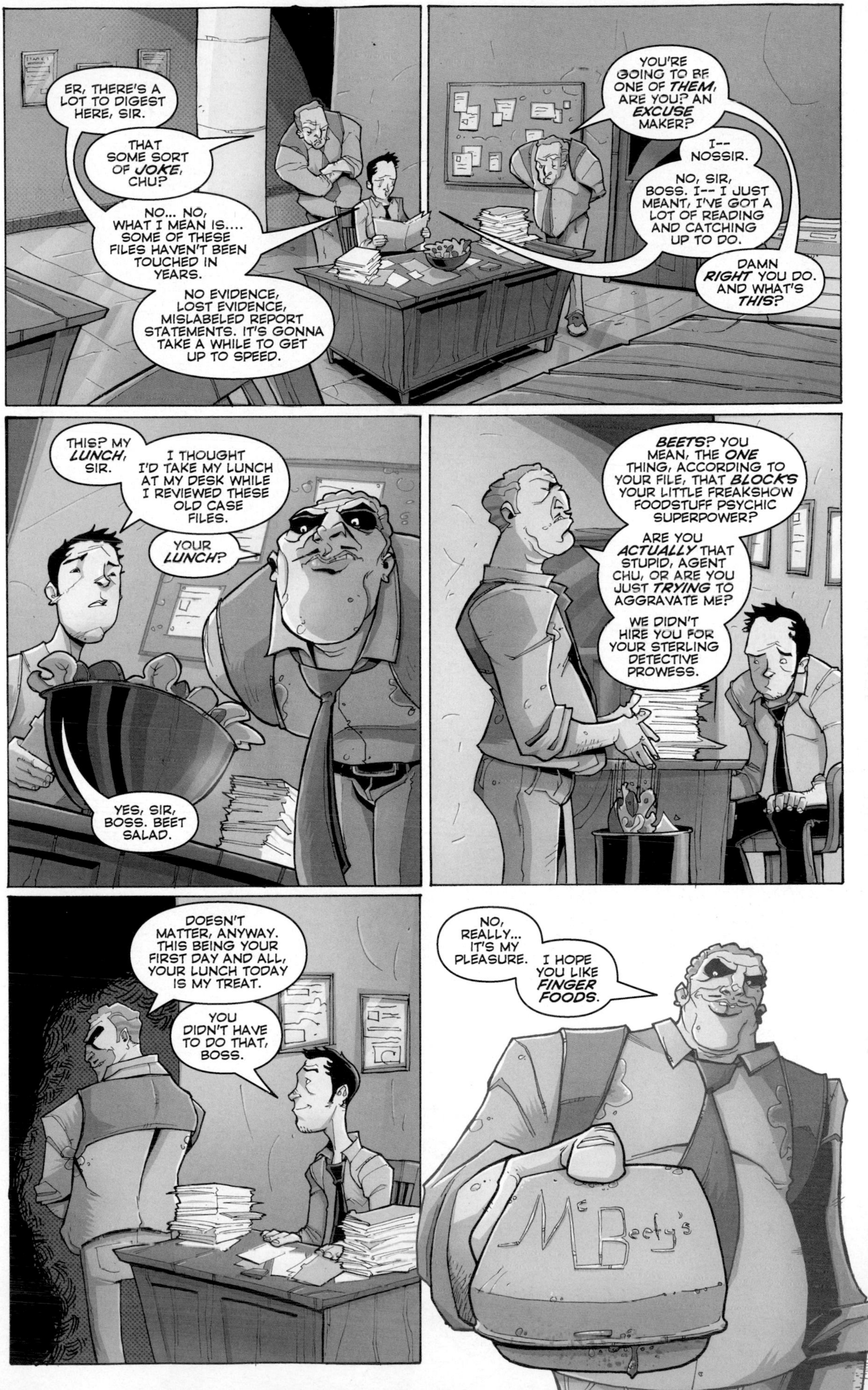
ER, THERE'S A LOT TO DIGEST HERE, SIR.
THAT SOME SORT OF JOKE, CHU?
NO... NO, WHAT I MEAN IS.... SOME OF THESE FILES HAVEN'T BEEN TOUCHED IN YEARS.
NO EVIDENCE, LOST EVIDENCE, MISLABELED REPORT STATEMENTS. IT'S GONNA TAKE A WHILE TO GET UP TO SPEED.
YOU'RE GOING TO BE ONE OF THEM, ARE YOU? AN EXCUSE MAKER?
I-- NOSSIR.
NO, SIR, BOSS. I-- I JUST MEANT, I'VE GOT A LOT OF READING AND CATCHING UP TO DO.
DAMN RIGHT YOU DO. AND WHAT'S THIS?
THIS? MY LUNCH, SIR.
I THOUGHT I'D TAKE MY LUNCH AT MY DESK WHILE I REVIEWED THESE OLD CASE FILES.
YOUR LUNCH?
YES, SIR, BOSS. BEET SALAD.
BEETS? YOU MEAN, THE ONE THING, ACCORDING TO YOUR FILE, THAT BLOCKS YOUR LITTLE FREAKSHOW FOODSTUFF PSYCHIC SUPERPOWER?
ARE YOU ACTUALLY THAT STUPID, AGENT CHU, OR ARE YOU JUST TRYING TO AGGRAVATE ME?
WE DIDN'T HIRE YOU FOR YOUR STERLING DETECTIVE PROWESS.
DOESN'T MATTER, ANYWAY. THIS BEING YOUR FIRST DAY AND ALL, YOUR LUNCH TODAY IS MY TREAT.
YOU DIDN'T HAVE TO DO THAT, BOSS.
NO, REALLY... IT'S MY PLEASURE.
I HOPE YOU LIKE FINGER FOODS.
McBeefy's

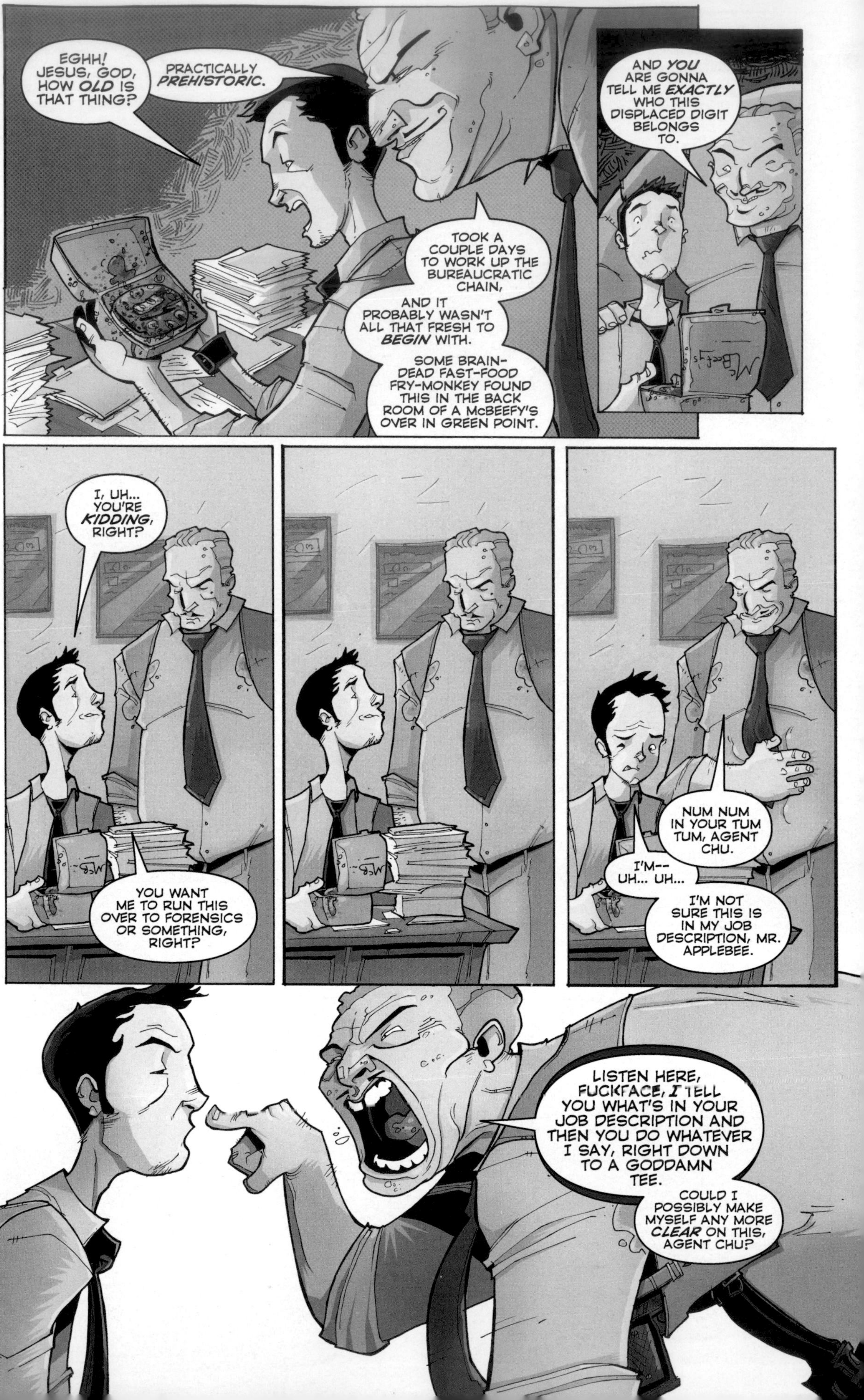
EGHH! JESUS, GOD, HOW OLD IS THAT THING?
PRACTICALLY PREHISTORIC.
TOOK A COUPLE DAYS TO WORK UP THE BUREAUCRATIC CHAIN,
AND IT PROBABLY WASN'T ALL THAT FRESH TO BEGIN WITH.
SOME BRAIN-DEAD FAST-FOOD FRY-MONKEY FOUND THIS IN THE BACK ROOM OF A McBEEFY'S OVER IN GREEN POINT.
AND YOU ARE GONNA TELL ME EXACTLY WHO THIS DISPLACED DIGIT BELONGS TO.
I, UH... YOU'RE KIDDING, RIGHT?
YOU WANT ME TO RUN THIS OVER TO FORENSICS OR SOMETHING, RIGHT?
NUM NUM IN YOUR TUM TUM, AGENT CHU.
I'M-- UH... UH...
I'M NOT SURE THIS IS IN MY JOB DESCRIPTION, MR. APPLEBEE.
LISTEN HERE, FUCKFACE, I TELL YOU WHAT'S IN YOUR JOB DESCRIPTION AND THEN YOU DO WHATEVER I SAY, RIGHT DOWN TO A GODDAMN TEE.
COULD I POSSIBLY MAKE MYSELF ANY MORE CLEAR ON THIS, AGENT CHU?

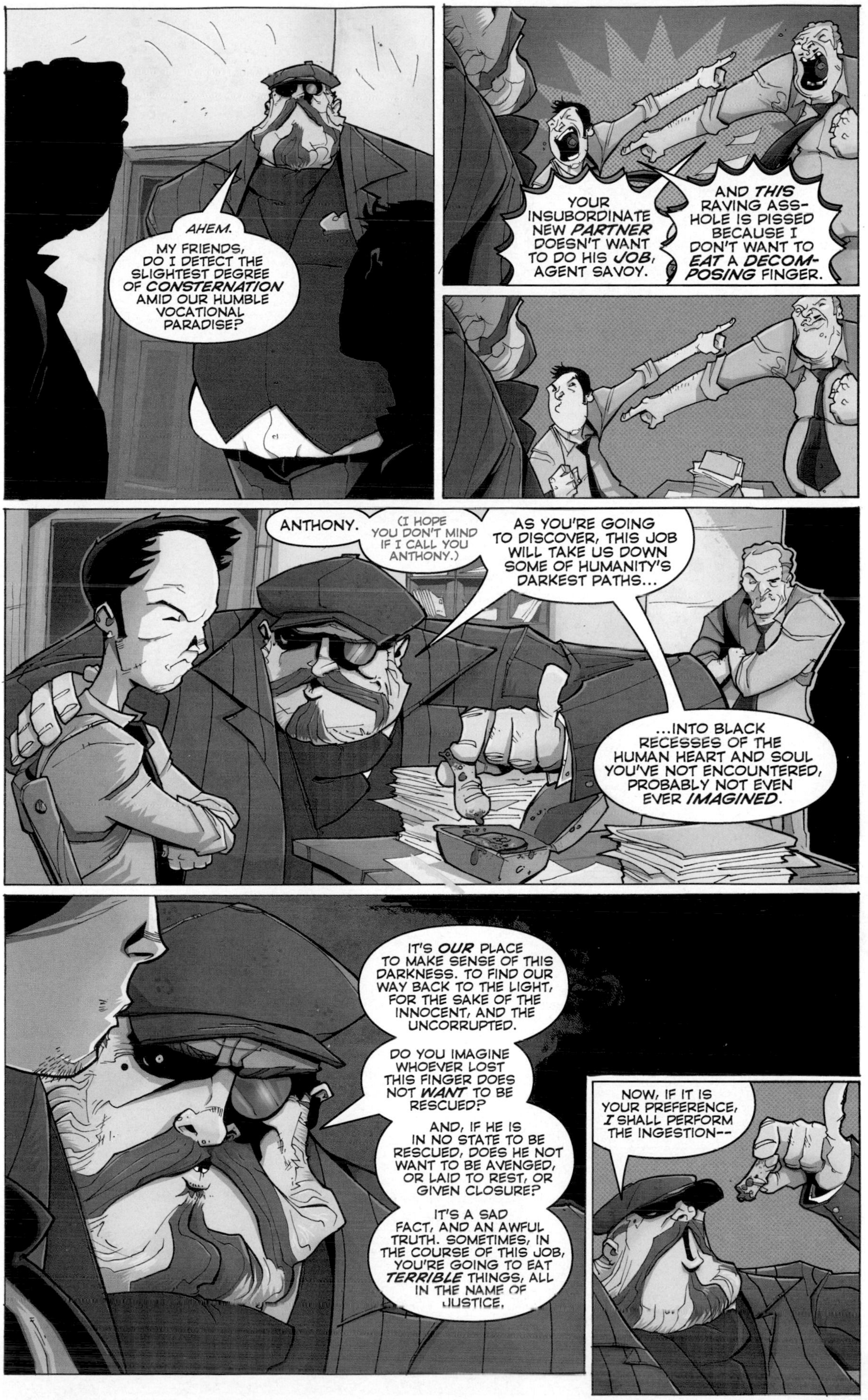
AHEM.
MY FRIENDS, DO I DETECT THE SLIGHTEST DEGREE OF CONSTERNATION AMID OUR HUMBLE VOCATIONAL PARADISE?
YOUR INSUBORDINATE NEW PARTNER DOESN'T WANT TO DO HIS JOB, AGENT SAVOY.
AND THIS RAVING ASS-HOLE IS PISSED BECAUSE I DON'T WANT TO EAT A DECOM-POSING FINGER.
ANTHONY.
(I HOPE YOU DON'T MIND IF I CALL YOU ANTHONY.)
AS YOU'RE GOING TO DISCOVER, THIS JOB WILL TAKE US DOWN SOME OF HUMANITY'S DARKEST PATHS...
...INTO BLACK RECESSES OF THE HUMAN HEART AND SOUL YOU'VE NOT ENCOUNTERED, PROBABLY NOT EVEN EVER IMAGINED.
IT'S OUR PLACE TO MAKE SENSE OF THIS DARKNESS. TO FIND OUR WAY BACK TO THE LIGHT, FOR THE SAKE OF THE INNOCENT, AND THE UNCORRUPTED.
DO YOU IMAGINE WHOEVER LOST THIS FINGER DOES NOT WANT TO BE RESCUED?
AND, IF HE IS IN NO STATE TO BE RESCUED, DOES HE NOT WANT TO BE AVENGED, OR LAID TO REST, OR GIVEN CLOSURE?
IT'S A SAD FACT, AND AN AWFUL TRUTH. SOMETIMES, IN THE COURSE OF THIS JOB, YOU'RE GOING TO EAT TERRIBLE THINGS, ALL IN THE NAME OF JUSTICE.
NOW, IF IT IS YOUR PREFERENCE, I SHALL PERFORM THE INGESTION--

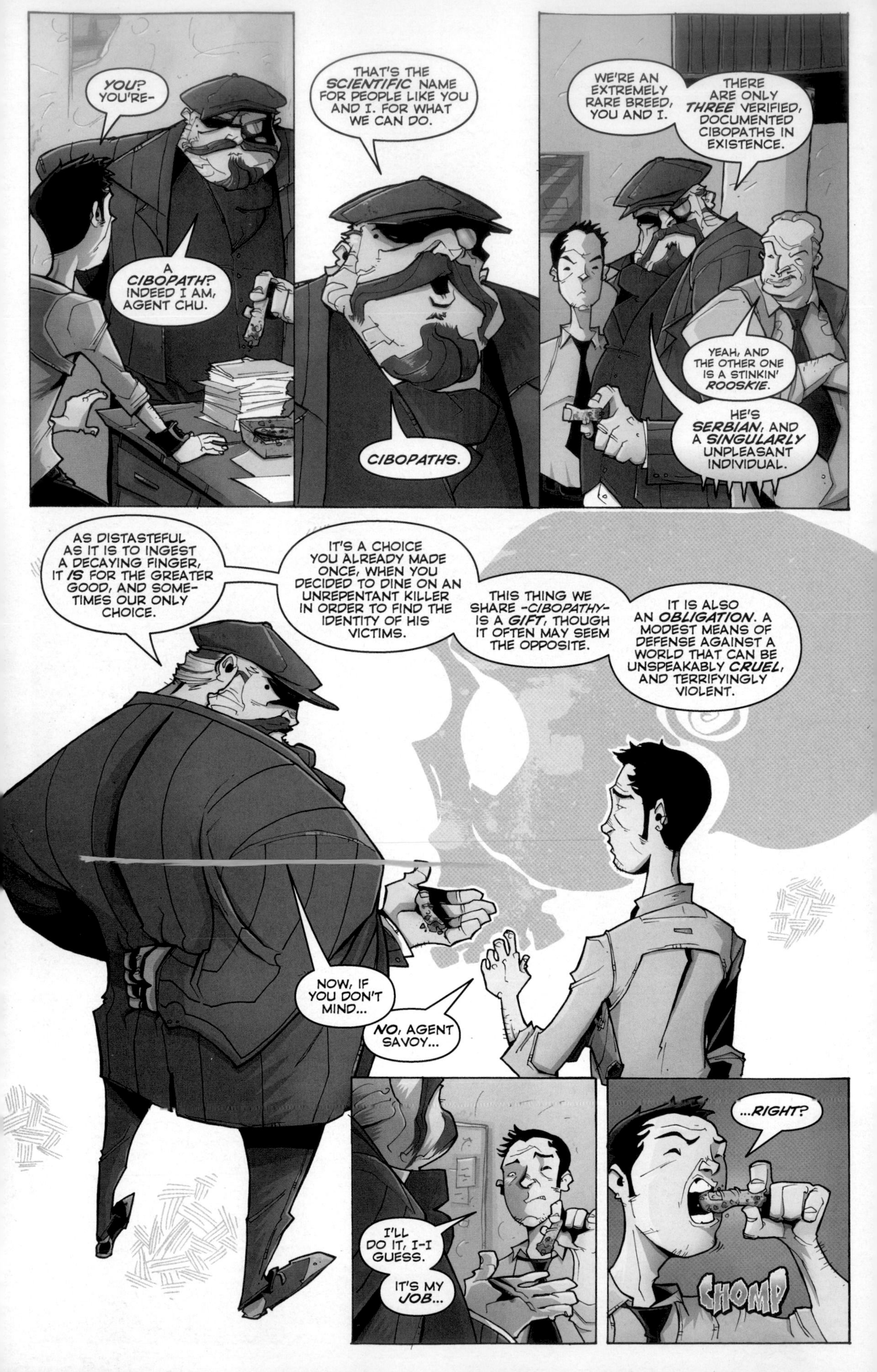

YOU? YOU'RE-
A CIBOPATH? INDEED I AM, AGENT CHU.
THAT'S THE SCIENTIFIC NAME FOR PEOPLE LIKE YOU AND I. FOR WHAT WE CAN DO.
CIBOPATHS.
WE'RE AN EXTREMELY RARE BREED, YOU AND I.
THERE ARE ONLY THREE VERIFIED, DOCUMENTED CIBOPATHS IN EXISTENCE.
YEAH, AND THE OTHER ONE IS A STINKIN' ROOSKIE.
HE'S SERBIAN, AND A SINGULARLY UNPLEASANT INDIVIDUAL.
AS DISTASTEFUL AS IT IS TO INGEST A DECAYING FINGER, IT IS FOR THE GREATER GOOD, AND SOMETIMES OUR ONLY CHOICE.
IT'S A CHOICE YOU ALREADY MADE ONCE, WHEN YOU DECIDED TO DINE ON AN UNREPENTANT KILLER IN ORDER TO FIND THE IDENTITY OF HIS VICTIMS.
THIS THING WE SHARE -CIBOPATHY- IS A GIFT, THOUGH IT OFTEN MAY SEEM THE OPPOSITE.
IT IS ALSO AN OBLIGATION. A MODEST MEANS OF DEFENSE AGAINST A WORLD THAT CAN BE UNSPEAKABLY CRUEL, AND TERRIFYINGLY VIOLENT.
NOW, IF YOU DON'T MIND...
NO, AGENT SAVOY...
I'LL DO IT, I-I GUESS.
IT'S MY JOB...
...RIGHT?
CHOMP

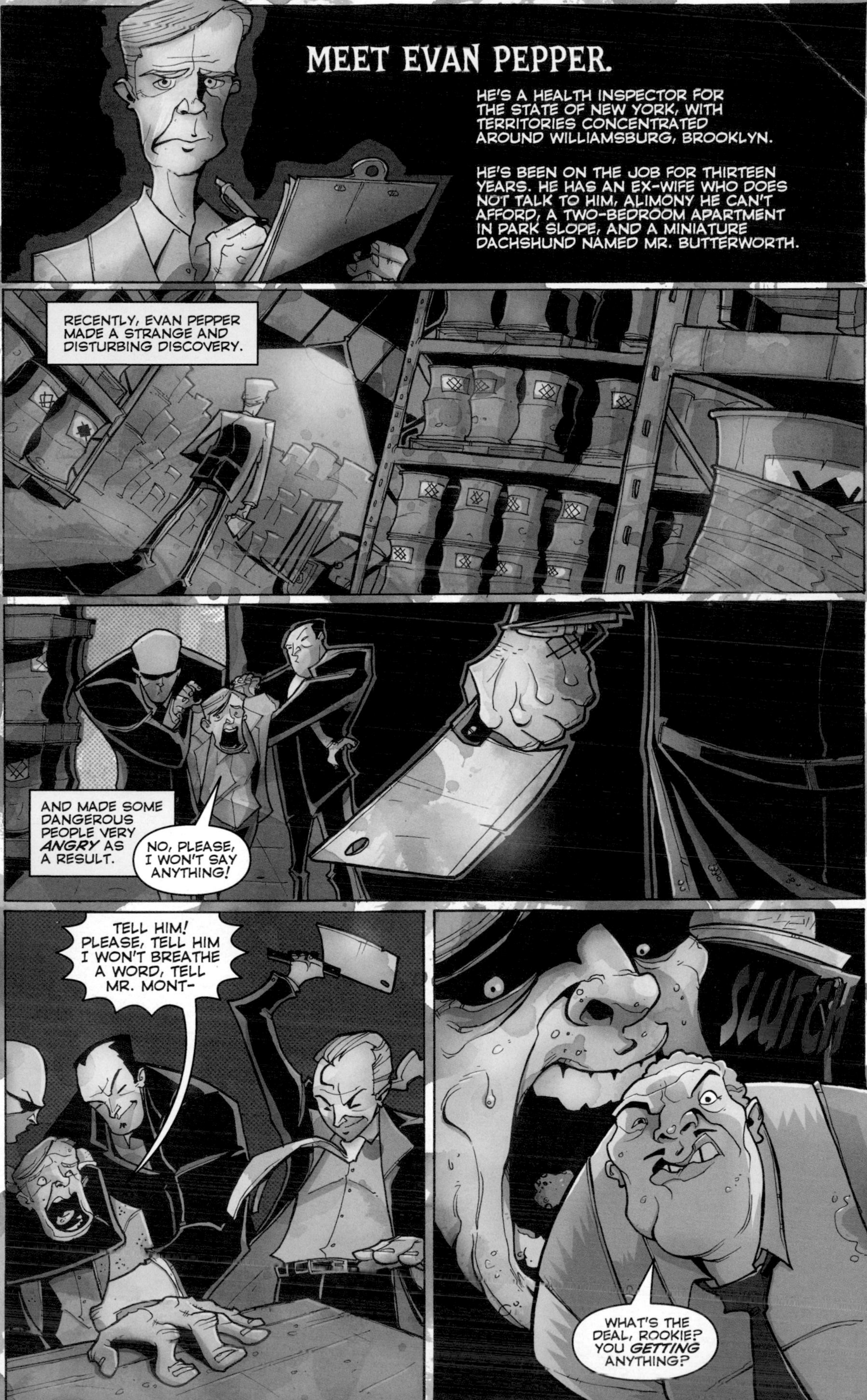
MEET EVAN PEPPER.
HE'S A HEALTH INSPECTOR FOR THE STATE OF NEW YORK, WITH TERRITORIES CONCENTRATED AROUND WILLIAMSBURG, BROOKLYN.
HE'S BEEN ON THE JOB FOR THIRTEEN YEARS. HE HAS AN EX-WIFE WHO DOES NOT TALK TO HIM, ALIMONY HE CAN'T AFFORD, A TWO-BEDROOM APARTMENT IN PARK SLOPE, AND A MINIATURE DACHSHUND NAMED MR. BUTTERWORTH.
RECENTLY, EVAN PEPPER MADE A STRANGE AND DISTURBING DISCOVERY.
AND MADE SOME DANGEROUS PEOPLE VERY *ANGRY* AS A RESULT.
NO, PLEASE, I WON'T SAY ANYTHING!
TELL HIM! PLEASE, TELL HIM I WON'T BREATHE A WORD, TELL MR. MONT-
SLUTCH
WHAT'S THE DEAL, ROOKIE? YOU *GETTING* ANYTHING?

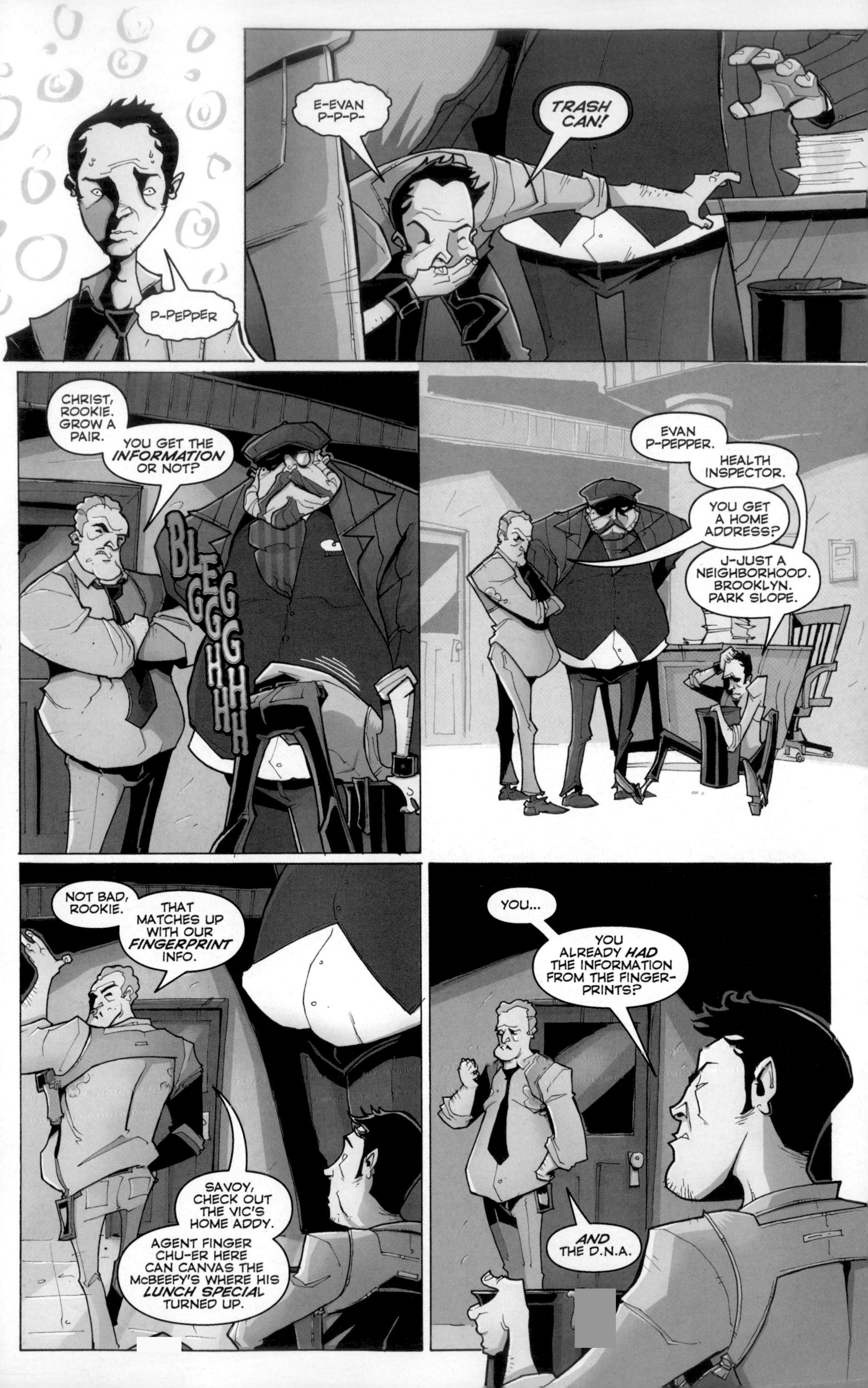
P-PEPPER
E-EVAN P-P-P-
TRASH CAN!
CHRIST, ROOKIE. GROW A PAIR.
YOU GET THE *INFORMATION* OR NOT?
BLEGGGHHHH
EVAN P-PEPPER.
HEALTH INSPECTOR.
YOU GET A HOME ADDRESS?
J-JUST A NEIGHBORHOOD. BROOKLYN. PARK SLOPE.
NOT BAD, ROOKIE.
THAT MATCHES UP WITH OUR *FINGERPRINT* INFO.
SAVOY, CHECK OUT THE VIC'S HOME ADDY.
AGENT FINGER CHU-ER HERE CAN CANVAS THE McBEEFY'S WHERE HIS *LUNCH SPECIAL* TURNED UP.
YOU...
YOU ALREADY *HAD* THE INFORMATION FROM THE FINGER-PRINTS?
AND THE D.N.A.

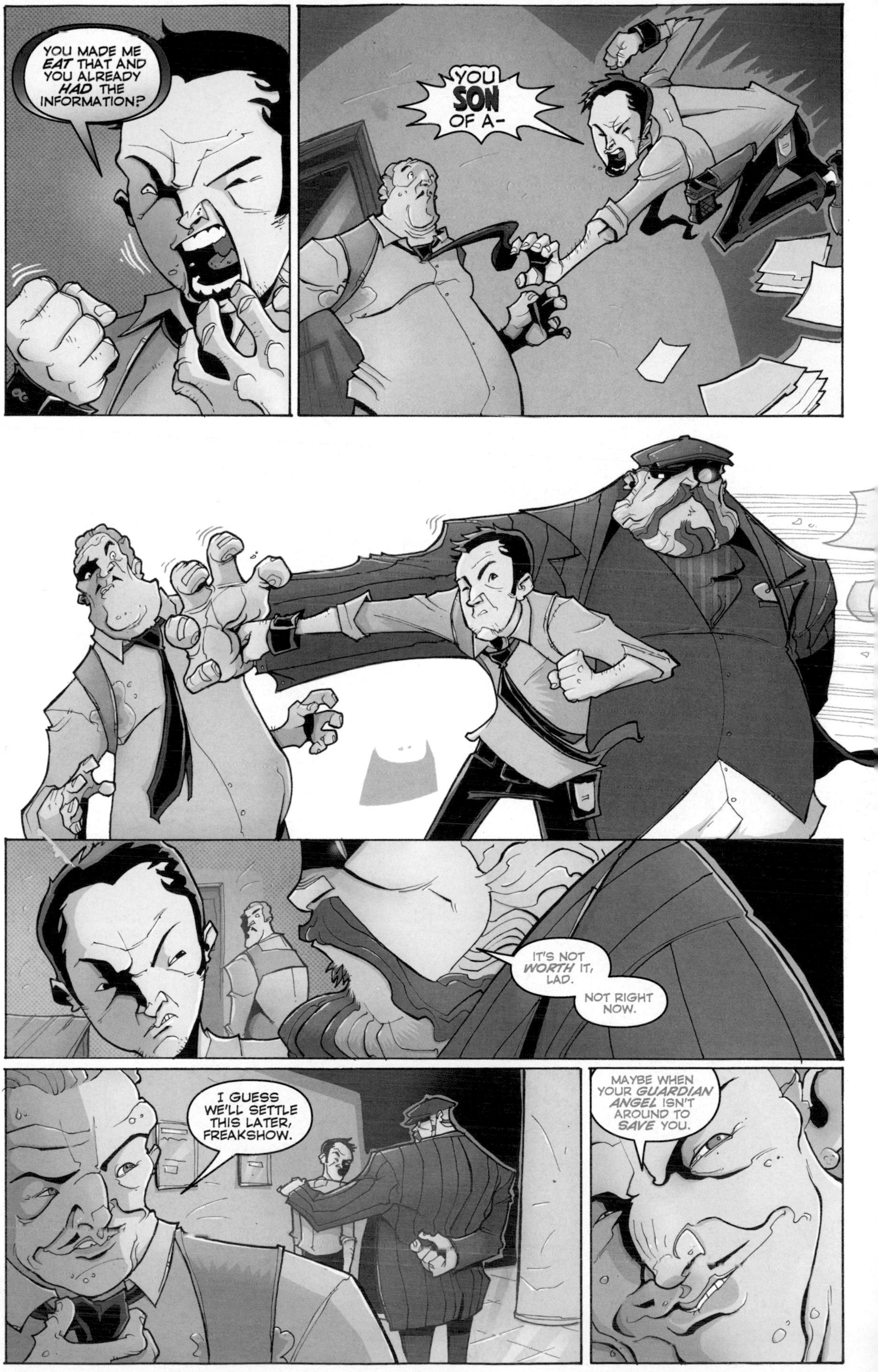

YOU MADE ME *EAT* THAT AND YOU ALREADY *HAD* THE INFORMATION?
YOU **SON** OF A-
IT'S NOT *WORTH* IT, LAD.
NOT RIGHT NOW.
I GUESS WE'LL SETTLE THIS LATER, FREAKSHOW.
MAYBE WHEN YOUR *GUARDIAN ANGEL* ISN'T AROUND TO *SAVE* YOU.

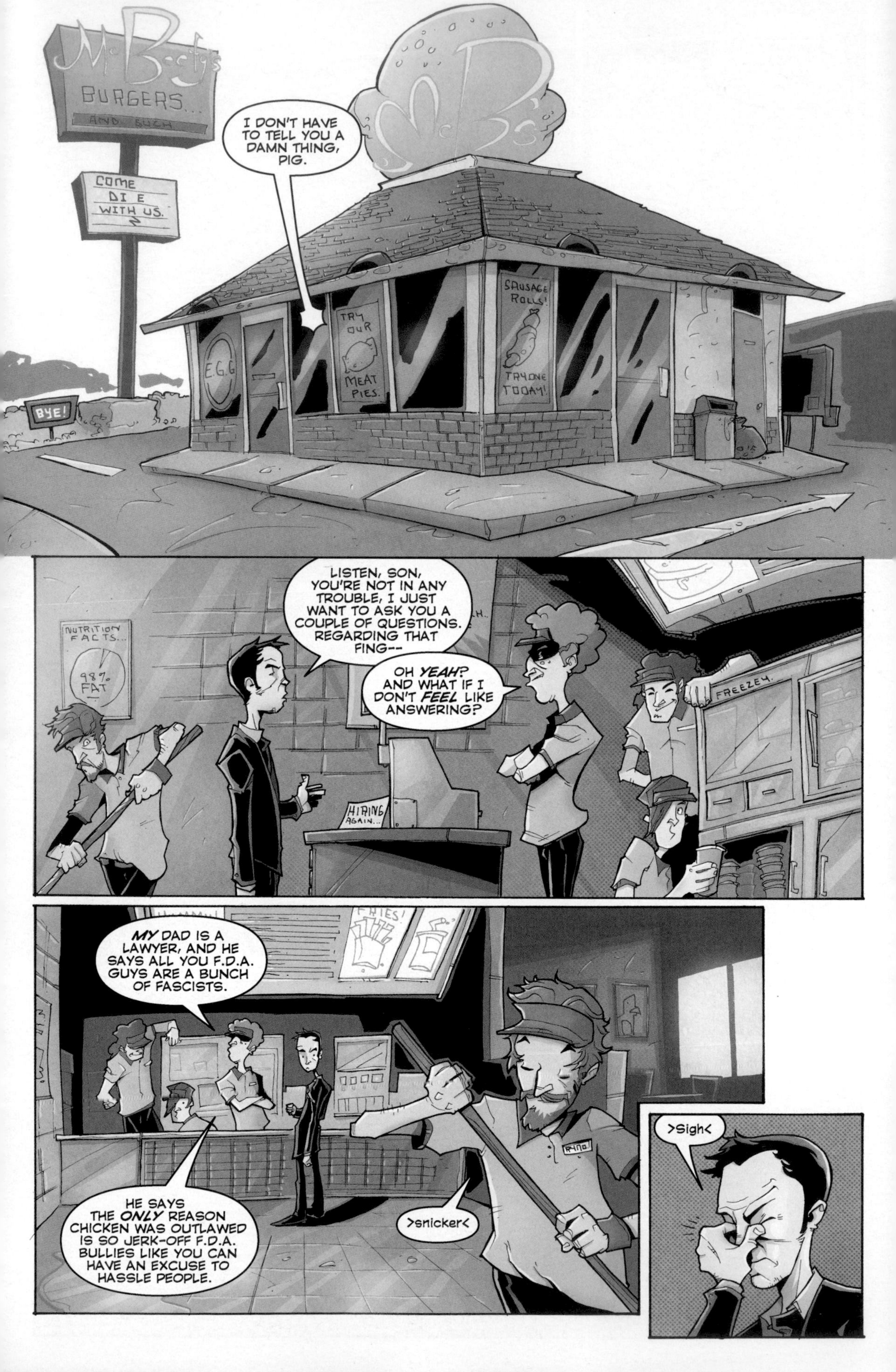
BURGERS...
AND SUCH
COME DI E WITH US.
BYE!
I DON'T HAVE TO TELL YOU A DAMN THING, PIG.
E.G.G
TRY OUR MEAT PIES.
SAUSAGE ROLLS! TRY ONE TODAY!
NUTRITION FACTS... 98% FAT
LISTEN, SON, YOU'RE NOT IN ANY TROUBLE, I JUST WANT TO ASK YOU A COUPLE OF QUESTIONS. REGARDING THAT FING--
OH *YEAH*? AND WHAT IF I DON'T *FEEL* LIKE ANSWERING?
HIRING AGAIN...
FREEZEY.
FRIES!
MY DAD IS A LAWYER, AND HE SAYS ALL YOU F.D.A. GUYS ARE A BUNCH OF FASCISTS.
HE SAYS THE *ONLY* REASON CHICKEN WAS OUTLAWED IS SO JERK-OFF F.D.A. BULLIES LIKE YOU CAN HAVE AN EXCUSE TO HASSLE PEOPLE.
>snicker<
>Sigh<

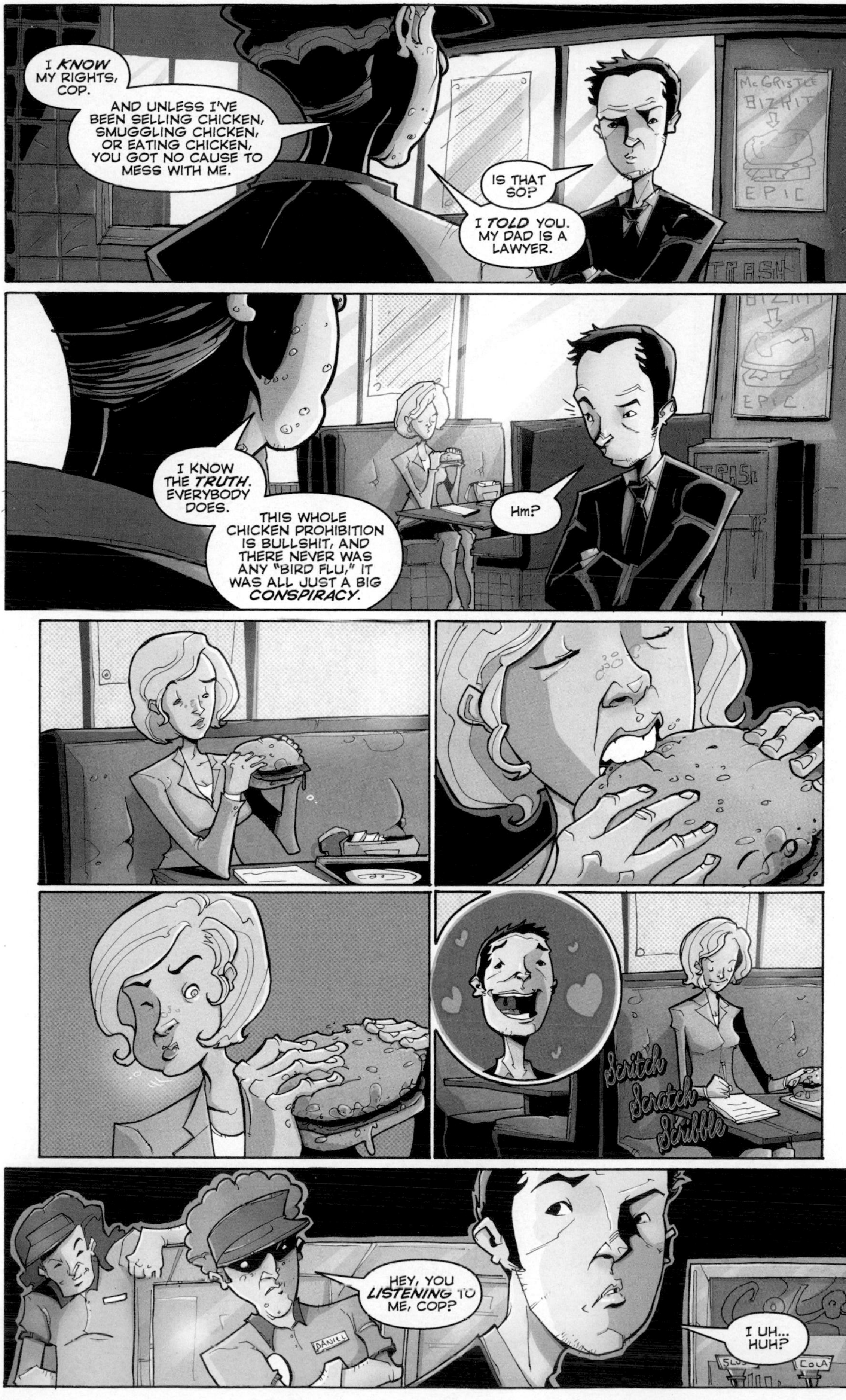

I KNOW MY RIGHTS, COP.
AND UNLESS I'VE BEEN SELLING CHICKEN, SMUGGLING CHICKEN, OR EATING CHICKEN, YOU GOT NO CAUSE TO MESS WITH ME.
McGRISTLE BIZKIT
EPIC
IS THAT SO?
I TOLD YOU. MY DAD IS A LAWYER.
TRASH
BIZKIT
EPIC
I KNOW THE TRUTH. EVERYBODY DOES.
THIS WHOLE CHICKEN PROHIBITION IS BULLSHIT, AND THERE NEVER WAS ANY "BIRD FLU," IT WAS ALL JUST A BIG CONSPIRACY.
Hm?
TRASH
Scritch
Scratch
Scribble
HEY, YOU LISTENING TO ME, COP?
DANIEL
I UH... HUH?
COLA

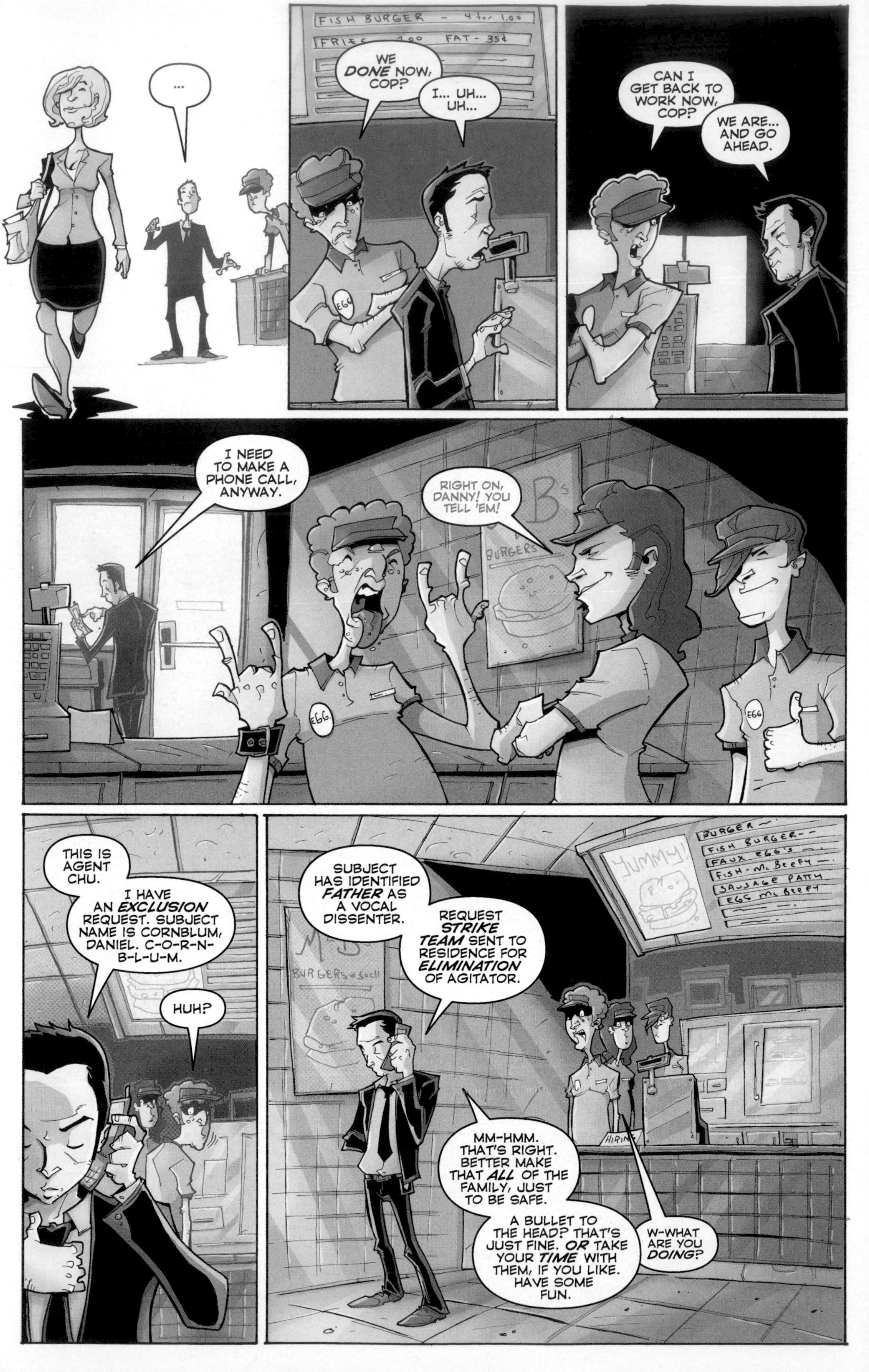
...
FISH BURGER - 4 for 1.00
FRIES 1.00 FAT - 35¢
WE DONE NOW, COP?
I... UH... UH...
CAN I GET BACK TO WORK NOW, COP?
WE ARE... AND GO AHEAD.
I NEED TO MAKE A PHONE CALL, ANYWAY.
RIGHT ON, DANNY! YOU TELL 'EM!
BURGERS
THIS IS AGENT CHU.
I HAVE AN EXCLUSION REQUEST. SUBJECT NAME IS CORNBLUM, DANIEL. C-O-R-N-B-L-U-M.
HUH?
BURGER
FISH BURGER
FAUX EGG'S
FISH-McBEEFY
SAUSAGE PATTY
EGG McBEEFY
YUMMY!
BURGERS & Such
SUBJECT HAS IDENTIFIED FATHER AS A VOCAL DISSENTER.
REQUEST STRIKE TEAM SENT TO RESIDENCE FOR ELIMINATION OF AGITATOR.
MM-HMM. THAT'S RIGHT. BETTER MAKE THAT ALL OF THE FAMILY, JUST TO BE SAFE.
A BULLET TO THE HEAD? THAT'S JUST FINE. OR TAKE YOUR TIME WITH THEM, IF YOU LIKE. HAVE SOME FUN.
W-WHAT ARE YOU DOING?

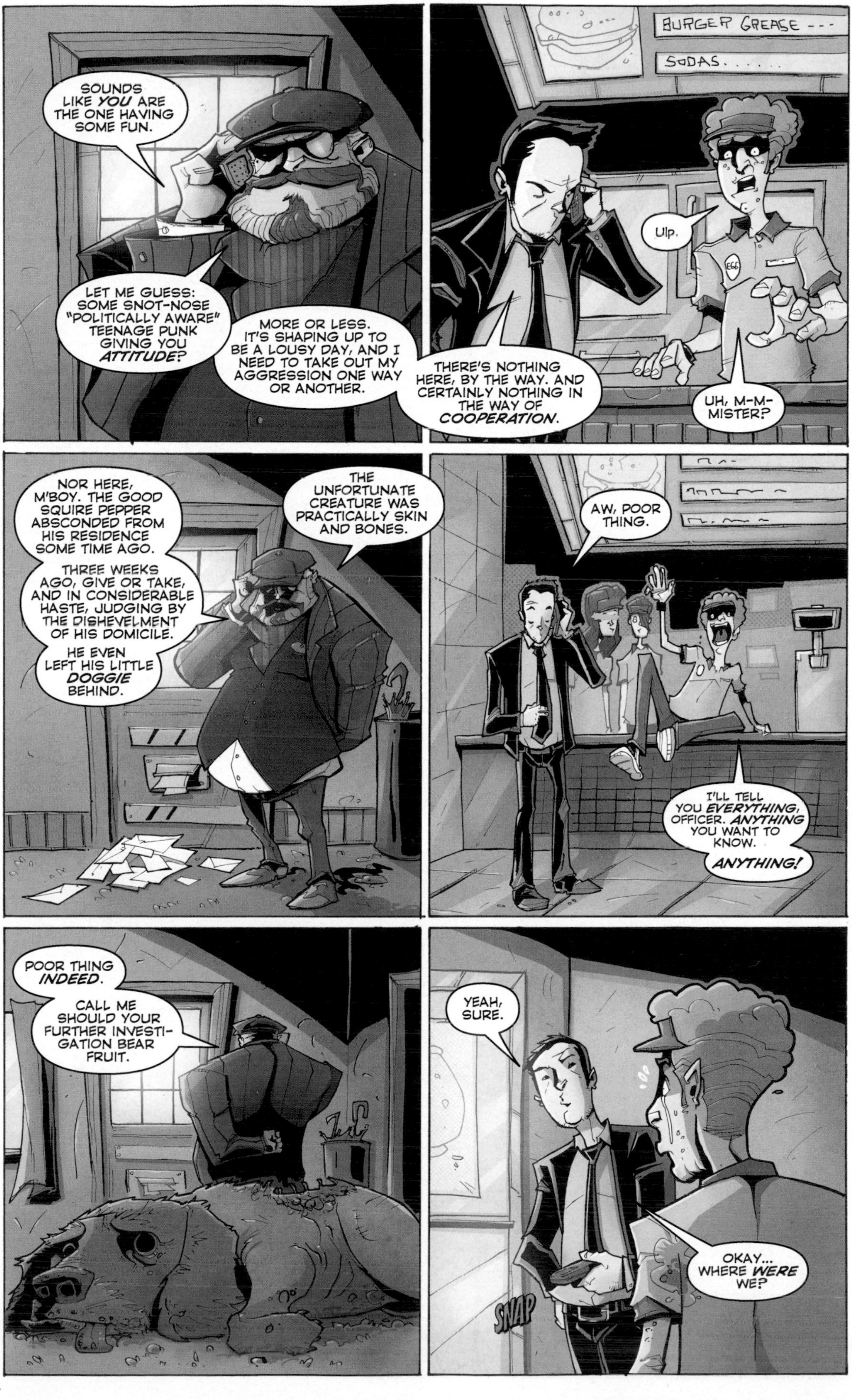

SOUNDS LIKE *YOU* ARE THE ONE HAVING SOME FUN.
LET ME GUESS: SOME SNOT-NOSE "POLITICALLY AWARE" TEENAGE PUNK GIVING YOU *ATTITUDE*?
MORE OR LESS. IT'S SHAPING UP TO BE A LOUSY DAY, AND I NEED TO TAKE OUT MY AGGRESSION ONE WAY OR ANOTHER.
BURGER GREASE ---
SODAS......
Ulp.
THERE'S NOTHING HERE, BY THE WAY. AND CERTAINLY NOTHING IN THE WAY OF *COOPERATION*.
UH, M-M-MISTER?
NOR HERE, M'BOY. THE GOOD SQUIRE PEPPER ABSCONDED FROM HIS RESIDENCE SOME TIME AGO.
THREE WEEKS AGO, GIVE OR TAKE, AND IN CONSIDERABLE HASTE, JUDGING BY THE DISHEVELMENT OF HIS DOMICILE.
HE EVEN LEFT HIS LITTLE *DOGGIE* BEHIND.
THE UNFORTUNATE CREATURE WAS PRACTICALLY SKIN AND BONES.
AW, POOR THING.
I'LL TELL YOU *EVERYTHING*, OFFICER. *ANYTHING* YOU WANT TO KNOW.
ANYTHING!
POOR THING *INDEED*.
CALL ME SHOULD YOUR FURTHER INVESTI-GATION BEAR FRUIT.
YEAH, SURE.
SNAP
OKAY... WHERE *WERE* WE?

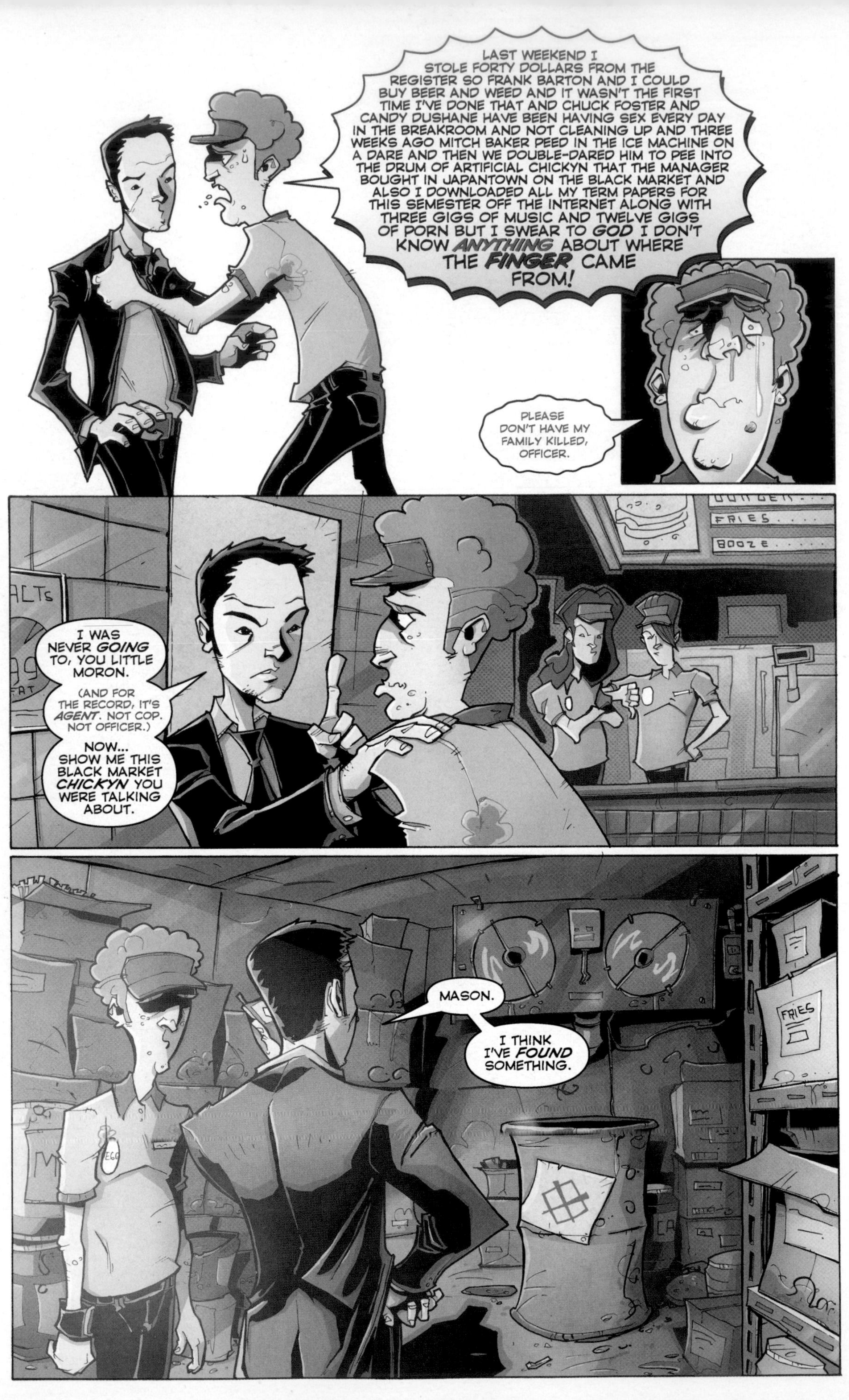
LAST WEEKEND I STOLE FORTY DOLLARS FROM THE REGISTER SO FRANK BARTON AND I COULD BUY BEER AND WEED AND IT WASN'T THE FIRST TIME I'VE DONE THAT AND CHUCK FOSTER AND CANDY DUSHANE HAVE BEEN HAVING SEX EVERY DAY IN THE BREAKROOM AND NOT CLEANING UP AND THREE WEEKS AGO MITCH BAKER PEED IN THE ICE MACHINE ON A DARE AND THEN WE DOUBLE-DARED HIM TO PEE INTO THE DRUM OF ARTIFICIAL CHICKYN THAT THE MANAGER BOUGHT IN JAPANTOWN ON THE BLACK MARKET AND ALSO I DOWNLOADED ALL MY TERM PAPERS FOR THIS SEMESTER OFF THE INTERNET ALONG WITH THREE GIGS OF MUSIC AND TWELVE GIGS OF PORN BUT I SWEAR TO GOD I DON'T KNOW ANYTHING ABOUT WHERE THE FINGER CAME FROM!
PLEASE DON'T HAVE MY FAMILY KILLED, OFFICER.
FRIES
BOOZE
I WAS NEVER GOING TO, YOU LITTLE MORON.
(AND FOR THE RECORD, IT'S AGENT. NOT COP. NOT OFFICER.)
NOW... SHOW ME THIS BLACK MARKET CHICKYN YOU WERE TALKING ABOUT.
MASON.
I THINK I'VE FOUND SOMETHING.
FRIES

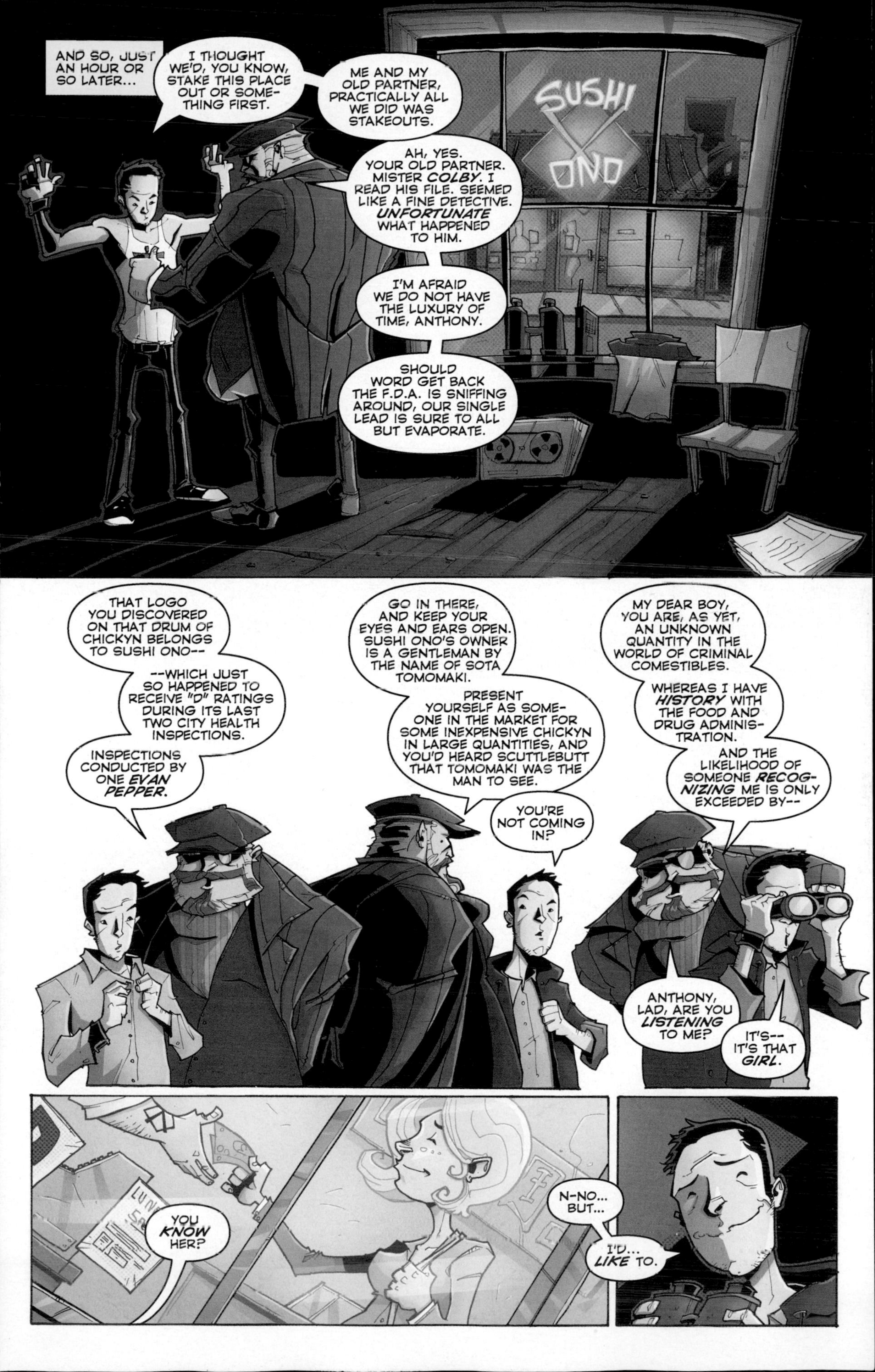
AND SO, JUST AN HOUR OR SO LATER...
I THOUGHT WE'D, YOU KNOW, STAKE THIS PLACE OUT OR SOMETHING FIRST.
ME AND MY OLD PARTNER, PRACTICALLY ALL WE DID WAS STAKEOUTS.
SUSHI ONO
AH, YES. YOUR OLD PARTNER. MISTER COLBY. I READ HIS FILE. SEEMED LIKE A FINE DETECTIVE. UNFORTUNATE WHAT HAPPENED TO HIM.
I'M AFRAID WE DO NOT HAVE THE LUXURY OF TIME, ANTHONY.
SHOULD WORD GET BACK THE F.D.A. IS SNIFFING AROUND, OUR SINGLE LEAD IS SURE TO ALL BUT EVAPORATE.
THAT LOGO YOU DISCOVERED ON THAT DRUM OF CHICKYN BELONGS TO SUSHI ONO--
--WHICH JUST SO HAPPENED TO RECEIVE "D" RATINGS DURING ITS LAST TWO CITY HEALTH INSPECTIONS.
INSPECTIONS CONDUCTED BY ONE EVAN PEPPER.
GO IN THERE, AND KEEP YOUR EYES AND EARS OPEN. SUSHI ONO'S OWNER IS A GENTLEMAN BY THE NAME OF SOTA TOMOMAKI.
PRESENT YOURSELF AS SOMEONE IN THE MARKET FOR SOME INEXPENSIVE CHICKYN IN LARGE QUANTITIES, AND YOU'D HEARD SCUTTLEBUTT THAT TOMOMAKI WAS THE MAN TO SEE.
YOU'RE NOT COMING IN?
MY DEAR BOY, YOU ARE, AS YET, AN UNKNOWN QUANTITY IN THE WORLD OF CRIMINAL COMESTIBLES.
WHEREAS I HAVE HISTORY WITH THE FOOD AND DRUG ADMINISTRATION.
AND THE LIKELIHOOD OF SOMEONE RECOGNIZING ME IS ONLY EXCEEDED BY--
ANTHONY, LAD, ARE YOU LISTENING TO ME?
IT'S-- IT'S THAT GIRL.
YOU KNOW HER?
N-NO... BUT...
I'D... LIKE TO.

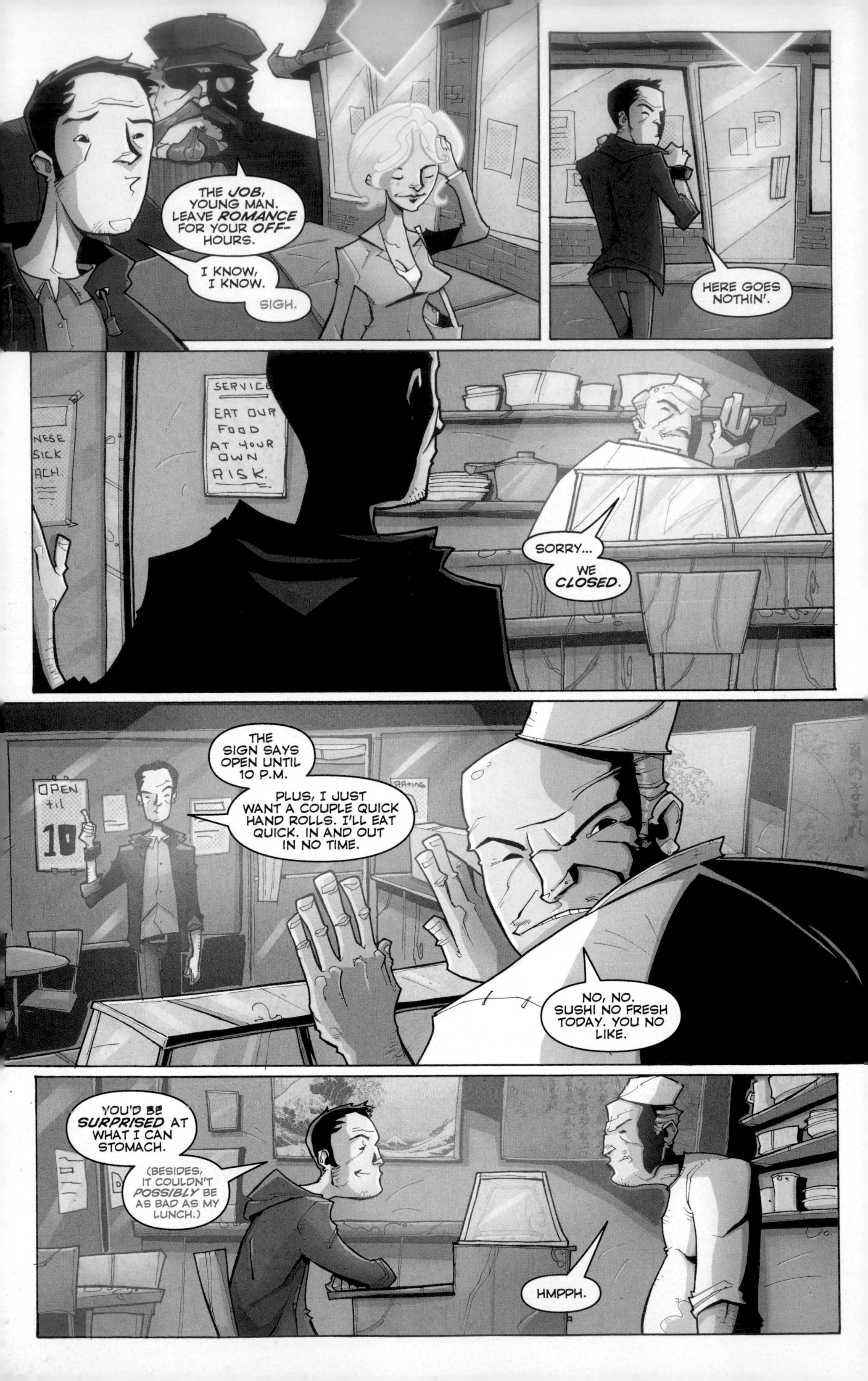
THE JOB, YOUNG MAN. LEAVE ROMANCE FOR YOUR OFF-HOURS.
I KNOW, I KNOW.
SIGH.
HERE GOES NOTHIN'.
SERVICE
EAT OUR FOOD AT YOUR OWN RISK.
SORRY... WE CLOSED.
OPEN til 10
THE SIGN SAYS OPEN UNTIL 10 P.M.
PLUS, I JUST WANT A COUPLE QUICK HAND ROLLS. I'LL EAT QUICK. IN AND OUT IN NO TIME.
NO, NO. SUSHI NO FRESH TODAY. YOU NO LIKE.
YOU'D BE SURPRISED AT WHAT I CAN STOMACH.
(BESIDES, IT COULDN'T POSSIBLY BE AS BAD AS MY LUNCH.)
HMPPH.

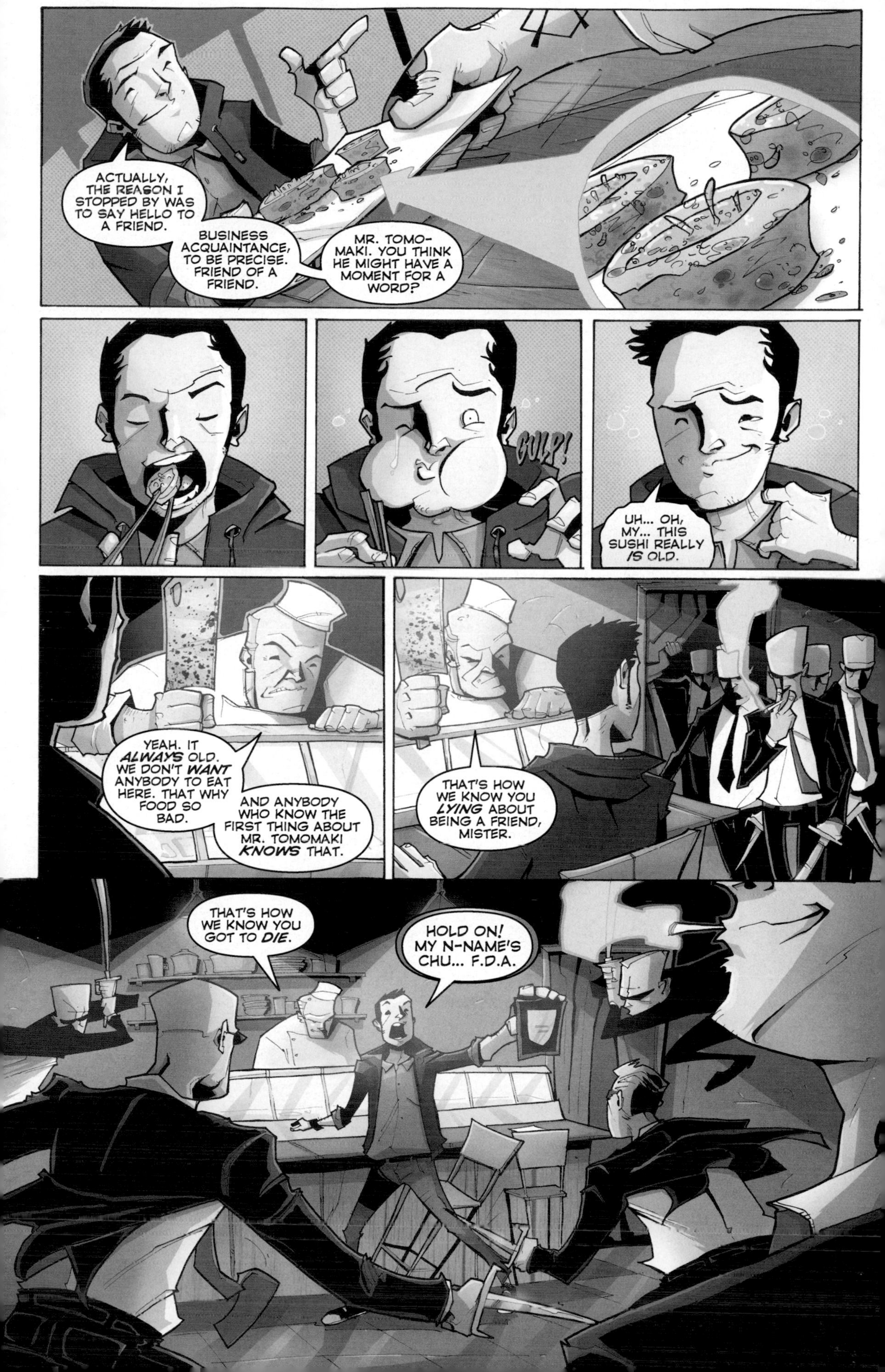
ACTUALLY, THE REASON I STOPPED BY WAS TO SAY HELLO TO A FRIEND.
BUSINESS ACQUAINTANCE, TO BE PRECISE. FRIEND OF A FRIEND.
MR. TOMOMAKI. YOU THINK HE MIGHT HAVE A MOMENT FOR A WORD?
GULP!
UH... OH, MY... THIS SUSHI REALLY *IS* OLD.
YEAH. IT *ALWAYS* OLD. WE DON'T *WANT* ANYBODY TO EAT HERE. THAT WHY FOOD SO BAD.
AND ANYBODY WHO KNOW THE FIRST THING ABOUT MR. TOMOMAKI *KNOWS* THAT.
THAT'S HOW WE KNOW YOU *LYING* ABOUT BEING A FRIEND, MISTER.
THAT'S HOW WE KNOW YOU GOT TO *DIE*.
HOLD ON! MY N-NAME'S CHU... F.D.A.

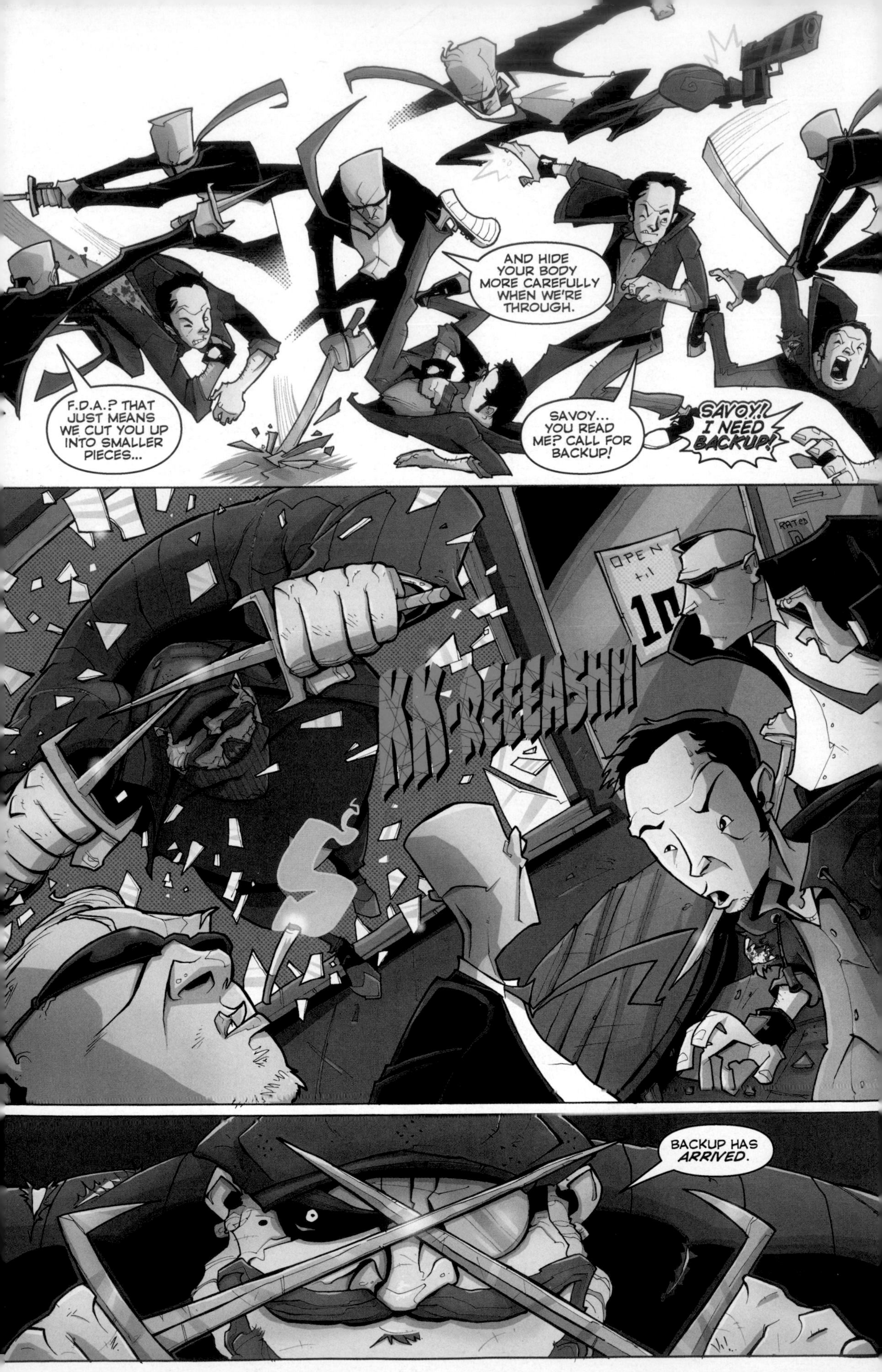
AND HIDE YOUR BODY MORE CAREFULLY WHEN WE'RE THROUGH.
F.D.A.? THAT JUST MEANS WE CUT YOU UP INTO SMALLER PIECES...
SAVOY... YOU READ ME? CALL FOR BACKUP!
SAVOY!! I NEED BACKUP!
KK-REEEASHH
OPEN til 10
RATED
BACKUP HAS ARRIVED.

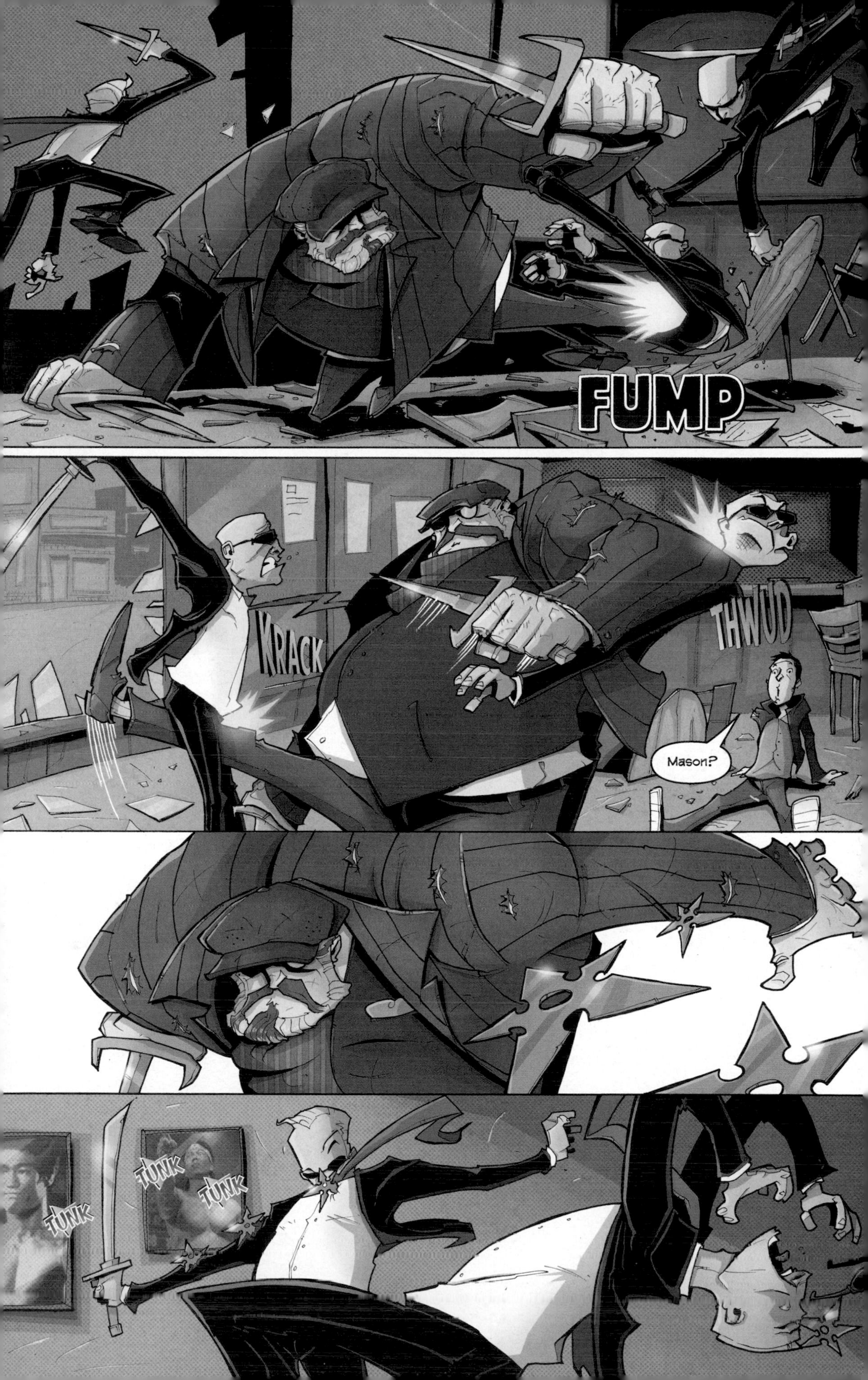
FUMP
KRACK
THWUD
Mason?
TUNK
TUNK
TUNK

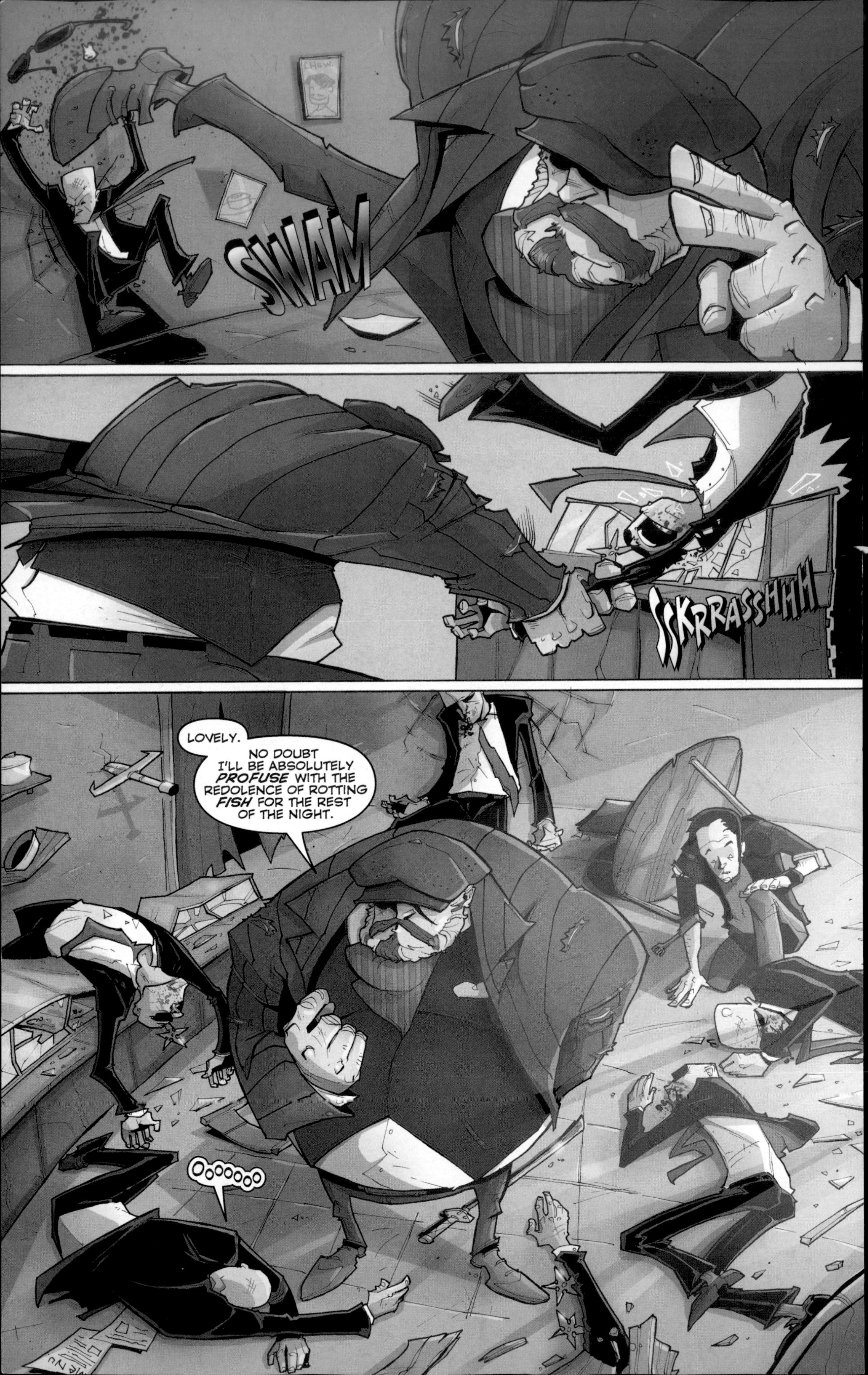

SWAM
SKRRASSHHH
LOVELY.
NO DOUBT I'LL BE ABSOLUTELY *PROFUSE* WITH THE REDOLENCE OF ROTTING *FISH* FOR THE REST OF THE NIGHT.
OOOOOOO

AND SO LATER:

SUSHI ONO

YOU... YOU WERE *AMAZING* IN THERE.

ALL IN A DAY'S WORK, M'BOY.

DID YOU THINK YOU WOULD JUST BE SOME FILE SORTER AND PENCIL PUSHER?

YOU'RE IN THE *F.D.A.* NOW. THIS SORT OF STUFF HAPPENS *ALL* THE TIME.

AND *YOU'LL* NEED TO BE PREPARED FOR IT AS WELL.

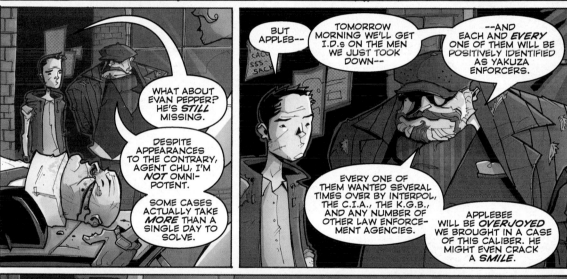

WHAT ABOUT EVAN PEPPER? HE'S *STILL* MISSING.

DESPITE APPEARANCES TO THE CONTRARY, AGENT CHU, I'M *NOT* OMNIPOTENT.

SOME CASES ACTUALLY TAKE *MORE* THAN A SINGLE DAY TO SOLVE.

BUT APPLEB--

TOMORROW MORNING WE'LL GET I.D.s ON THE MEN WE JUST TOOK DOWN--

--AND EACH AND *EVERY* ONE OF THEM WILL BE POSITIVELY IDENTIFIED AS YAKUZA ENFORCERS.

EVERY ONE OF THEM WANTED SEVERAL TIMES OVER BY INTERPOL, THE C.I.A., THE K.G.B., AND ANY NUMBER OF OTHER LAW ENFORCEMENT AGENCIES.

APPLEBEE WILL BE *OVERJOYED* WE BROUGHT IN A CASE OF THIS CALIBER. HE MIGHT EVEN CRACK A *SMILE*.

BUCK UP, LAD. THIS IS WHAT WE REFER TO AS "THE END OF A GOOD DAY."

ENJOY IT, BECAUSE, IN *THIS* JOB, THIS IS ABOUT AS CLOSE TO A HAPPY ENDING AS WE GET.

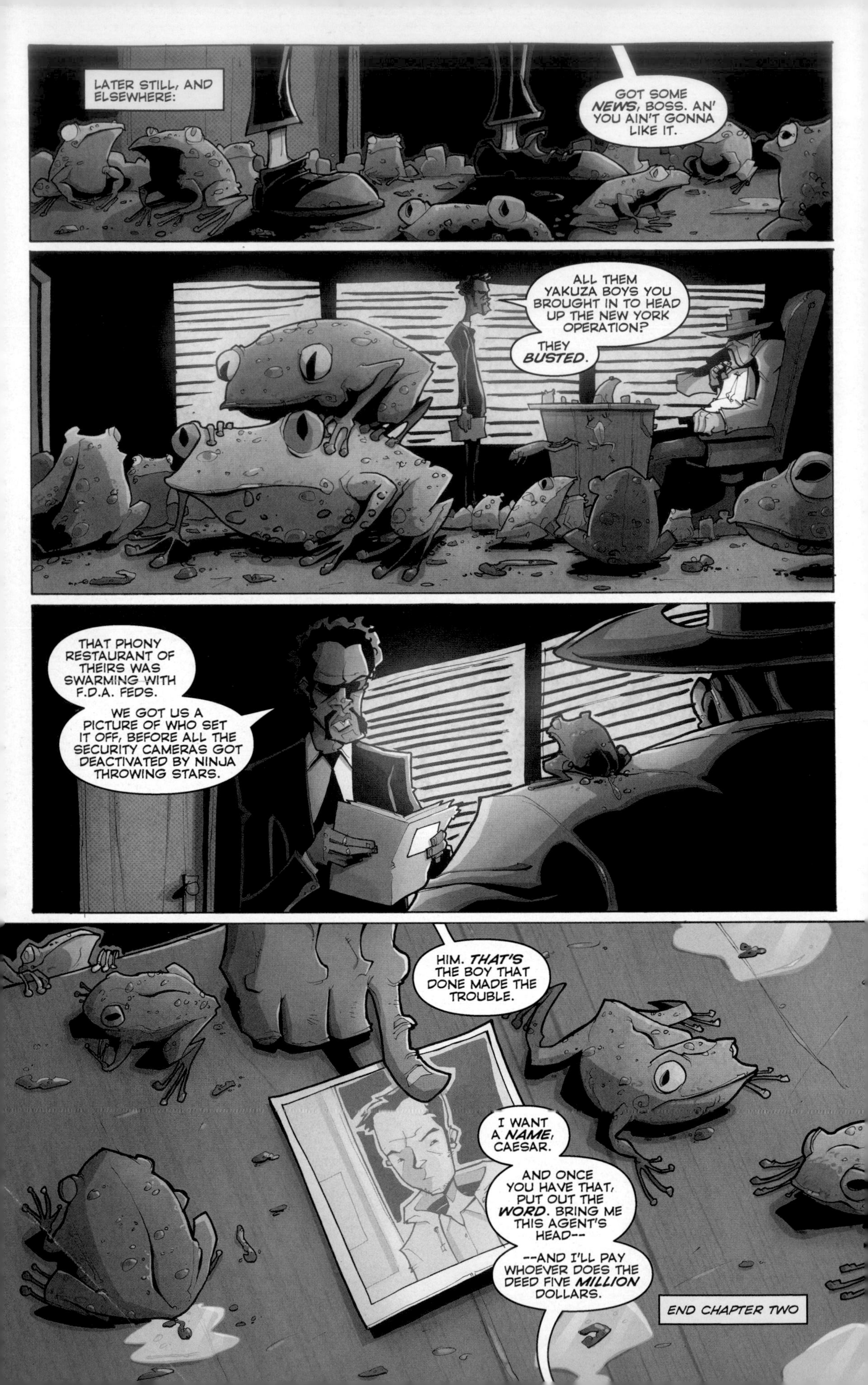

LATER STILL, AND ELSEWHERE:
GOT SOME NEWS, BOSS. AN' YOU AIN'T GONNA LIKE IT.
ALL THEM YAKUZA BOYS YOU BROUGHT IN TO HEAD UP THE NEW YORK OPERATION?
THEY BUSTED.
THAT PHONY RESTAURANT OF THEIRS WAS SWARMING WITH F.D.A. FEDS.
WE GOT US A PICTURE OF WHO SET IT OFF, BEFORE ALL THE SECURITY CAMERAS GOT DEACTIVATED BY NINJA THROWING STARS.
HIM. THAT'S THE BOY THAT DONE MADE THE TROUBLE.
I WANT A NAME, CAESAR.
AND ONCE YOU HAVE THAT, PUT OUT THE WORD. BRING ME THIS AGENT'S HEAD--
--AND I'LL PAY WHOEVER DOES THE DEED FIVE MILLION DOLLARS.
END CHAPTER TWO

Chapter 3

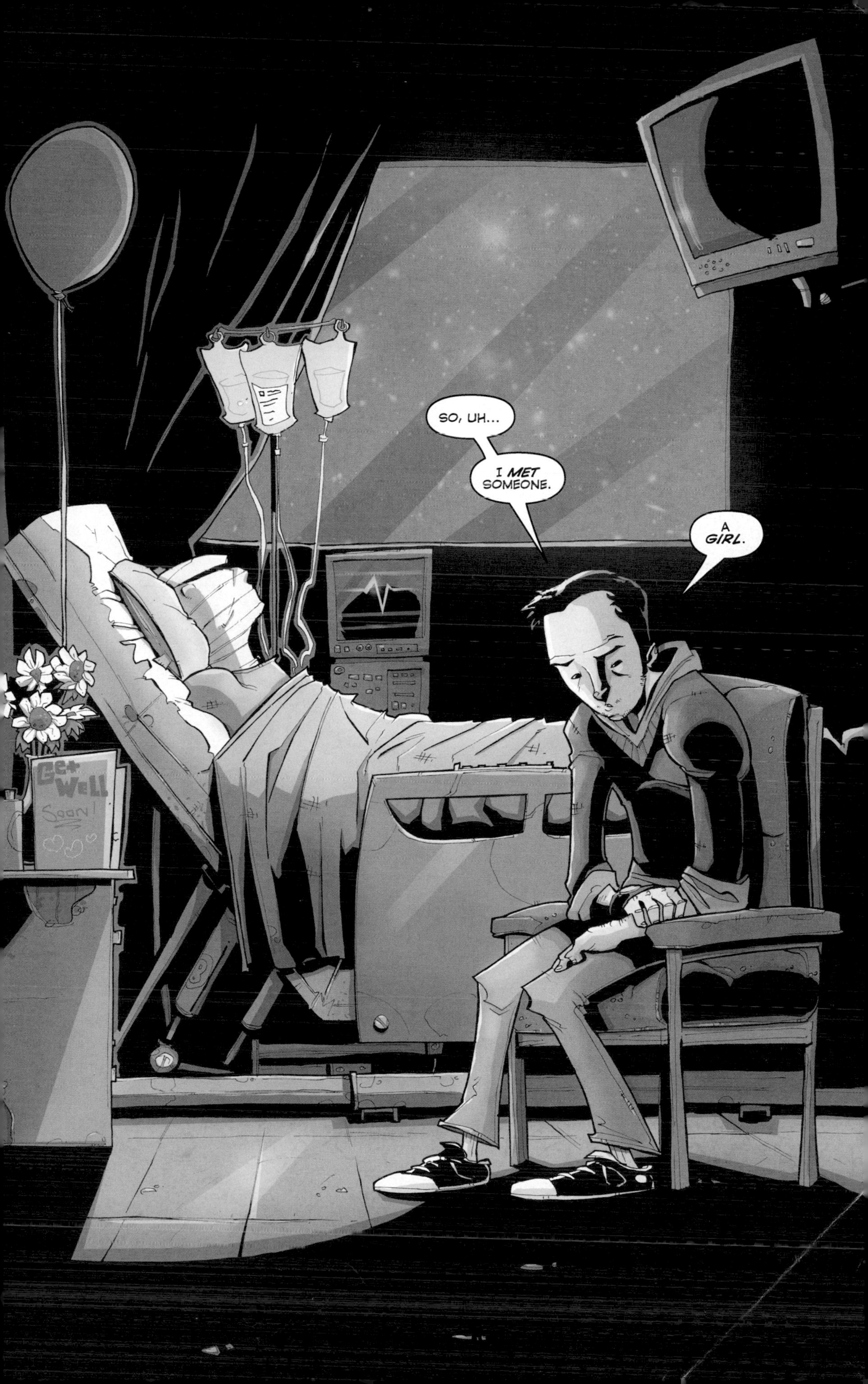
SO, UH...
I MET SOMEONE.
A GIRL.
Get Well Soon!

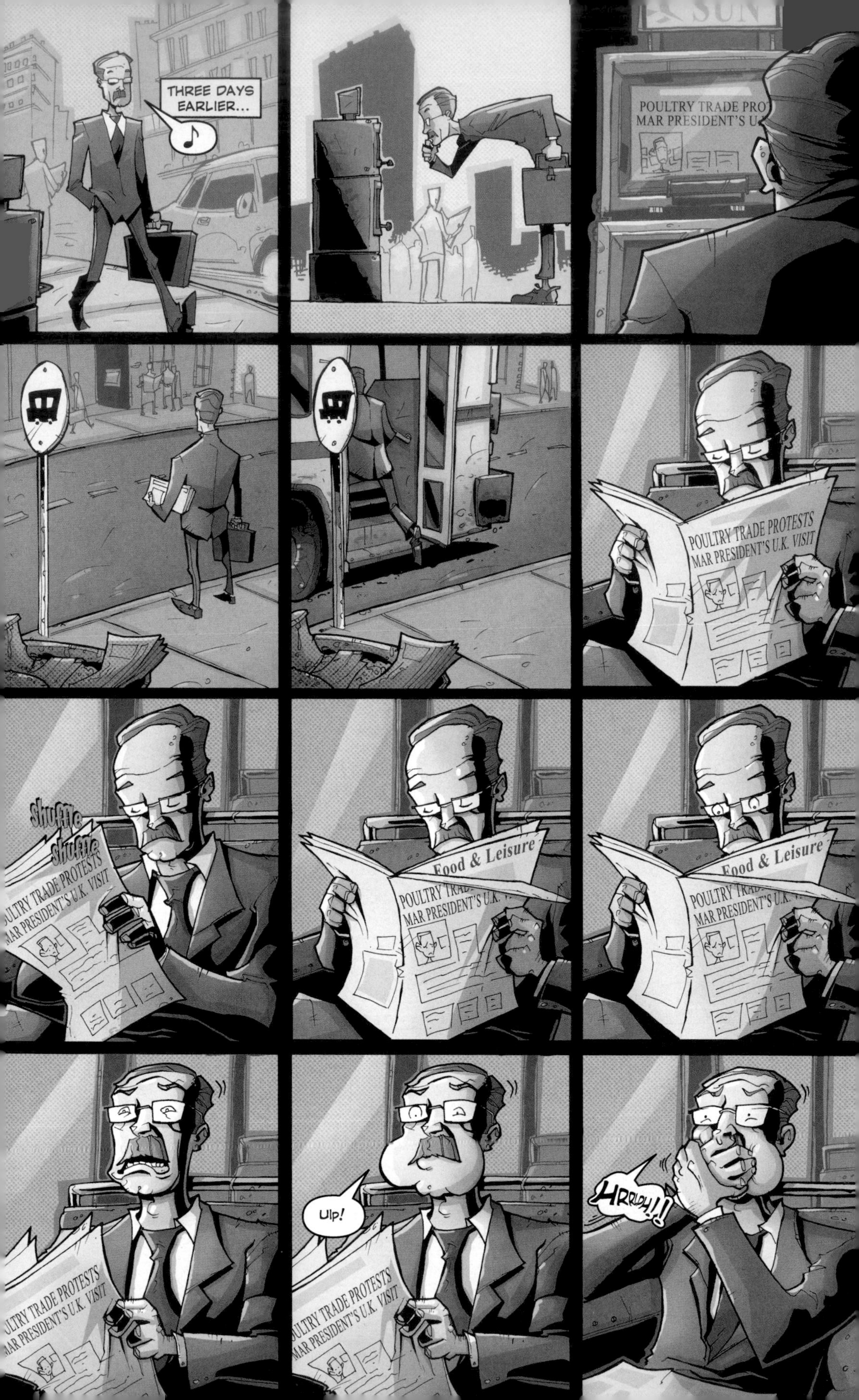
THREE DAYS EARLIER...
♪
SUN
POULTRY TRADE PROT
MAR PRESIDENT'S U
POULTRY TRADE PROTESTS
MAR PRESIDENT'S U.K. VISIT
shuffle
shuffle
ULTRY TRADE PROTESTS
MAR PRESIDENT'S U.K. VISIT
Food & Leisure
Food & Leisure
ULTRY TRADE PROTESTS
MAR PRESIDENT'S U.K. VISIT
Ulp!
ULTRY TRADE PROTESTS
MAR PRESIDENT'S U.K. VISIT
HRRUGH!!

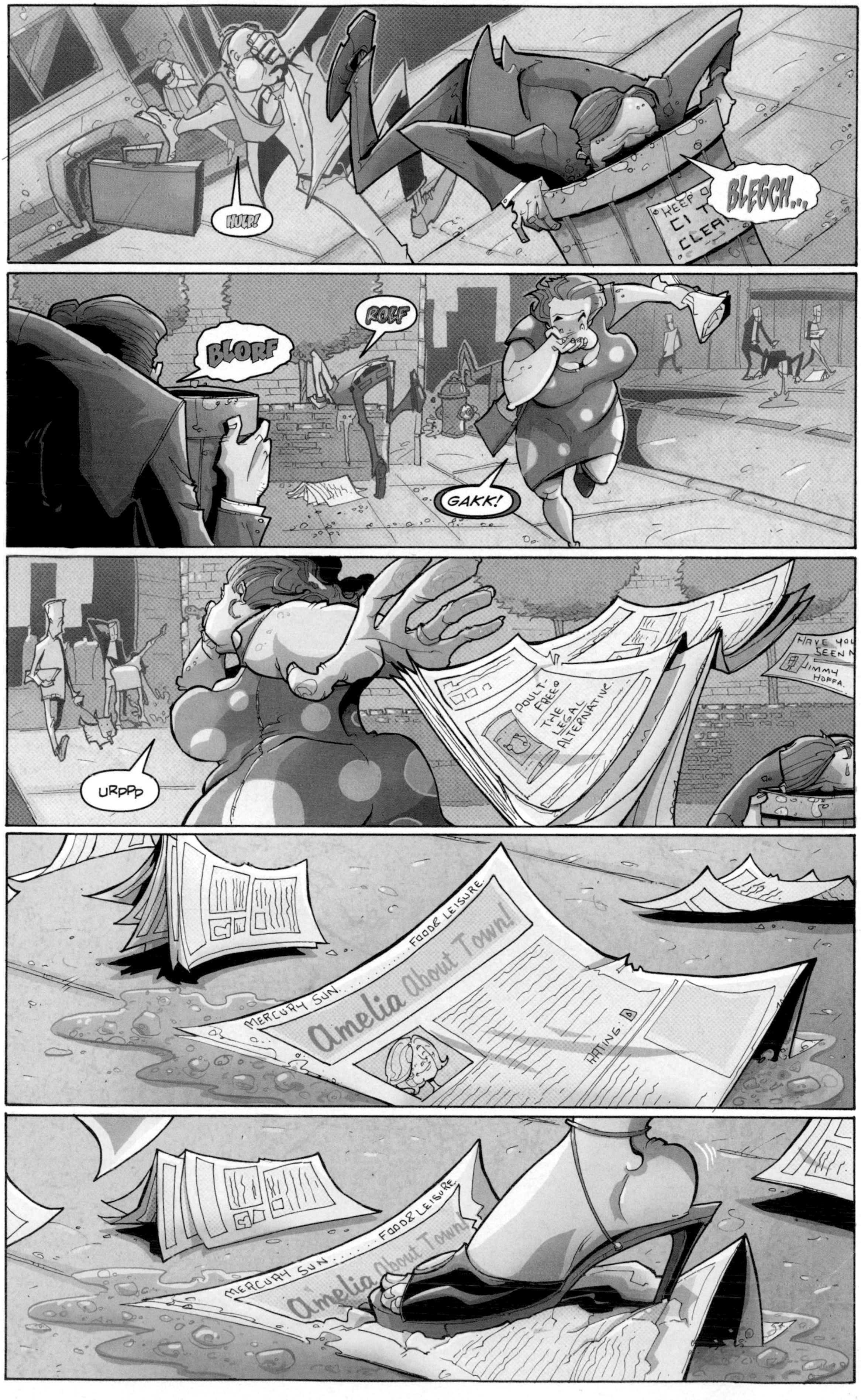
HULP!
BLEGCH...
BLORF
ROLF
GAKK!
URPPP
POULT-FREE© THE LEGAL ALTERNATIVE
HAVE YOU SEEN
JIMMY HOFFA.
MERCURY SUN.......FOOD& LEISURE.
Amelia About Town!
RATING: D
MERCURY SUN.......FOOD& LEISURE.
Amelia About Town!

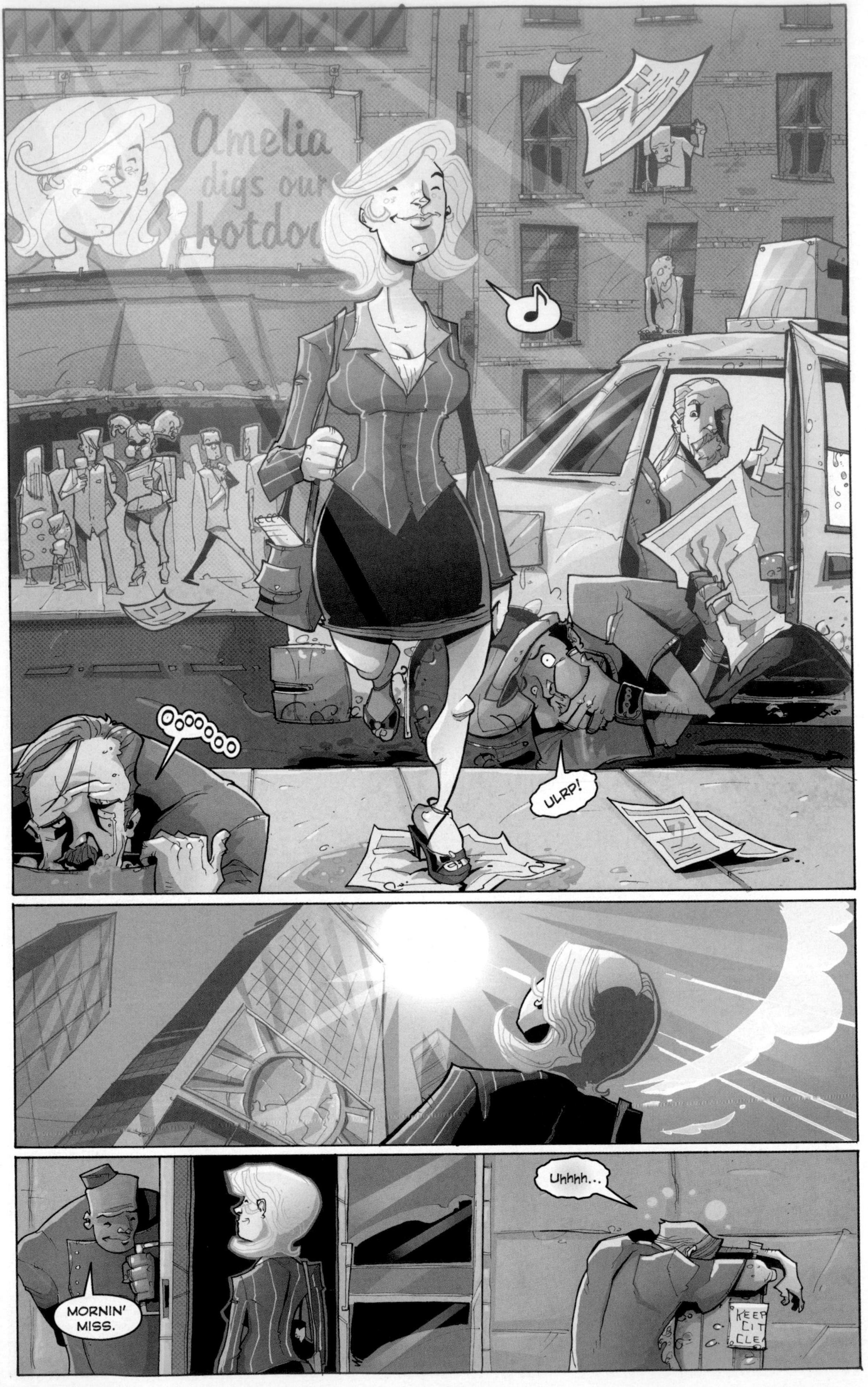
Amelia
digs our
hotdo
OOOOOOO
ULRP!
MORNIN' MISS.
Uhhhh...

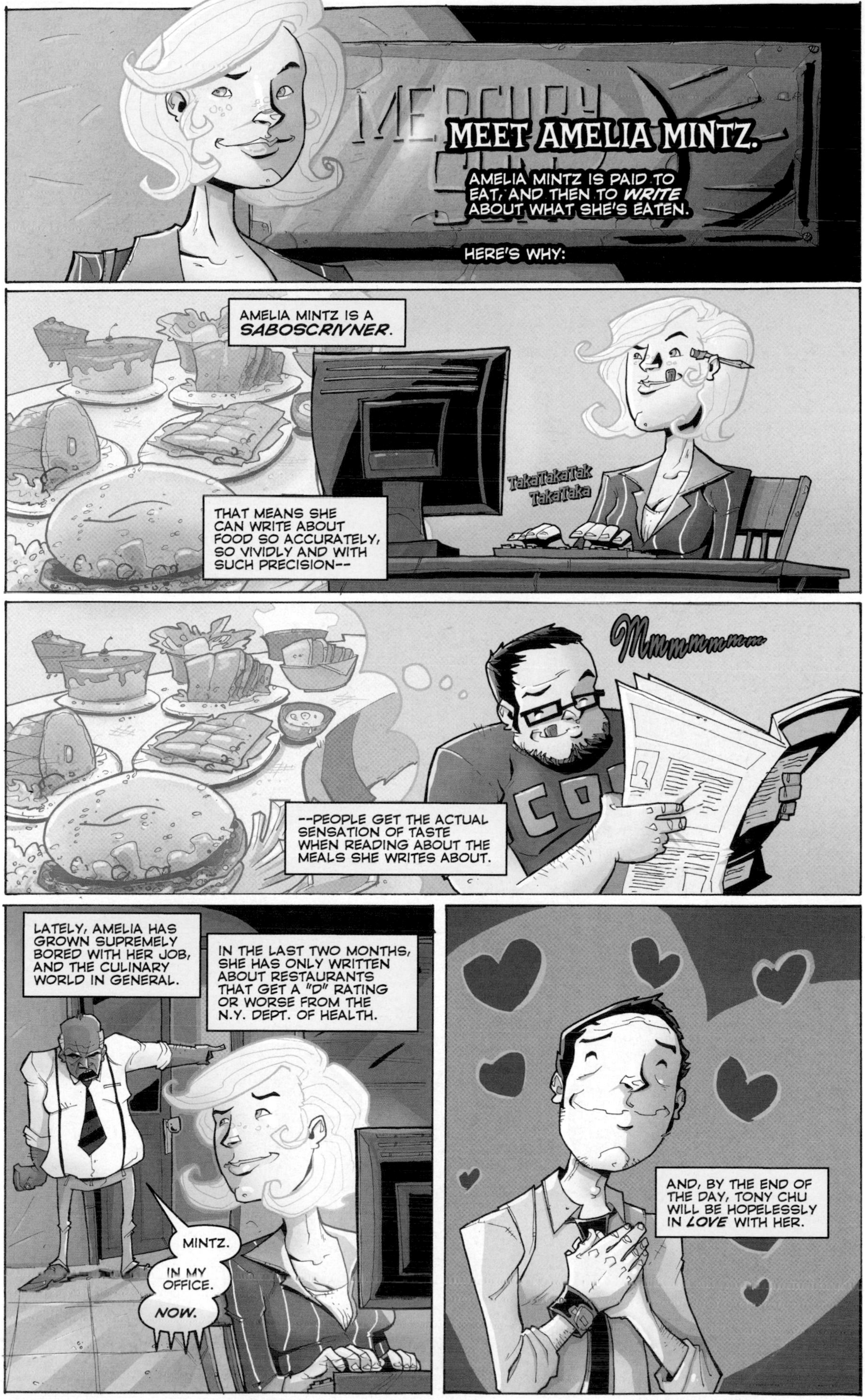
MEET AMELIA MINTZ.
AMELIA MINTZ IS PAID TO EAT, AND THEN TO *WRITE* ABOUT WHAT SHE'S EATEN.
HERE'S WHY:
AMELIA MINTZ IS A *SABOSCRIVNER*.
TakaTakaTak TakaTaka
THAT MEANS SHE CAN WRITE ABOUT FOOD SO ACCURATELY, SO VIVIDLY AND WITH SUCH PRECISION--
Mmmmmmm...
--PEOPLE GET THE ACTUAL SENSATION OF TASTE WHEN READING ABOUT THE MEALS SHE WRITES ABOUT.
LATELY, AMELIA HAS GROWN SUPREMELY BORED WITH HER JOB, AND THE CULINARY WORLD IN GENERAL.
IN THE LAST TWO MONTHS, SHE HAS ONLY WRITTEN ABOUT RESTAURANTS THAT GET A "D" RATING OR WORSE FROM THE N.Y. DEPT. OF HEALTH.
MINTZ.
IN MY OFFICE.
NOW.
AND, BY THE END OF THE DAY, TONY CHU WILL BE HOPELESSLY IN *LOVE* WITH HER.

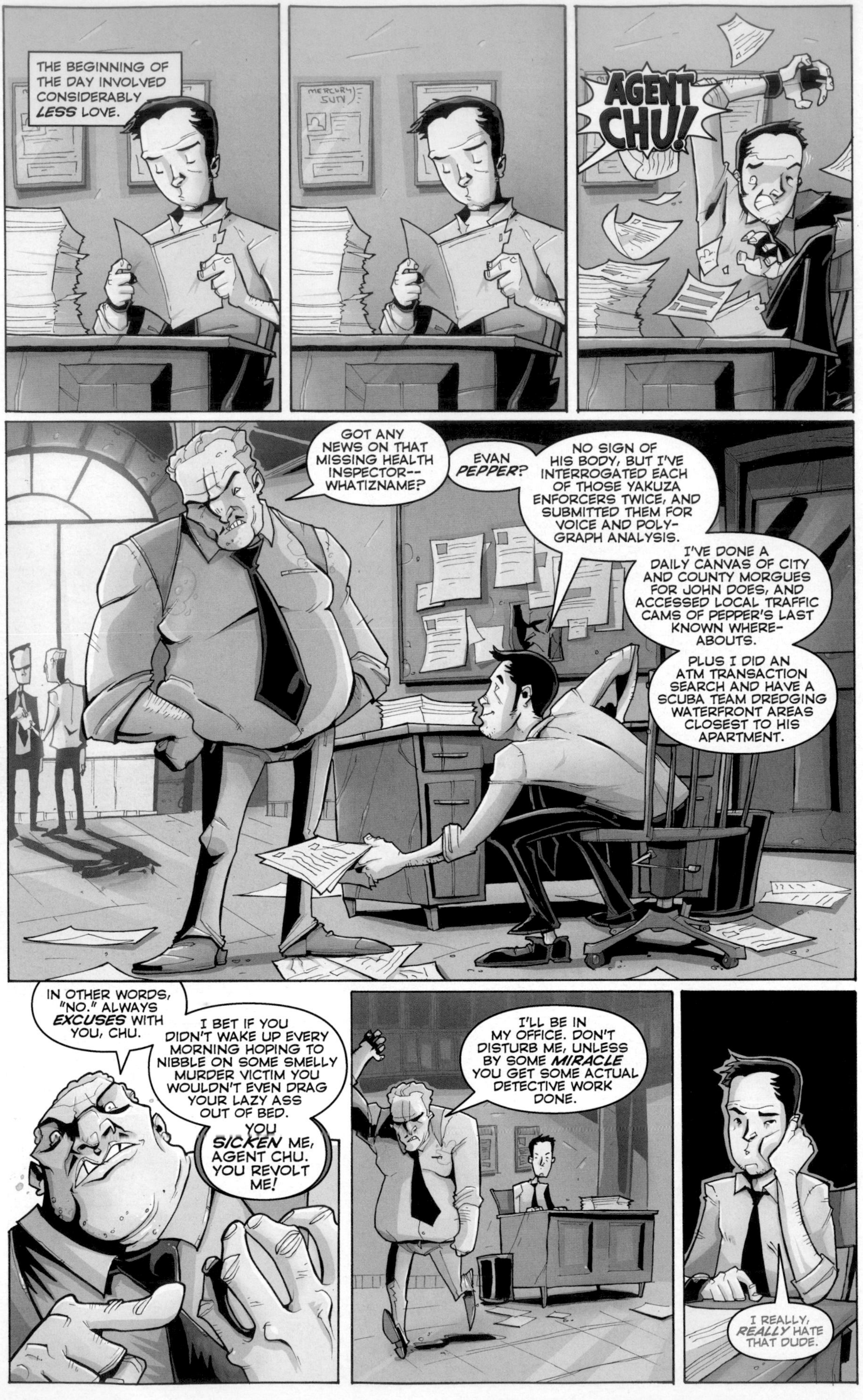
THE BEGINNING OF THE DAY INVOLVED CONSIDERABLY *LESS* LOVE.
MERCURY SUTY
AGENT CHU!
GOT ANY NEWS ON THAT MISSING HEALTH INSPECTOR-- WHATIZNAME?
EVAN *PEPPER*?
NO SIGN OF HIS BODY, BUT I'VE INTERROGATED EACH OF THOSE YAKUZA ENFORCERS TWICE, AND SUBMITTED THEM FOR VOICE AND POLY-GRAPH ANALYSIS.
I'VE DONE A DAILY CANVAS OF CITY AND COUNTY MORGUES FOR JOHN DOES, AND ACCESSED LOCAL TRAFFIC CAMS OF PEPPER'S LAST KNOWN WHERE-ABOUTS.
PLUS I DID AN ATM TRANSACTION SEARCH AND HAVE A SCUBA TEAM DREDGING WATERFRONT AREAS CLOSEST TO HIS APARTMENT.
IN OTHER WORDS, "NO." ALWAYS *EXCUSES* WITH YOU, CHU.
I BET IF YOU DIDN'T WAKE UP EVERY MORNING HOPING TO NIBBLE ON SOME SMELLY MURDER VICTIM YOU WOULDN'T EVEN DRAG YOUR LAZY ASS OUT OF BED.
YOU *SICKEN* ME, AGENT CHU. YOU REVOLT ME!
I'LL BE IN MY OFFICE. DON'T DISTURB ME, UNLESS BY SOME *MIRACLE* YOU GET SOME ACTUAL DETECTIVE WORK DONE.
I REALLY, *REALLY* HATE THAT DUDE.

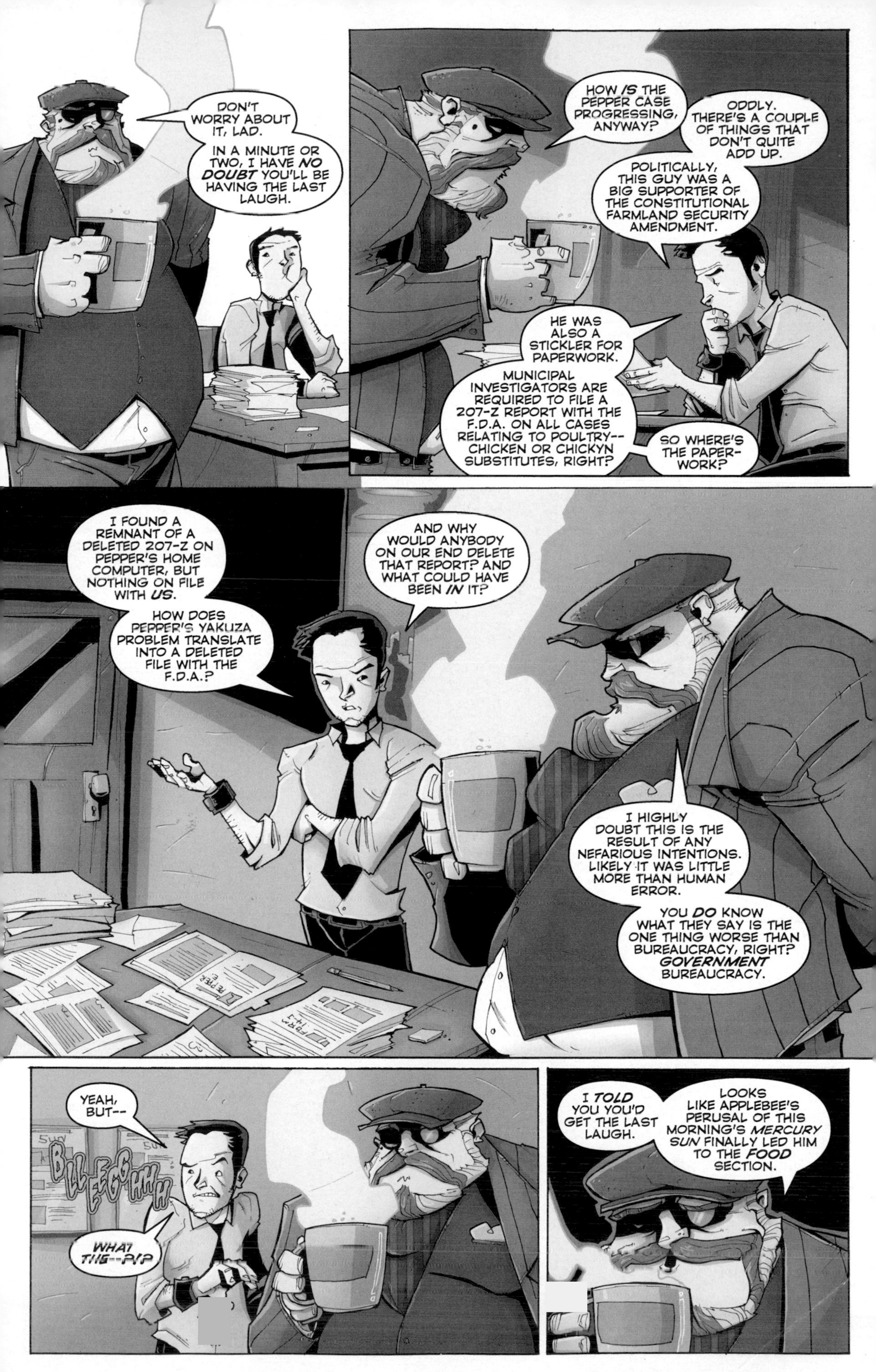
DON'T WORRY ABOUT IT, LAD.
IN A MINUTE OR TWO, I HAVE *NO DOUBT* YOU'LL BE HAVING THE LAST LAUGH.
HOW *IS* THE PEPPER CASE PROGRESSING, ANYWAY?
ODDLY. THERE'S A COUPLE OF THINGS THAT DON'T QUITE ADD UP.
POLITICALLY, THIS GUY WAS A BIG SUPPORTER OF THE CONSTITUTIONAL FARMLAND SECURITY AMENDMENT.
HE WAS ALSO A STICKLER FOR PAPERWORK.
MUNICIPAL INVESTIGATORS ARE REQUIRED TO FILE A 207-Z REPORT WITH THE F.D.A. ON ALL CASES RELATING TO POULTRY-- CHICKEN OR CHICKYN SUBSTITUTES, RIGHT?
SO WHERE'S THE PAPER-WORK?
I FOUND A REMNANT OF A DELETED 207-Z ON PEPPER'S HOME COMPUTER, BUT NOTHING ON FILE WITH *US*.
HOW DOES PEPPER'S YAKUZA PROBLEM TRANSLATE INTO A DELETED FILE WITH THE F.D.A.?
AND WHY WOULD ANYBODY ON OUR END DELETE THAT REPORT? AND WHAT COULD HAVE BEEN *IN* IT?
I HIGHLY DOUBT THIS IS THE RESULT OF ANY NEFARIOUS INTENTIONS. LIKELY IT WAS LITTLE MORE THAN HUMAN ERROR.
YOU *DO* KNOW WHAT THEY SAY IS THE ONE THING WORSE THAN BUREAUCRACY, RIGHT? *GOVERNMENT* BUREAUCRACY.
YEAH, BUT--
BLLEEGGHHH
WHAT THE--?!?
I *TOLD* YOU YOU'D GET THE LAST LAUGH.
LOOKS LIKE APPLEBEE'S PERUSAL OF THIS MORNING'S *MERCURY SUN* FINALLY LED HIM TO THE *FOOD* SECTION.

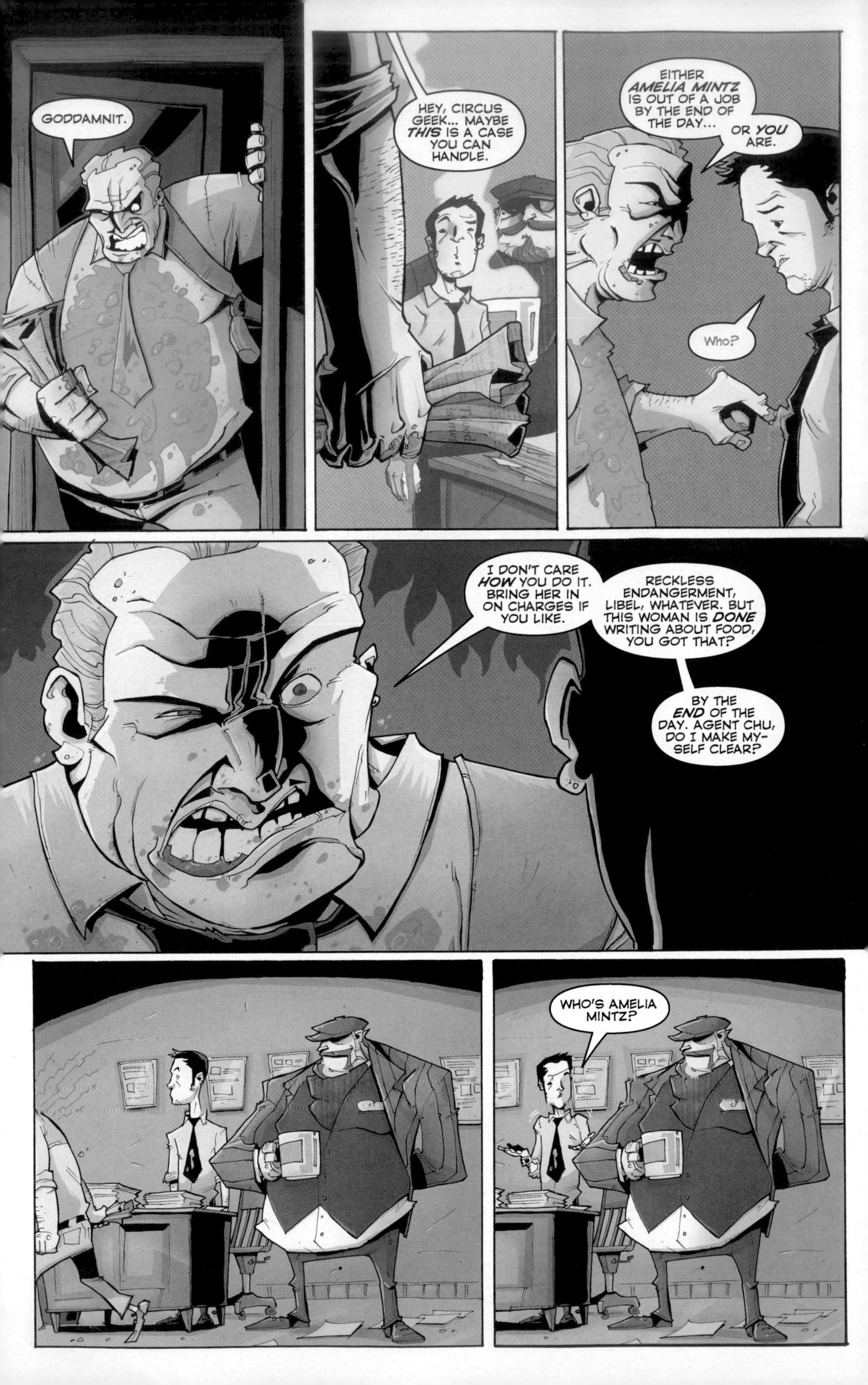
GODDAMNIT.
HEY, CIRCUS GEEK... MAYBE THIS IS A CASE YOU CAN HANDLE.
EITHER AMELIA MINTZ IS OUT OF A JOB BY THE END OF THE DAY...
OR YOU ARE.
Who?
I DON'T CARE HOW YOU DO IT. BRING HER IN ON CHARGES IF YOU LIKE.
RECKLESS ENDANGERMENT, LIBEL, WHATEVER. BUT THIS WOMAN IS DONE WRITING ABOUT FOOD, YOU GOT THAT?
BY THE END OF THE DAY. AGENT CHU, DO I MAKE MY-SELF CLEAR?
WHO'S AMELIA MINTZ?

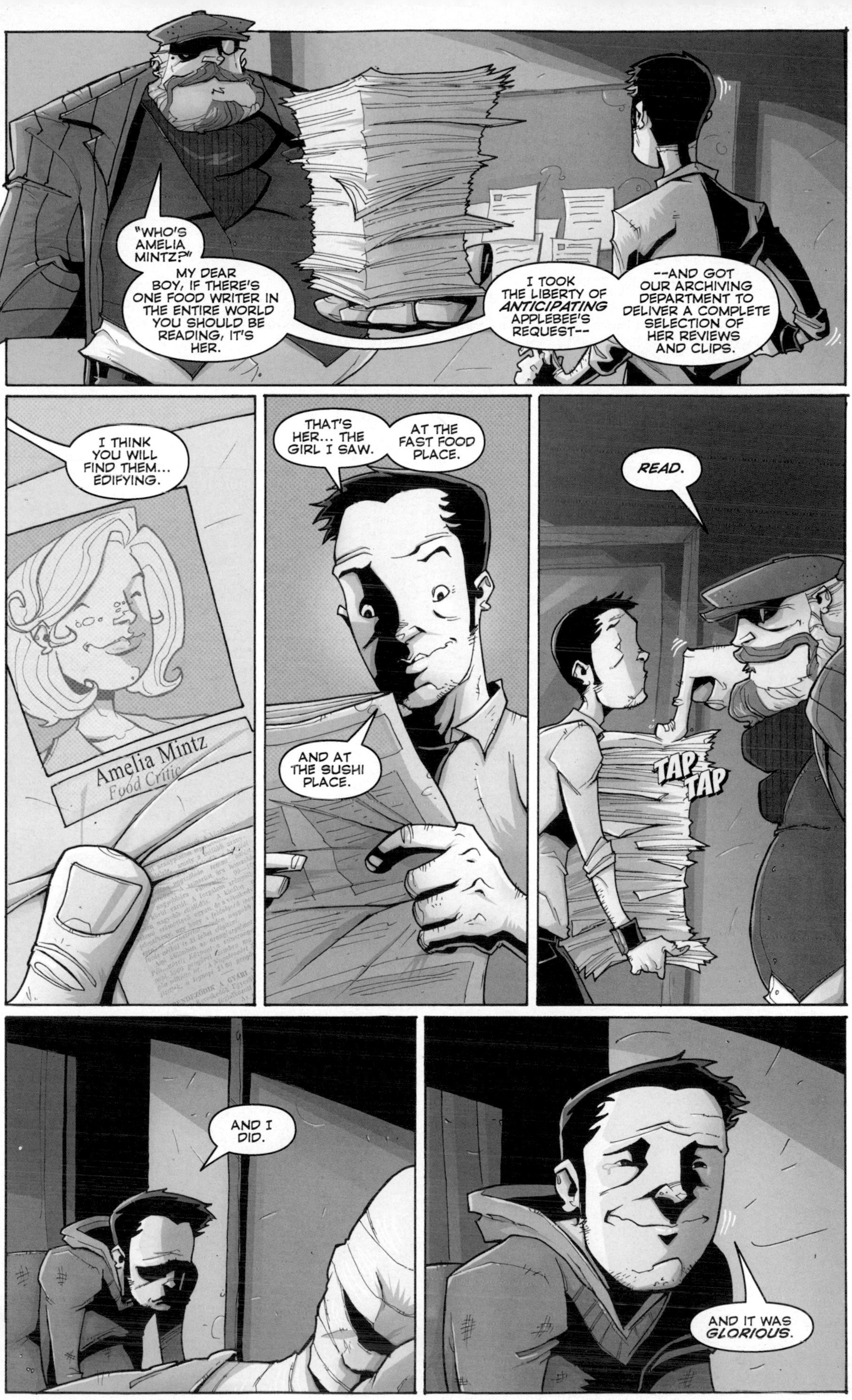

"WHO'S AMELIA MINTZ?"
MY DEAR BOY, IF THERE'S ONE FOOD WRITER IN THE ENTIRE WORLD YOU SHOULD BE READING, IT'S HER.
I TOOK THE LIBERTY OF *ANTICIPATING* APPLEBEE'S REQUEST--
--AND GOT OUR ARCHIVING DEPARTMENT TO DELIVER A COMPLETE SELECTION OF HER REVIEWS AND CLIPS.
I THINK YOU WILL FIND THEM... EDIFYING.
Amelia Mintz
Food Critic
THAT'S HER... THE GIRL I SAW.
AT THE FAST FOOD PLACE.
AND AT THE SUSHI PLACE.
READ.
TAP TAP
AND I DID.
AND IT WAS *GLORIOUS*.

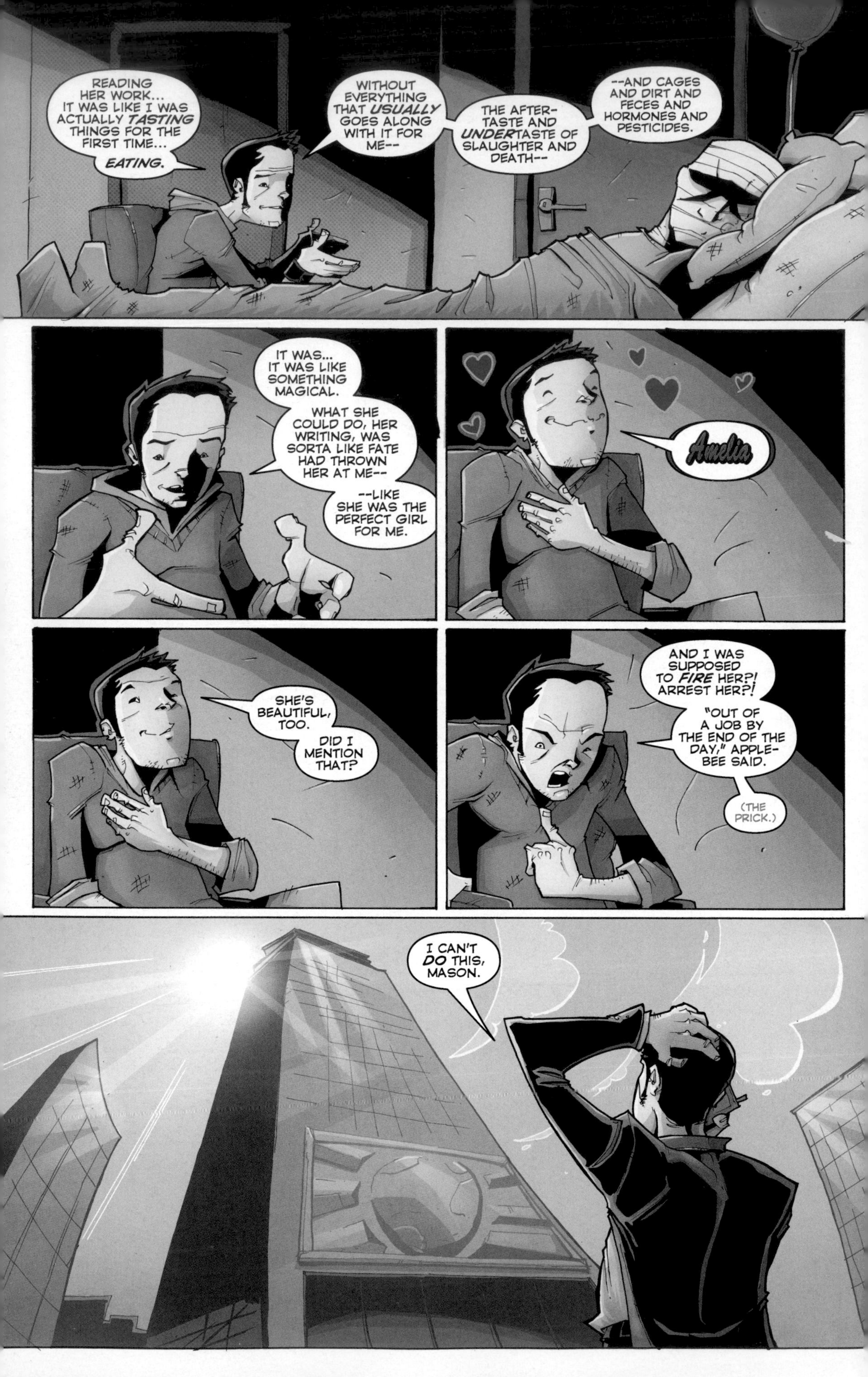
READING HER WORK... IT WAS LIKE I WAS ACTUALLY TASTING THINGS FOR THE FIRST TIME... EATING.
WITHOUT EVERYTHING THAT USUALLY GOES ALONG WITH IT FOR ME--
THE AFTER-TASTE AND UNDERTASTE OF SLAUGHTER AND DEATH--
--AND CAGES AND DIRT AND FECES AND HORMONES AND PESTICIDES.
IT WAS... IT WAS LIKE SOMETHING MAGICAL.
WHAT SHE COULD DO, HER WRITING, WAS SORTA LIKE FATE HAD THROWN HER AT ME--
--LIKE SHE WAS THE PERFECT GIRL FOR ME.
Amelia
SHE'S BEAUTIFUL, TOO.
DID I MENTION THAT?
AND I WAS SUPPOSED TO FIRE HER?! ARREST HER?!
"OUT OF A JOB BY THE END OF THE DAY," APPLE-BEE SAID.
(THE PRICK.)
I CAN'T DO THIS, MASON.

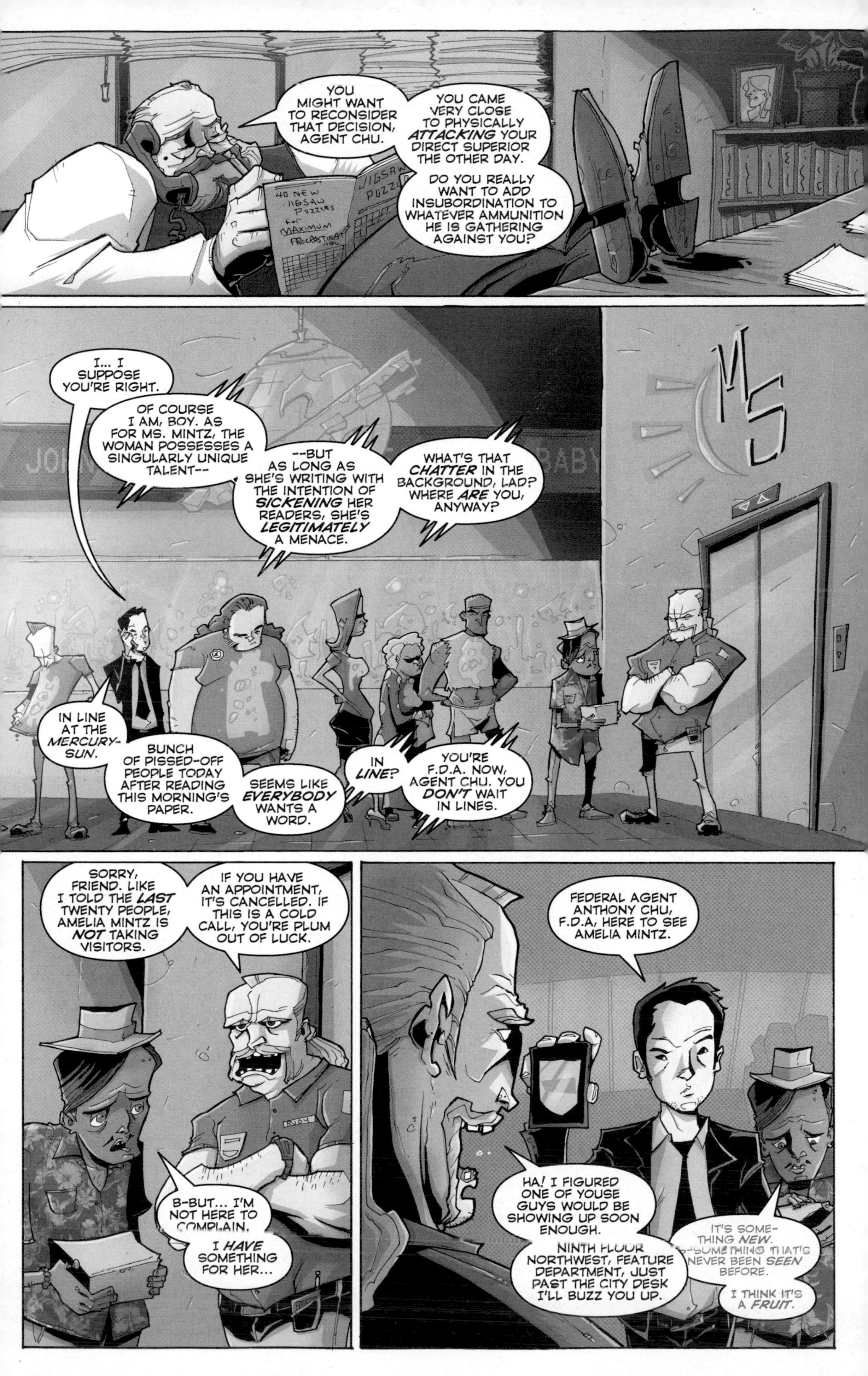
YOU MIGHT WANT TO RECONSIDER THAT DECISION, AGENT CHU.
YOU CAME VERY CLOSE TO PHYSICALLY *ATTACKING* YOUR DIRECT SUPERIOR THE OTHER DAY.
DO YOU REALLY WANT TO ADD INSUBORDINATION TO WHATEVER AMMUNITION HE IS GATHERING AGAINST YOU?
I... I SUPPOSE YOU'RE RIGHT.
OF COURSE I AM, BOY. AS FOR MS. MINTZ, THE WOMAN POSSESSES A SINGULARLY UNIQUE TALENT--
--BUT AS LONG AS SHE'S WRITING WITH THE INTENTION OF *SICKENING* HER READERS, SHE'S *LEGITIMATELY* A MENACE.
WHAT'S THAT *CHATTER* IN THE BACKGROUND, LAD? WHERE *ARE* YOU, ANYWAY?
IN LINE AT THE *MERCURY-SUN*.
BUNCH OF PISSED-OFF PEOPLE TODAY AFTER READING THIS MORNING'S PAPER.
SEEMS LIKE *EVERYBODY* WANTS A WORD.
IN *LINE*?
YOU'RE F.D.A. NOW, AGENT CHU. YOU *DON'T* WAIT IN LINES.
SORRY, FRIEND. LIKE I TOLD THE *LAST* TWENTY PEOPLE, AMELIA MINTZ IS *NOT* TAKING VISITORS.
IF YOU HAVE AN APPOINTMENT, IT'S CANCELLED. IF THIS IS A COLD CALL, YOU'RE PLUM OUT OF LUCK.
B-BUT... I'M NOT HERE TO COMPLAIN, I *HAVE* SOMETHING FOR HER...
FEDERAL AGENT ANTHONY CHU, F.D.A, HERE TO SEE AMELIA MINTZ.
HA! I FIGURED ONE OF YOUSE GUYS WOULD BE SHOWING UP SOON ENOUGH.
NINTH FLOOR NORTHWEST, FEATURE DEPARTMENT, JUST PAST THE CITY DESK I'LL BUZZ YOU UP.
IT'S SOMETHING *NEW*. SOMETHING THAT'S NEVER BEEN *SEEN* BEFORE.
I THINK IT'S A *FRUIT*.

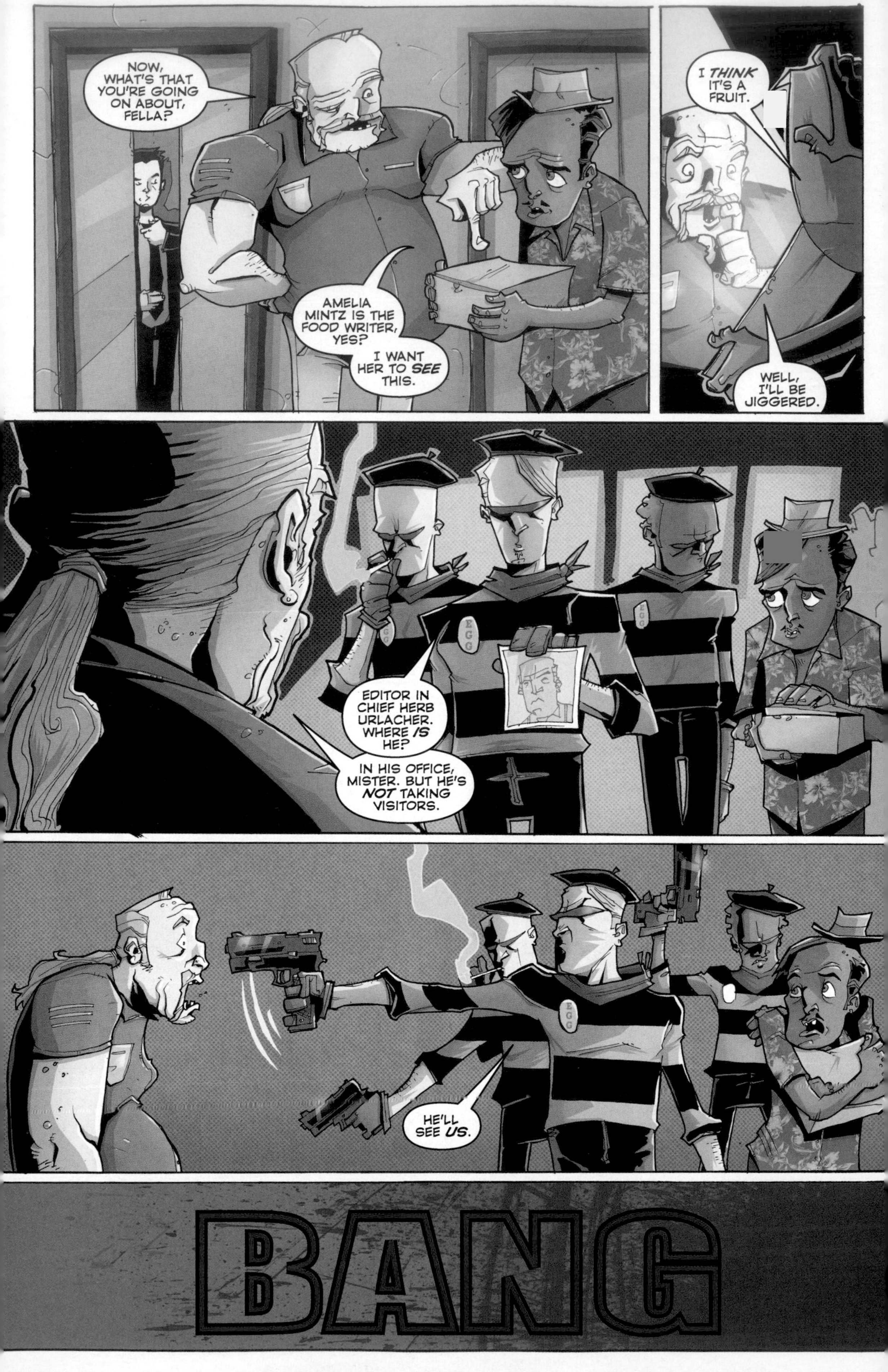
NOW, WHAT'S THAT YOU'RE GOING ON ABOUT, FELLA?
AMELIA MINTZ IS THE FOOD WRITER, YES?
I WANT HER TO *SEE* THIS.
I *THINK* IT'S A FRUIT.
WELL, I'LL BE JIGGERED.
EDITOR IN CHIEF HERB URLACHER. WHERE *IS* HE?
IN HIS OFFICE, MISTER. BUT HE'S *NOT* TAKING VISITORS.
HE'LL SEE *US*.
BANG

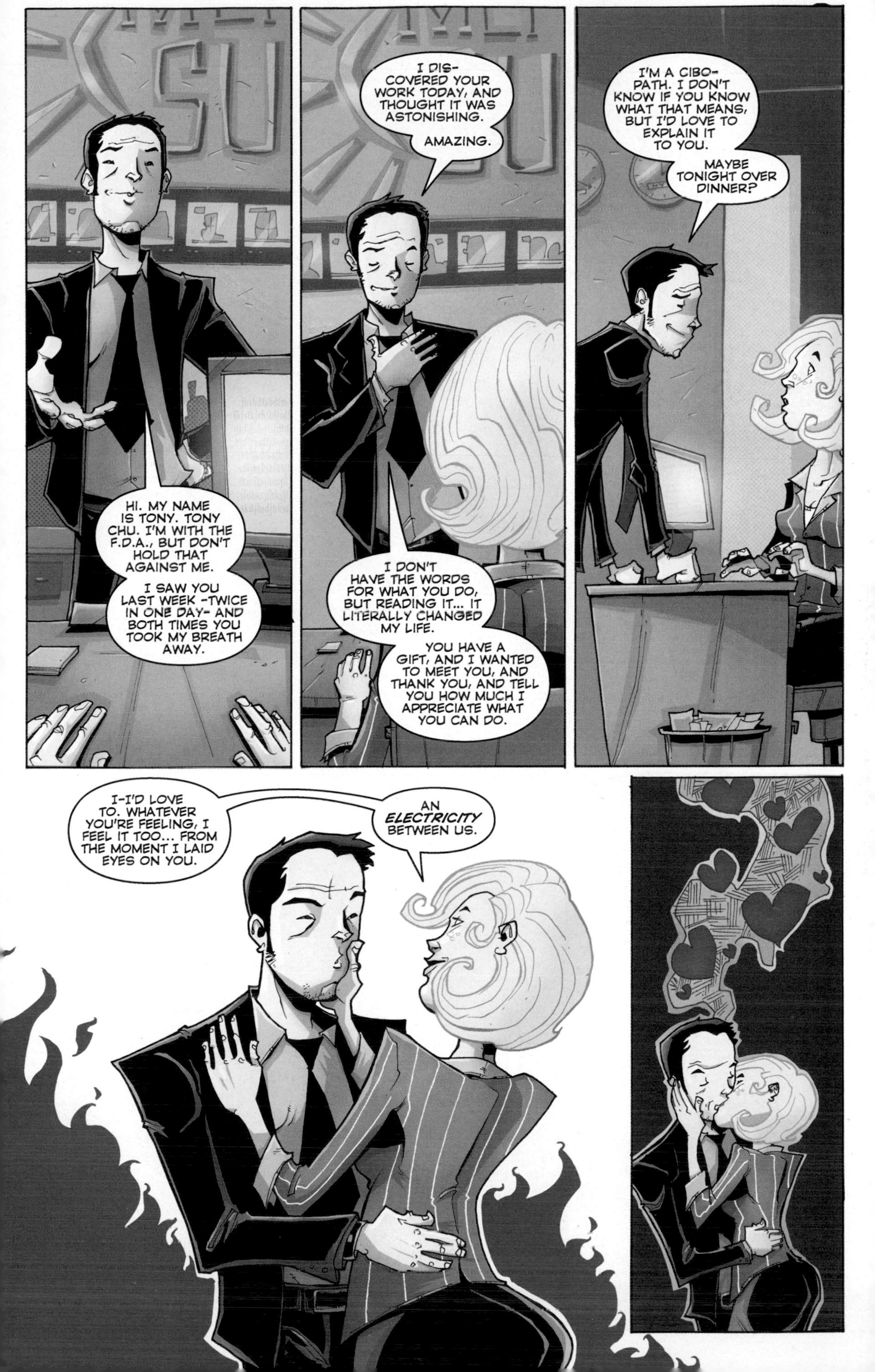
HI. MY NAME IS TONY. TONY CHU. I'M WITH THE F.D.A., BUT DON'T HOLD THAT AGAINST ME.
I SAW YOU LAST WEEK -TWICE IN ONE DAY- AND BOTH TIMES YOU TOOK MY BREATH AWAY.
I DIS-COVERED YOUR WORK TODAY, AND THOUGHT IT WAS ASTONISHING.
AMAZING.
I DON'T HAVE THE WORDS FOR WHAT YOU DO, BUT READING IT... IT LITERALLY CHANGED MY LIFE.
YOU HAVE A GIFT, AND I WANTED TO MEET YOU, AND THANK YOU, AND TELL YOU HOW MUCH I APPRECIATE WHAT YOU CAN DO.
I'M A CIBO-PATH. I DON'T KNOW IF YOU KNOW WHAT THAT MEANS, BUT I'D LOVE TO EXPLAIN IT TO YOU.
MAYBE TONIGHT OVER DINNER?
I-I'D LOVE TO. WHATEVER YOU'RE FEELING, I FEEL IT TOO... FROM THE MOMENT I LAID EYES ON YOU.
AN *ELECTRICITY* BETWEEN US.

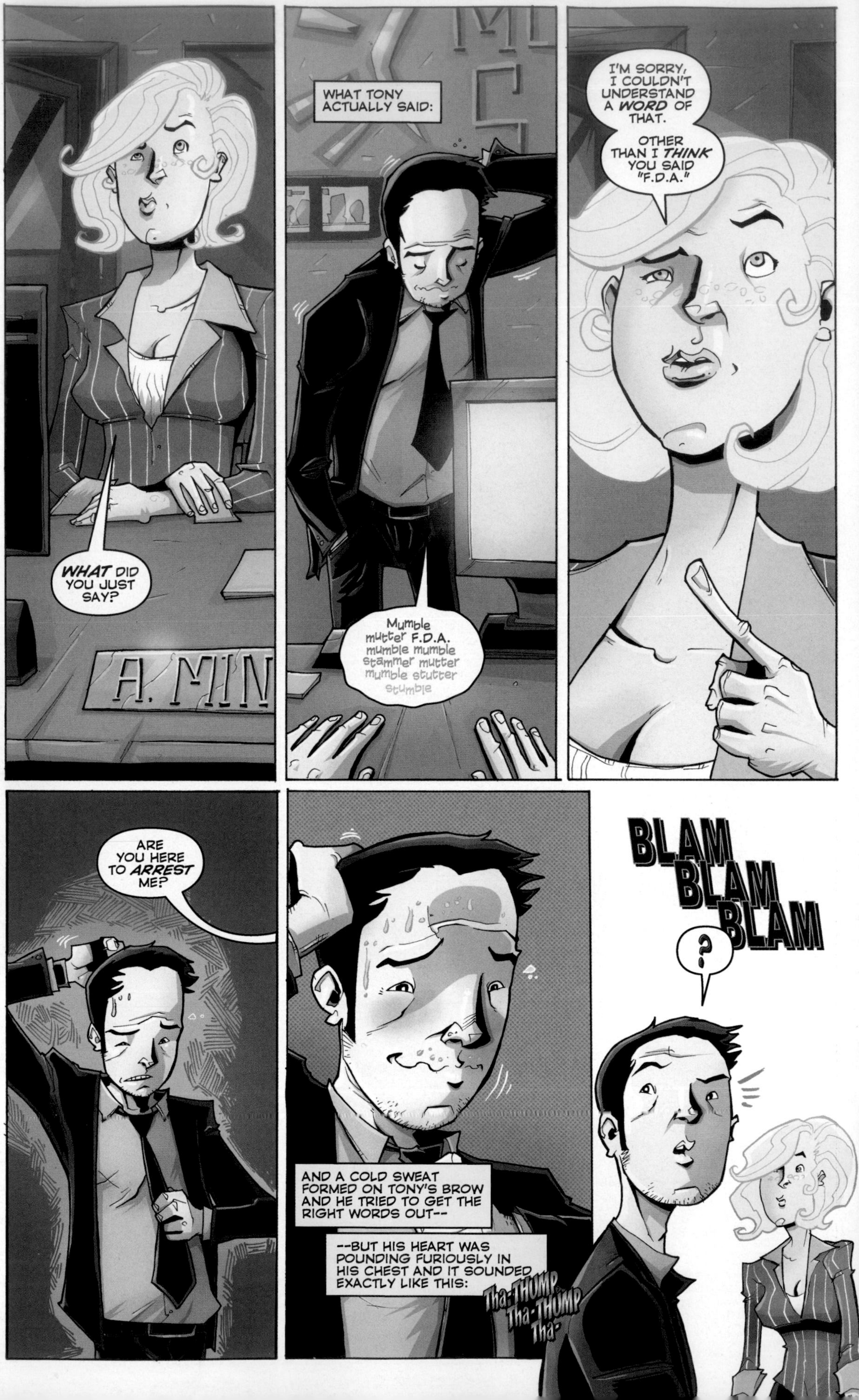
WHAT DID YOU JUST SAY?
A. MIN
WHAT TONY ACTUALLY SAID:
Mumble mutter F.D.A. mumble mumble stammer mutter mumble stutter stumble
I'M SORRY, I COULDN'T UNDERSTAND A WORD OF THAT.
OTHER THAN I THINK YOU SAID "F.D.A."
ARE YOU HERE TO ARREST ME?
AND A COLD SWEAT FORMED ON TONY'S BROW AND HE TRIED TO GET THE RIGHT WORDS OUT--
--BUT HIS HEART WAS POUNDING FURIOUSLY IN HIS CHEST AND IT SOUNDED EXACTLY LIKE THIS:
Tha-THUMP Tha-THUMP Tha-
BLAM BLAM BLAM
?

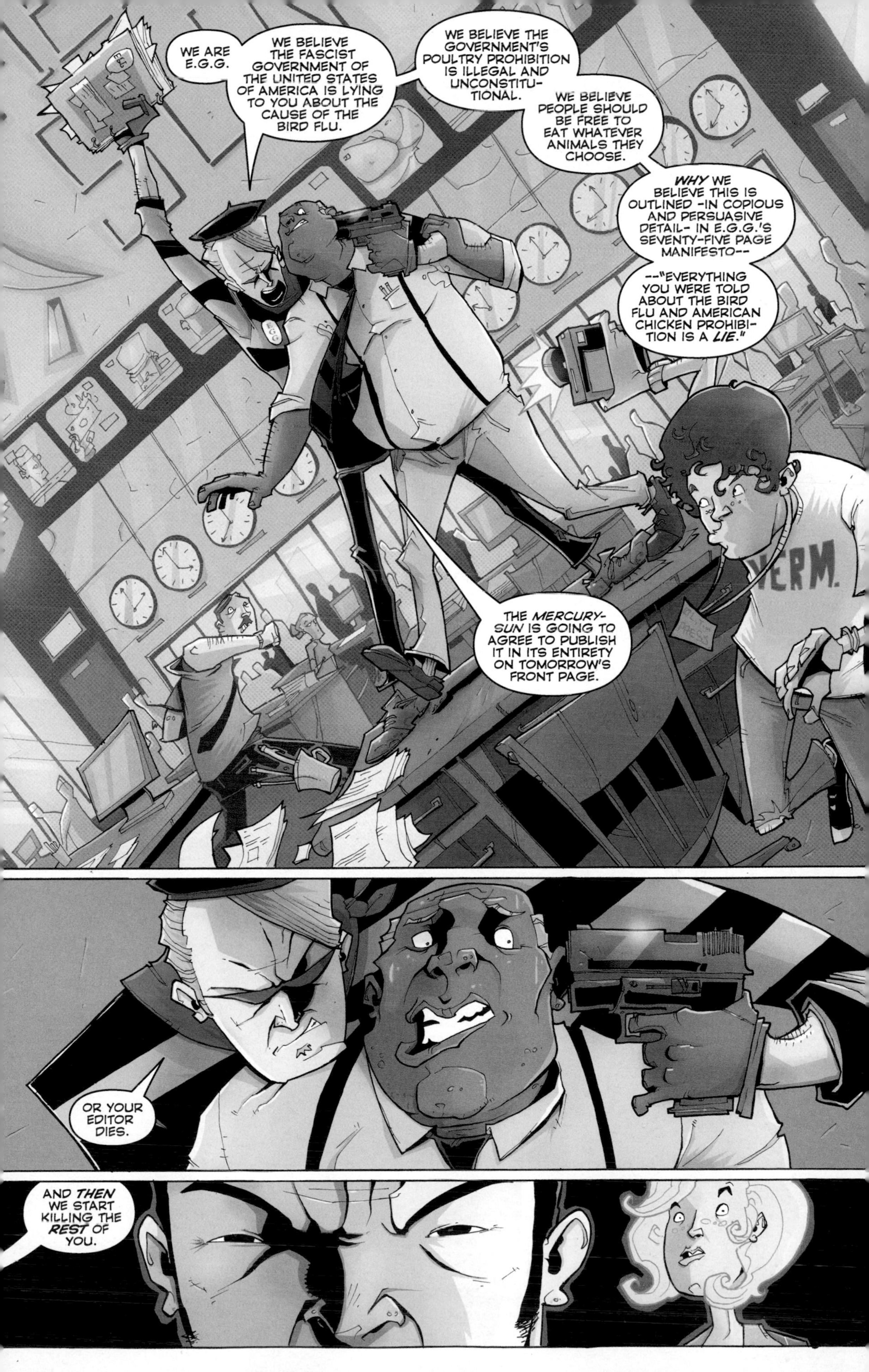

WE ARE E.G.G.
WE BELIEVE THE FASCIST GOVERNMENT OF THE UNITED STATES OF AMERICA IS LYING TO YOU ABOUT THE CAUSE OF THE BIRD FLU.
WE BELIEVE THE GOVERNMENT'S POULTRY PROHIBITION IS ILLEGAL AND UNCONSTITU-TIONAL.
WE BELIEVE PEOPLE SHOULD BE FREE TO EAT WHATEVER ANIMALS THEY CHOOSE.
WHY WE BELIEVE THIS IS OUTLINED -IN COPIOUS AND PERSUASIVE DETAIL- IN E.G.G.'S SEVENTY-FIVE PAGE MANIFESTO--
--"EVERYTHING YOU WERE TOLD ABOUT THE BIRD FLU AND AMERICAN CHICKEN PROHIBI-TION IS A LIE."
THE MERCURY-SUN IS GOING TO AGREE TO PUBLISH IT IN ITS ENTIRETY ON TOMORROW'S FRONT PAGE.
OR YOUR EDITOR DIES.
AND THEN WE START KILLING THE REST OF YOU.

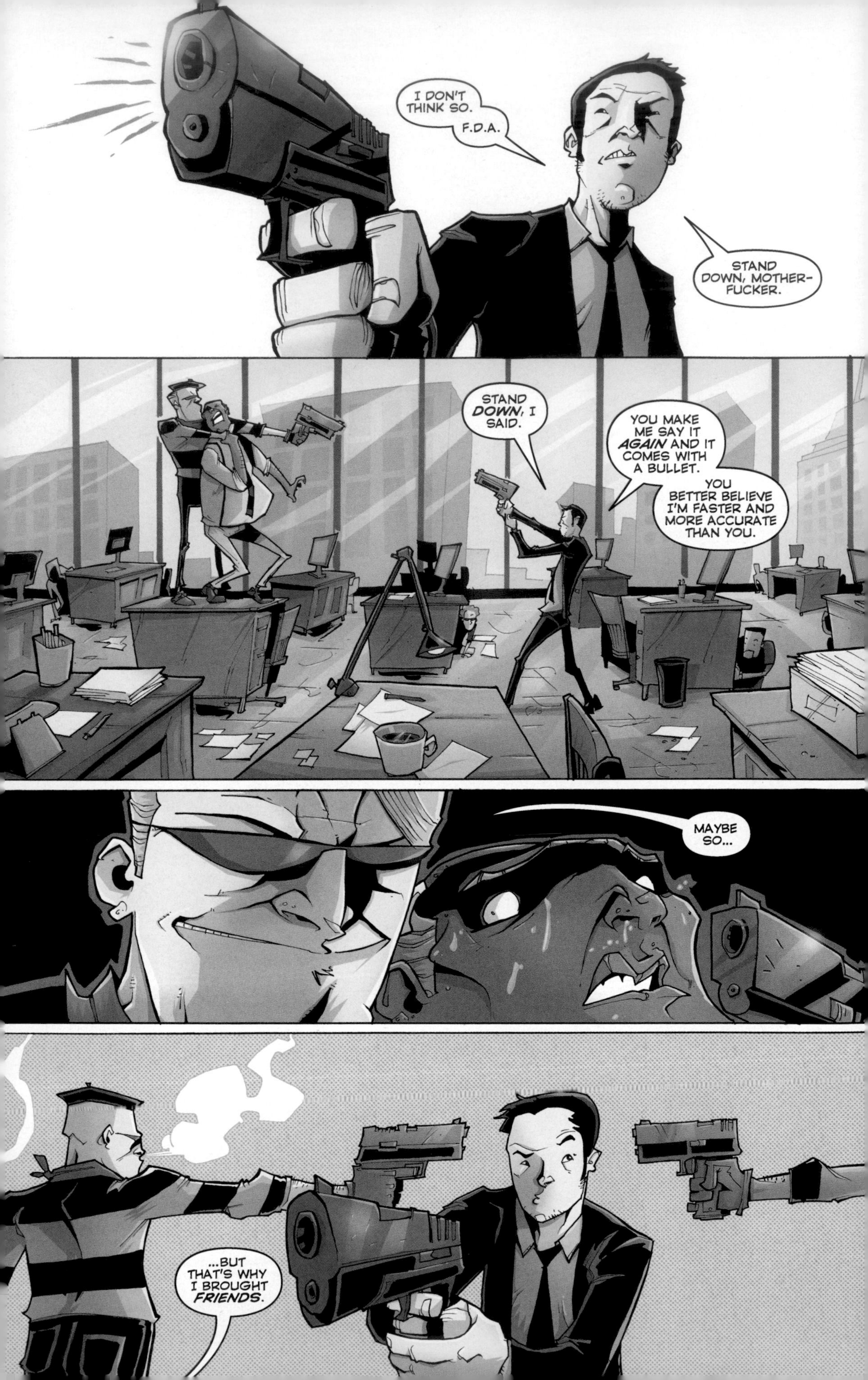

I DON'T THINK SO.
F.D.A.
STAND DOWN, MOTHER-FUCKER.
STAND *DOWN*, I SAID.
YOU MAKE ME SAY IT *AGAIN* AND IT COMES WITH A BULLET.
YOU BETTER BELIEVE I'M FASTER AND MORE ACCURATE THAN YOU.
MAYBE SO...
...BUT THAT'S WHY I BROUGHT *FRIENDS*.

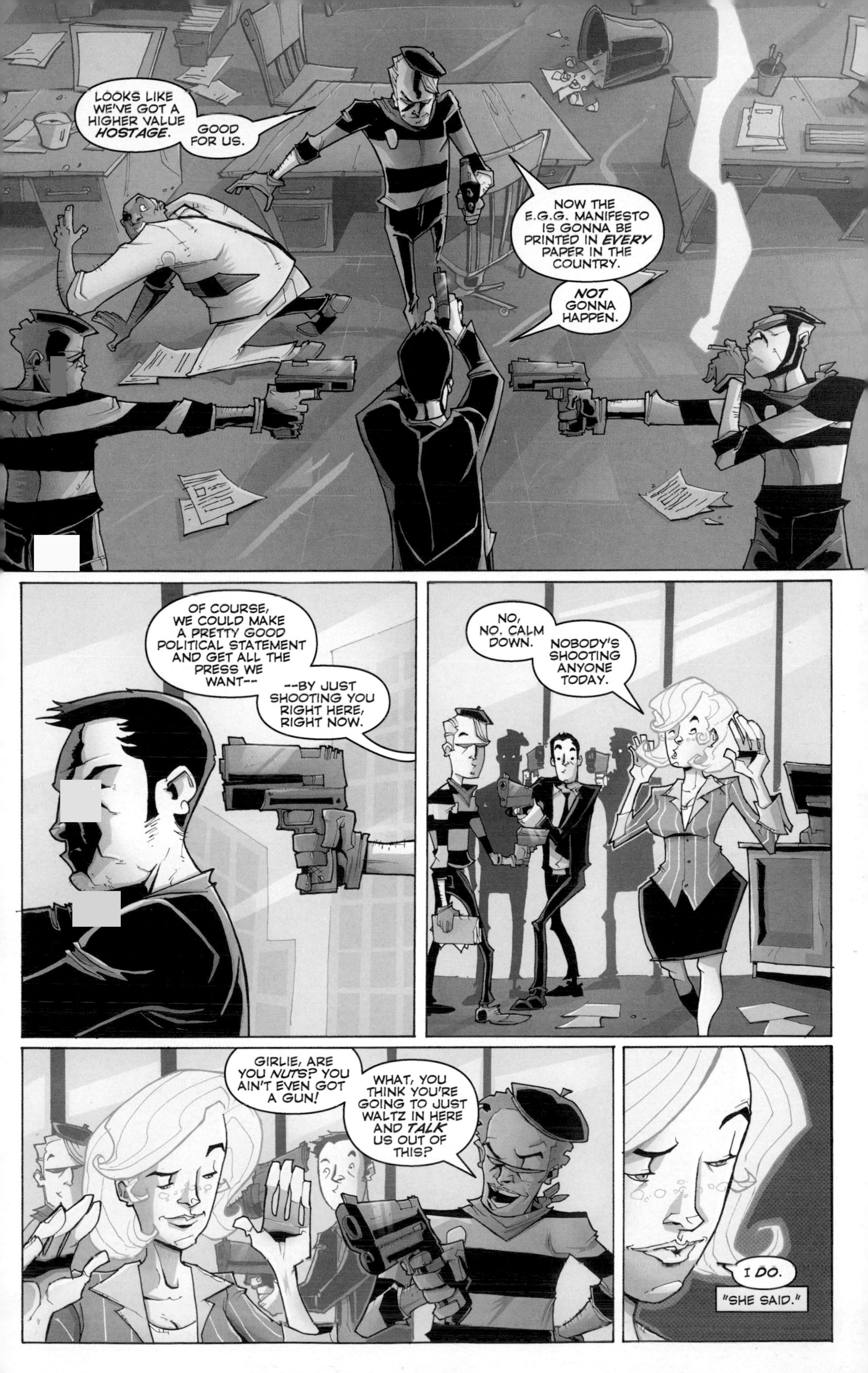
LOOKS LIKE WE'VE GOT A HIGHER VALUE *HOSTAGE*.
GOOD FOR US.
NOW THE E.G.G. MANIFESTO IS GONNA BE PRINTED IN *EVERY* PAPER IN THE COUNTRY.
NOT GONNA HAPPEN.
OF COURSE, WE COULD MAKE A PRETTY GOOD POLITICAL STATEMENT AND GET ALL THE PRESS WE WANT--
--BY JUST SHOOTING YOU RIGHT HERE, RIGHT NOW.
NO, NO. CALM DOWN.
NOBODY'S SHOOTING ANYONE TODAY.
GIRLIE, ARE YOU *NUTS*? YOU AIN'T EVEN GOT A GUN!
WHAT, YOU THINK YOU'RE GOING TO JUST WALTZ IN HERE AND *TALK* US OUT OF THIS?
I *DO*.
"SHE SAID."

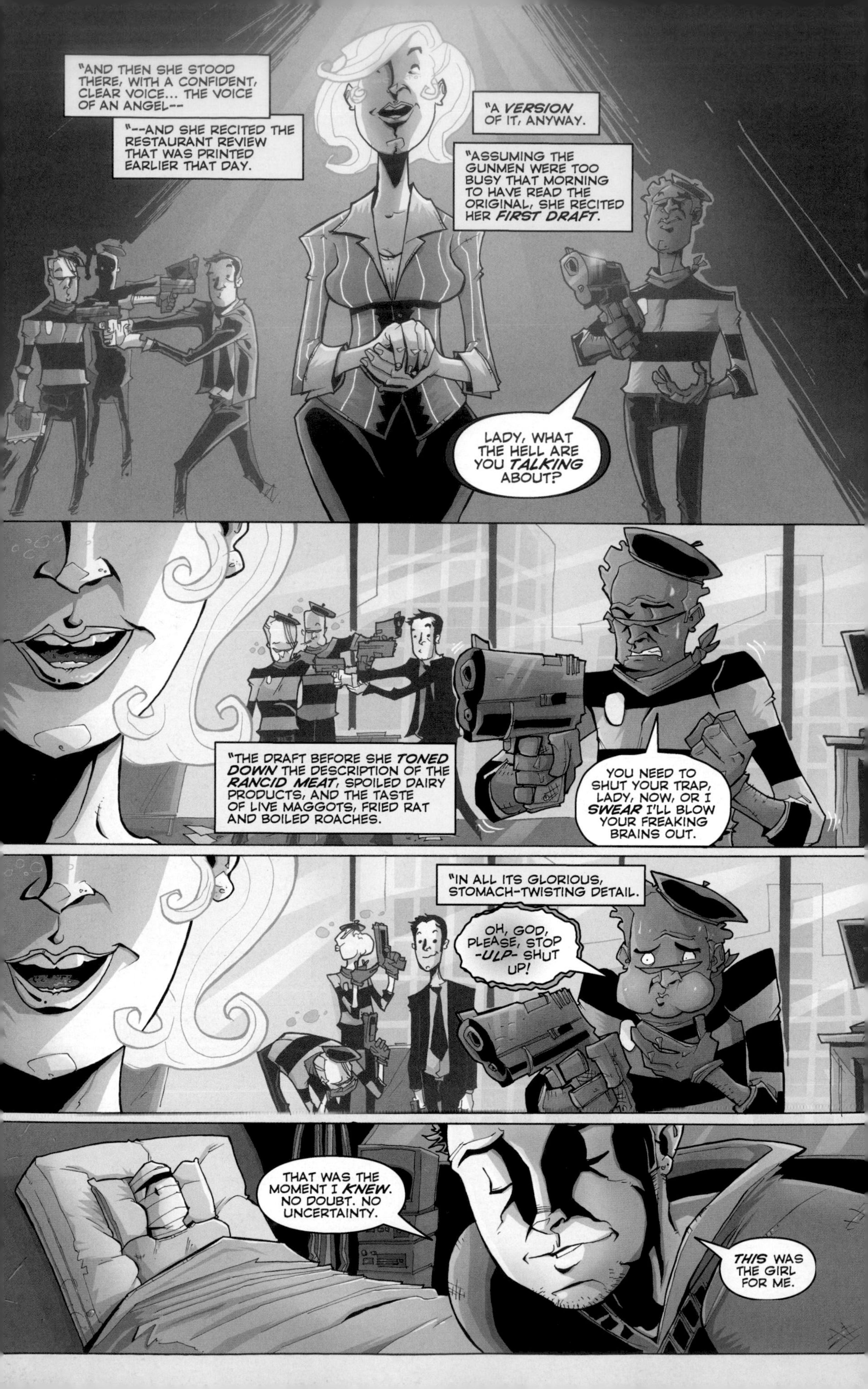
"AND THEN SHE STOOD THERE, WITH A CONFIDENT, CLEAR VOICE... THE VOICE OF AN ANGEL--
"--AND SHE RECITED THE RESTAURANT REVIEW THAT WAS PRINTED EARLIER THAT DAY.
"A VERSION OF IT, ANYWAY.
"ASSUMING THE GUNMEN WERE TOO BUSY THAT MORNING TO HAVE READ THE ORIGINAL, SHE RECITED HER FIRST DRAFT.
LADY, WHAT THE HELL ARE YOU TALKING ABOUT?
"THE DRAFT BEFORE SHE TONED DOWN THE DESCRIPTION OF THE RANCID MEAT, SPOILED DAIRY PRODUCTS, AND THE TASTE OF LIVE MAGGOTS, FRIED RAT AND BOILED ROACHES.
YOU NEED TO SHUT YOUR TRAP, LADY, NOW, OR I SWEAR I'LL BLOW YOUR FREAKING BRAINS OUT.
"IN ALL ITS GLORIOUS, STOMACH-TWISTING DETAIL.
OH, GOD, PLEASE, STOP -ULP- SHUT UP!
THAT WAS THE MOMENT I KNEW. NO DOUBT. NO UNCERTAINTY.
THIS WAS THE GIRL FOR ME.

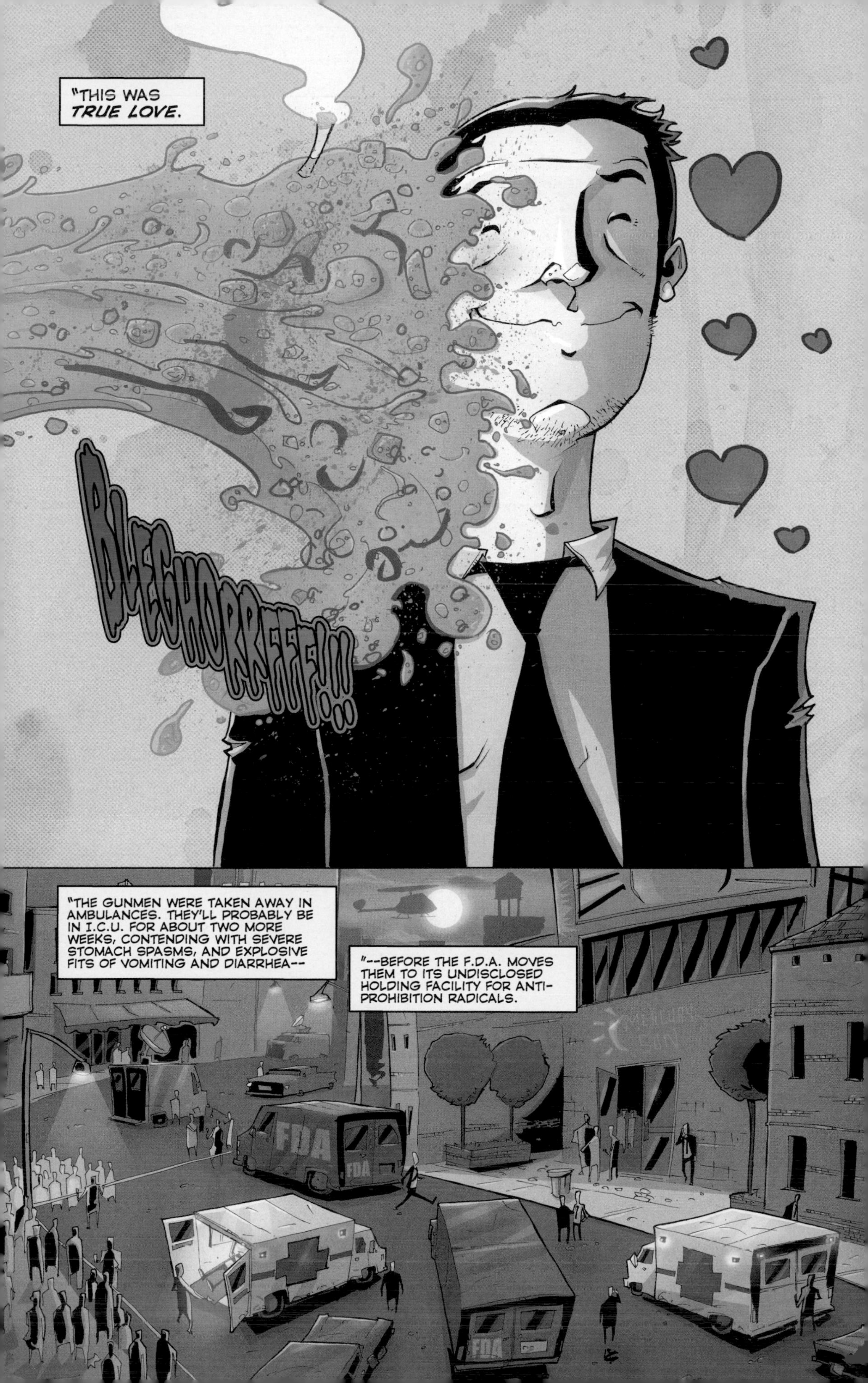
"THIS WAS *TRUE LOVE.*
BLEGHORRFFF!!!
"THE GUNMEN WERE TAKEN AWAY IN AMBULANCES. THEY'LL PROBABLY BE IN I.C.U. FOR ABOUT TWO MORE WEEKS, CONTENDING WITH SEVERE STOMACH SPASMS, AND EXPLOSIVE FITS OF VOMITING AND DIARRHEA--
"--BEFORE THE F.D.A. MOVES THEM TO ITS UNDISCLOSED HOLDING FACILITY FOR ANTI-PROHIBITION RADICALS.
FDA
FDA
FDA

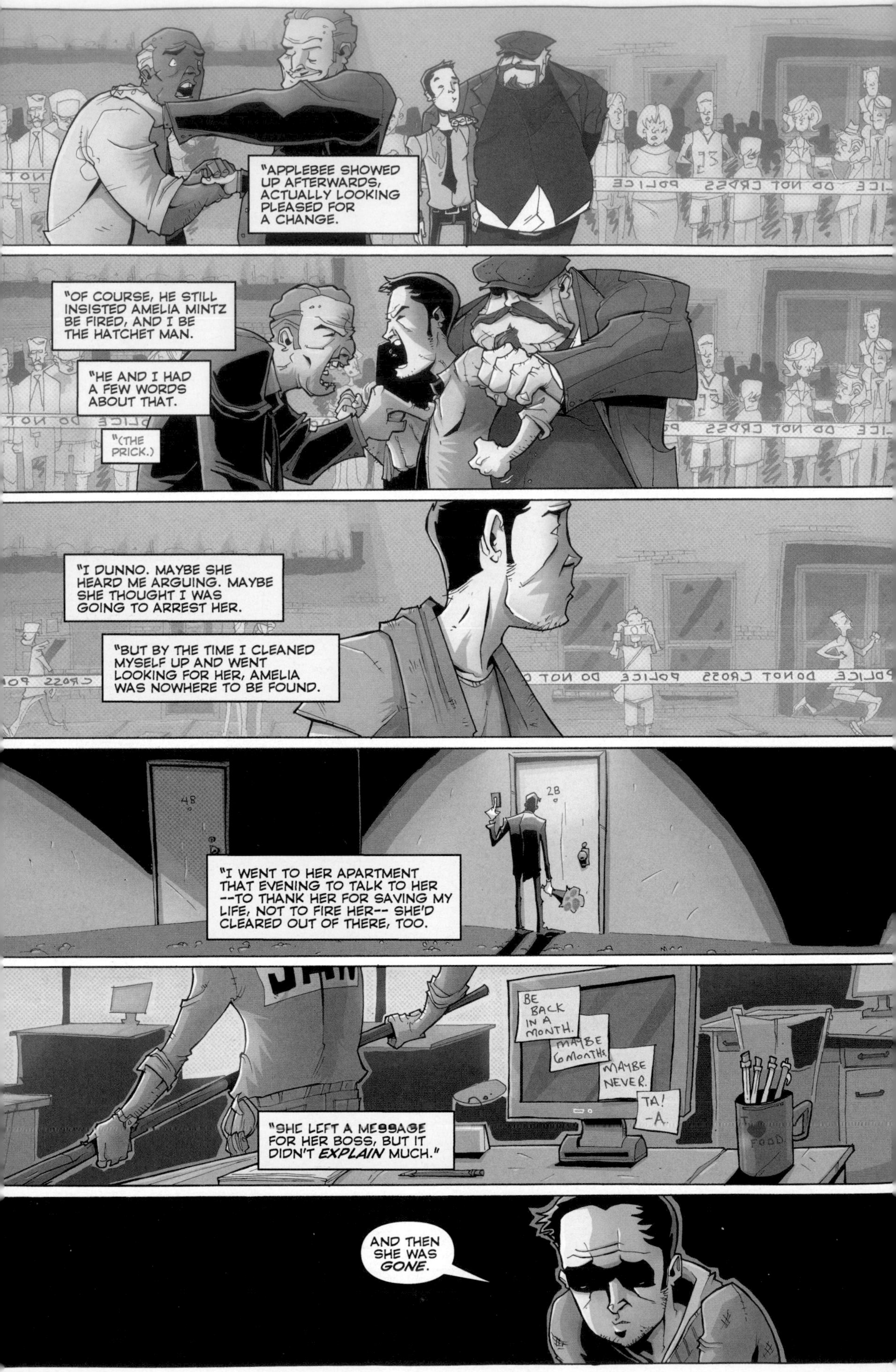
"APPLEBEE SHOWED UP AFTERWARDS, ACTUALLY LOOKING PLEASED FOR A CHANGE.
POLICE DO NOT CROSS
"OF COURSE, HE STILL INSISTED AMELIA MINTZ BE FIRED, AND I BE THE HATCHET MAN.
"HE AND I HAD A FEW WORDS ABOUT THAT.
"(THE PRICK.)
"I DUNNO. MAYBE SHE HEARD ME ARGUING. MAYBE SHE THOUGHT I WAS GOING TO ARREST HER.
"BUT BY THE TIME I CLEANED MYSELF UP AND WENT LOOKING FOR HER, AMELIA WAS NOWHERE TO BE FOUND.
4B
2B
"I WENT TO HER APARTMENT THAT EVENING TO TALK TO HER --TO THANK HER FOR SAVING MY LIFE, NOT TO FIRE HER-- SHE'D CLEARED OUT OF THERE, TOO.
BE BACK IN A MONTH.
MAYBE 6 MONTHS.
MAYBE NEVER.
TA! -A.
"SHE LEFT A MESSAGE FOR HER BOSS, BUT IT DIDN'T *EXPLAIN* MUCH."
AND THEN SHE WAS *GONE*.

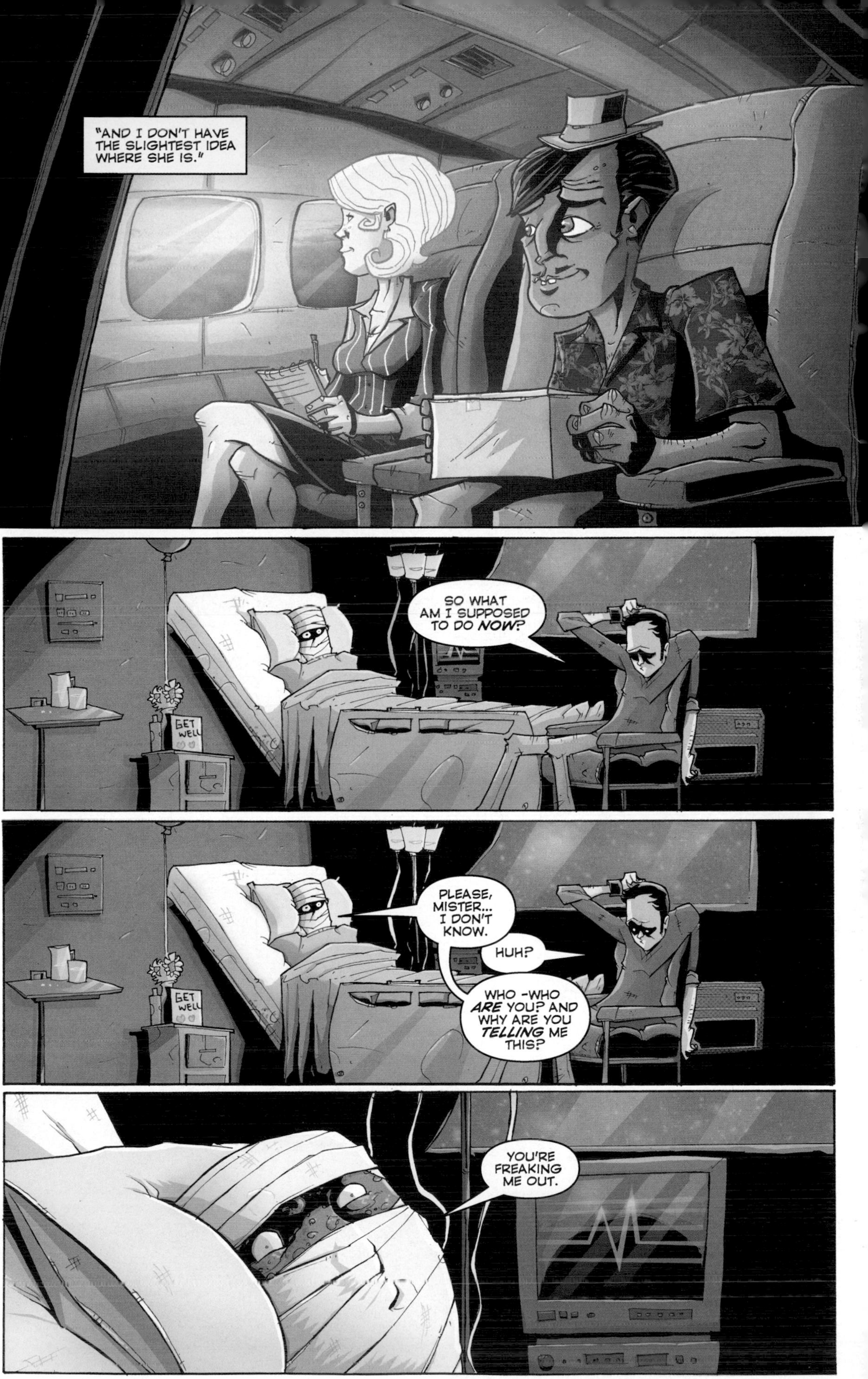
"AND I DON'T HAVE THE SLIGHTEST IDEA WHERE SHE IS."
SO WHAT AM I SUPPOSED TO DO *NOW*?
GET WELL
PLEASE, MISTER... I DON'T KNOW.
HUH?
WHO -WHO *ARE* YOU? AND WHY ARE YOU *TELLING* ME THIS?
GET WELL
YOU'RE FREAKING ME OUT.

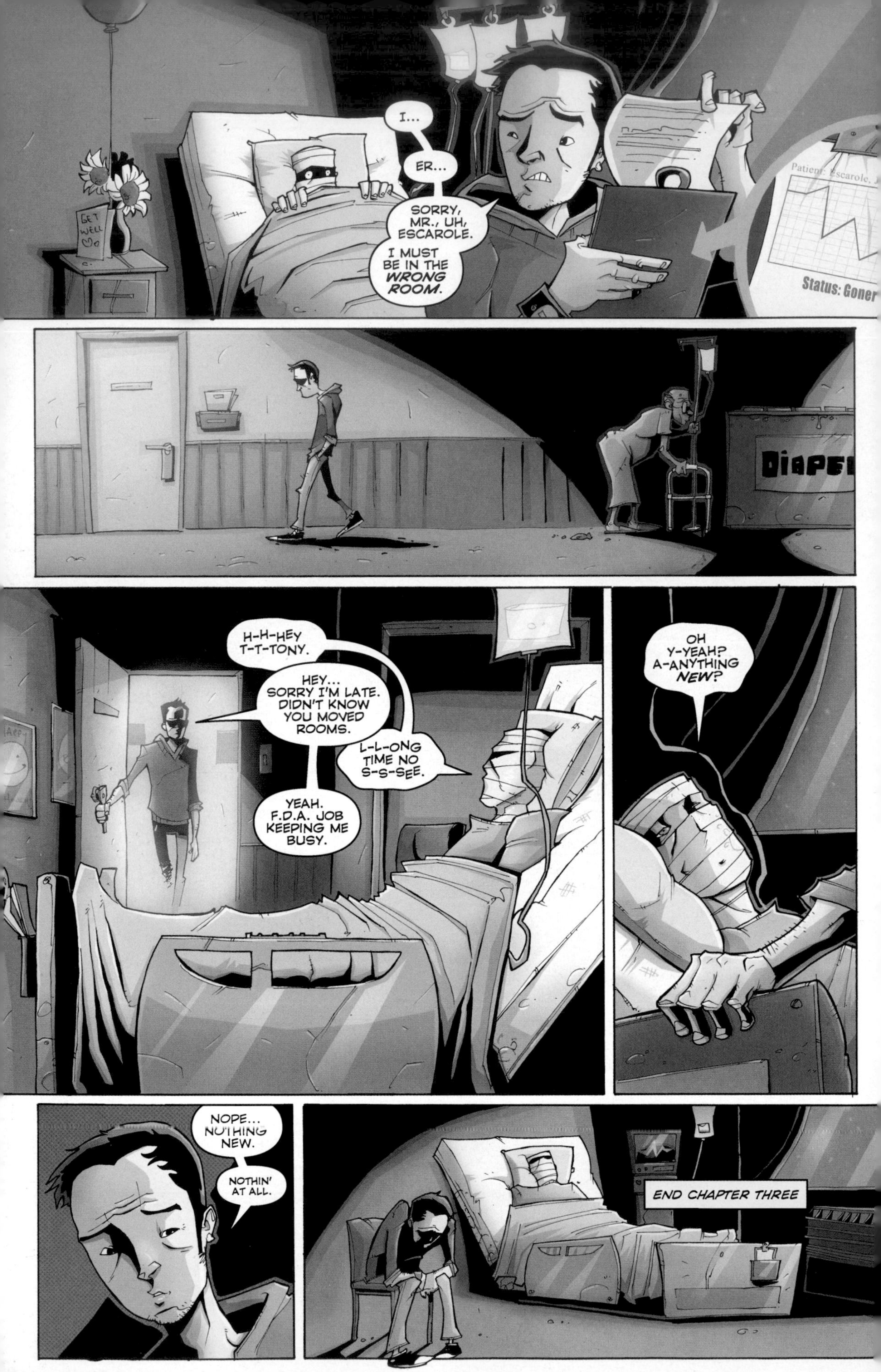
I...
ER...
SORRY, MR., UH, ESCAROLE.
I MUST BE IN THE WRONG ROOM.
Patient: Escarole,
Status: Goner
GET WELL
DIAPE
H-H-HEY T-T-TONY.
HEY... SORRY I'M LATE. DIDN'T KNOW YOU MOVED ROOMS.
L-L-ONG TIME NO S-S-SEE.
YEAH. F.D.A. JOB KEEPING ME BUSY.
OH Y-YEAH? A-ANYTHING NEW?
NOPE... NOTHING NEW.
NOTHIN' AT ALL.
END CHAPTER THREE

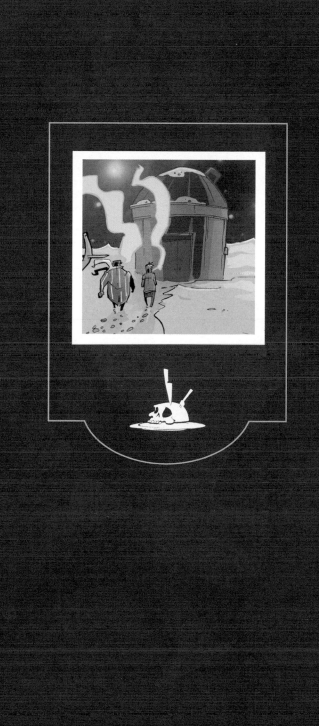

Chapter 4

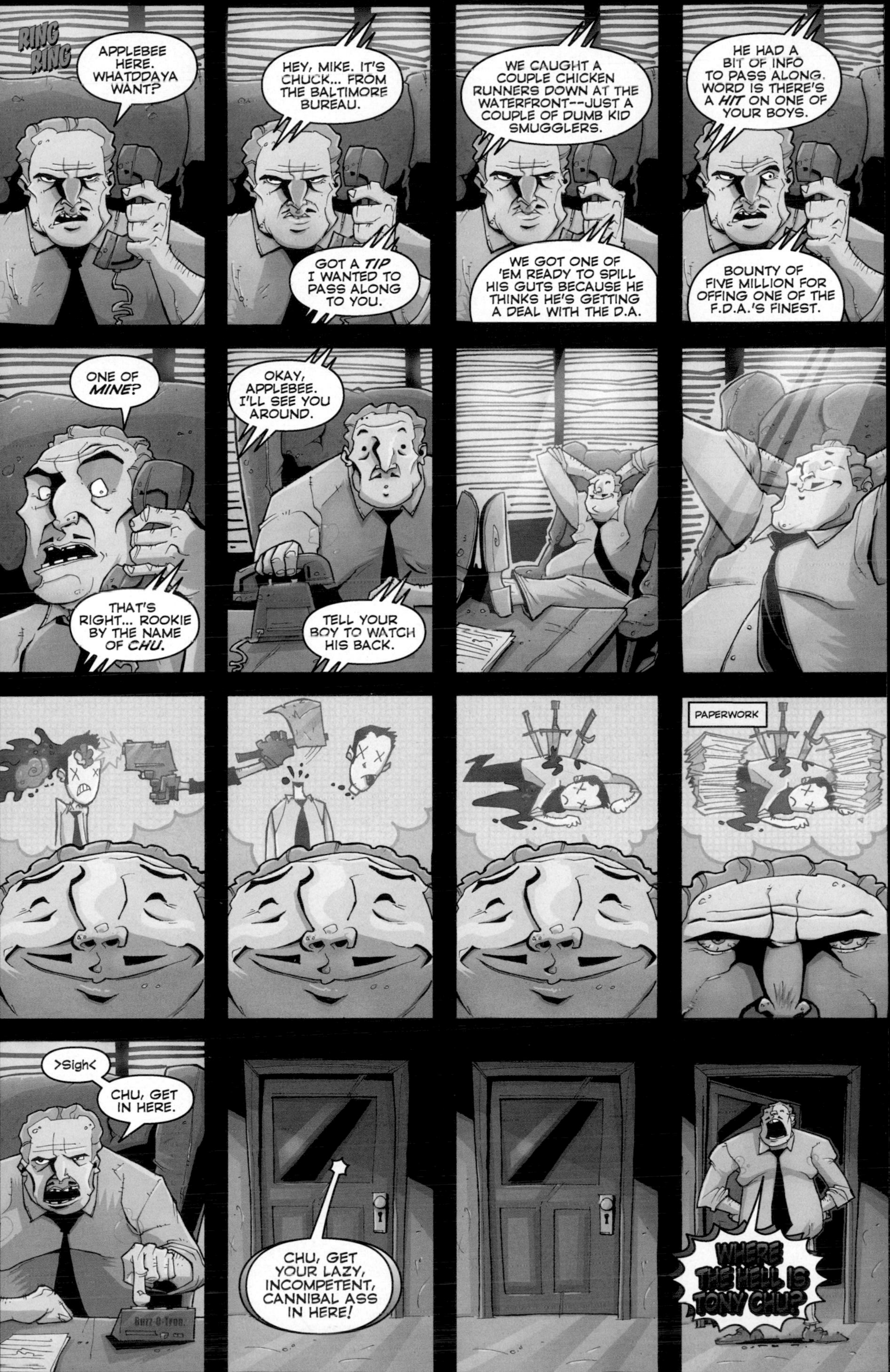
RING RING
APPLEBEE HERE. WHATDDAYA WANT?
HEY, MIKE. IT'S CHUCK... FROM THE BALTIMORE BUREAU.
GOT A TIP I WANTED TO PASS ALONG TO YOU.
WE CAUGHT A COUPLE CHICKEN RUNNERS DOWN AT THE WATERFRONT--JUST A COUPLE OF DUMB KID SMUGGLERS.
WE GOT ONE OF 'EM READY TO SPILL HIS GUTS BECAUSE HE THINKS HE'S GETTING A DEAL WITH THE D.A.
HE HAD A BIT OF INFO TO PASS ALONG. WORD IS THERE'S A HIT ON ONE OF YOUR BOYS.
BOUNTY OF FIVE MILLION FOR OFFING ONE OF THE F.D.A.'S FINEST.
ONE OF MINE?
THAT'S RIGHT... ROOKIE BY THE NAME OF CHU.
OKAY, APPLEBEE. I'LL SEE YOU AROUND.
TELL YOUR BOY TO WATCH HIS BACK.
PAPERWORK
>Sigh<
CHU, GET IN HERE.
CHU, GET YOUR LAZY, INCOMPETENT, CANNIBAL ASS IN HERE!
WHERE THE HELL IS TONY CHU?

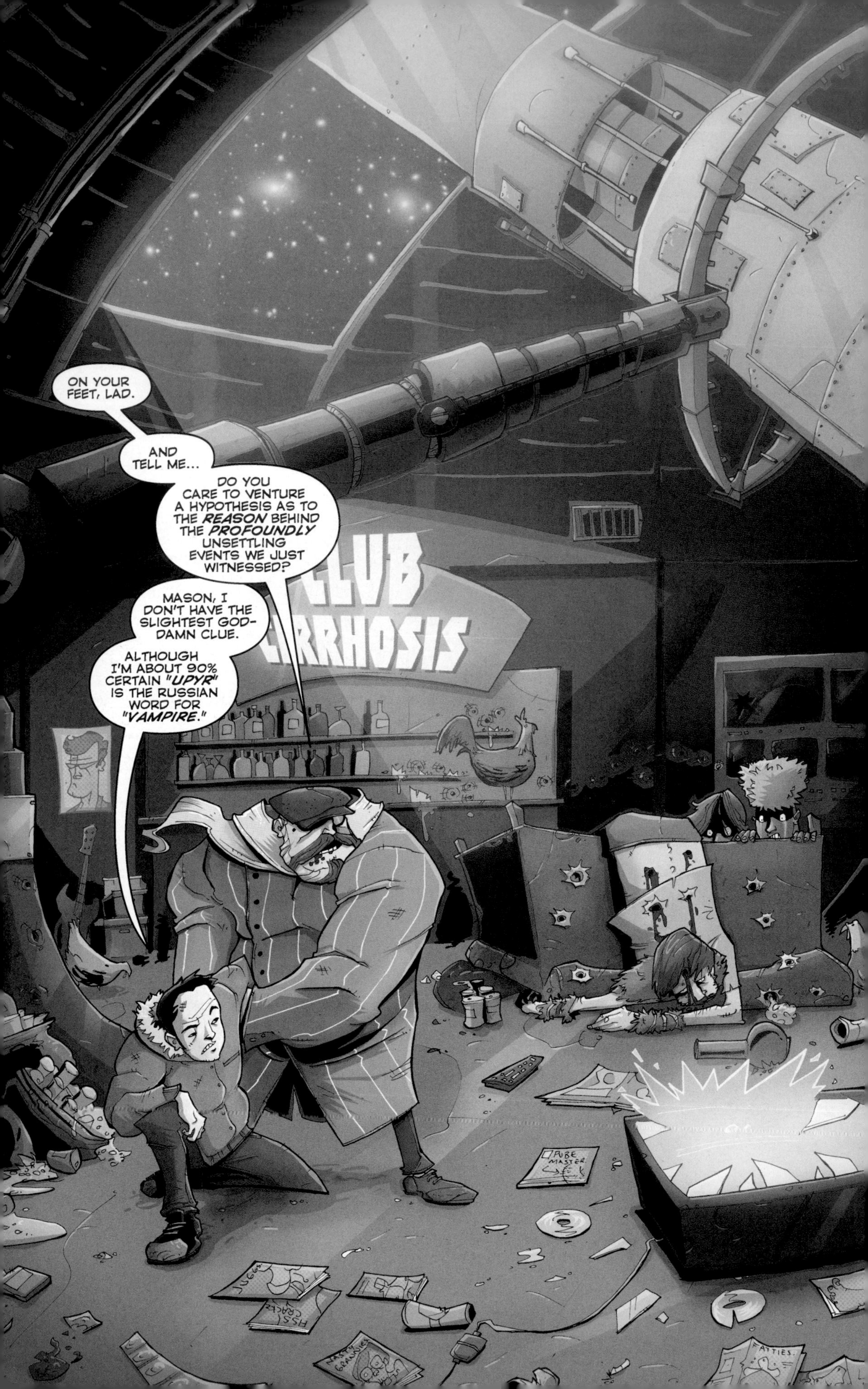
ON YOUR FEET, LAD.
AND TELL ME...
DO YOU CARE TO VENTURE A HYPOTHESIS AS TO THE *REASON* BEHIND THE *PROFOUNDLY* UNSETTLING EVENTS WE JUST WITNESSED?
MASON, I DON'T HAVE THE SLIGHTEST GOD-DAMN CLUE.
ALTHOUGH I'M ABOUT 90% CERTAIN *"UPYR"* IS THE RUSSIAN WORD FOR *"VAMPIRE."*

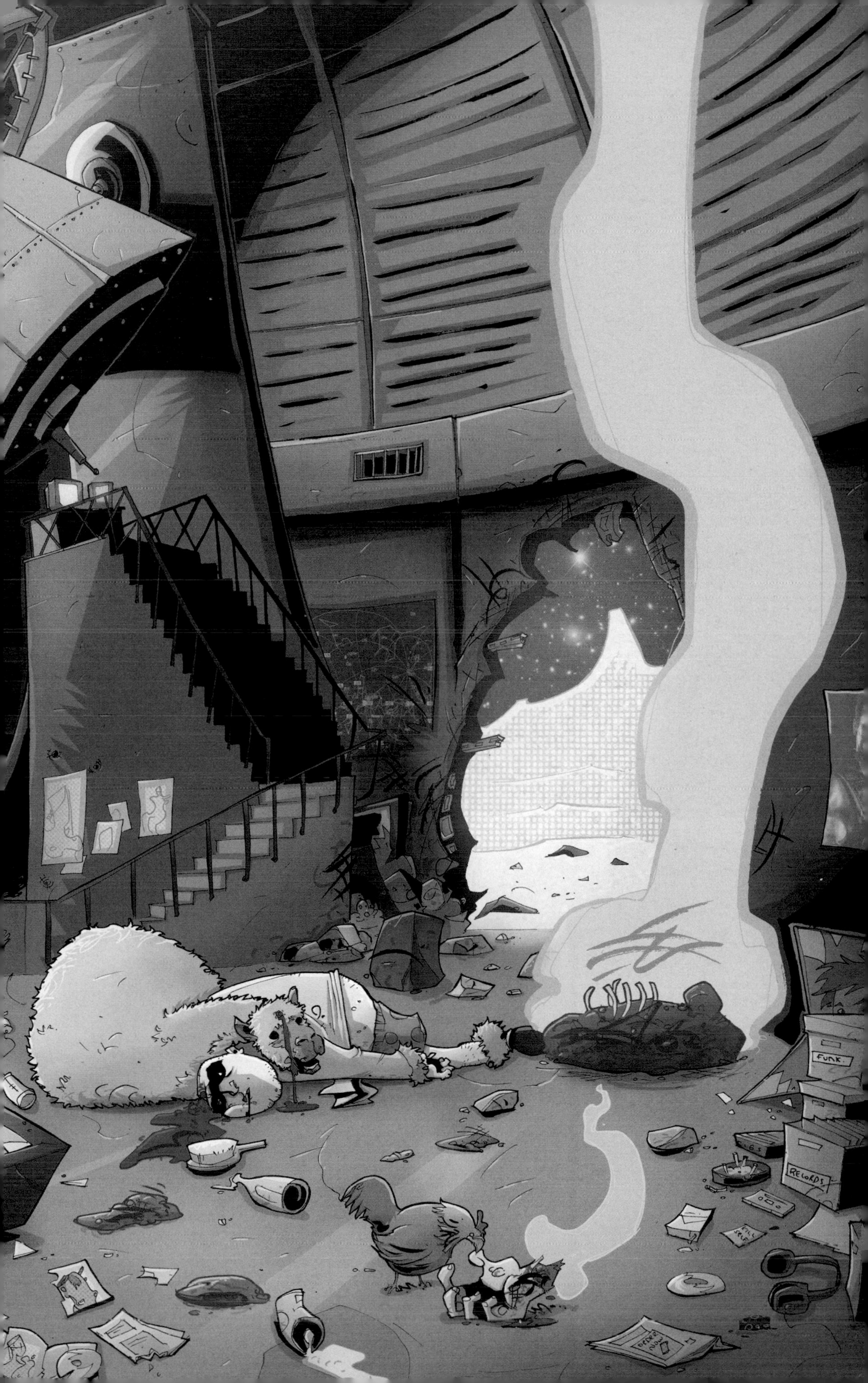
FUNK.
RECORDS

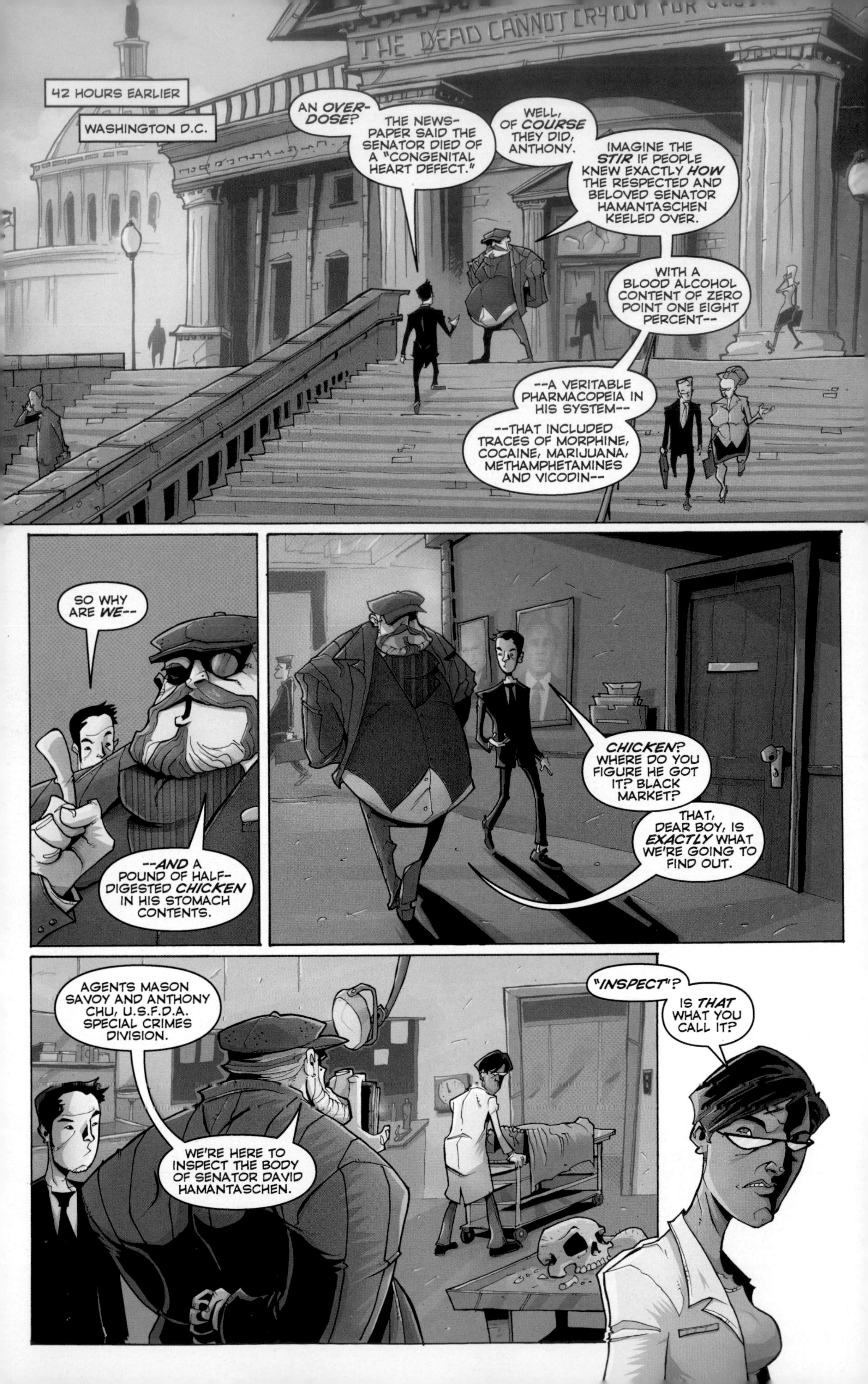
THE DEAD CANNOT CRY OUT FOR
42 HOURS EARLIER
WASHINGTON D.C.
AN OVER-DOSE?
THE NEWS-PAPER SAID THE SENATOR DIED OF A "CONGENITAL HEART DEFECT."
WELL, OF COURSE THEY DID, ANTHONY.
IMAGINE THE STIR IF PEOPLE KNEW EXACTLY HOW THE RESPECTED AND BELOVED SENATOR HAMANTASCHEN KEELED OVER.
WITH A BLOOD ALCOHOL CONTENT OF ZERO POINT ONE EIGHT PERCENT--
--A VERITABLE PHARMACOPEIA IN HIS SYSTEM--
--THAT INCLUDED TRACES OF MORPHINE, COCAINE, MARIJUANA, METHAMPHETAMINES AND VICODIN--
SO WHY ARE WE--
--AND A POUND OF HALF-DIGESTED CHICKEN IN HIS STOMACH CONTENTS.
CHICKEN? WHERE DO YOU FIGURE HE GOT IT? BLACK MARKET?
THAT, DEAR BOY, IS EXACTLY WHAT WE'RE GOING TO FIND OUT.
AGENTS MASON SAVOY AND ANTHONY CHU, U.S.F.D.A. SPECIAL CRIMES DIVISION.
WE'RE HERE TO INSPECT THE BODY OF SENATOR DAVID HAMANTASCHEN.
"INSPECT"?
IS THAT WHAT YOU CALL IT?

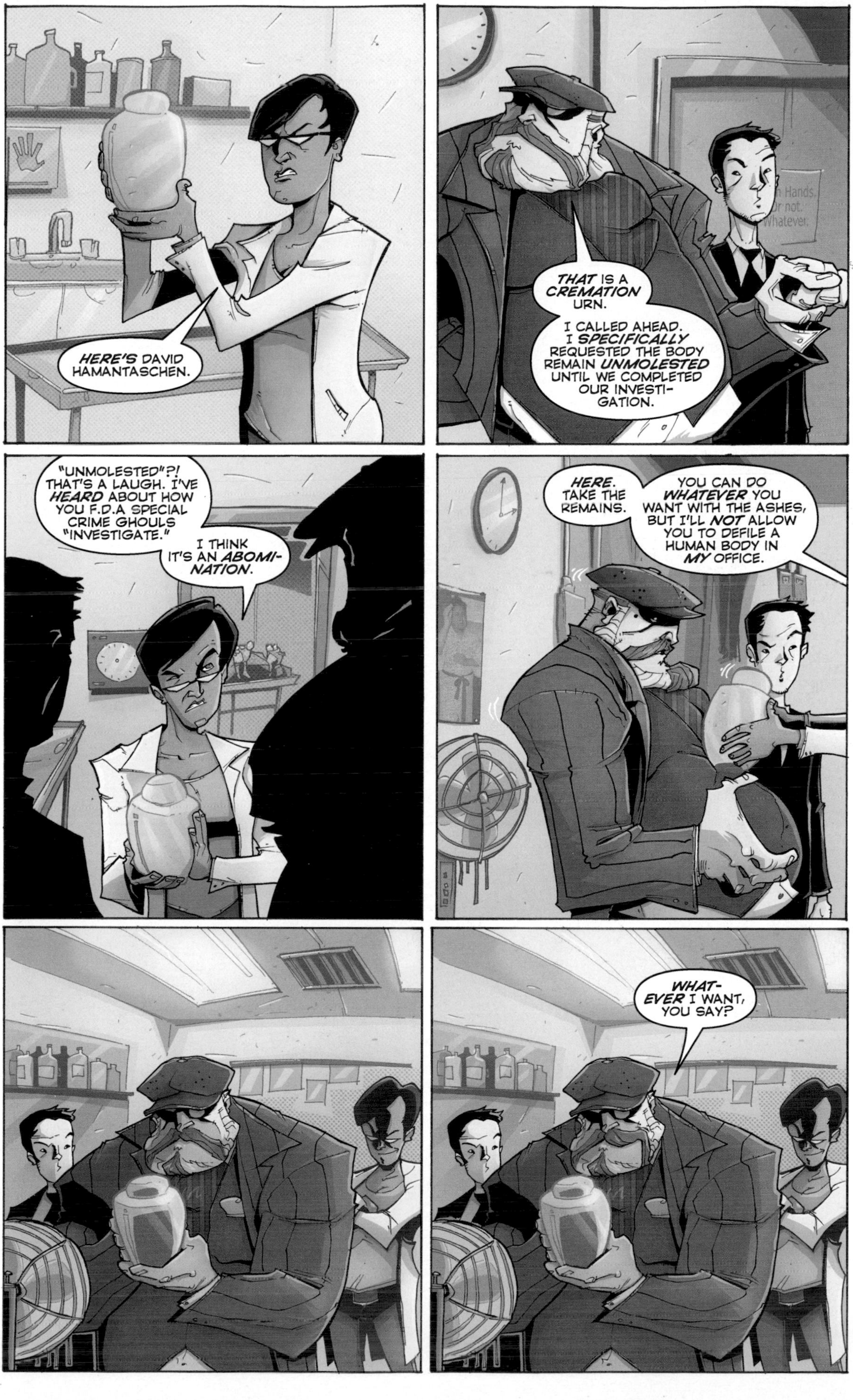
HERE'S DAVID HAMANTASCHEN.
THAT IS A CREMATION URN.
I CALLED AHEAD. I SPECIFICALLY REQUESTED THE BODY REMAIN UNMOLESTED UNTIL WE COMPLETED OUR INVESTI-GATION.
"UNMOLESTED"?! THAT'S A LAUGH. I'VE HEARD ABOUT HOW YOU F.D.A SPECIAL CRIME GHOULS "INVESTIGATE."
I THINK IT'S AN ABOMI-NATION.
HERE. TAKE THE REMAINS.
YOU CAN DO WHATEVER YOU WANT WITH THE ASHES, BUT I'LL NOT ALLOW YOU TO DEFILE A HUMAN BODY IN MY OFFICE.
WHAT-EVER I WANT, YOU SAY?

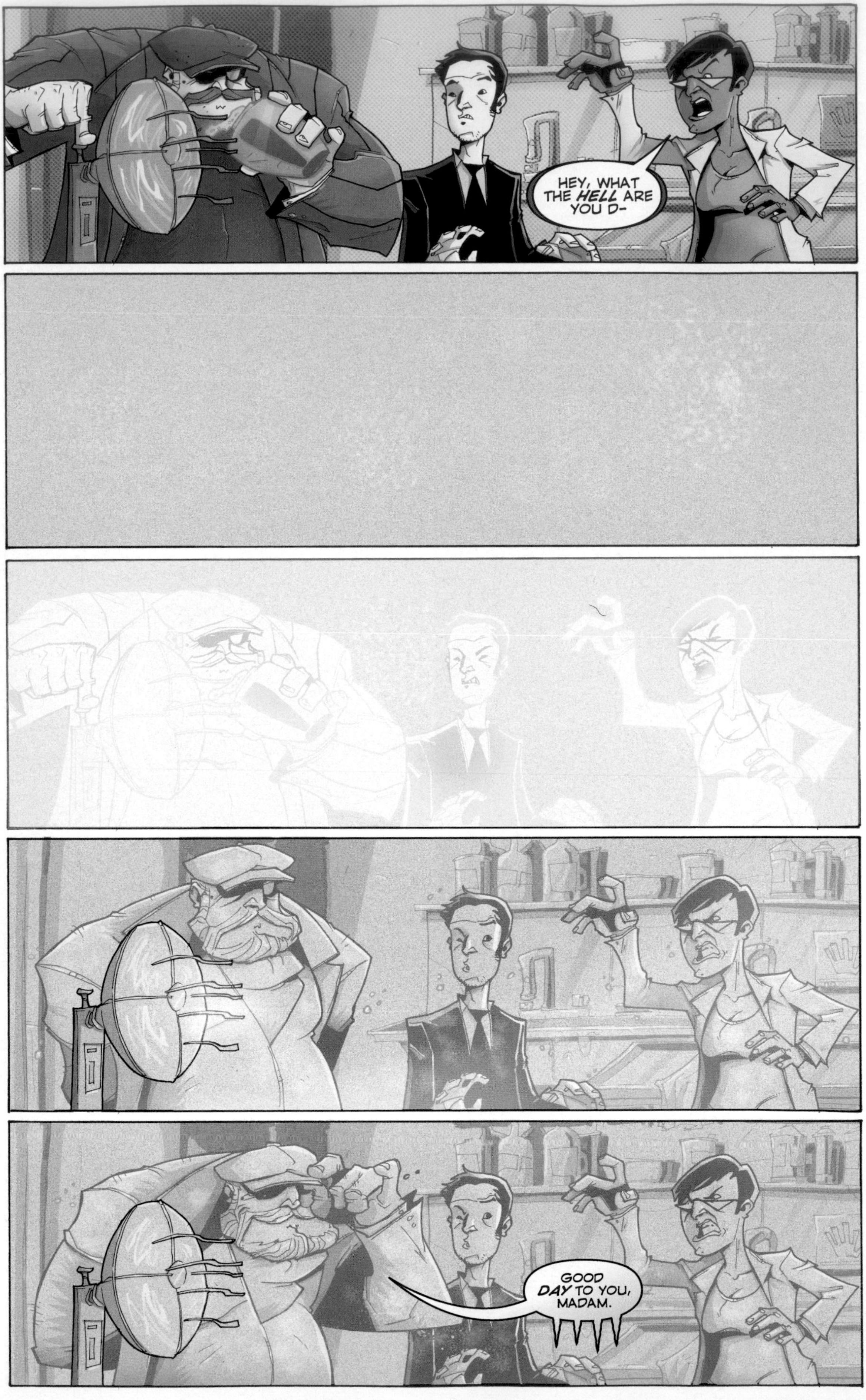
HEY, WHAT THE HELL ARE YOU D-
GOOD DAY TO YOU, MADAM.

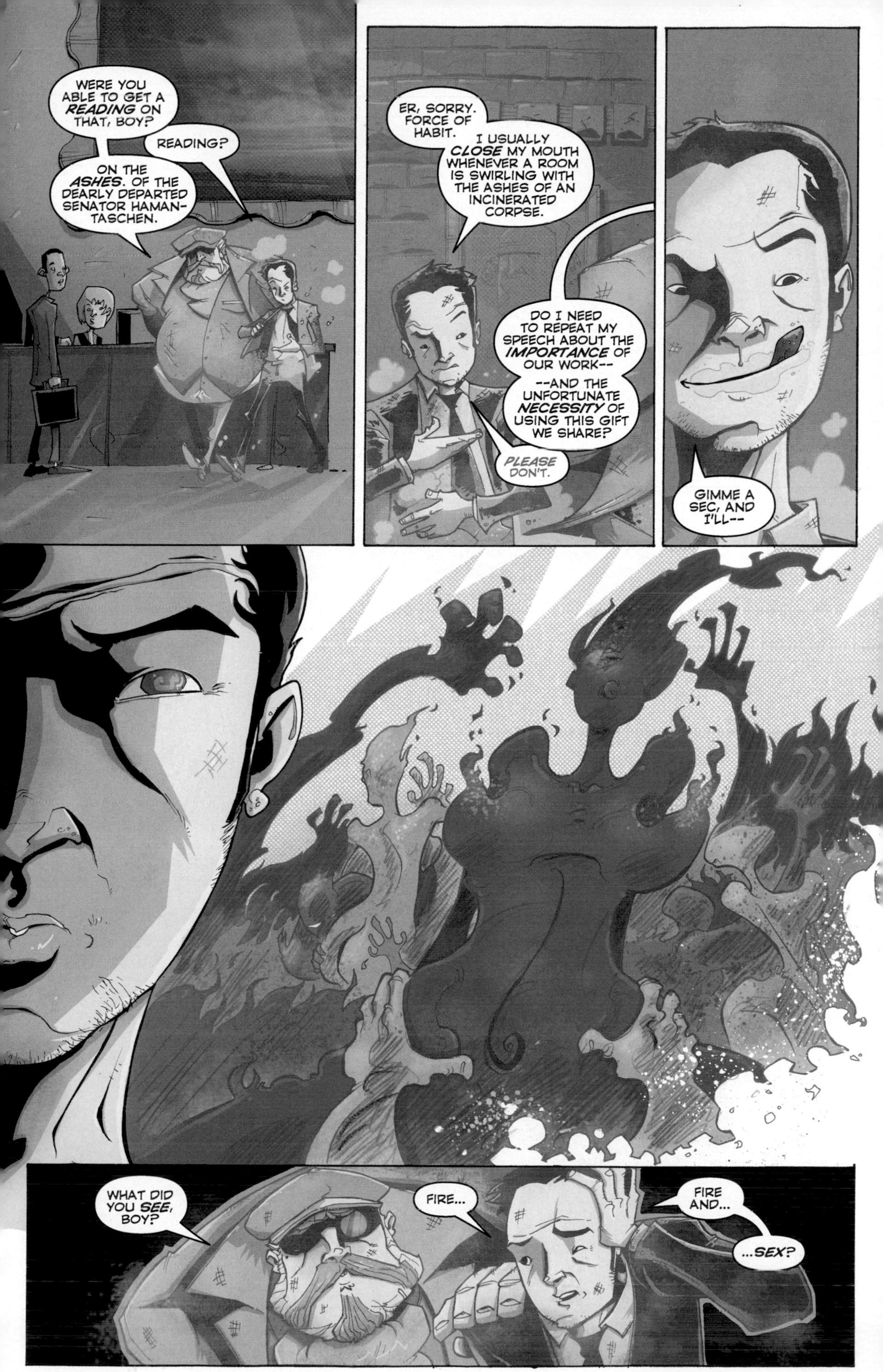
WERE YOU ABLE TO GET A *READING* ON THAT, BOY?
READING?
ON THE *ASHES*. OF THE DEARLY DEPARTED SENATOR HAMAN-TASCHEN.
ER, SORRY. FORCE OF HABIT.
I USUALLY *CLOSE* MY MOUTH WHENEVER A ROOM IS SWIRLING WITH THE ASHES OF AN INCINERATED CORPSE.
DO I NEED TO REPEAT MY SPEECH ABOUT THE *IMPORTANCE* OF OUR WORK--
--AND THE UNFORTUNATE *NECESSITY* OF USING THIS GIFT WE SHARE?
PLEASE DON'T.
GIMME A SEC, AND I'LL--
WHAT DID YOU *SEE*, BOY?
FIRE...
FIRE AND...
...*SEX*?

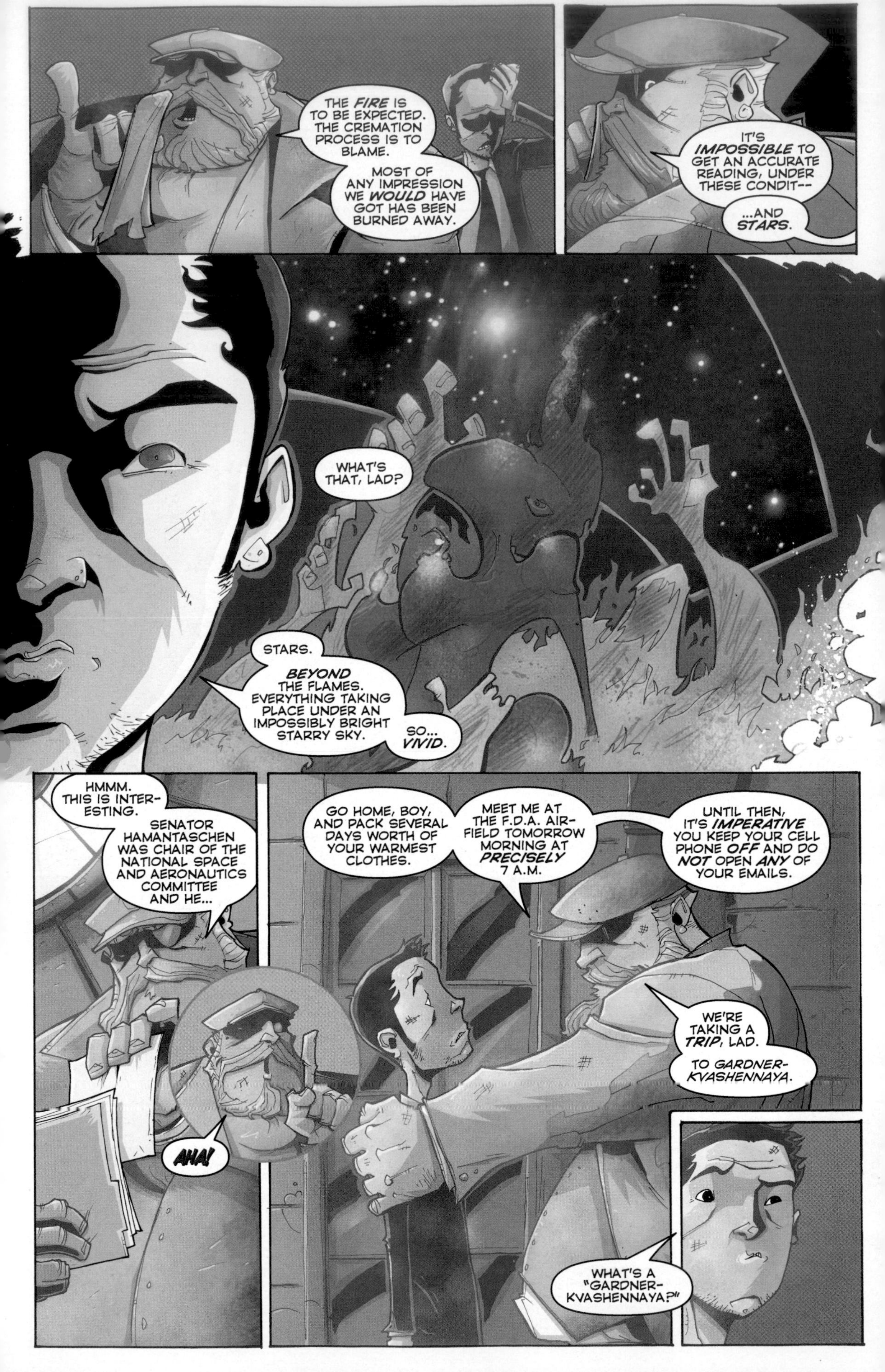
THE FIRE IS TO BE EXPECTED. THE CREMATION PROCESS IS TO BLAME.
MOST OF ANY IMPRESSION WE WOULD HAVE GOT HAS BEEN BURNED AWAY.
IT'S IMPOSSIBLE TO GET AN ACCURATE READING, UNDER THESE CONDIT--
...AND STARS.
WHAT'S THAT, LAD?
STARS.
BEYOND THE FLAMES. EVERYTHING TAKING PLACE UNDER AN IMPOSSIBLY BRIGHT STARRY SKY.
SO... VIVID.
HMMM. THIS IS INTER-ESTING.
SENATOR HAMANTASCHEN WAS CHAIR OF THE NATIONAL SPACE AND AERONAUTICS COMMITTEE AND HE...
AHA!
GO HOME, BOY, AND PACK SEVERAL DAYS WORTH OF YOUR WARMEST CLOTHES.
MEET ME AT THE F.D.A. AIR-FIELD TOMORROW MORNING AT PRECISELY 7 A.M.
UNTIL THEN, IT'S IMPERATIVE YOU KEEP YOUR CELL PHONE OFF AND DO NOT OPEN ANY OF YOUR EMAILS.
WE'RE TAKING A TRIP, LAD.
TO GARDNER-KVASHENNAYA.
WHAT'S A "GARDNER-KVASHENNAYA?"

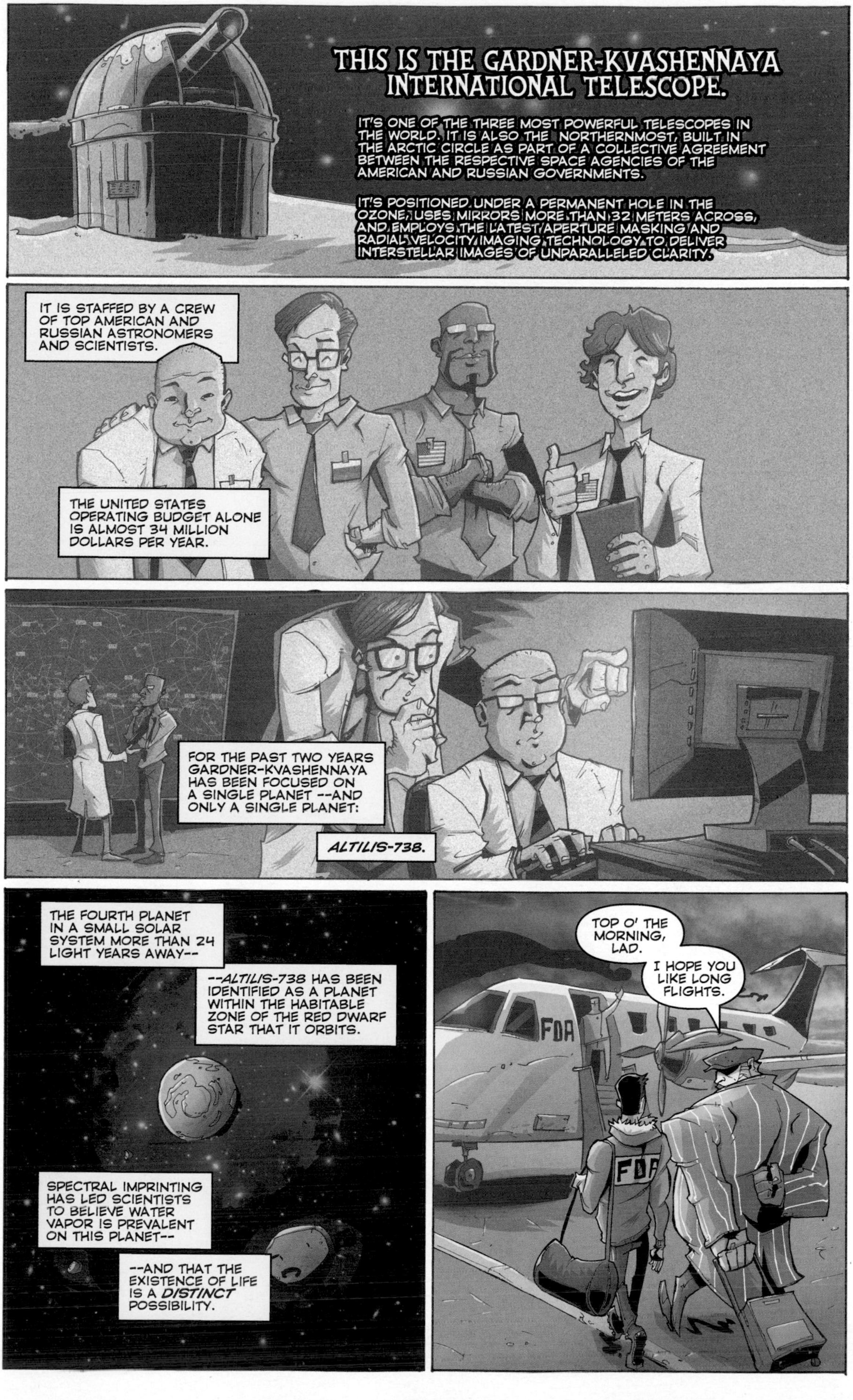
THIS IS THE GARDNER-KVASHENNAYA INTERNATIONAL TELESCOPE.
IT'S ONE OF THE THREE MOST POWERFUL TELESCOPES IN THE WORLD. IT IS ALSO THE NORTHERNMOST, BUILT IN THE ARCTIC CIRCLE AS PART OF A COLLECTIVE AGREEMENT BETWEEN THE RESPECTIVE SPACE AGENCIES OF THE AMERICAN AND RUSSIAN GOVERNMENTS.
IT'S POSITIONED UNDER A PERMANENT HOLE IN THE OZONE, USES MIRRORS MORE THAN 32 METERS ACROSS, AND EMPLOYS THE LATEST APERTURE MASKING AND RADIAL VELOCITY IMAGING TECHNOLOGY TO DELIVER INTERSTELLAR IMAGES OF UNPARALLELED CLARITY.
IT IS STAFFED BY A CREW OF TOP AMERICAN AND RUSSIAN ASTRONOMERS AND SCIENTISTS.
THE UNITED STATES OPERATING BUDGET ALONE IS ALMOST 34 MILLION DOLLARS PER YEAR.
FOR THE PAST TWO YEARS GARDNER-KVASHENNAYA HAS BEEN FOCUSED ON A SINGLE PLANET --AND ONLY A SINGLE PLANET:
ALTILIS-738.
THE FOURTH PLANET IN A SMALL SOLAR SYSTEM MORE THAN 24 LIGHT YEARS AWAY--
--*ALTILIS-738* HAS BEEN IDENTIFIED AS A PLANET WITHIN THE HABITABLE ZONE OF THE RED DWARF STAR THAT IT ORBITS.
SPECTRAL IMPRINTING HAS LED SCIENTISTS TO BELIEVE WATER VAPOR IS PREVALENT ON THIS PLANET--
--AND THAT THE EXISTENCE OF LIFE IS A *DISTINCT* POSSIBILITY.
FDA
TOP O' THE MORNING, LAD.
I HOPE YOU LIKE LONG FLIGHTS.
FDA

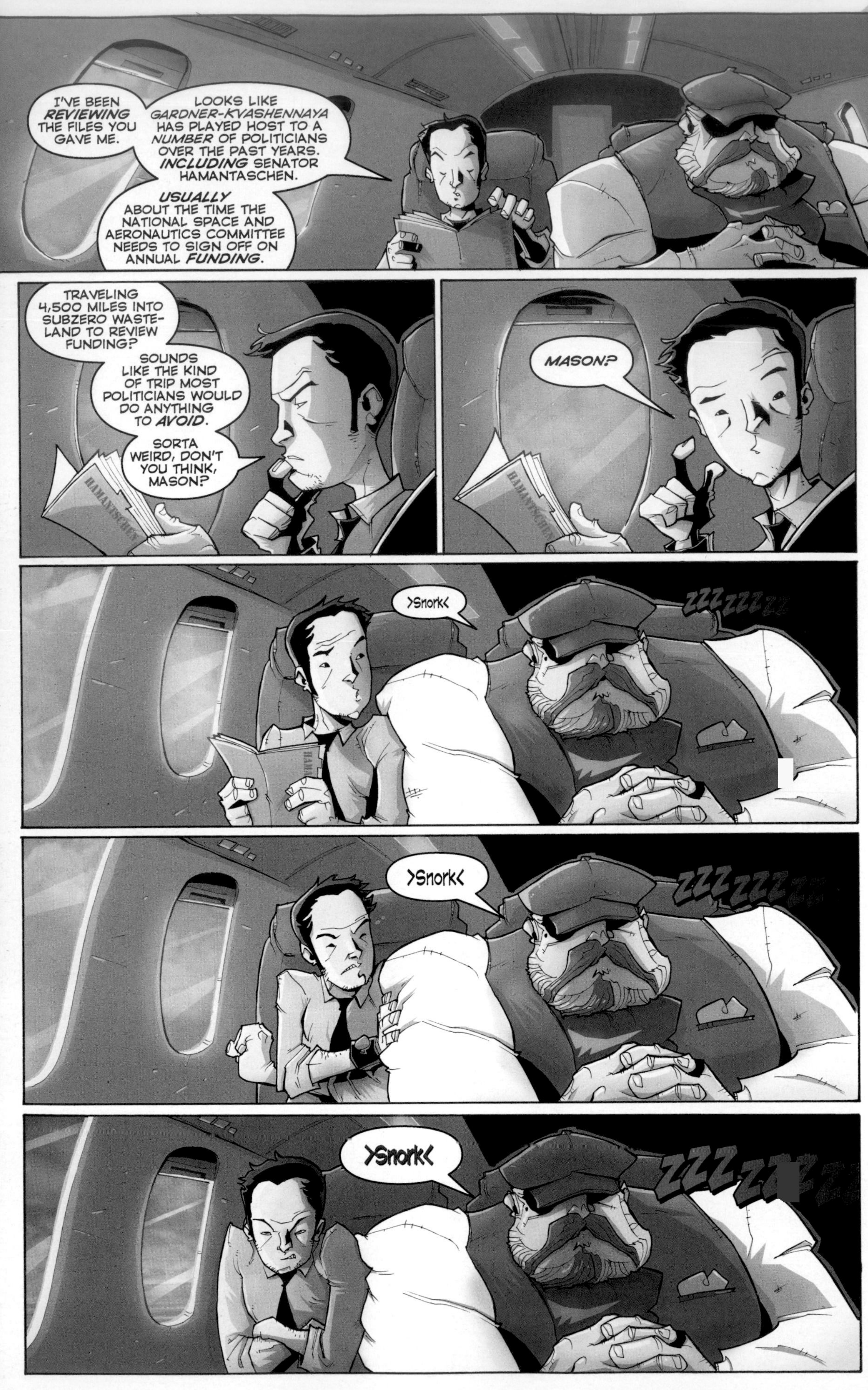
I'VE BEEN *REVIEWING* THE FILES YOU GAVE ME.
LOOKS LIKE *GARDNER-KVASHENNAYA* HAS PLAYED HOST TO A *NUMBER* OF POLITICIANS OVER THE PAST YEARS. *INCLUDING* SENATOR HAMANTASCHEN.
USUALLY ABOUT THE TIME THE NATIONAL SPACE AND AERONAUTICS COMMITTEE NEEDS TO SIGN OFF ON ANNUAL *FUNDING*.
TRAVELING 4,500 MILES INTO SUBZERO WASTE-LAND TO REVIEW FUNDING?
SOUNDS LIKE THE KIND OF TRIP MOST POLITICIANS WOULD DO ANYTHING TO *AVOID*.
SORTA WEIRD, DON'T YOU THINK, MASON?
HAMANTASCHEN
MASON?
HAMANTASCHEN
>Snork<
ZZZZZZZ
>Snork<
ZZZZZZZ
>Snork<
ZZZZ[redacted]

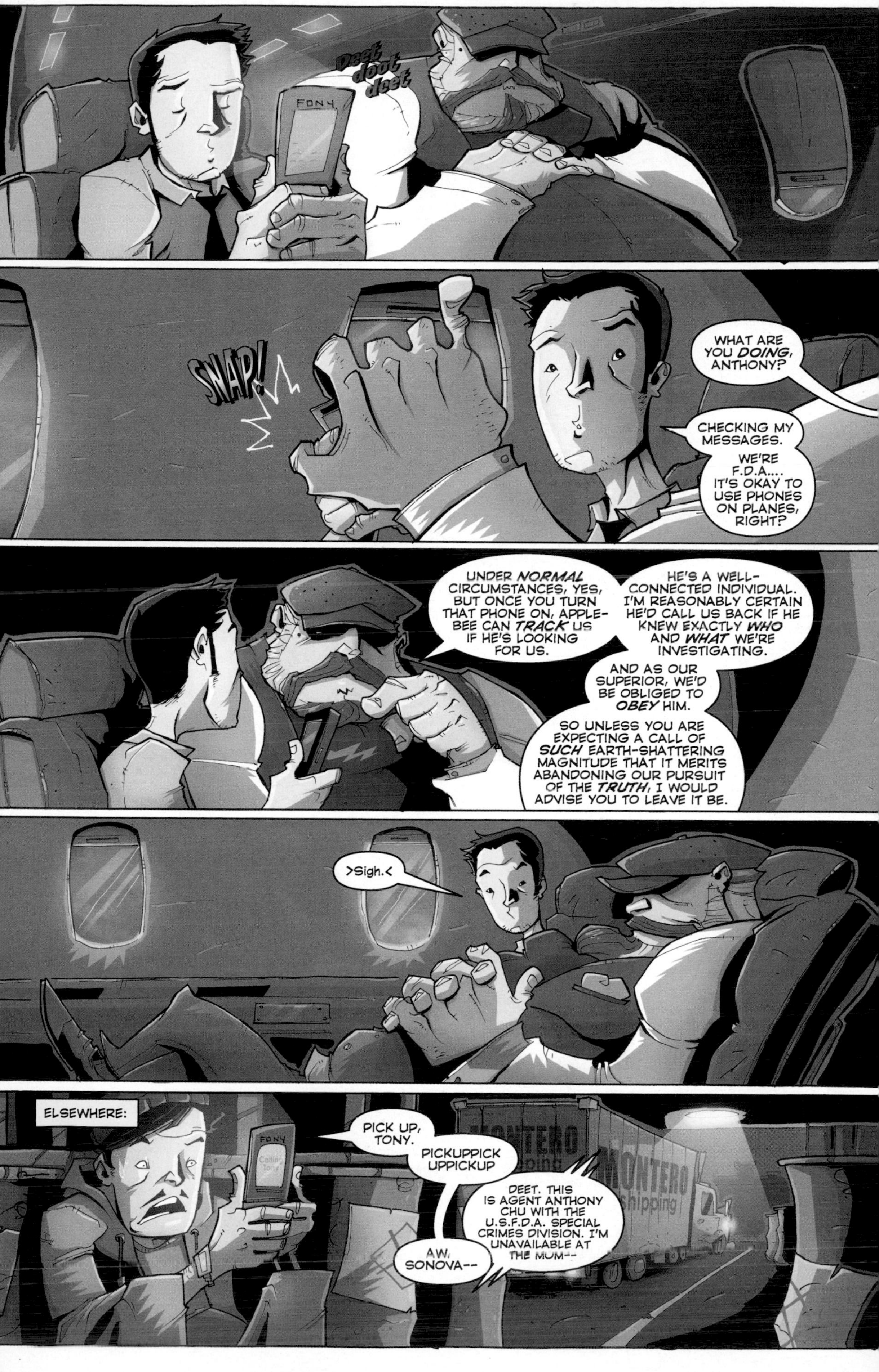
FONY
Deet doot deet
SNAP!
WHAT ARE YOU DOING, ANTHONY?
CHECKING MY MESSAGES.
WE'RE F.D.A.... IT'S OKAY TO USE PHONES ON PLANES, RIGHT?
UNDER NORMAL CIRCUMSTANCES, YES, BUT ONCE YOU TURN THAT PHONE ON, APPLEBEE CAN TRACK US IF HE'S LOOKING FOR US.
HE'S A WELL-CONNECTED INDIVIDUAL. I'M REASONABLY CERTAIN HE'D CALL US BACK IF HE KNEW EXACTLY WHO AND WHAT WE'RE INVESTIGATING.
AND AS OUR SUPERIOR, WE'D BE OBLIGED TO OBEY HIM.
SO UNLESS YOU ARE EXPECTING A CALL OF SUCH EARTH-SHATTERING MAGNITUDE THAT IT MERITS ABANDONING OUR PURSUIT OF THE TRUTH, I WOULD ADVISE YOU TO LEAVE IT BE.
>Sigh.<
ELSEWHERE:
FONY
PICK UP, TONY.
PICKUPPICK UPPICKUP
DEET. THIS IS AGENT ANTHONY CHU WITH THE U.S.F.D.A. SPECIAL CRIMES DIVISION. I'M UNAVAILABLE AT THE MOM--
A.W. SONOVA--
MONTERO Shipping
MONTERO Shipping

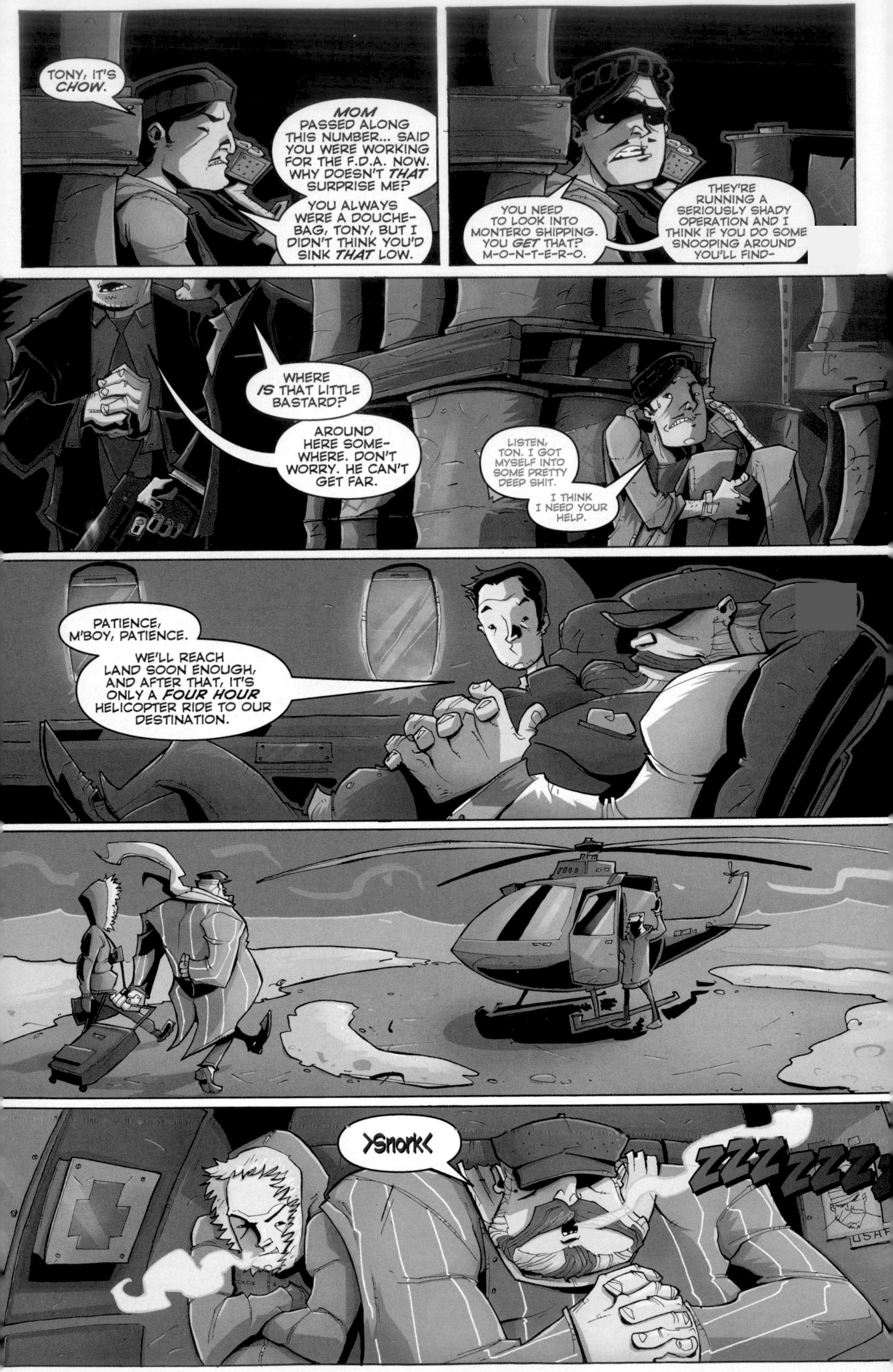
TONY, IT'S *CHOW*.
MOM PASSED ALONG THIS NUMBER... SAID YOU WERE WORKING FOR THE F.D.A. NOW. WHY DOESN'T *THAT* SURPRISE ME?
YOU ALWAYS WERE A DOUCHE-BAG, TONY, BUT I DIDN'T THINK YOU'D SINK *THAT* LOW.
YOU NEED TO LOOK INTO MONTERO SHIPPING. YOU *GET* THAT? M-O-N-T-E-R-O.
THEY'RE RUNNING A SERIOUSLY SHADY OPERATION AND I THINK IF YOU DO SOME SNOOPING AROUND YOU'LL FIND-
WHERE *IS* THAT LITTLE BASTARD?
AROUND HERE SOME-WHERE. DON'T WORRY. HE CAN'T GET FAR.
LISTEN, TON. I GOT MYSELF INTO SOME PRETTY DEEP SHIT.
I THINK I NEED YOUR HELP.
PATIENCE, M'BOY, PATIENCE.
WE'LL REACH LAND SOON ENOUGH, AND AFTER THAT, IT'S ONLY A *FOUR HOUR* HELICOPTER RIDE TO OUR DESTINATION.
>Snork<
ZZZZZZZ
USAF

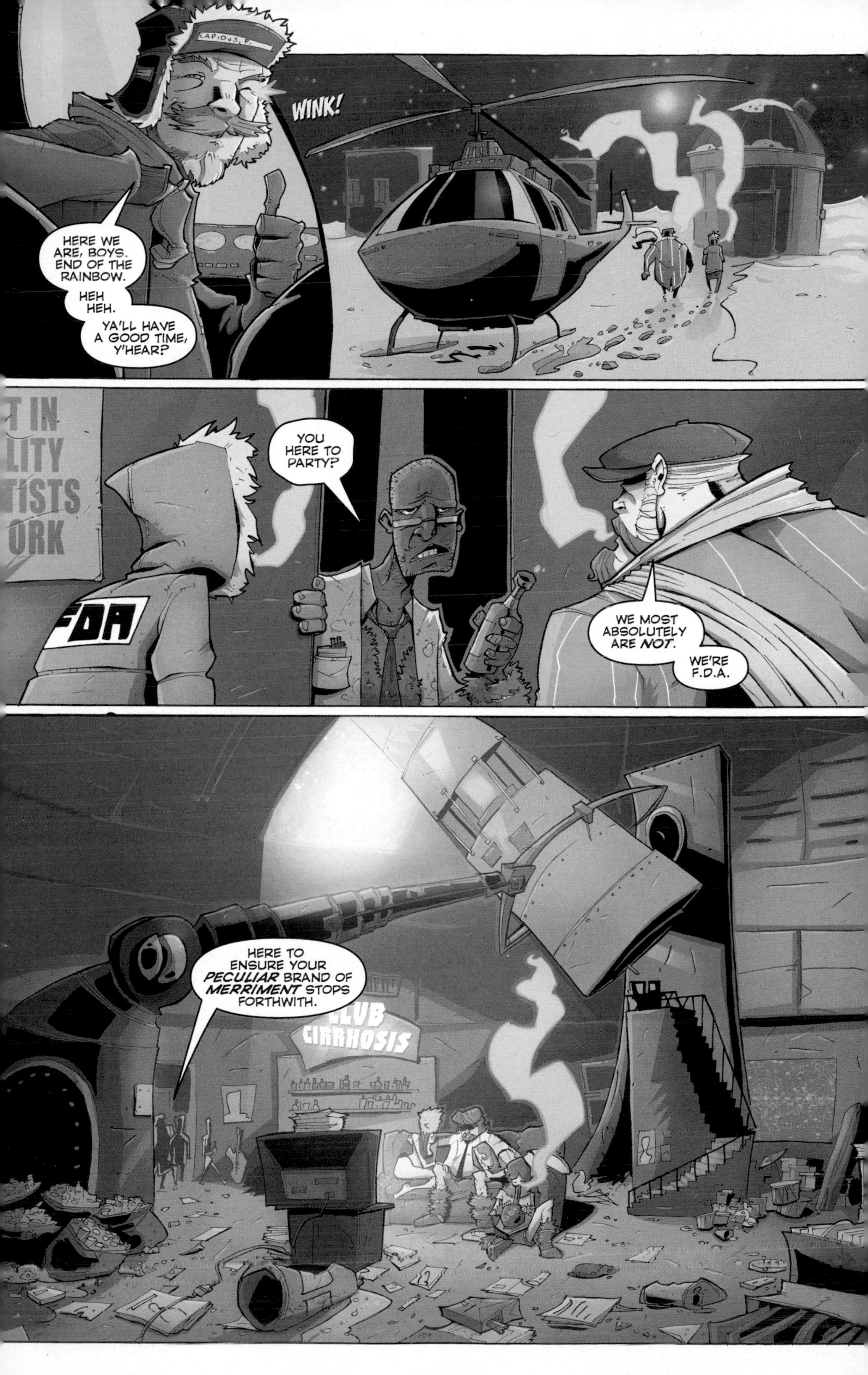
WINK!
HERE WE ARE, BOYS. END OF THE RAINBOW.
HEH HEH.
YA'LL HAVE A GOOD TIME, Y'HEAR?
YOU HERE TO PARTY?
FDA
WE MOST ABSOLUTELY ARE *NOT*.
WE'RE F.D.A.
HERE TO ENSURE YOUR ***PECULIAR*** BRAND OF ***MERRIMENT*** STOPS FORTHWITH.
CLUB CIRRHOSIS

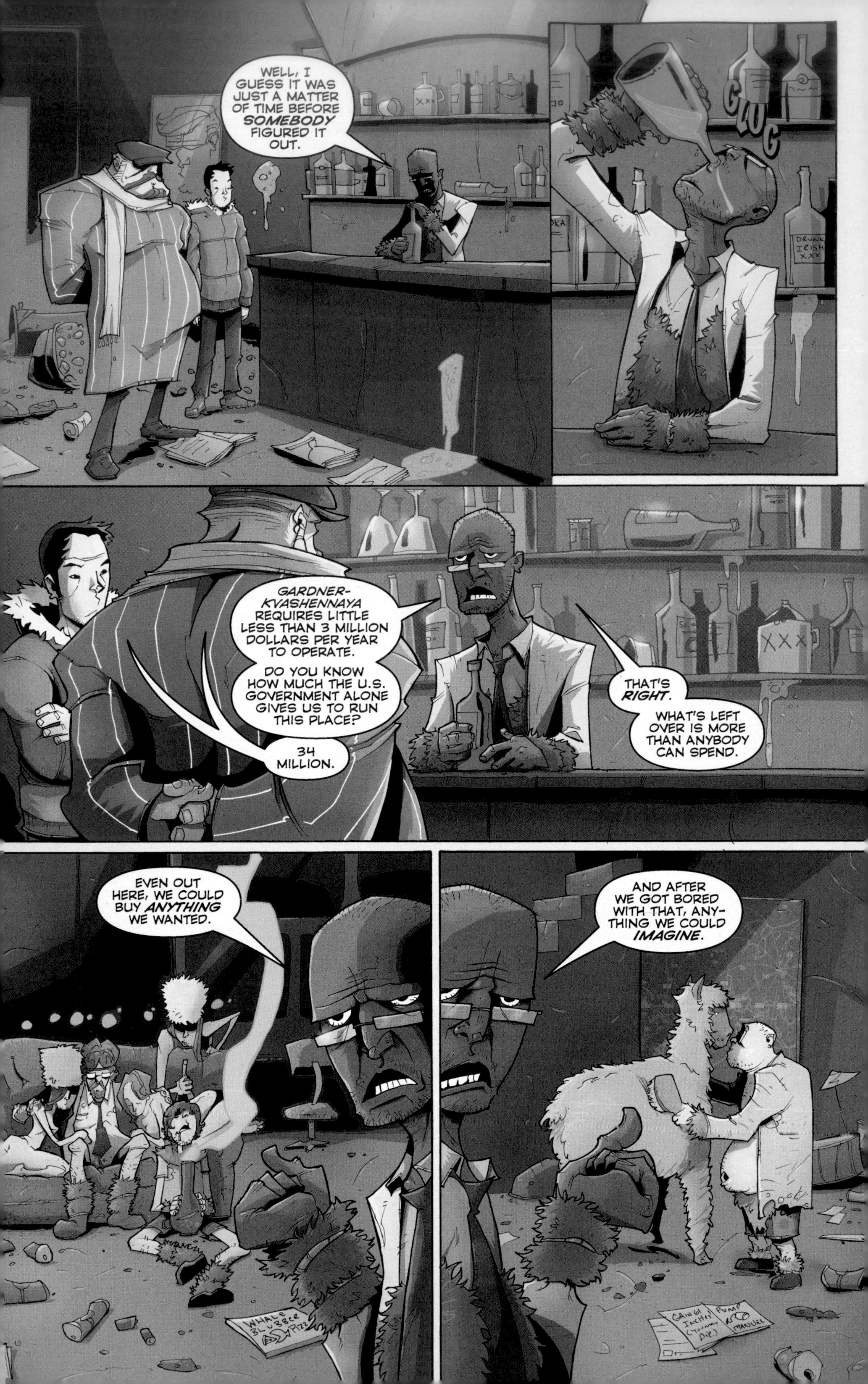

WELL, I GUESS IT WAS JUST A MATTER OF TIME BEFORE *SOMEBODY* FIGURED IT OUT.
GLUG
GARDNER-KVASHENNAYA REQUIRES LITTLE LESS THAN 3 MILLION DOLLARS PER YEAR TO OPERATE.
DO YOU KNOW HOW MUCH THE U.S. GOVERNMENT ALONE GIVES US TO RUN THIS PLACE?
34 MILLION.
THAT'S *RIGHT*.
WHAT'S LEFT OVER IS MORE THAN ANYBODY CAN SPEND.
EVEN OUT HERE, WE COULD BUY *ANYTHING* WE WANTED.
AND AFTER WE GOT BORED WITH THAT, ANY-THING WE COULD *IMAGINE*.

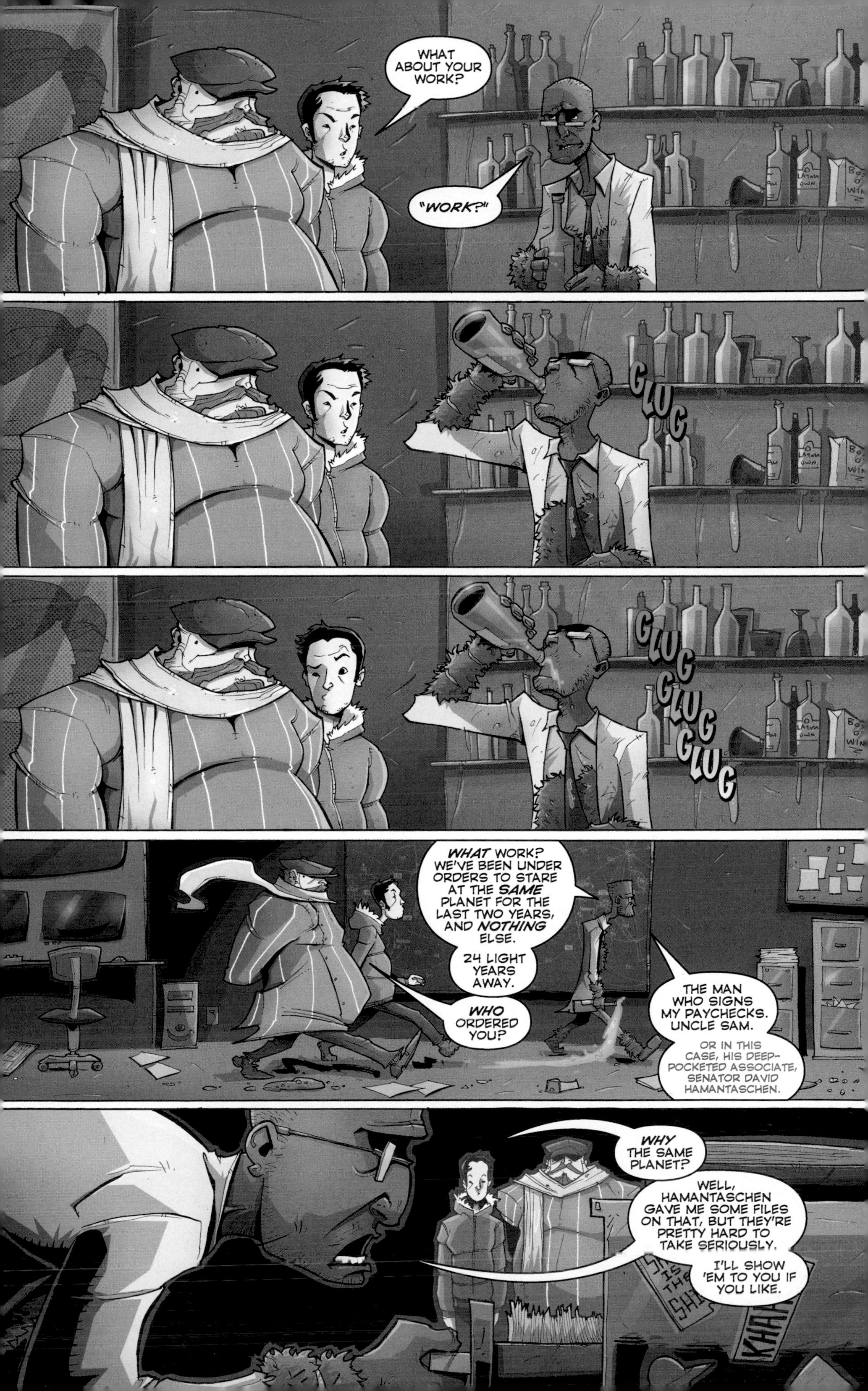
WHAT ABOUT YOUR WORK?
"WORK?"
GLUG
GLUG GLUG GLUG
WHAT WORK? WE'VE BEEN UNDER ORDERS TO STARE AT THE SAME PLANET FOR THE LAST TWO YEARS, AND NOTHING ELSE.
24 LIGHT YEARS AWAY.
WHO ORDERED YOU?
THE MAN WHO SIGNS MY PAYCHECKS. UNCLE SAM.
OR IN THIS CASE, HIS DEEP-POCKETED ASSOCIATE, SENATOR DAVID HAMANTASCHEN.
WHY THE SAME PLANET?
WELL, HAMANTASCHEN GAVE ME SOME FILES ON THAT, BUT THEY'RE PRETTY HARD TO TAKE SERIOUSLY.
I'LL SHOW 'EM TO YOU IF YOU LIKE.

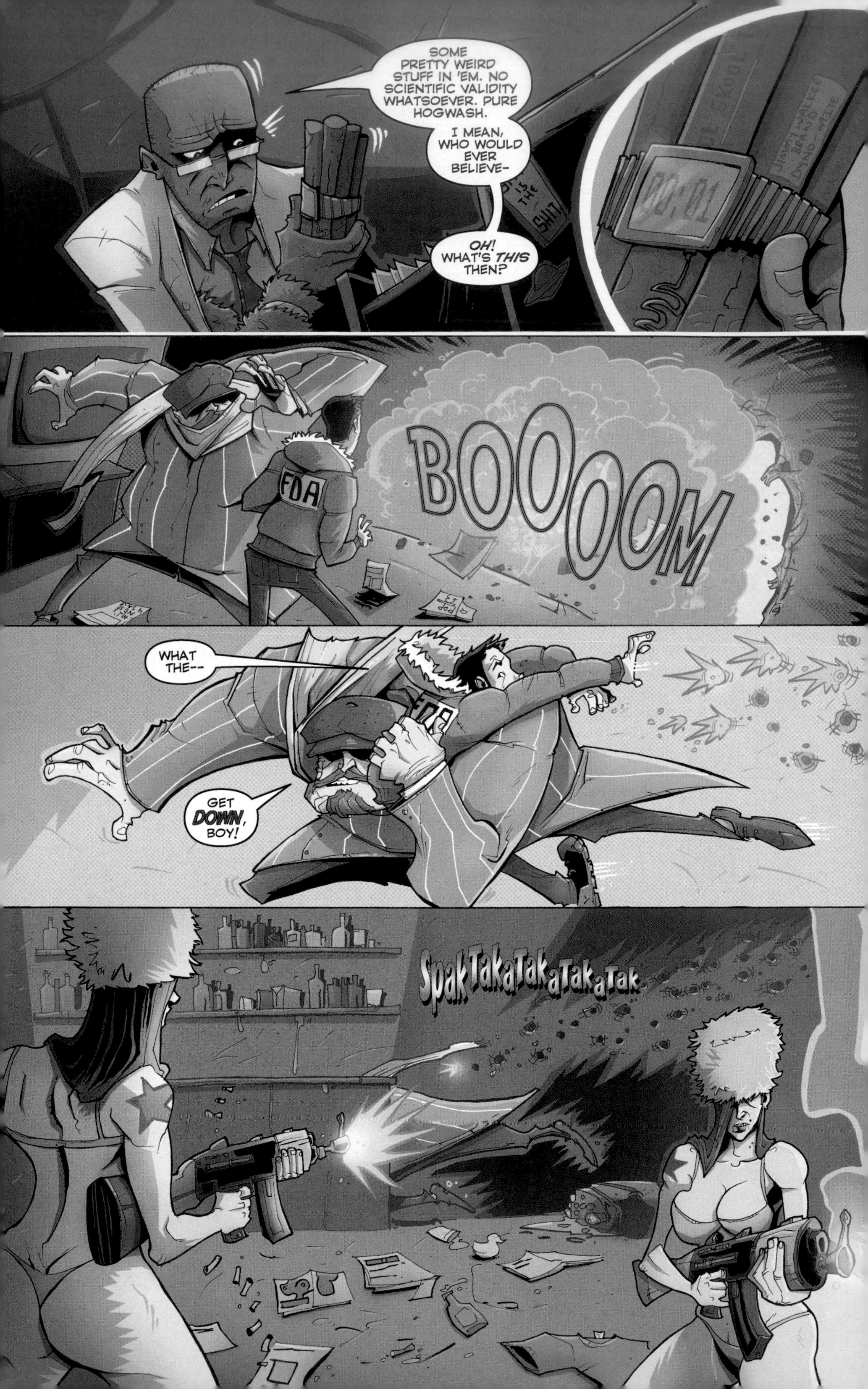
SOME PRETTY WEIRD STUFF IN 'EM. NO SCIENTIFIC VALIDITY WHATSOEVER. PURE HOGWASH.
I MEAN, WHO WOULD EVER BELIEVE-
OH! WHAT'S THIS THEN?
00:01
FDA
BOOOOOM
WHAT THE--
GET DOWN, BOY!
SpakTakaTakaTakaTak

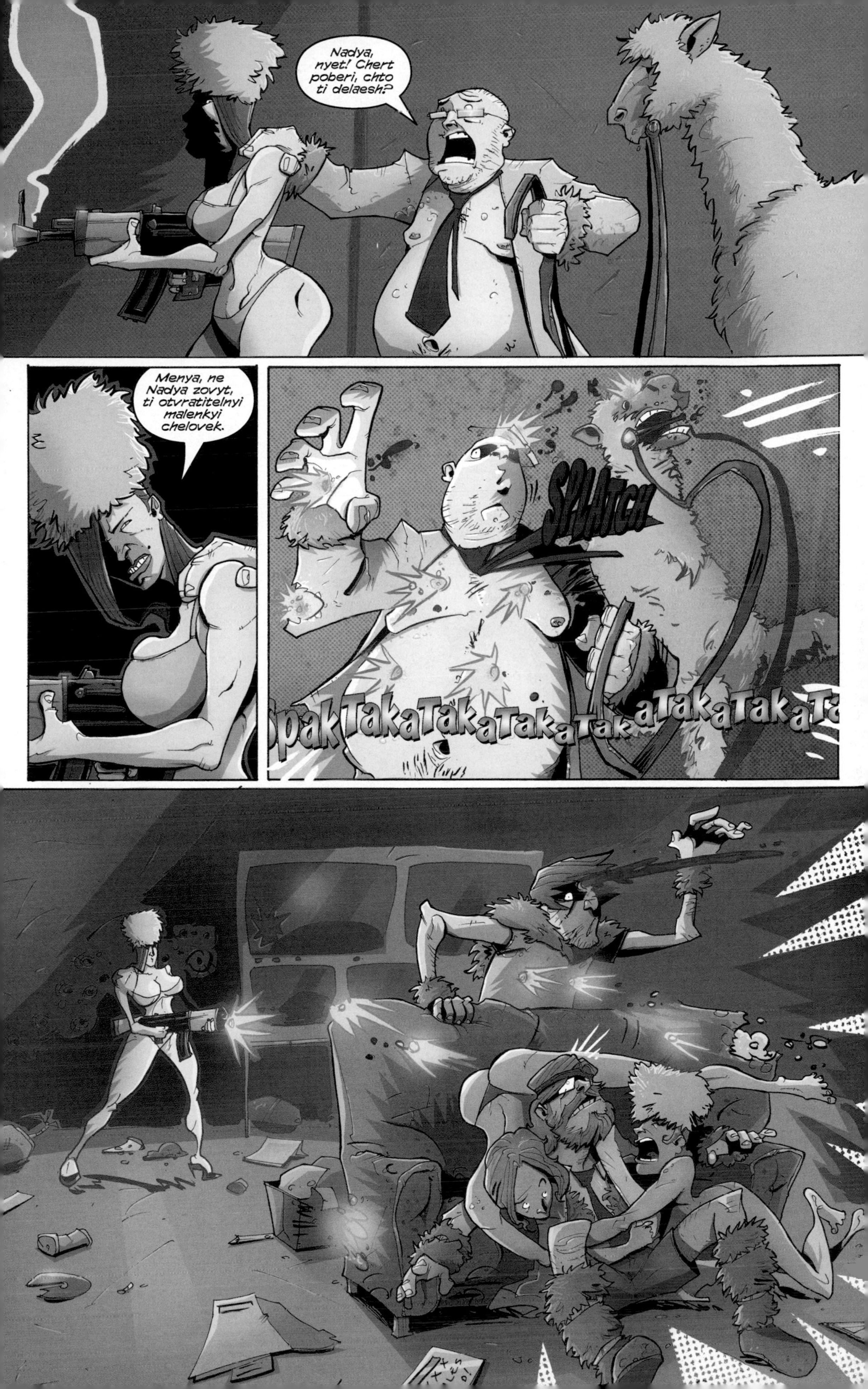
Nadya, nyet! Chert poberi, chto ti delaesh?
Menya, ne Nadya zovyt, ti otvratitelnyi malenkyi chelovek.
SPLATCH
pakTakaTakaTakaTakaTakaTakaTa

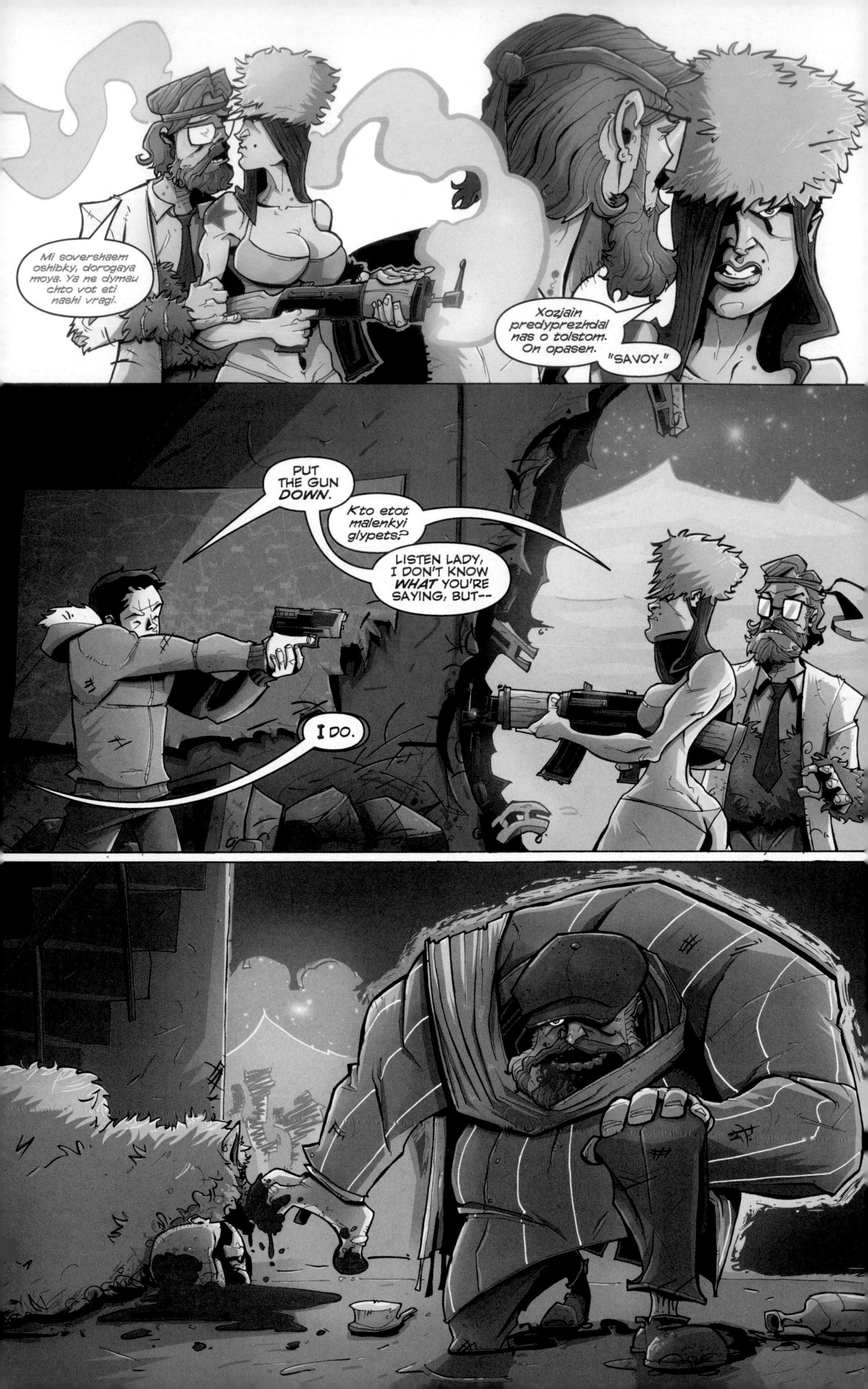
Mi sovershaem oshibky, dorogaya moya. Ya ne dymau chto vot eti nashi vragi.
Xozjain predyprezhdal nas o tolstom. On opasen.
"SAVOY."
PUT THE GUN DOWN.
Kto etot malenkyi glypets?
LISTEN LADY, I DON'T KNOW WHAT YOU'RE SAYING, BUT--
I DO.

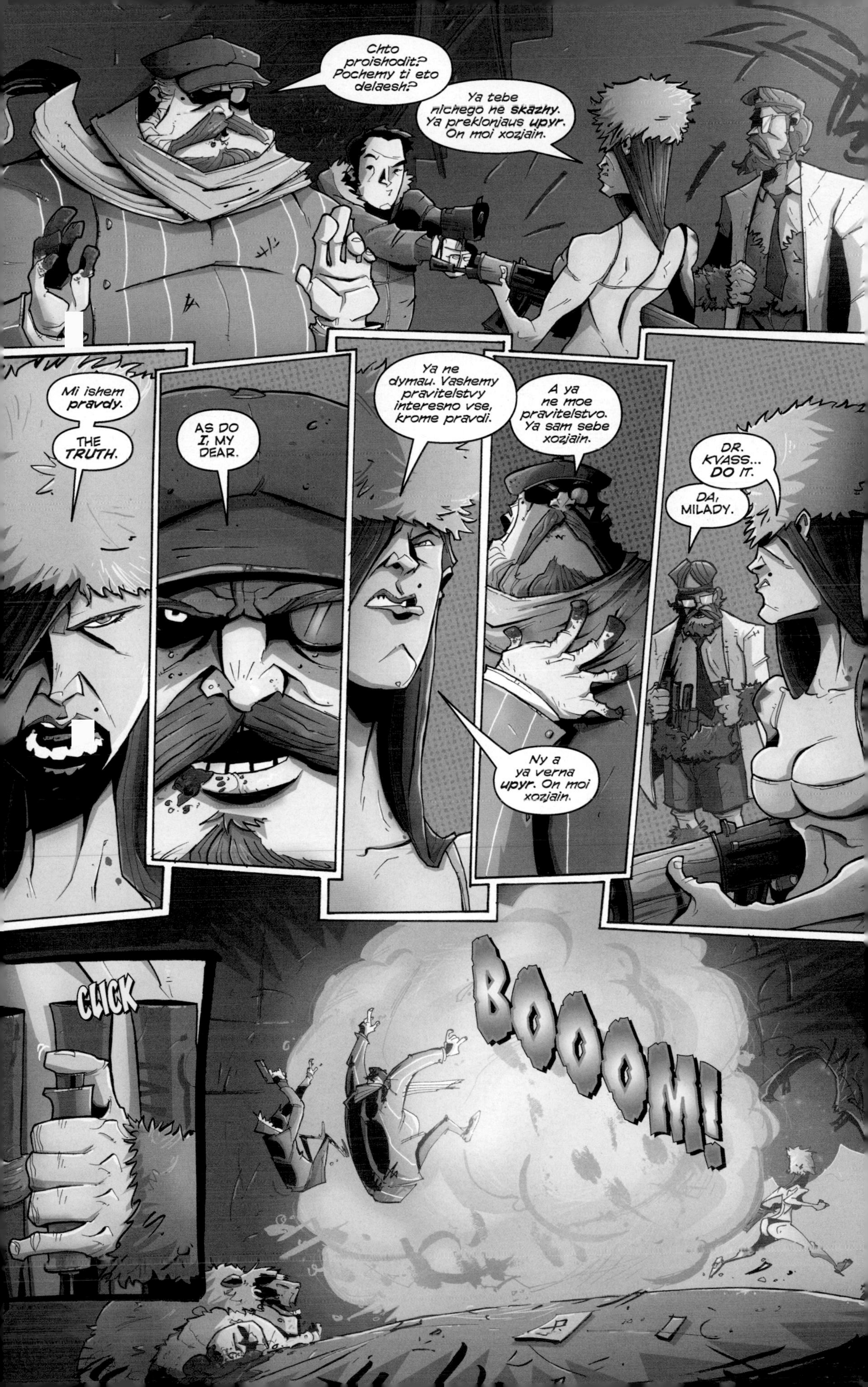
Chto proishodit? Pochemy ti eto delaesh?
Ya tebe nichego ne skazhy. Ya preklonjaus upyr. On moi xozjain.
Mi ishem pravdy.
THE TRUTH.
AS DO I, MY DEAR.
Ya ne dymau. Vashemy pravitelstvy interesno vse, krome pravdi.
A ya ne moe pravitelstvo. Ya sam sebe xozjain.
Ny a ya verna upyr. On moi xozjain.
DR. KVASS... DO IT.
DA, MILADY.
CLICK
BOOOOM!

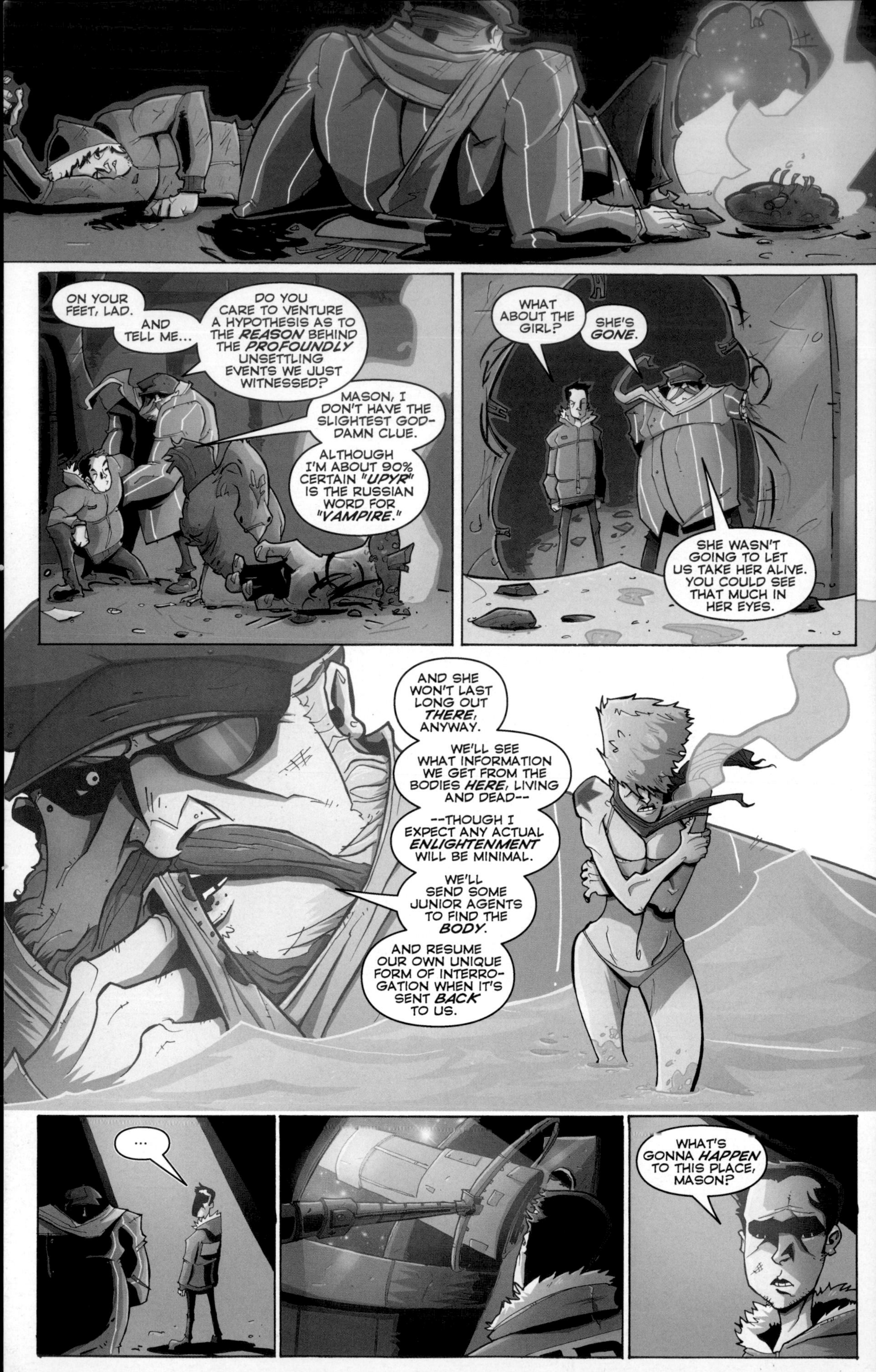

ON YOUR FEET, LAD.
AND TELL ME...
DO YOU CARE TO VENTURE A HYPOTHESIS AS TO THE *REASON* BEHIND THE *PROFOUNDLY* UNSETTLING EVENTS WE JUST WITNESSED?
MASON, I DON'T HAVE THE SLIGHTEST GOD-DAMN CLUE.
ALTHOUGH I'M ABOUT 90% CERTAIN *"UPYR"* IS THE RUSSIAN WORD FOR *"VAMPIRE."*
WHAT ABOUT THE GIRL?
SHE'S *GONE*.
SHE WASN'T GOING TO LET US TAKE HER ALIVE. YOU COULD SEE THAT MUCH IN HER EYES.
AND SHE WON'T LAST LONG OUT *THERE*, ANYWAY.
WE'LL SEE WHAT INFORMATION WE GET FROM THE BODIES *HERE*, LIVING AND DEAD--
--THOUGH I EXPECT ANY ACTUAL *ENLIGHTENMENT* WILL BE MINIMAL.
WE'LL SEND SOME JUNIOR AGENTS TO FIND THE *BODY*.
AND RESUME OUR OWN UNIQUE FORM OF INTERRO-GATION WHEN IT'S SENT *BACK* TO US.
...
WHAT'S GONNA *HAPPEN* TO THIS PLACE, MASON?

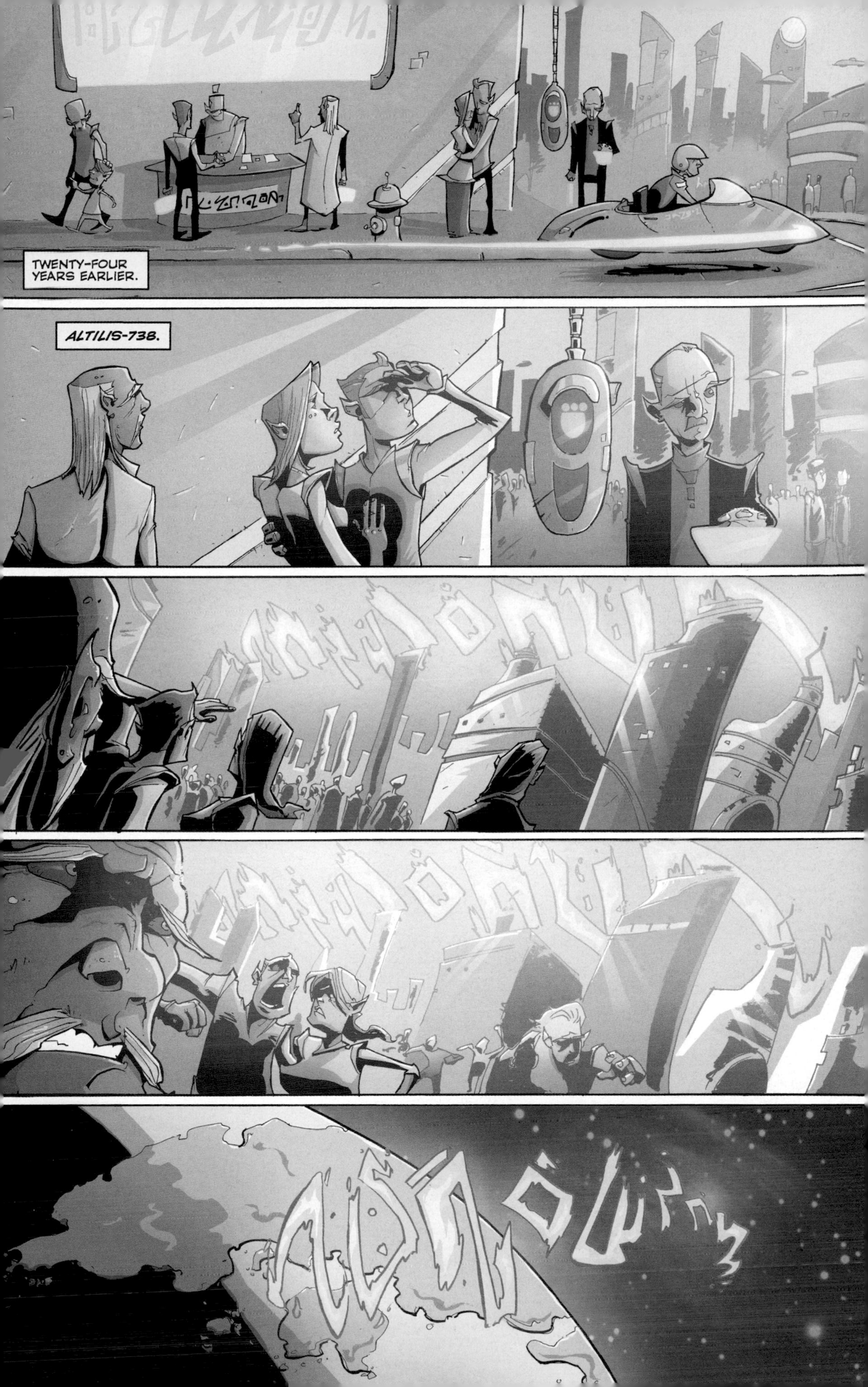
TWENTY-FOUR YEARS EARLIER.
ALTILIS-738.

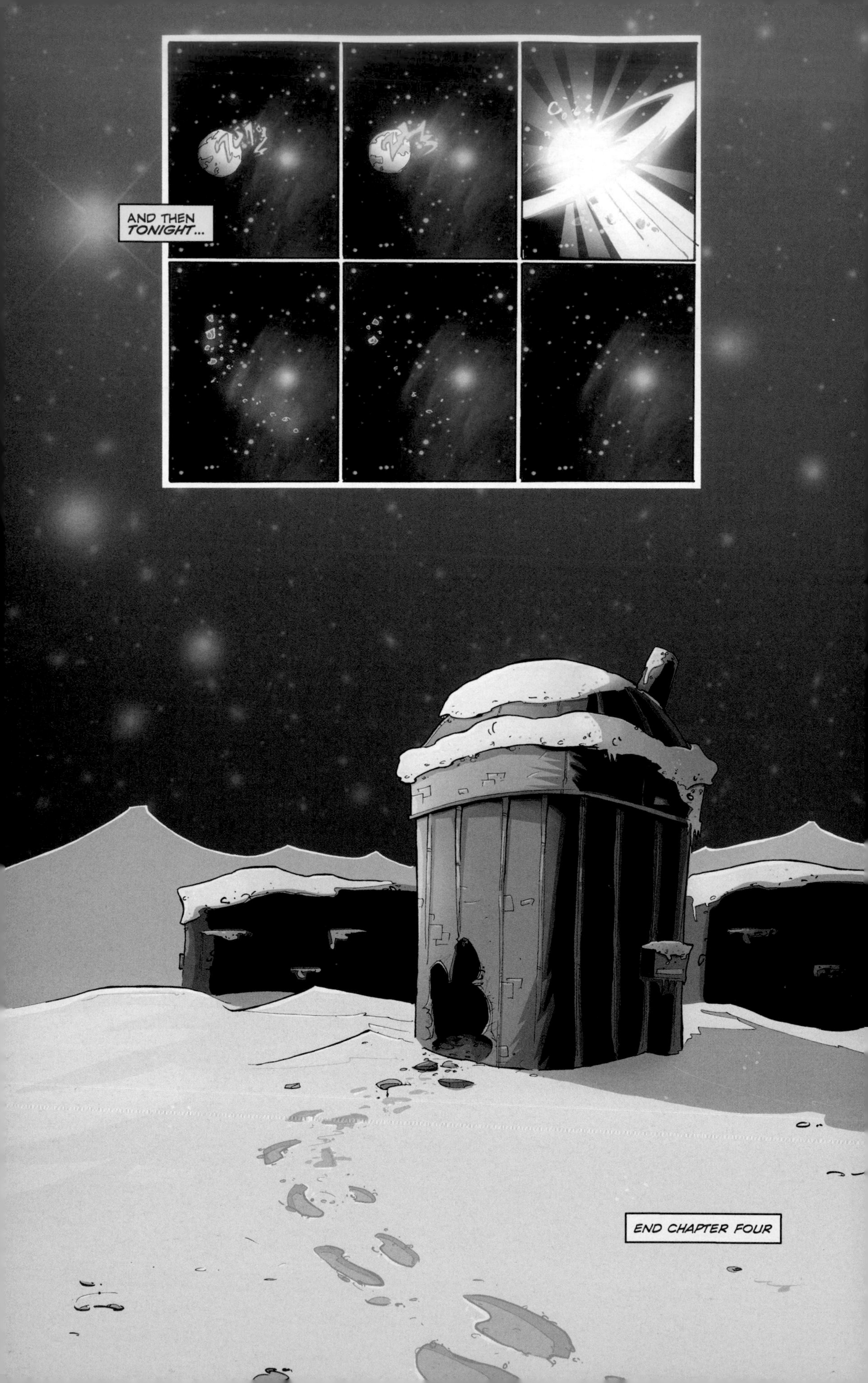
AND THEN *TONIGHT*...
END CHAPTER FOUR

Chapter 5

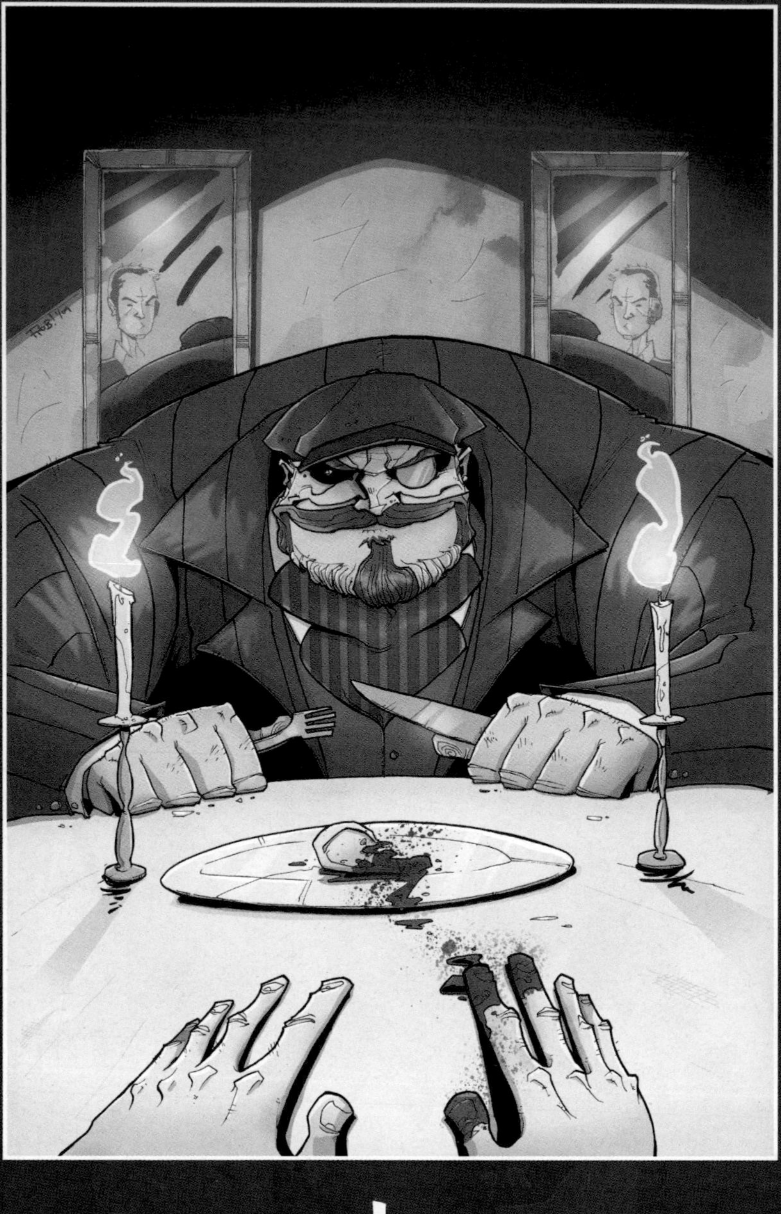

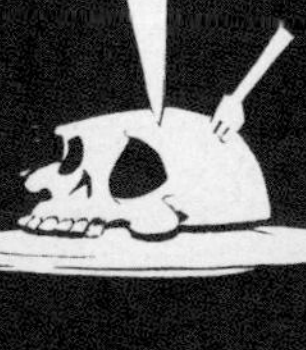

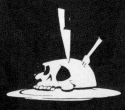

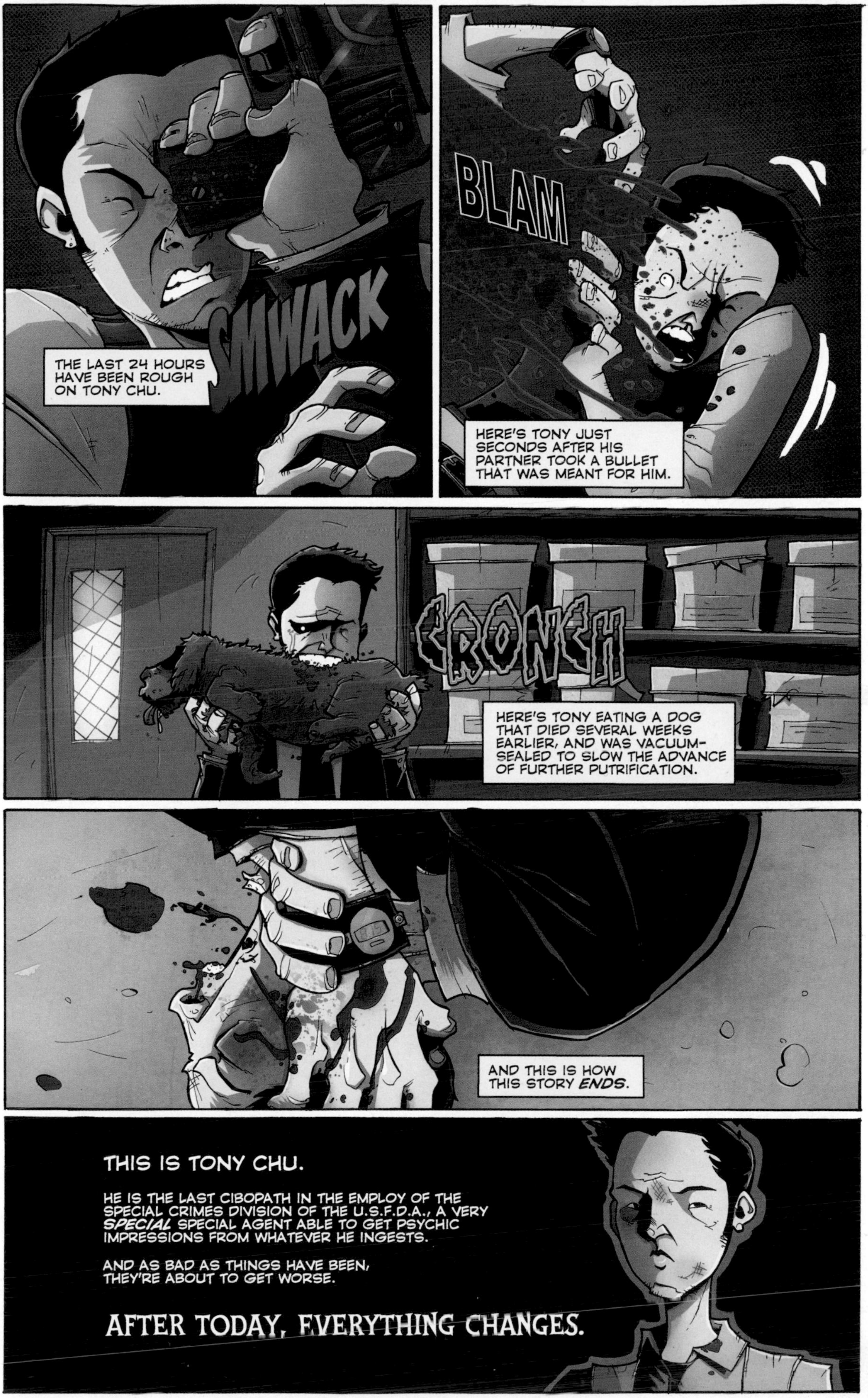
SMWACK
THE LAST 24 HOURS HAVE BEEN ROUGH ON TONY CHU.
BLAM
HERE'S TONY JUST SECONDS AFTER HIS PARTNER TOOK A BULLET THAT WAS MEANT FOR HIM.
CRONCH
HERE'S TONY EATING A DOG THAT DIED SEVERAL WEEKS EARLIER, AND WAS VACUUM-SEALED TO SLOW THE ADVANCE OF FURTHER PUTRIFICATION.
AND THIS IS HOW THIS STORY *ENDS*.
THIS IS TONY CHU.
HE IS THE LAST CIBOPATH IN THE EMPLOY OF THE SPECIAL CRIMES DIVISION OF THE U.S.F.D.A., A VERY *SPECIAL* SPECIAL AGENT ABLE TO GET PSYCHIC IMPRESSIONS FROM WHATEVER HE INGESTS.
AND AS BAD AS THINGS HAVE BEEN, THEY'RE ABOUT TO GET WORSE.
AFTER TODAY, EVERYTHING CHANGES.

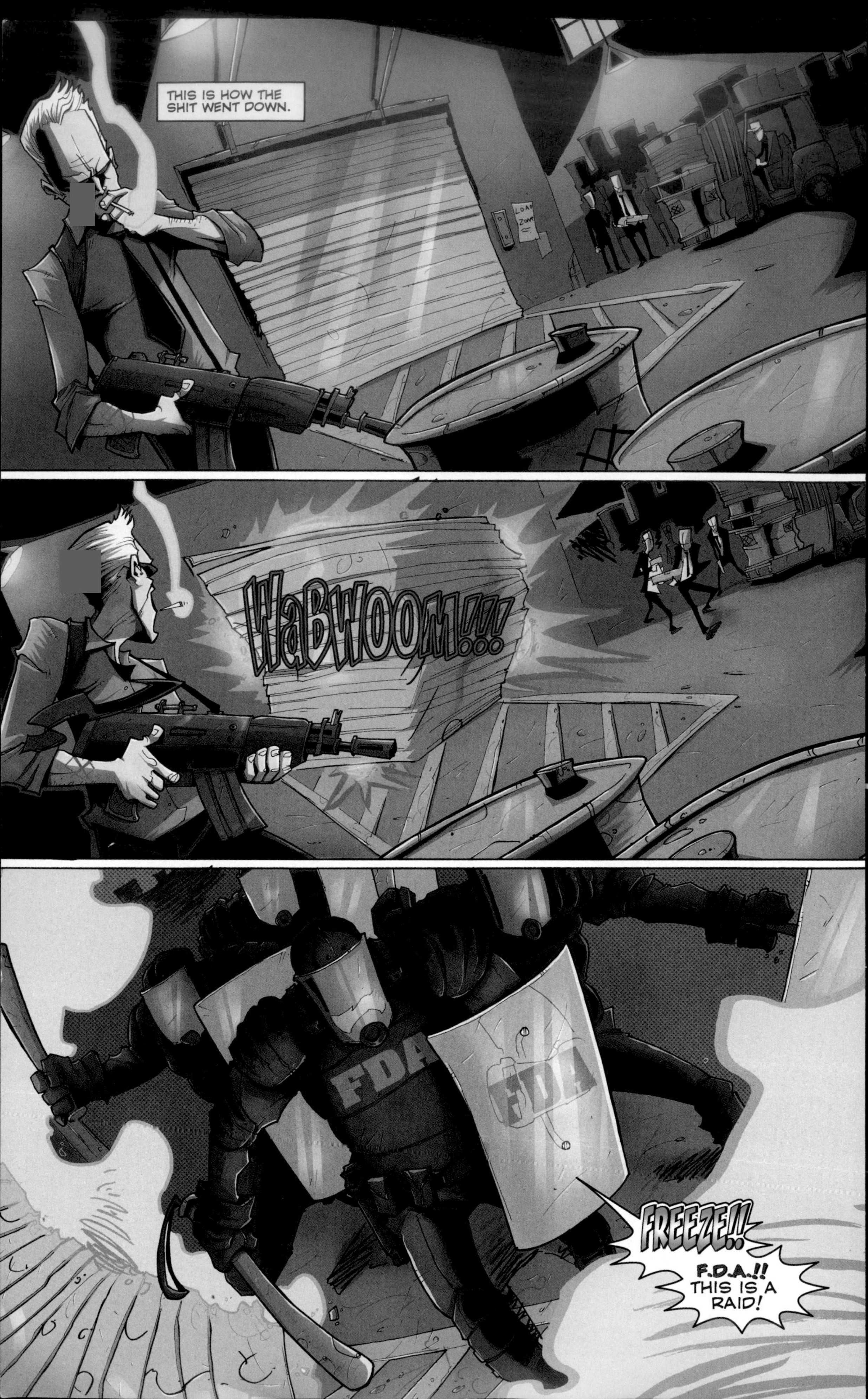
THIS IS HOW THE SHIT WENT DOWN.
WaBWOOM!!!
FDA
FDA
FREEZE!!
F.D.A.!! THIS IS A RAID!

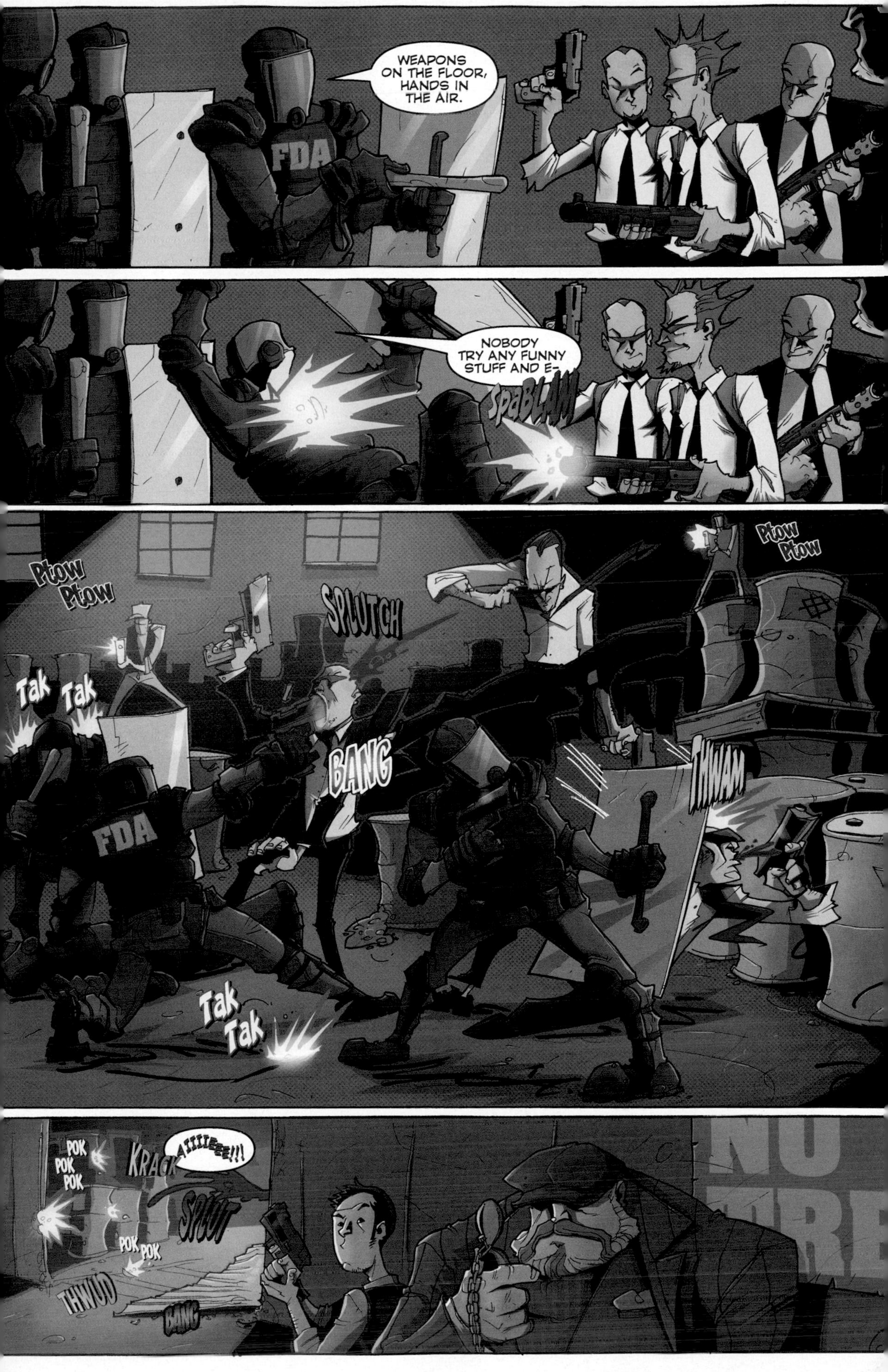
WEAPONS ON THE FLOOR, HANDS IN THE AIR.
FDA
NOBODY TRY ANY FUNNY STUFF AND E-
SpaBLAM
Ptow Ptow
Tak Tak
SPLUTCH
FDA
BANG
Ptow Ptow
THWAM
Tak Tak
POK POK POK
KRACK
AIIIIEEE!!!
SPLUT
POK POK
THWUD
BANG
NO

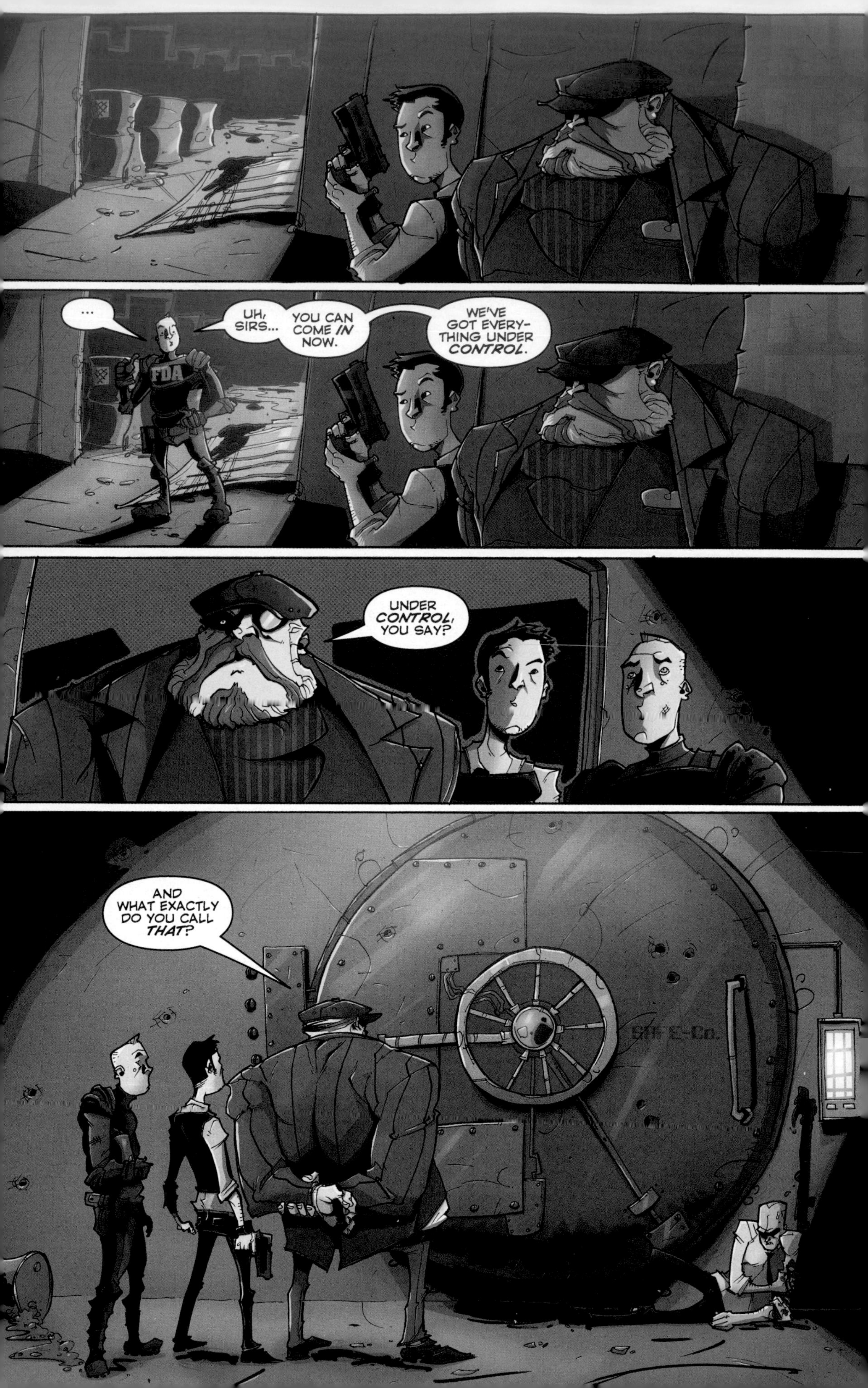
...
UH, SIRS...
YOU CAN COME *IN* NOW.
WE'VE GOT EVERYTHING UNDER *CONTROL*.
UNDER *CONTROL*, YOU SAY?
AND WHAT EXACTLY DO YOU CALL *THAT*?

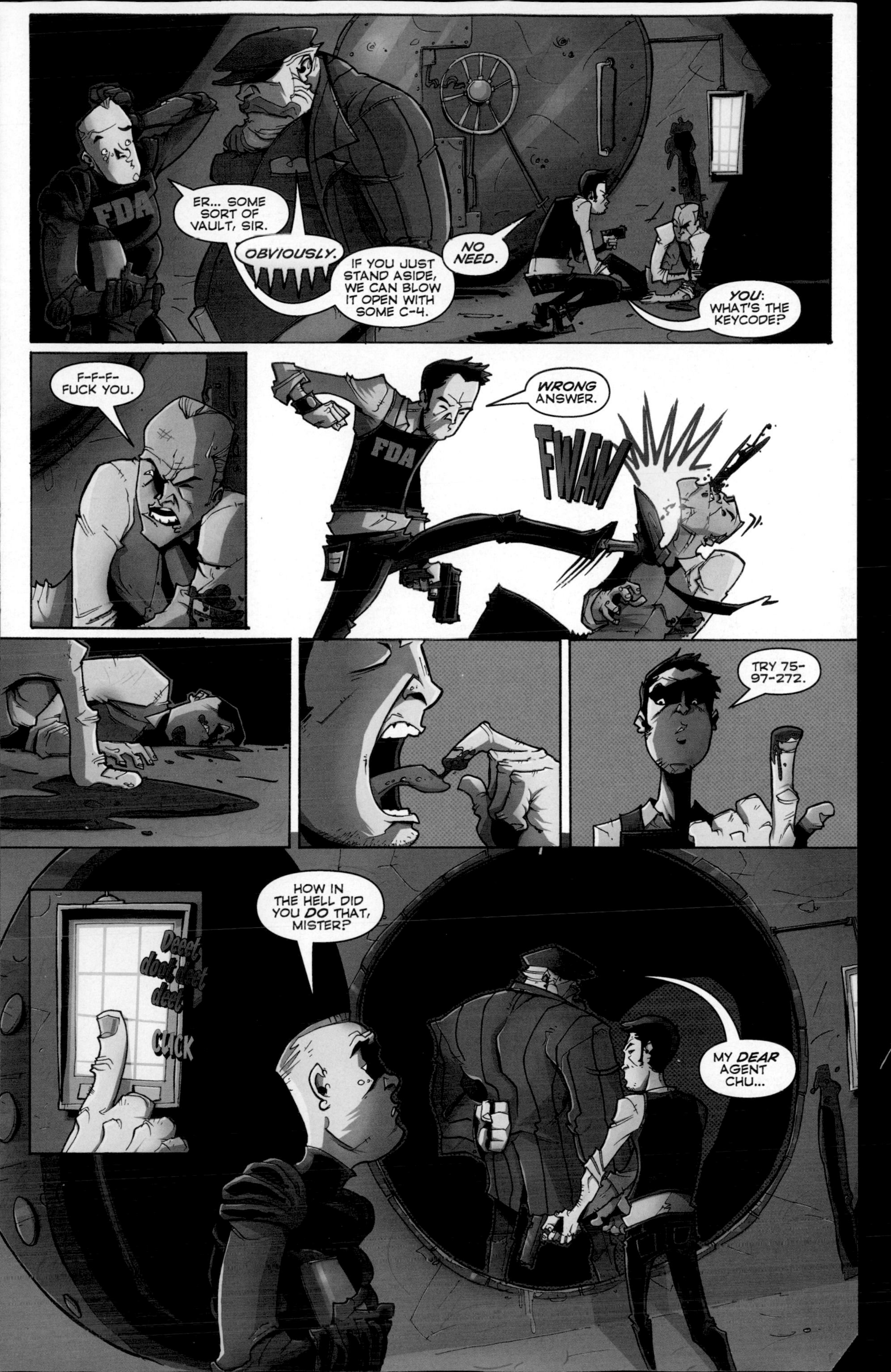
ER... SOME SORT OF VAULT, SIR.
OBVIOUSLY.
IF YOU JUST STAND ASIDE, WE CAN BLOW IT OPEN WITH SOME C-4.
NO NEED.
YOU: WHAT'S THE KEYCODE?
F-F-F- FUCK YOU.
WRONG ANSWER.
FWAM
TRY 75-97-272.
HOW IN THE HELL DID YOU DO THAT, MISTER?
Deeet doot deet deet
CLICK
MY DEAR AGENT CHU...

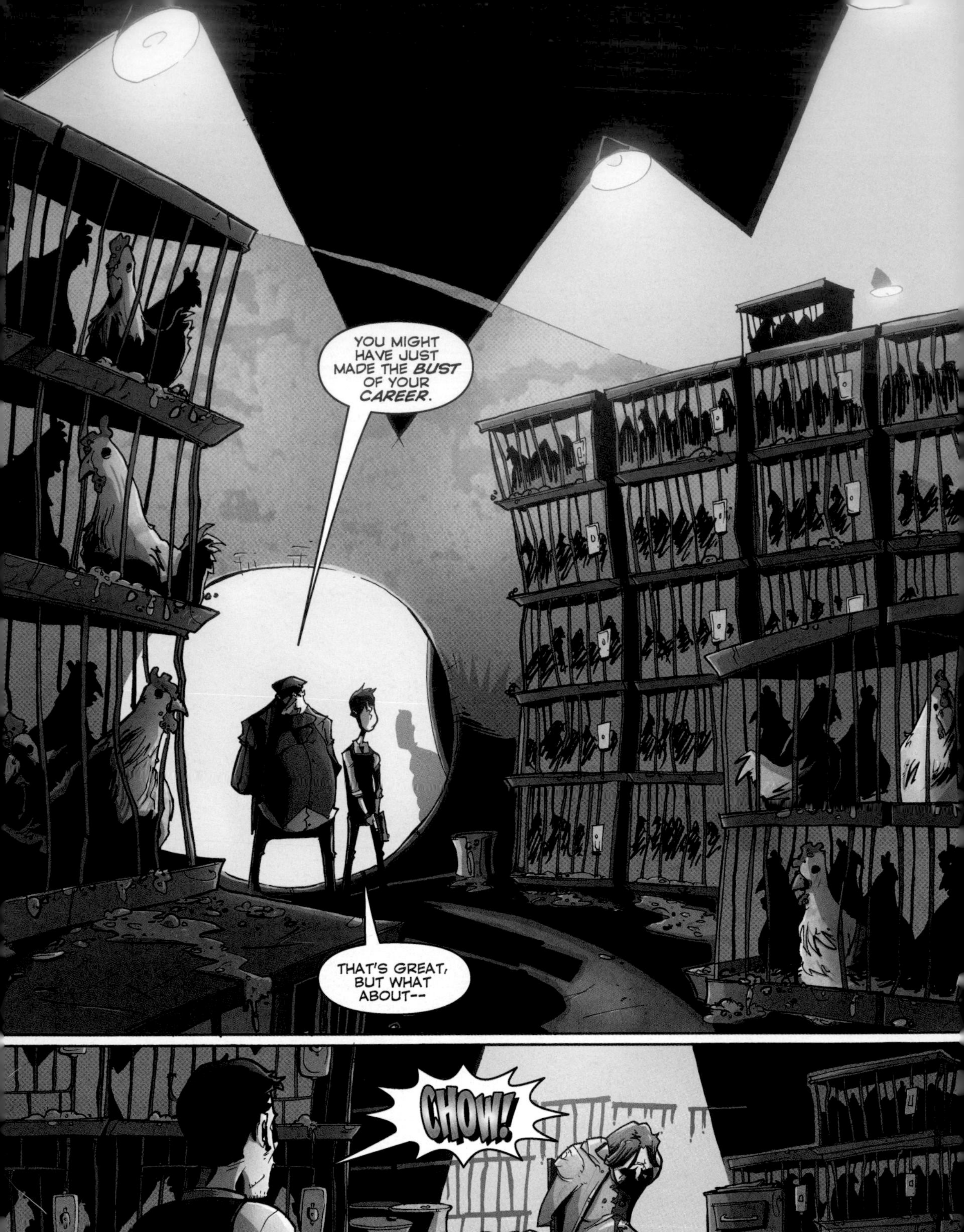
YOU MIGHT HAVE JUST MADE THE *BUST* OF YOUR *CAREER*.
THAT'S GREAT, BUT WHAT ABOUT--
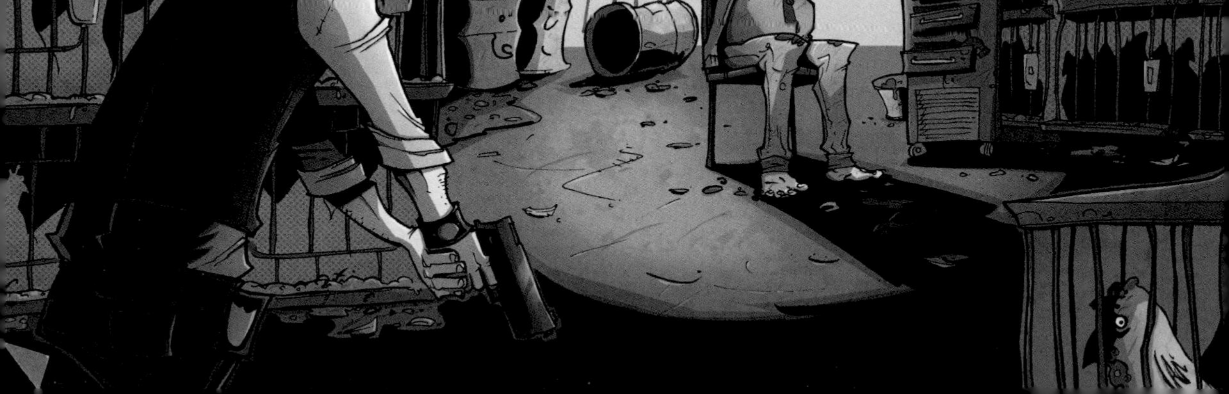
CHOW!

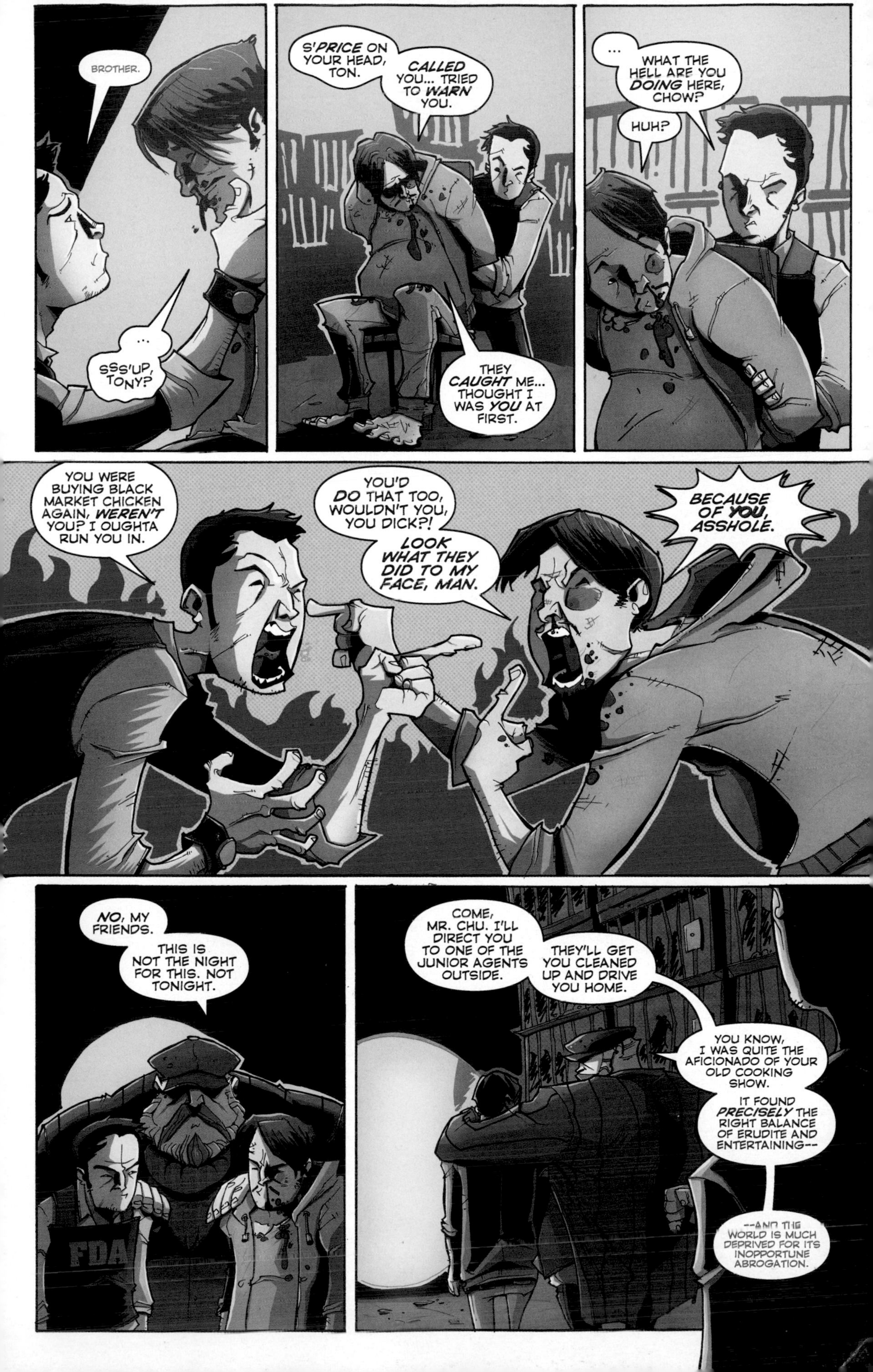
BROTHER.
...
SSS'UP, TONY?
S'PRICE ON YOUR HEAD, TON.
CALLED YOU... TRIED TO WARN YOU.
THEY CAUGHT ME... THOUGHT I WAS YOU AT FIRST.
...
WHAT THE HELL ARE YOU DOING HERE, CHOW?
HUH?
YOU WERE BUYING BLACK MARKET CHICKEN AGAIN, WEREN'T YOU? I OUGHTA RUN YOU IN.
YOU'D DO THAT TOO, WOULDN'T YOU, YOU DICK?!
LOOK WHAT THEY DID TO MY FACE, MAN.
BECAUSE OF YOU, ASSHOLE.
NO, MY FRIENDS.
THIS IS NOT THE NIGHT FOR THIS. NOT TONIGHT.
FDA
COME, MR. CHU. I'LL DIRECT YOU TO ONE OF THE JUNIOR AGENTS OUTSIDE.
THEY'LL GET YOU CLEANED UP AND DRIVE YOU HOME.
YOU KNOW, I WAS QUITE THE AFICIONADO OF YOUR OLD COOKING SHOW.
IT FOUND PRECISELY THE RIGHT BALANCE OF ERUDITE AND ENTERTAINING--
--AND THE WORLD IS MUCH DEPRIVED FOR ITS INOPPORTUNE ABROGATION.

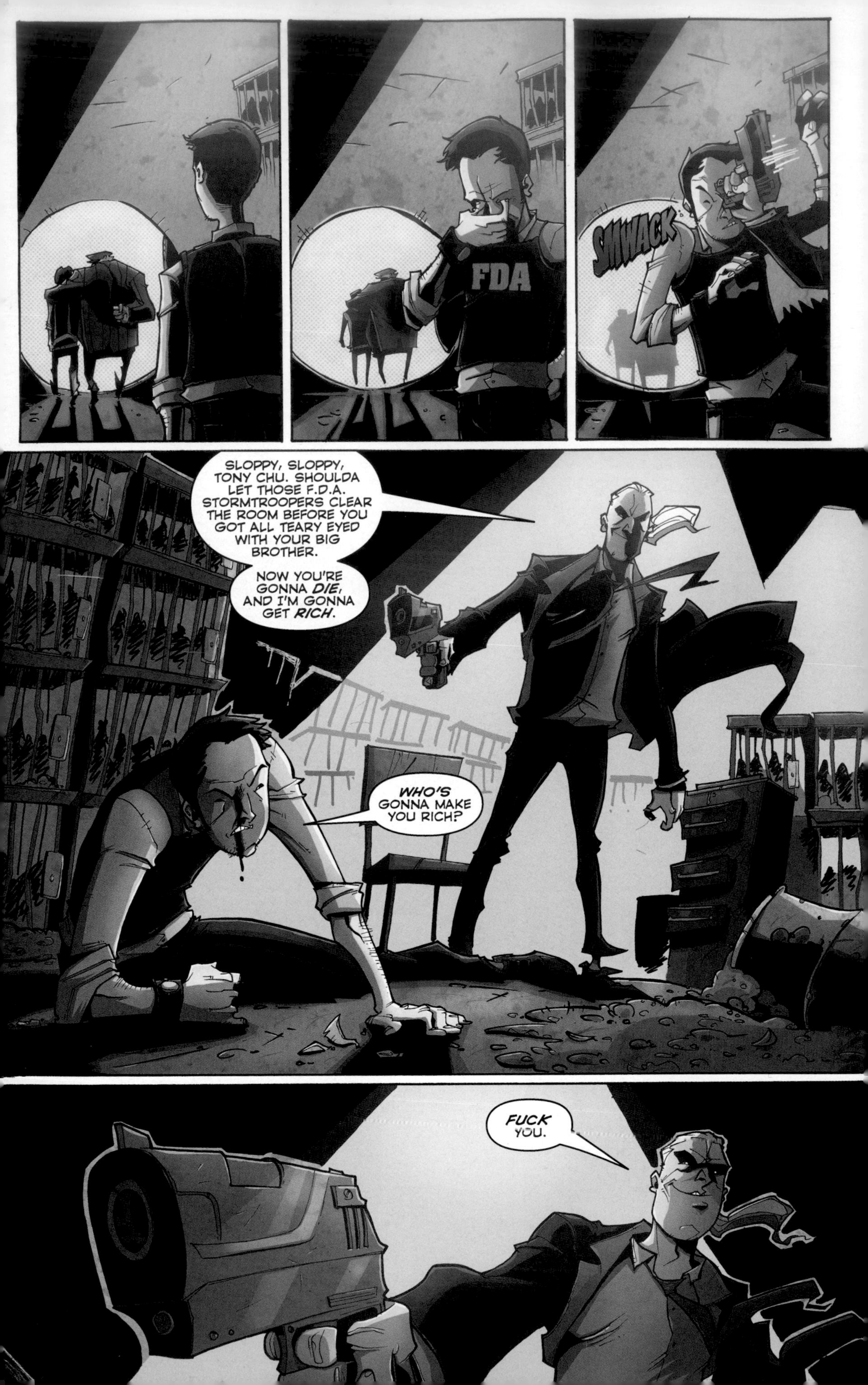
FDA
SMWACK
SLOPPY, SLOPPY, TONY CHU. SHOULDA LET THOSE F.D.A. STORMTROOPERS CLEAR THE ROOM BEFORE YOU GOT ALL TEARY EYED WITH YOUR BIG BROTHER.
NOW YOU'RE GONNA *DIE*, AND I'M GONNA GET *RICH*.
WHO'S GONNA MAKE YOU RICH?
FUCK YOU.

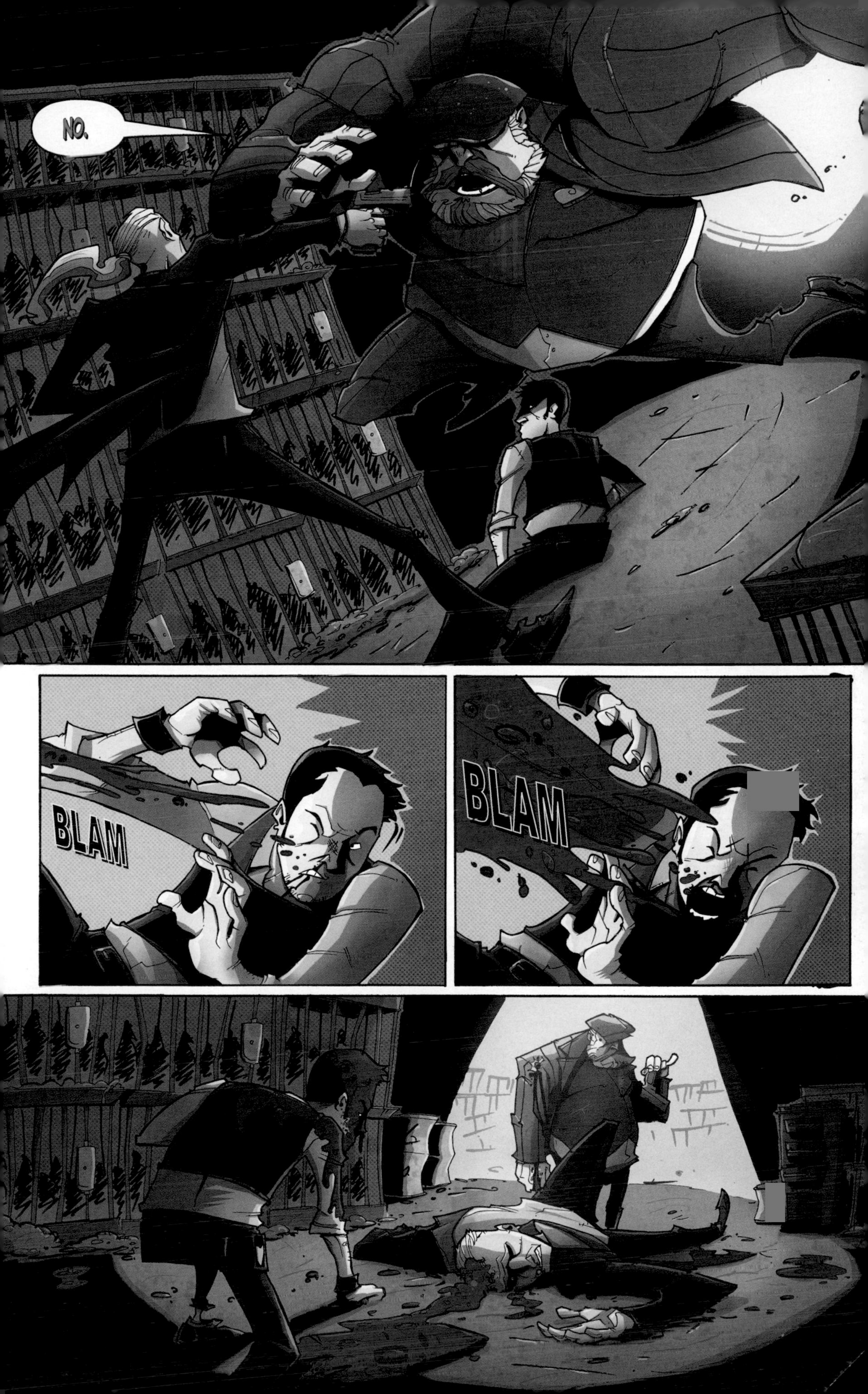
NO.
BLAM
BLAM

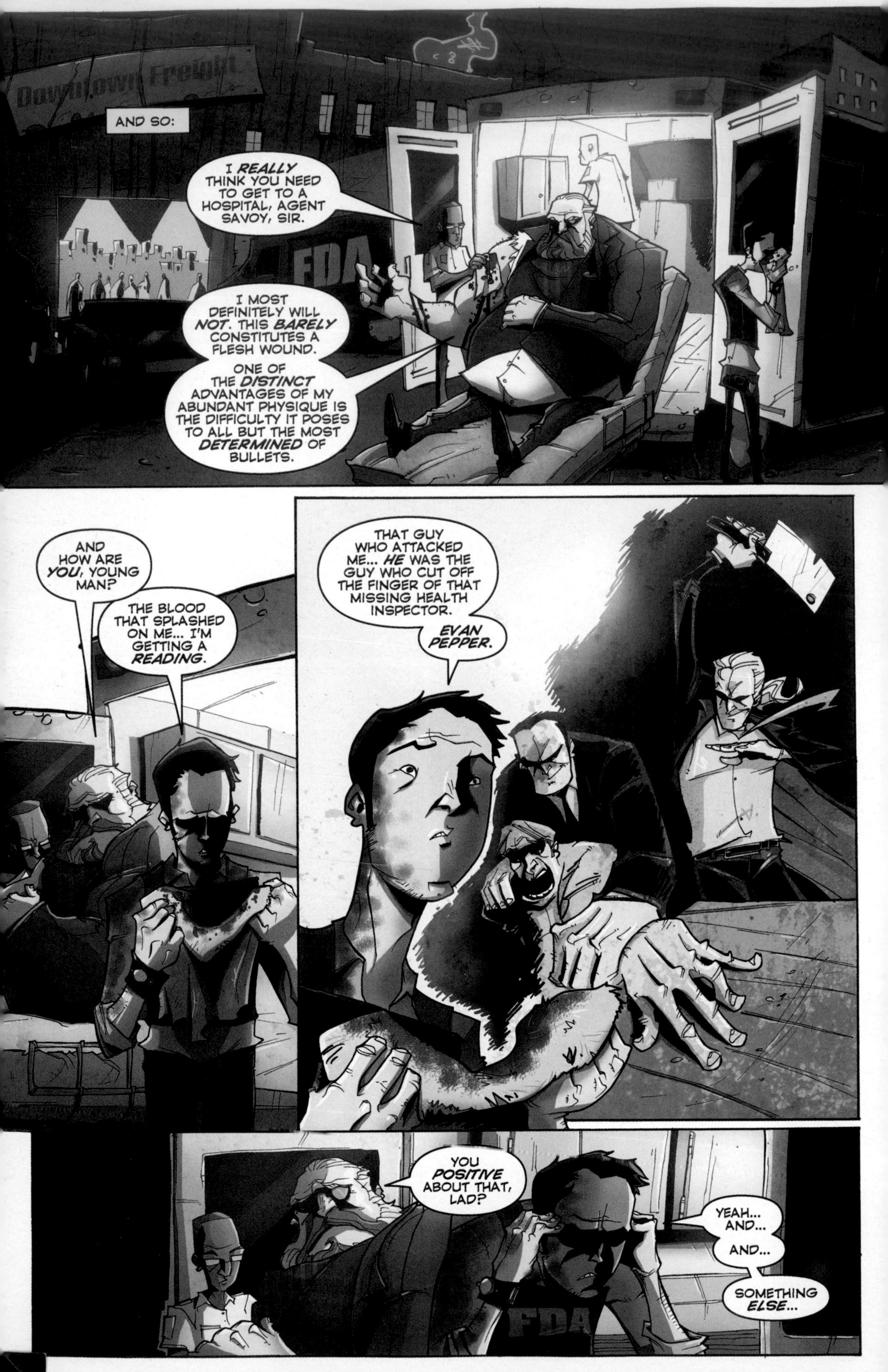
Downtown Freight
AND SO:
I *REALLY* THINK YOU NEED TO GET TO A HOSPITAL, AGENT SAVOY, SIR.
FDA
I MOST DEFINITELY WILL *NOT*. THIS *BARELY* CONSTITUTES A FLESH WOUND.
ONE OF THE *DISTINCT* ADVANTAGES OF MY ABUNDANT PHYSIQUE IS THE DIFFICULTY IT POSES TO ALL BUT THE MOST *DETERMINED* OF BULLETS.
AND HOW ARE *YOU*, YOUNG MAN?
THE BLOOD THAT SPLASHED ON ME... I'M GETTING A *READING*.
THAT GUY WHO ATTACKED ME... *HE* WAS THE GUY WHO CUT OFF THE FINGER OF THAT MISSING HEALTH INSPECTOR.
EVAN PEPPER.
YOU *POSITIVE* ABOUT THAT, LAD?
YEAH... AND...
AND...
SOMETHING *ELSE*...
FDA

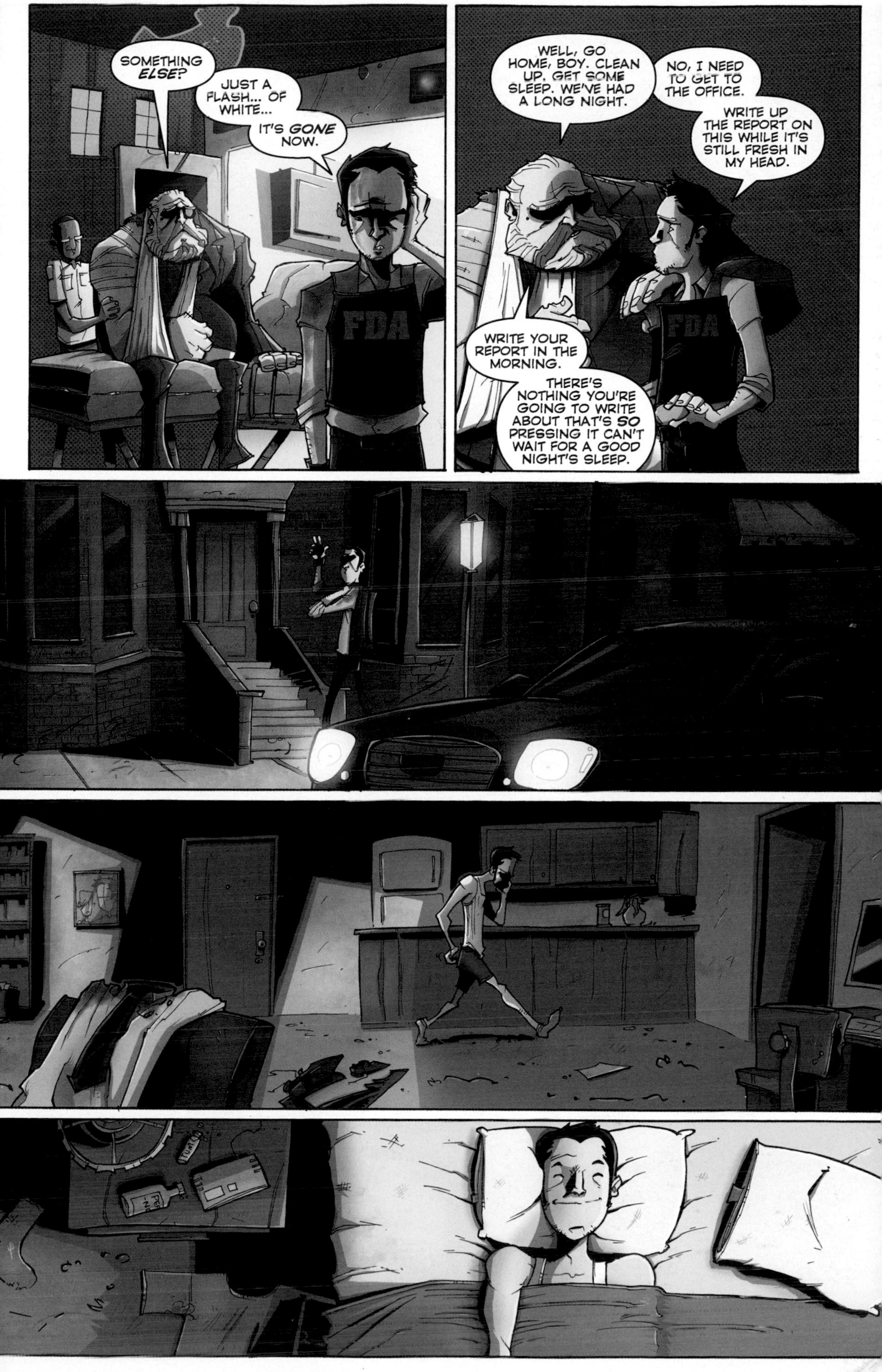

SOMETHING *ELSE*?
JUST A FLASH... OF WHITE...
IT'S *GONE* NOW.
WELL, GO HOME, BOY. CLEAN UP, GET SOME SLEEP. WE'VE HAD A LONG NIGHT.
NO, I NEED TO GET TO THE OFFICE.
WRITE UP THE REPORT ON THIS WHILE IT'S STILL FRESH IN MY HEAD.
WRITE YOUR REPORT IN THE MORNING.
THERE'S NOTHING YOU'RE GOING TO WRITE ABOUT THAT'S **SO** PRESSING IT CAN'T WAIT FOR A GOOD NIGHT'S SLEEP.
FDA
FDA

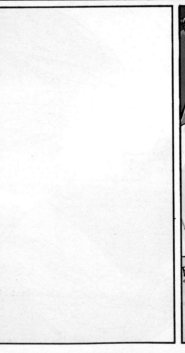

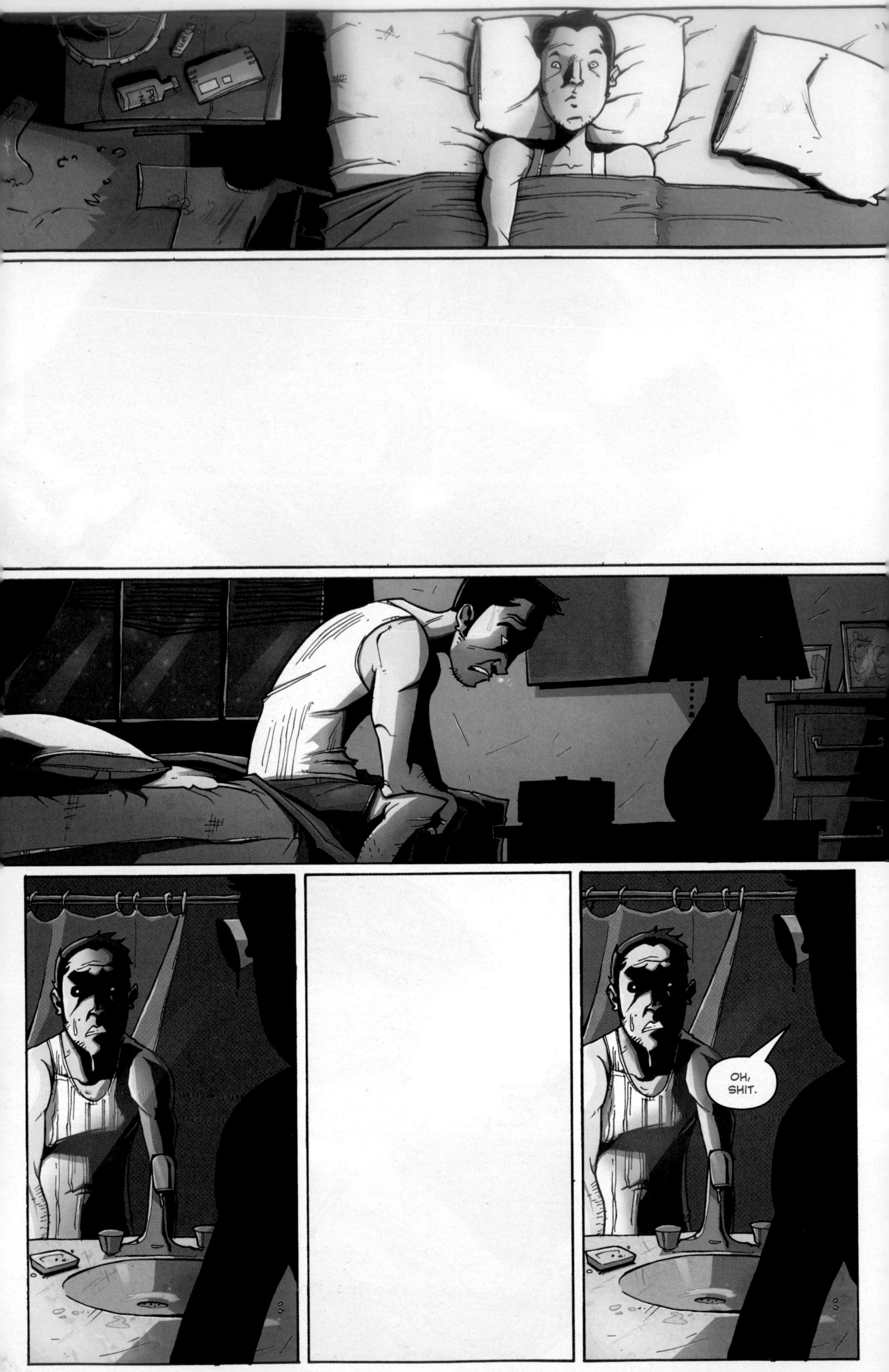
OH, SHIT.

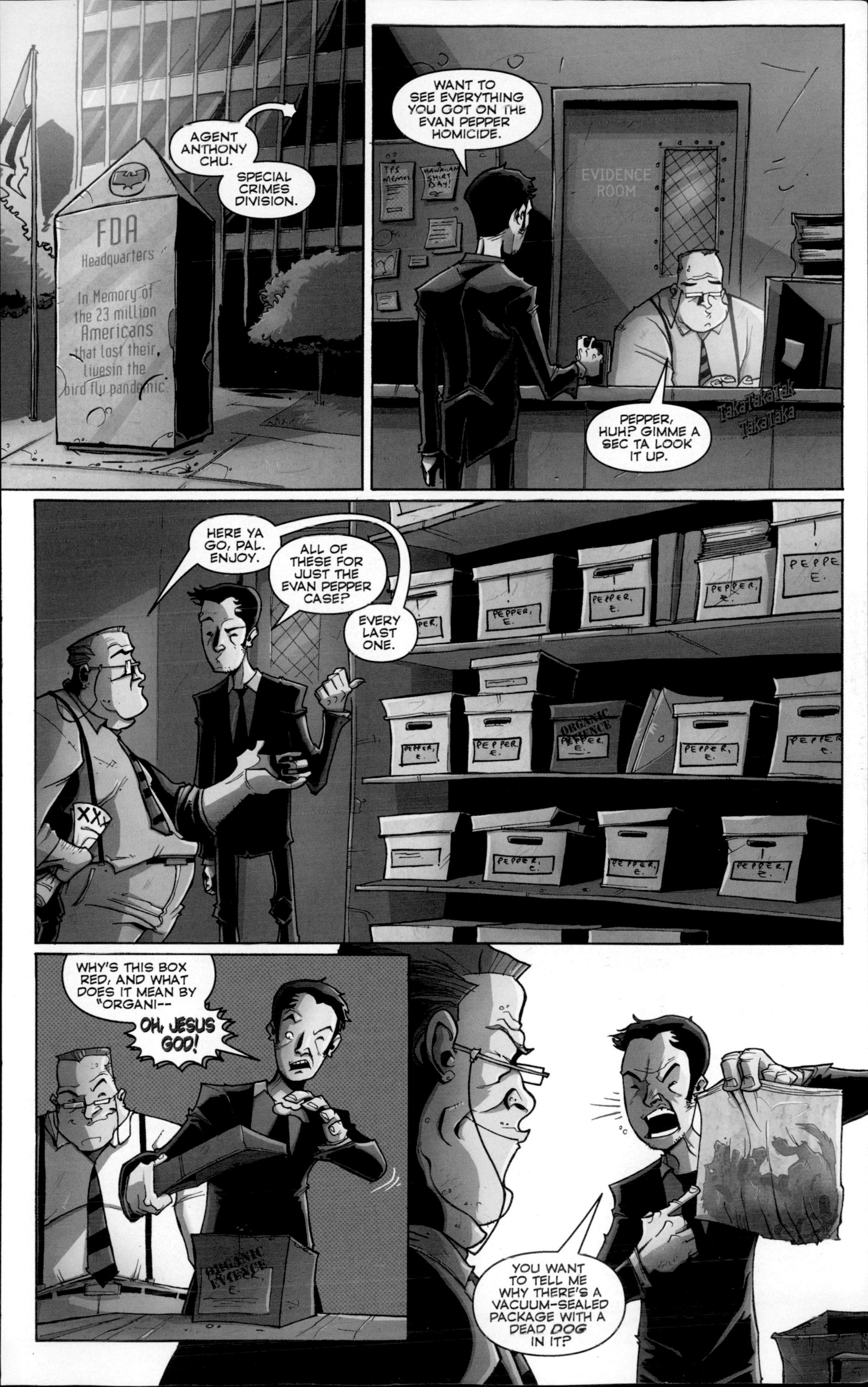
AGENT ANTHONY CHU.
SPECIAL CRIMES DIVISION.
FDA Headquarters
In Memory of the 23 million Americans that lost their livesin the bird flu pandemic.
WANT TO SEE EVERYTHING YOU GOT ON THE EVAN PEPPER HOMICIDE.
EVIDENCE ROOM
TPS MEMOS
HAWAIIAN SHIRT DAY!
PEPPER, HUH? GIMME A SEC TA LOOK IT UP.
TakaTakaTak TakaTaka
HERE YA GO, PAL. ENJOY.
ALL OF THESE FOR JUST THE EVAN PEPPER CASE?
EVERY LAST ONE.
PEPPER, E.
ORGANIC EVIDENCE
WHY'S THIS BOX RED, AND WHAT DOES IT MEAN BY "ORGANI--
OH, JESUS GOD!
YOU WANT TO TELL ME WHY THERE'S A VACUUM-SEALED PACKAGE WITH A DEAD DOG IN IT?

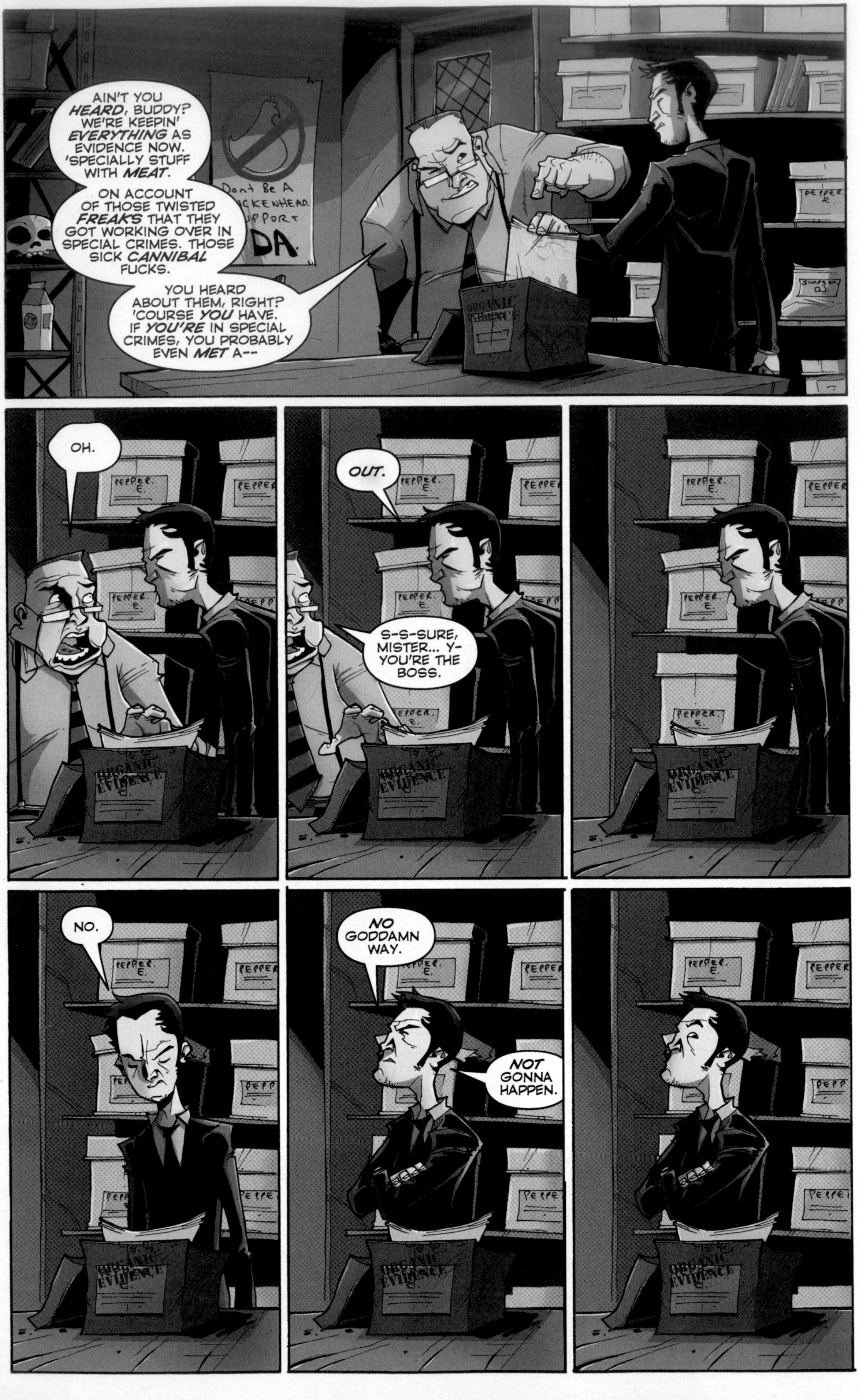
AIN'T YOU HEARD, BUDDY? WE'RE KEEPIN' EVERYTHING AS EVIDENCE NOW. 'SPECIALLY STUFF WITH MEAT.
ON ACCOUNT OF THOSE TWISTED FREAKS THAT THEY GOT WORKING OVER IN SPECIAL CRIMES. THOSE SICK CANNIBAL FUCKS.
YOU HEARD ABOUT THEM, RIGHT? 'COURSE YOU HAVE. IF YOU'RE IN SPECIAL CRIMES, YOU PROBABLY EVEN MET A--
OH.
OUT.
S-S-SURE, MISTER... Y-YOU'RE THE BOSS.
NO.
NO GODDAMN WAY.
NOT GONNA HAPPEN.

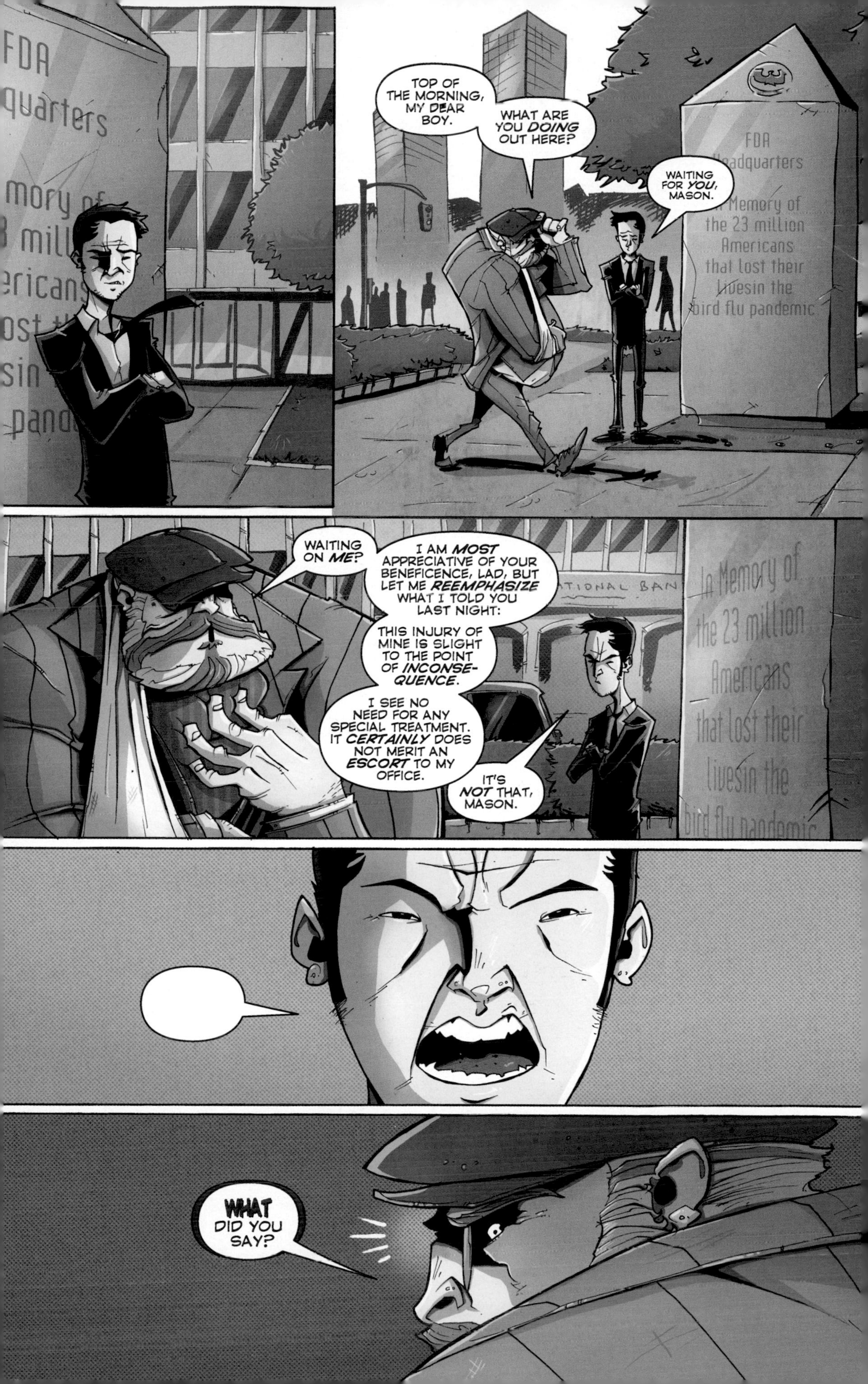

TOP OF THE MORNING, MY DEAR BOY.
WHAT ARE YOU DOING OUT HERE?
FDA Headquarters
WAITING FOR YOU, MASON.
In Memory of the 23 million Americans that lost their livesin the bird flu pandemic
WAITING ON ME?
I AM MOST APPRECIATIVE OF YOUR BENEFICENCE, LAD, BUT LET ME REEMPHASIZE WHAT I TOLD YOU LAST NIGHT:
THIS INJURY OF MINE IS SLIGHT TO THE POINT OF INCONSE-QUENCE.
I SEE NO NEED FOR ANY SPECIAL TREATMENT. IT CERTAINLY DOES NOT MERIT AN ESCORT TO MY OFFICE.
IT'S NOT THAT, MASON.
WHAT DID YOU SAY?

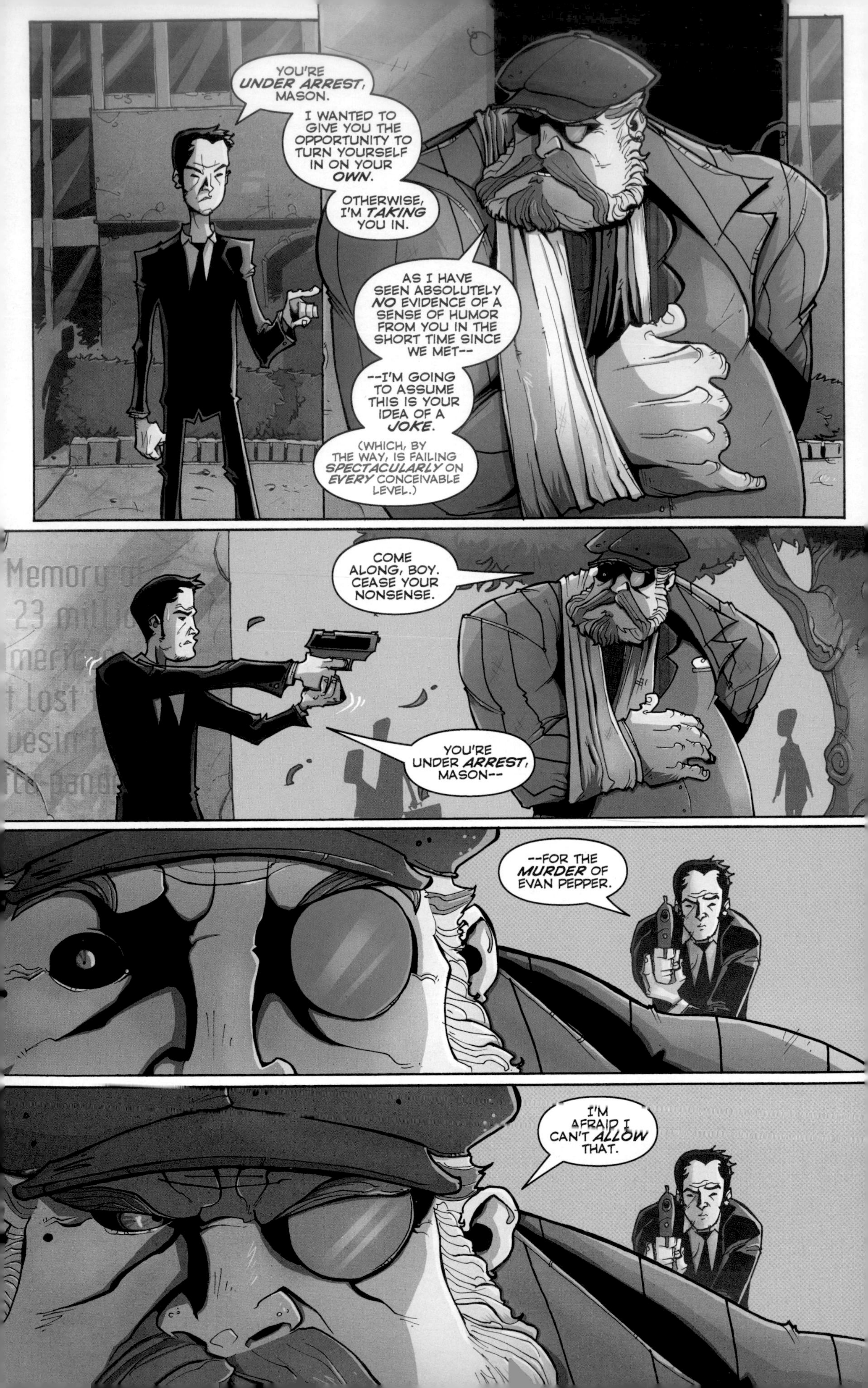
YOU'RE UNDER ARREST, MASON.
I WANTED TO GIVE YOU THE OPPORTUNITY TO TURN YOURSELF IN ON YOUR OWN.
OTHERWISE, I'M TAKING YOU IN.
AS I HAVE SEEN ABSOLUTELY NO EVIDENCE OF A SENSE OF HUMOR FROM YOU IN THE SHORT TIME SINCE WE MET--
--I'M GOING TO ASSUME THIS IS YOUR IDEA OF A JOKE.
(WHICH, BY THE WAY, IS FAILING SPECTACULARLY ON EVERY CONCEIVABLE LEVEL.)
Memory of
COME ALONG, BOY. CEASE YOUR NONSENSE.
YOU'RE UNDER ARREST, MASON--
--FOR THE MURDER OF EVAN PEPPER.
I'M AFRAID I CAN'T ALLOW THAT.

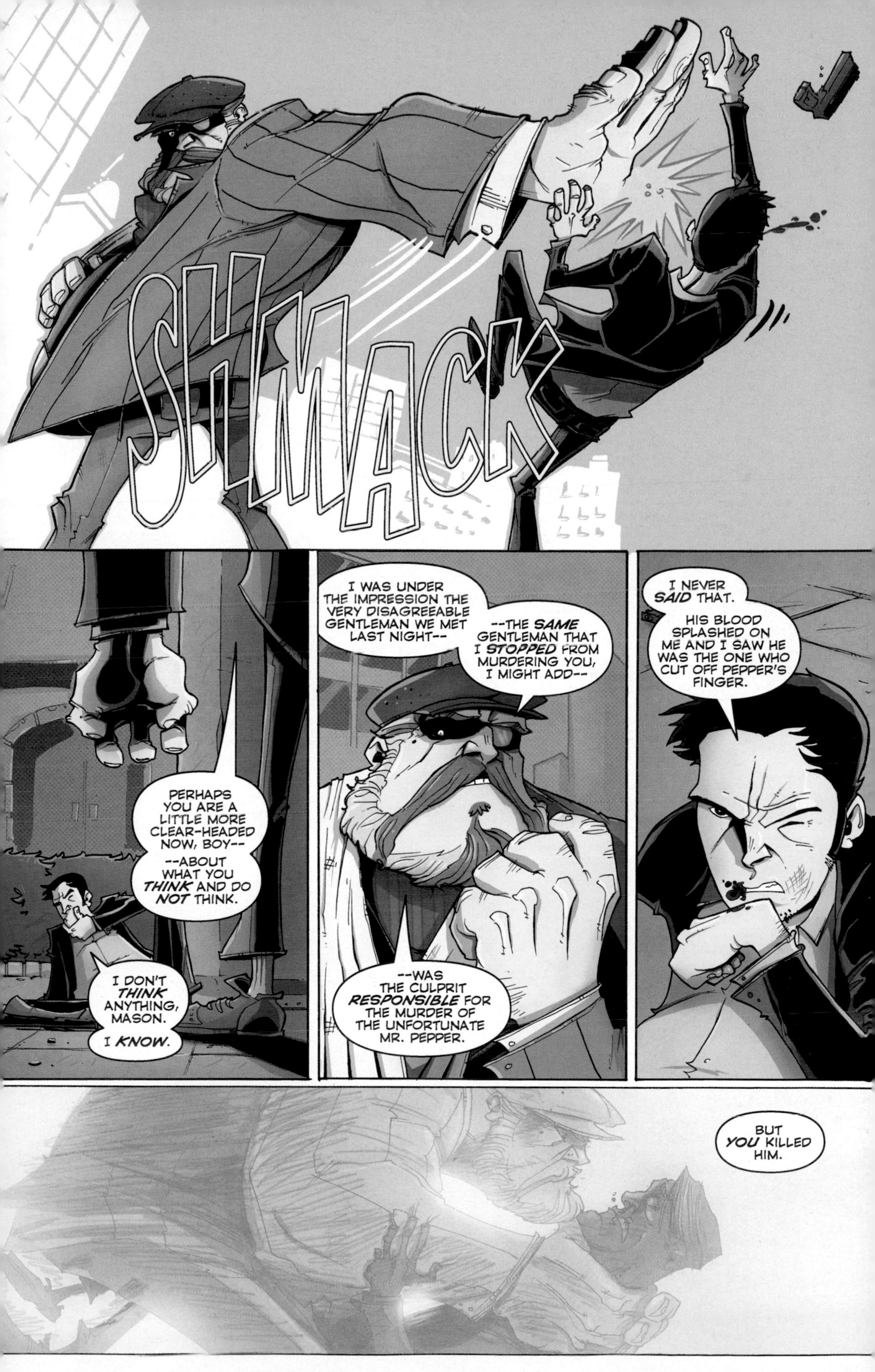
SHMACK
PERHAPS YOU ARE A LITTLE MORE CLEAR-HEADED NOW, BOY--
--ABOUT WHAT YOU THINK AND DO NOT THINK.
I DON'T THINK ANYTHING, MASON.
I KNOW.
I WAS UNDER THE IMPRESSION THE VERY DISAGREEABLE GENTLEMAN WE MET LAST NIGHT--
--THE SAME GENTLEMAN THAT I STOPPED FROM MURDERING YOU, I MIGHT ADD--
--WAS THE CULPRIT RESPONSIBLE FOR THE MURDER OF THE UNFORTUNATE MR. PEPPER.
I NEVER SAID THAT.
HIS BLOOD SPLASHED ON ME AND I SAW HE WAS THE ONE WHO CUT OFF PEPPER'S FINGER.
BUT YOU KILLED HIM.

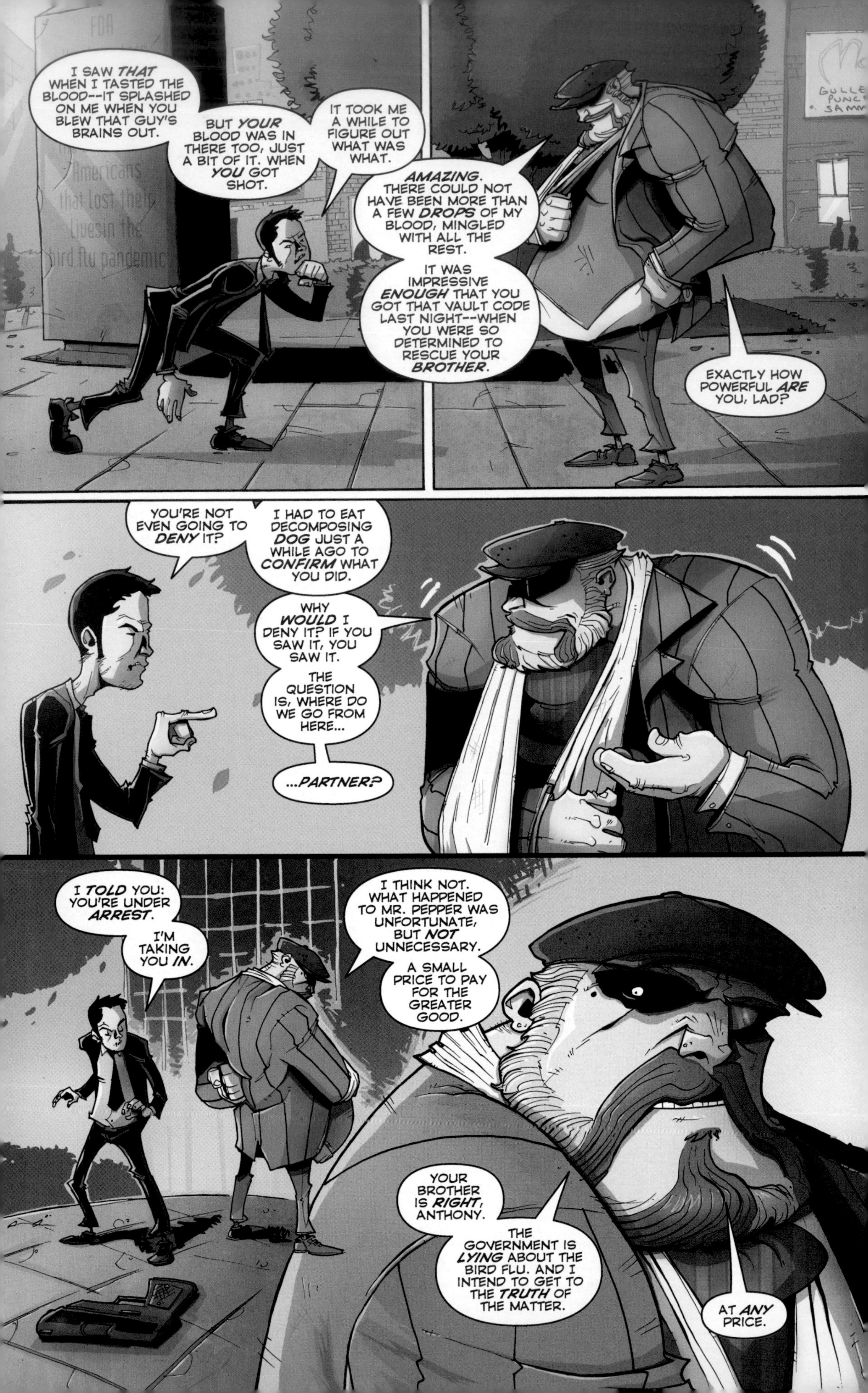
I SAW THAT WHEN I TASTED THE BLOOD--IT SPLASHED ON ME WHEN YOU BLEW THAT GUY'S BRAINS OUT.
BUT YOUR BLOOD WAS IN THERE TOO, JUST A BIT OF IT. WHEN YOU GOT SHOT.
IT TOOK ME A WHILE TO FIGURE OUT WHAT WAS WHAT.
AMAZING. THERE COULD NOT HAVE BEEN MORE THAN A FEW DROPS OF MY BLOOD, MINGLED WITH ALL THE REST.
IT WAS IMPRESSIVE ENOUGH THAT YOU GOT THAT VAULT CODE LAST NIGHT--WHEN YOU WERE SO DETERMINED TO RESCUE YOUR BROTHER.
EXACTLY HOW POWERFUL ARE YOU, LAD?
YOU'RE NOT EVEN GOING TO DENY IT?
I HAD TO EAT DECOMPOSING DOG JUST A WHILE AGO TO CONFIRM WHAT YOU DID.
WHY WOULD I DENY IT? IF YOU SAW IT, YOU SAW IT.
THE QUESTION IS, WHERE DO WE GO FROM HERE...
...PARTNER?
I TOLD YOU: YOU'RE UNDER ARREST.
I'M TAKING YOU IN.
I THINK NOT. WHAT HAPPENED TO MR. PEPPER WAS UNFORTUNATE, BUT NOT UNNECESSARY.
A SMALL PRICE TO PAY FOR THE GREATER GOOD.
YOUR BROTHER IS RIGHT, ANTHONY.
THE GOVERNMENT IS LYING ABOUT THE BIRD FLU. AND I INTEND TO GET TO THE TRUTH OF THE MATTER.
AT ANY PRICE.

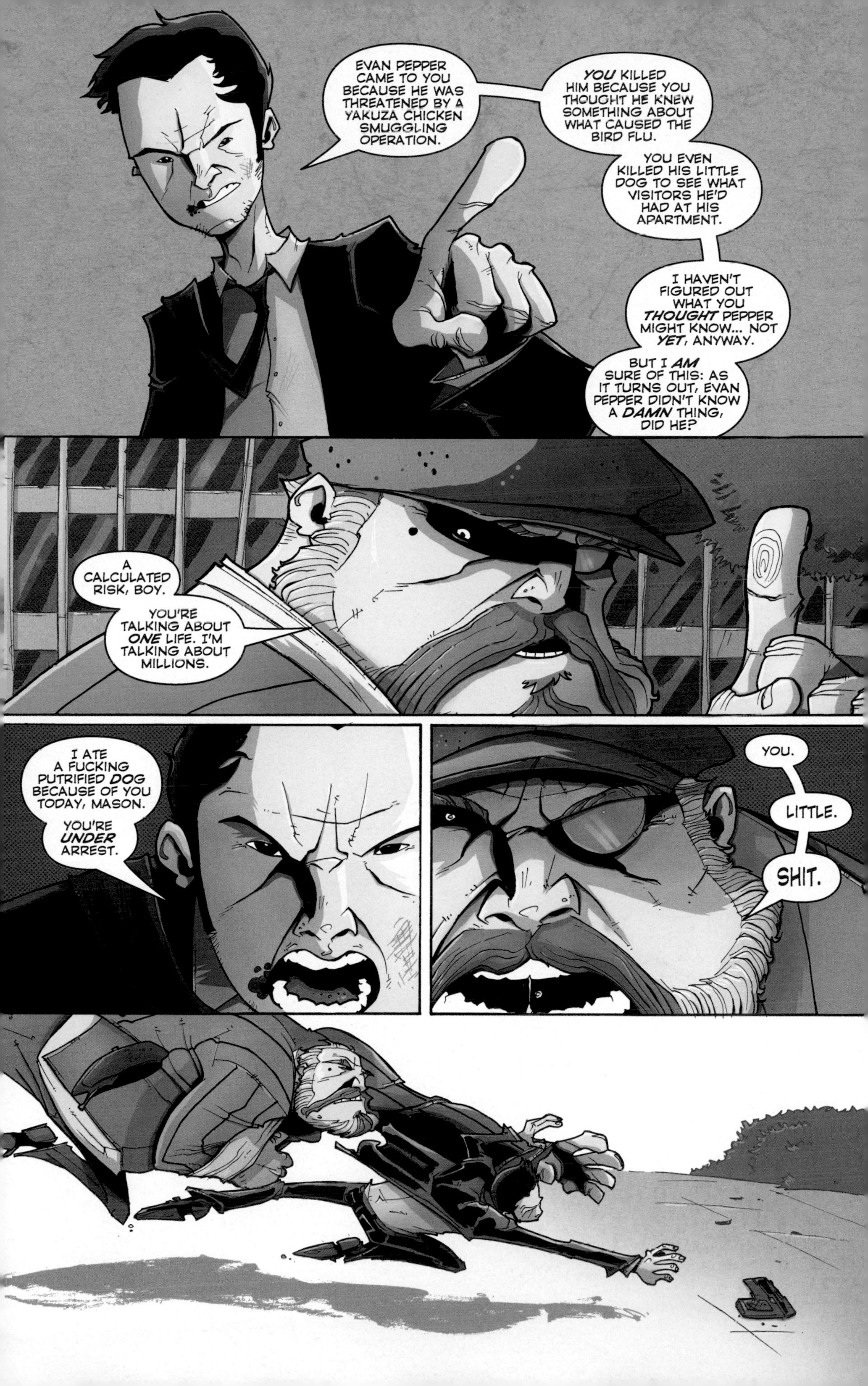
EVAN PEPPER CAME TO YOU BECAUSE HE WAS THREATENED BY A YAKUZA CHICKEN SMUGGLING OPERATION.
YOU KILLED HIM BECAUSE YOU THOUGHT HE KNEW SOMETHING ABOUT WHAT CAUSED THE BIRD FLU.
YOU EVEN KILLED HIS LITTLE DOG TO SEE WHAT VISITORS HE'D HAD AT HIS APARTMENT.
I HAVEN'T FIGURED OUT WHAT YOU THOUGHT PEPPER MIGHT KNOW... NOT YET, ANYWAY.
BUT I AM SURE OF THIS: AS IT TURNS OUT, EVAN PEPPER DIDN'T KNOW A DAMN THING, DID HE?
A CALCULATED RISK, BOY.
YOU'RE TALKING ABOUT ONE LIFE. I'M TALKING ABOUT MILLIONS.
I ATE A FUCKING PUTRIFIED DOG BECAUSE OF YOU TODAY, MASON.
YOU'RE UNDER ARREST.
YOU.
LITTLE.
SHIT.

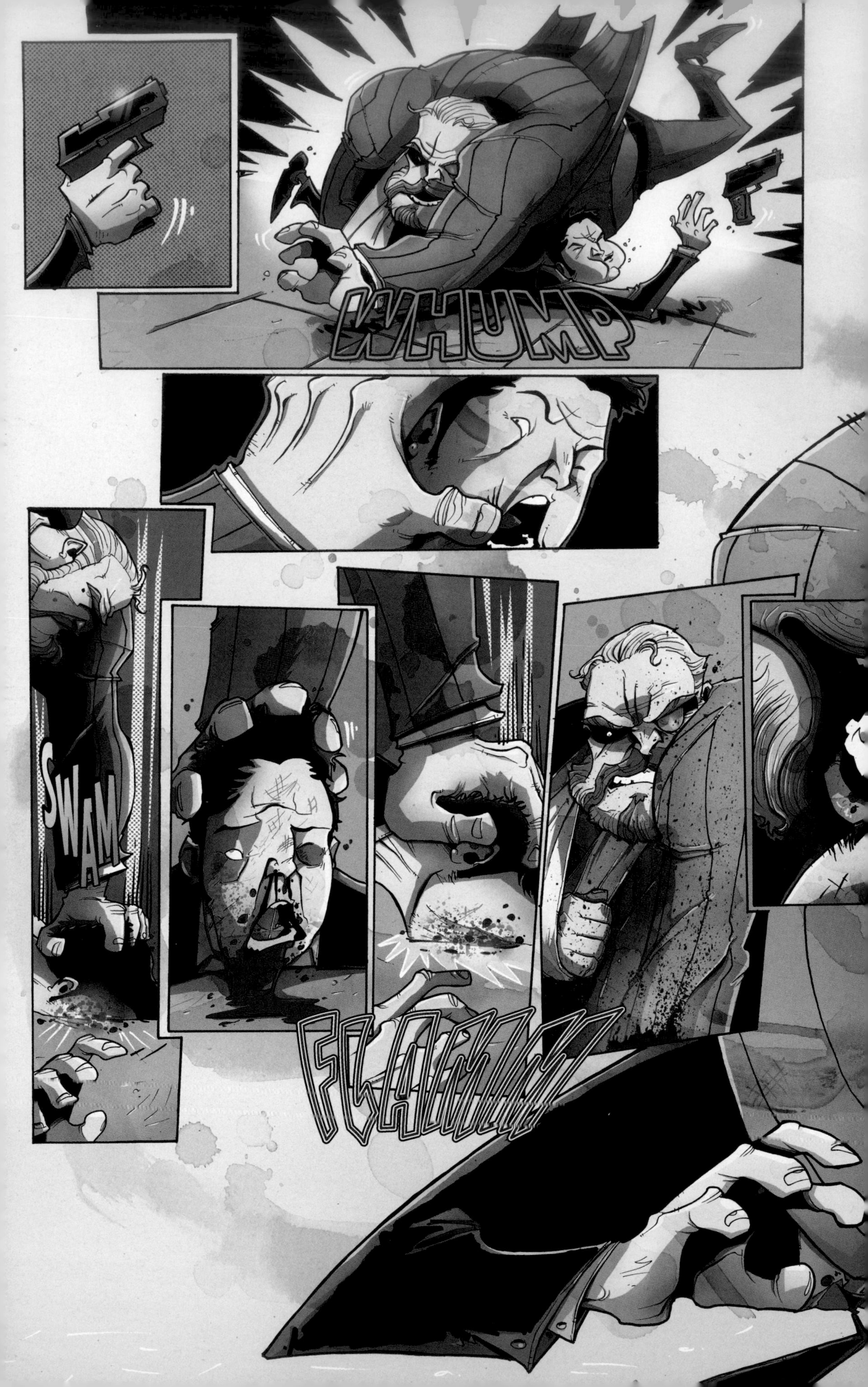
WHUMP
SWAM
FCLACK

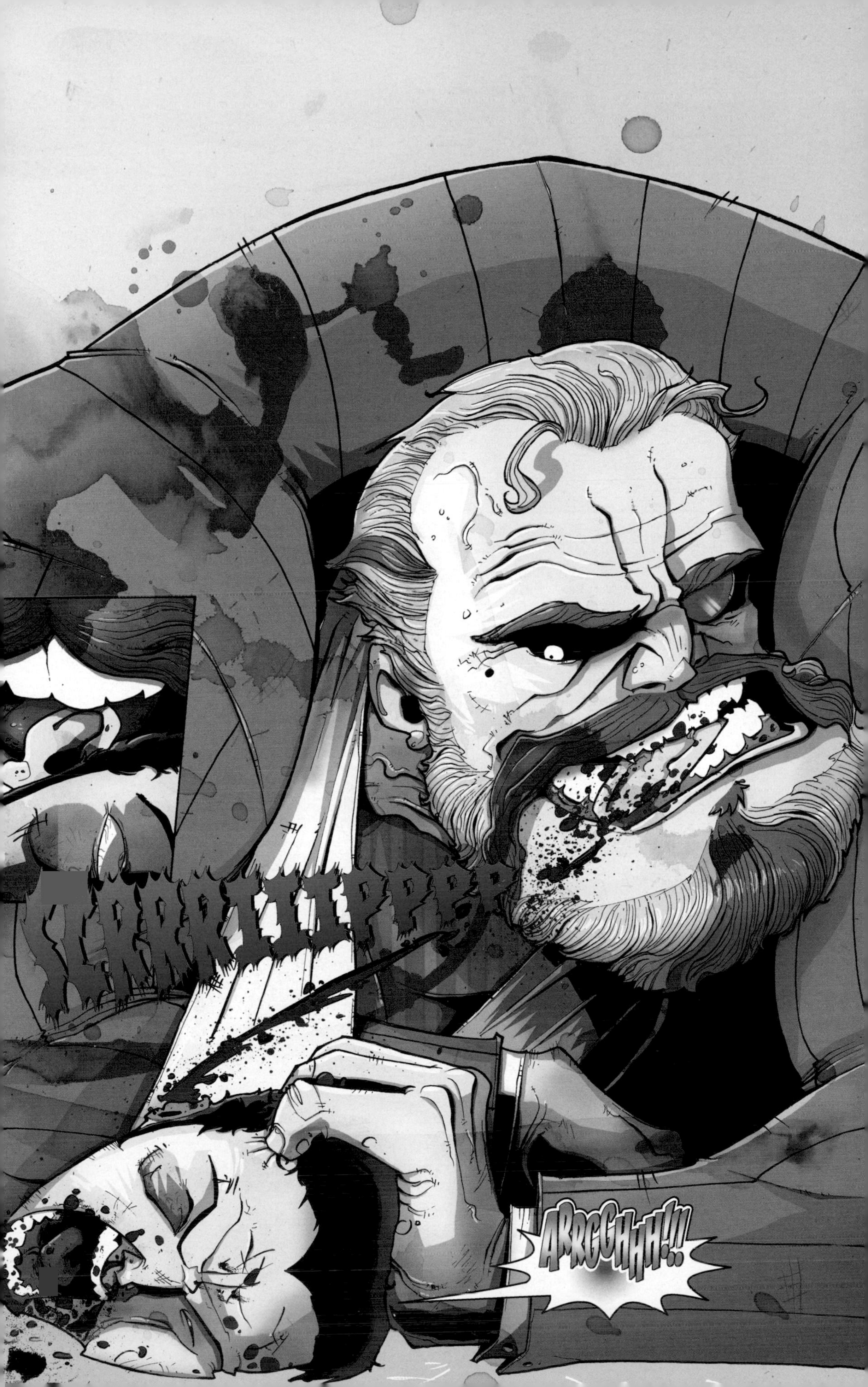
SCRRRIIIPPPP
ARRGGHHH!!!

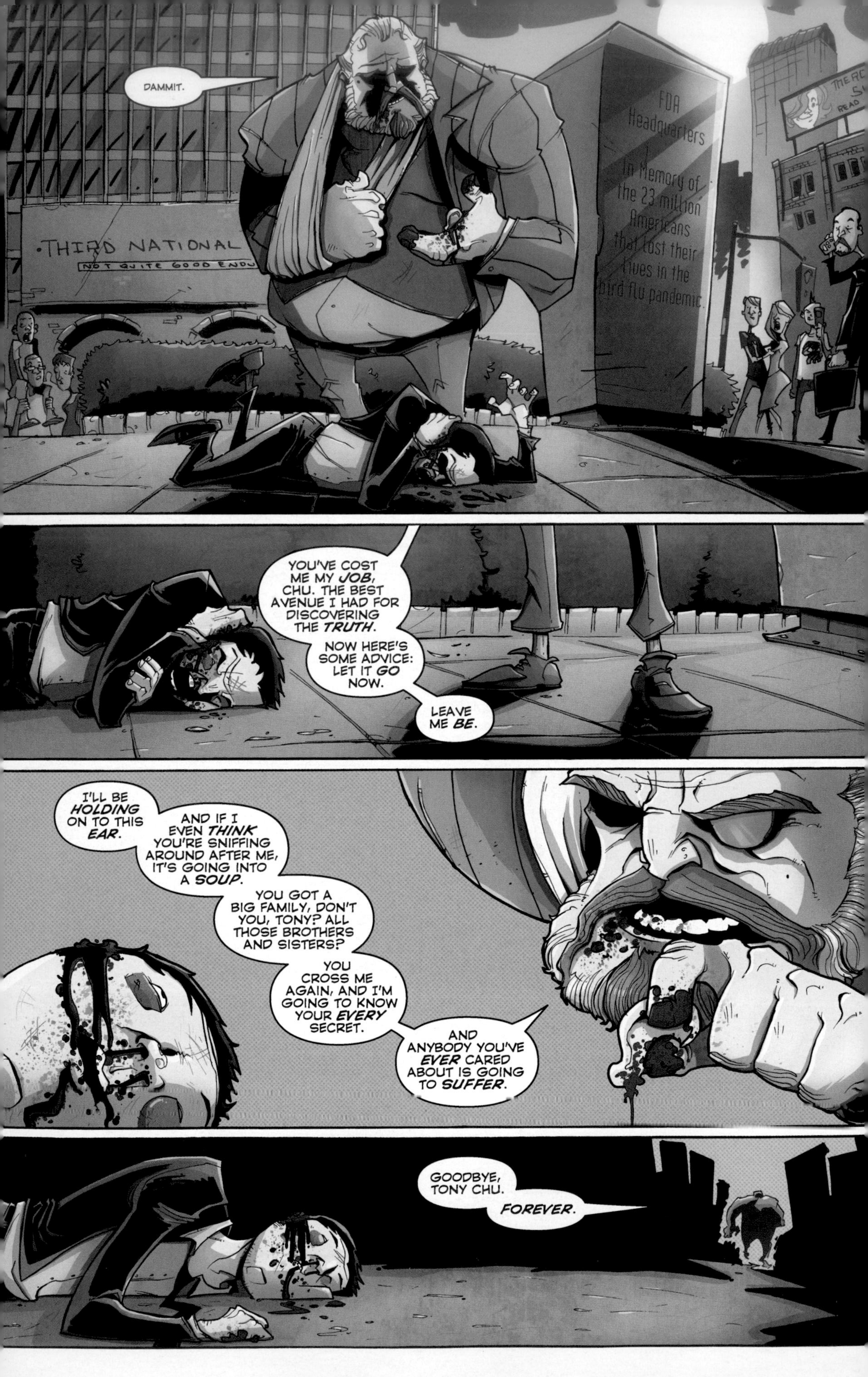
DAMMIT.
THIRD NATIONAL
FDA Headquarters
In Memory of the 23 million Americans that lost their lives in the bird flu pandemic.
YOU'VE COST ME MY JOB, CHU. THE BEST AVENUE I HAD FOR DISCOVERING THE TRUTH.
NOW HERE'S SOME ADVICE: LET IT GO NOW.
LEAVE ME BE.
I'LL BE HOLDING ON TO THIS EAR.
AND IF I EVEN THINK YOU'RE SNIFFING AROUND AFTER ME, IT'S GOING INTO A SOUP.
YOU GOT A BIG FAMILY, DON'T YOU, TONY? ALL THOSE BROTHERS AND SISTERS?
YOU CROSS ME AGAIN, AND I'M GOING TO KNOW YOUR EVERY SECRET.
AND ANYBODY YOU'VE EVER CARED ABOUT IS GOING TO SUFFER.
GOODBYE, TONY CHU.
FOREVER.

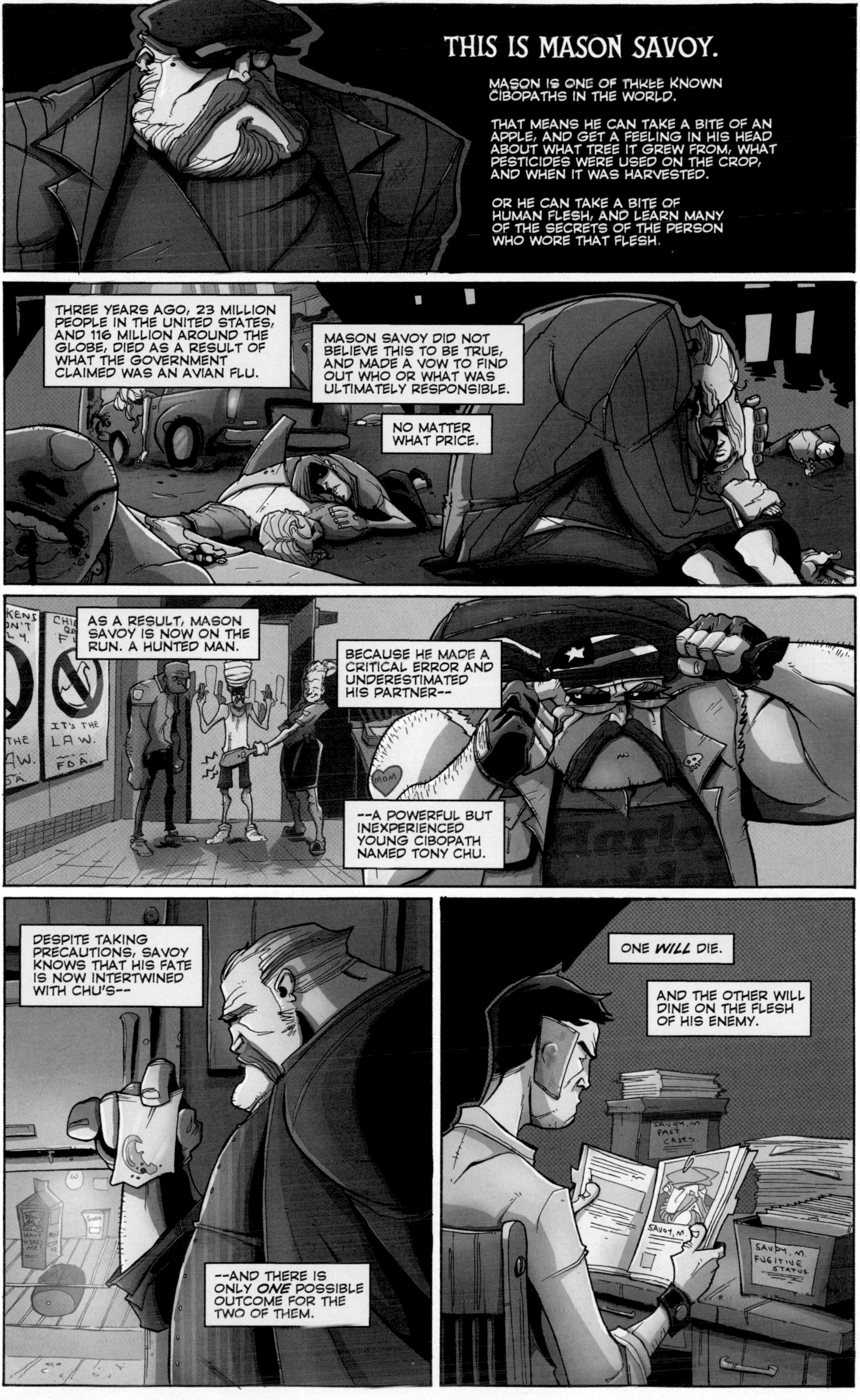
THIS IS MASON SAVOY.
MASON IS ONE OF THREE KNOWN CIBOPATHS IN THE WORLD.
THAT MEANS HE CAN TAKE A BITE OF AN APPLE, AND GET A FEELING IN HIS HEAD ABOUT WHAT TREE IT GREW FROM, WHAT PESTICIDES WERE USED ON THE CROP, AND WHEN IT WAS HARVESTED.
OR HE CAN TAKE A BITE OF HUMAN FLESH, AND LEARN MANY OF THE SECRETS OF THE PERSON WHO WORE THAT FLESH.
THREE YEARS AGO, 23 MILLION PEOPLE IN THE UNITED STATES, AND 116 MILLION AROUND THE GLOBE, DIED AS A RESULT OF WHAT THE GOVERNMENT CLAIMED WAS AN AVIAN FLU.
MASON SAVOY DID NOT BELIEVE THIS TO BE TRUE, AND MADE A VOW TO FIND OUT WHO OR WHAT WAS ULTIMATELY RESPONSIBLE.
NO MATTER WHAT PRICE.
AS A RESULT, MASON SAVOY IS NOW ON THE RUN. A HUNTED MAN.
IT'S THE LAW.
FDA.
BECAUSE HE MADE A CRITICAL ERROR AND UNDERESTIMATED HIS PARTNER--
MOM
--A POWERFUL BUT INEXPERIENCED YOUNG CIBOPATH NAMED TONY CHU.
DESPITE TAKING PRECAUTIONS, SAVOY KNOWS THAT HIS FATE IS NOW INTERTWINED WITH CHU'S--
SODA
--AND THERE IS ONLY *ONE* POSSIBLE OUTCOME FOR THE TWO OF THEM.
ONE ***WILL*** DIE.
AND THE OTHER WILL DINE ON THE FLESH OF HIS ENEMY.
SAVOY, M. PAST CASES
SAVOY, M.
SAVOY, M. FUGITIVE STATUS

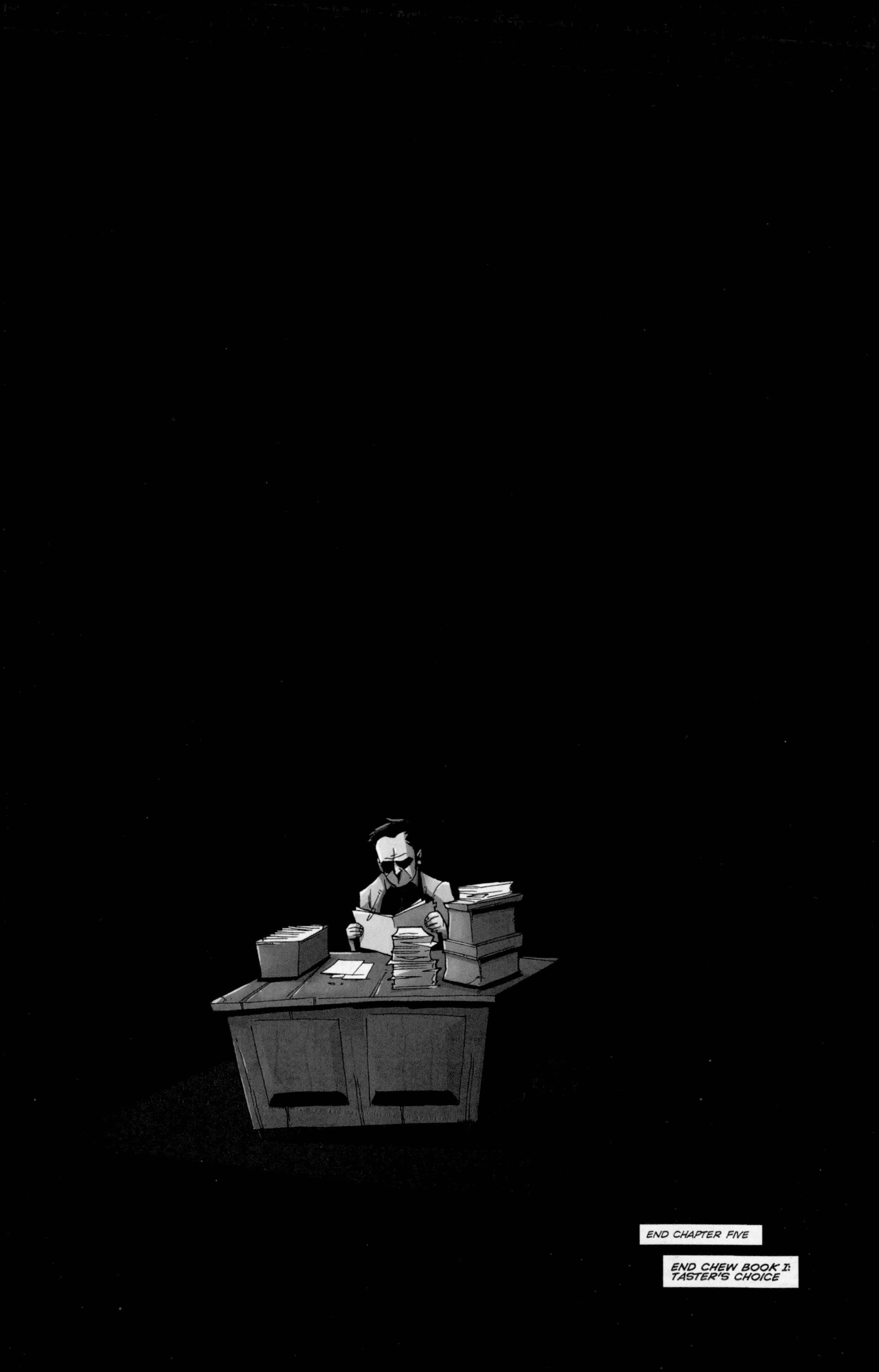
END CHAPTER FIVE
END CHEW BOOK I:
TASTER'S CHOICE

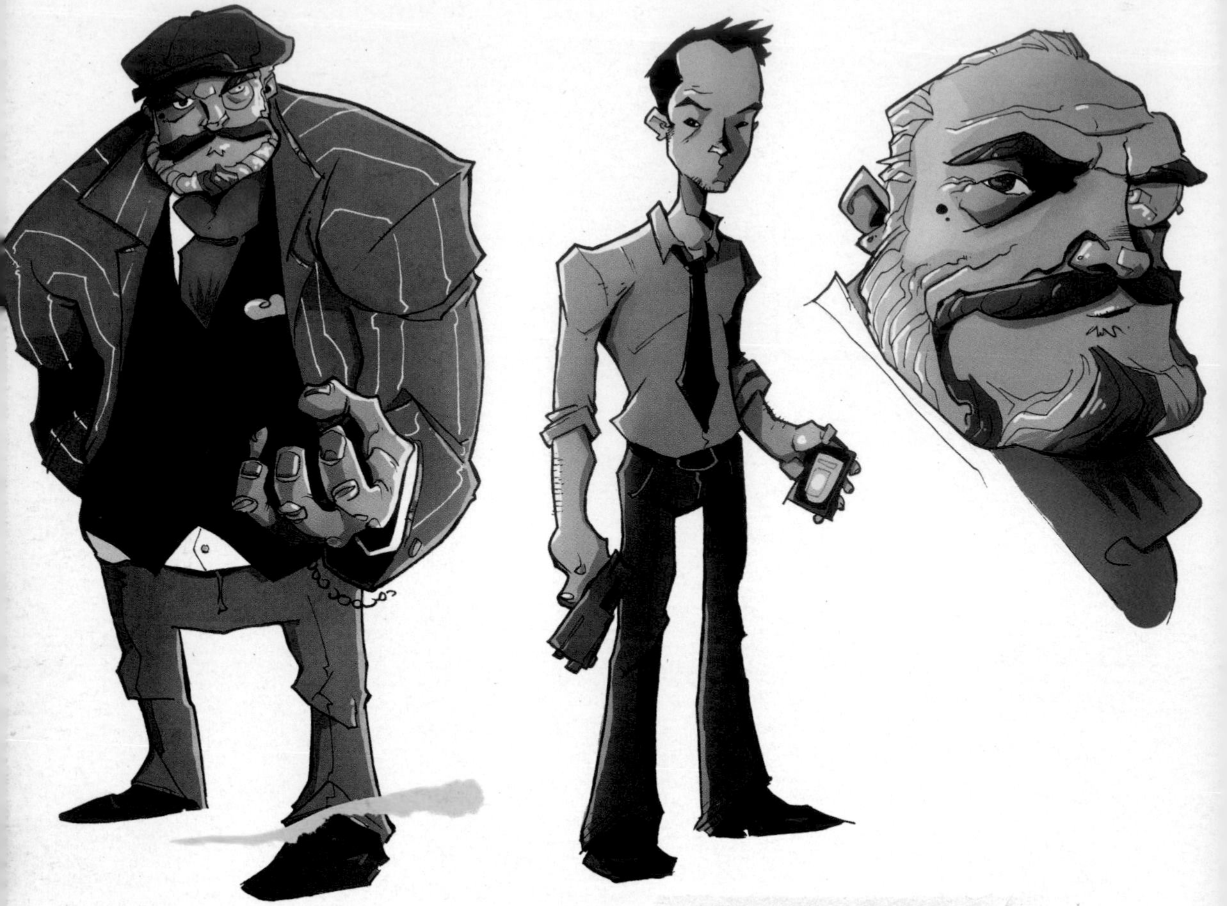

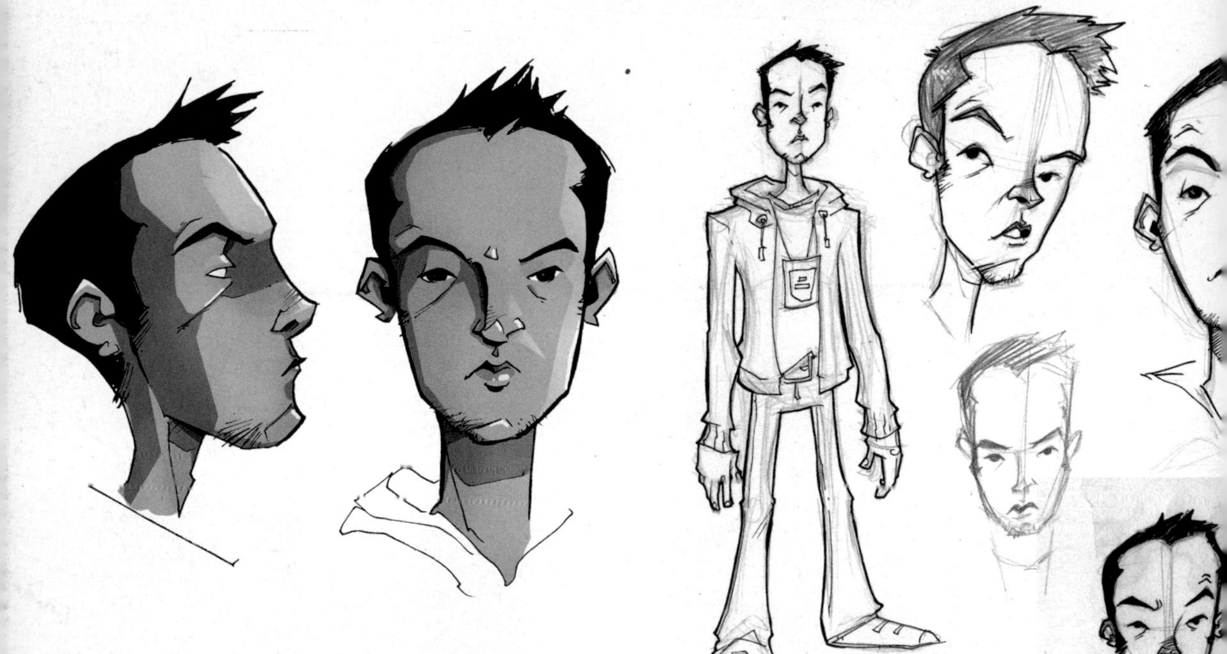

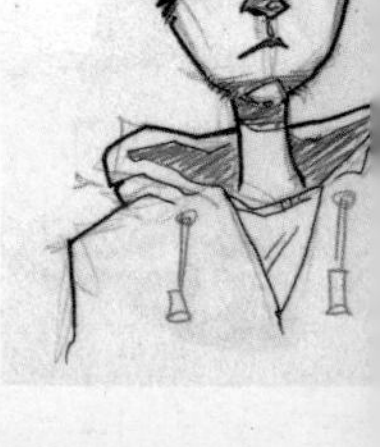

First sketches for Tony and Mason. We wanted Chu to be a totally unstereotypical Asian-American. Mason is the lovechild of Orson Welles and a grizzly bear.

CHEW #4: The Translation

Page 17, Panel 1

SCIENTIST: *“Nadya, No! What the hell are you doing?”*

Page 17, Panel 2

RUSSIAN CHICK: *“My name is not Nadya, you disgusting little man.”*

Page 18, Panel 1

RUSSIAN SCIENTIST: *“We are making a mistake, milady. I do not think that these are our enemies.”*

R.CHICK: *“The master warned us about the fat one. He is dangerous. Savoy.”*

Page 18, Panel 2

R.CHICK: *“Who is this little fool?”*

Page 19, Panel 1

SAVOY: *“What’s going on? Why are you doing this? “*

R.CHICK: *“I’ll tell you nothing. I serve The Vampire. He is my master.”*

Page 19, Panel 2

R.CHICK: *"We seek The Truth."*

Page 19, Panel 4

R.CHICK: *“I think not. Your government is interested in anything but the truth."*

Page 19, Panel 5

SAVOY: *“I am not my government. I am my own master.”*

R.CHICK: *“And I am loyal to The Vampire. He is my master.”*

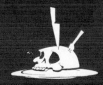

JOHN LAYMAN *is terrifically old and has suffered terribly throughout his entire life. Every day, every step, every breath brings him a new and terrible type of pain and, yet, he perseveres. For you, dear reader, for you. He has one wife, and one kid, and three cats. The cats are named Rufus, Bumble Buzz and Batty. He lives in San Jose, California, but will likely be in Phoenix, Arizona, by the time this book sees print. In his spare time he plays harpsichord and hunts pelicans with a buck knife.*

ROB GUILLORY *is a young freelance artist who has been a square peg in the round hole of life for as long as he cares to remember. Dedicated to breaking into comics on his terms, CHEW is his first "Big Break". He lives with his wife April and his two cats, Emma and George in the posh metropolis that is Lafayette, Louisiana. He has no spare time, but in the miraculous event that he does, he enjoys sitting on his ass and watching the grass grow. He also likes Sunday driving and the tour de force known as CSI: Miami. Visit* **RobGuillory.com**.

ChewComic.com